CW00566385

THE HONEY AND THE STING

CHRIS HUNT

THE HONEY AND THE STING

THE GAY MEN'S PRESS

First published 1999 by The Gay Men's Press,
GMP Publishers Ltd in association with Prowler Press Ltd,
3 Broadbent Close, London N6 5GG

World Copyright © 1999 Chris Hunt

Chris Hunt has asserted her right to be identified as the author of this work
in accordance with the Copyright, Designs and Patents Act 1988

A CIP catalogue record for this book is available
from the British Library

ISBN 0 85449 283 6

Distributed in Europe by Central Books,
99 Wallis Rd, London E9 5LN

Distributed in North America by InBook/LPC Group,
1436 West Randolph, Chicago, IL 60607

Distributed in Australia by Bulldog Books,
P O Box 300, Beaconsfield, NSW 2014

Printed and bound in the EU by WSOY, Juva, Finland

"It is good to carry yourself fair . . . to keep a good distance and to play your own game, showing yourself to have, as the bee hath, both of the honey and of the sting."

— Sir Francis Bacon

to Sal and Co.

CHAPTER ONE

They say that the court of a prince resembles a fountain, whose clear water should refresh the land; but if corruption enters near the head, the infected streams bring poison.

We were like boys that bathed and splashed in that same fountain, never guessing at its depth, nor seeing the murky darkness beneath. All that was hidden by the dazzle of the sun.

The three of us were country bred, raised from our sphere by circumstance. I, Giles Rawlins, came from Oxfordshire, and the Midland shires have always found me most at my ease. Robbie, it was admiringly surmised, came from the realm of Elfland, like the young Tam Lin, who appears in a glow of green when the seeker tugs at a wild rose; but in sober truth he was from Jedburgh in the Scottish Border country. Thomas my cousin was Warwickshire born, though he had turned his back on all that smacked of the rustic; and by his mingling with the great and his familiarity with the Cheapside tavern poets and the wayward discontented lawyers he made us all believe he was as able to intrigue, conspire and plot as any courtier of long standing. He certainly believed it himself. A more self-conceited fellow you would search hard to find, and I say so who admired him.

In the autumn of the year 1601 Thomas had just returned from Scotland, where he had been sent upon a mission of diplomacy – secret, of course, and monstrous important, as all Tom's ventures were – and he was lodging at his father's house at Bourton-on-the-Hill in Gloucestershire. I was summoned to attend him and receive the gifts he had brought from the north, and I went gladly – Tom was a figure of glamour and authority to me, being, at twenty, five years older than myself, and on close terms, he said, with lords and ladies at the court, and, for all I knew, attendant on the aged queen and privy to her counsel.

I rode up from Moreton-in-Marsh on a morning of overcast sky and low cloud through which the sun showed as a blurred white shape of eerie brightness. It was the day of St Simon and St Jude, a day by which the cider pressing should have begun, and, no doubt the one following from the other, a day for peeling an apple and casting into the future for a sight of the unknown beloved.

It was all so very quiet. Even the wind was still. The air hung heavy with the scent of rotting leaves. There was nothing to indicate that as I made my slow way forward I was riding into danger, nothing that gave warning of the thing to come – a tale as ominous and violent as any story from our stage, with lust and passion, hatred and betrayal . . . and murder. And little did I know that I, Giles Rawlins, was to find my name coupled with those of villains of vilest degree – some of noble blood and some poor wretches caught in others' toils, and one worse than all, that even now was growing, all unknown to me, wayward, vigorous and lethal, like a hemlock in a ditch.

I rode on, unaware.

Cider making was somewhat in my thoughts, as I had left my parents engrossed in a discourse of some moment – the apples gathered earlier in the month and spread out in the stable loft, had they yet sweated enough? Some had been green and maybe needed longer, but the rotted ones were very much ready for the press. The general conclusion seemed to be, then, that tomorrow would be the day of pressing, and the bulk of it done before All Hallows when the brimming brew might tempt the wandering souls to tarry as they pushed and jostled for their places by the hearth.

I passed along a hedgerow that was purpled with sloes. We had an old servant who swore a grey lady had picked sloes with him last year. An Aftermath, he called her, something transparent, something like a spider's web. He could put his hand through her, but he had not been afraid. And once, where the old hall used to be, he saw another of more startling appearance.

"She were leanin' over the wall and she had no head."

"If she had no head, how did you know she leaned?"

"Why, she leaned just like you and I would do, with her hands gripping the wall, the only difference being that she had no head."

I rode slowly up the lower slopes of the hill. The hedgerows thinned and dwindled and the open fields showed, treeless, ribbed with green turf. Down towards the Evenlode the cattle grazed. The ascent was now hard going, the road miry and waterlogged. I dismounted, mare and I plodding on laboriously.

A man from Bourton was bringing a cartload of logs down from the wood, drawn by a shaggy farmhorse. He was taking his logs as a gift to his cousin; he told me so. He was Master Upton, yeoman farmer, an acquaintance.

"I know 'e, don't I, Master Rawlins' son? You are he that went away to Burford School to gain his book learning?"

I admitted as much.

"Ah, better unborn than untaught," he quoted sagely. "But now what, Master Giles? What can you do with your book learning here?"

A fair question, surrounded as we were by empty fields and sky and misty moisty distances.

"I don't intend to stay here, Master Upton."

He shook his head.

"I know your dad," he said. "A good country man. I cannot understand why folks want to go somewhere else. What can you learn elsewhere that you cannot learn here? If you can write a letter and your name and read your prayers and count your money, you are well set up, and all the rest your dad can teach you – ploughing, sowing, planting, pruning, and to live within the law and serve the queen."

As he did, to my certain knowledge. He had been in all his days no further afield than Stow-on-the-Wold.

He grinned, guessing my thoughts. "Aye," he agreed, "I'm no traveller."

"Neither am I today," I said. "I go no further than Bourton. I'm on my way to Justice Overbury's house."

"You have a wasted journey then – the squire's from home. I heard he's far away in Warwickshire."

I laughed. "And that's not so far. But I'm not visiting Squire Overbury; so no matter."

"Ah, then 't will be one of the daughters," decided Master Upton comfortably. I was redeemed. Restless I might be, but my natural leanings were as they should be. "All beauties, every one."

How folks' minds did run on one thing!

"It is not," I said. "It's Thomas."

"Ah . . ." A weight of disapproval, disappointment and dislike was conveyed in Master Upton's response. Our conversation halted. We said our farewells and separated. We wished each other good day.

The houses of the village clustered about me and I drew level with the church; but there was yet more incline before level ground; then beyond a low hedge and set amongst trees, Tom's house showed, a little way back from the road.

My aunt and her daughters made me welcome and would have hurried me to dine.

"You are surely tired from your journey, Giles; you surely long to eat and drink?"

"He is not and he does not," Thomas called from above. "He wishes to come upstairs and hear my news from Scotland. Leave him alone. He's come to see me, not to eat."

We all looked up to where Thomas lounged at the head of the stairs, in the pose of one who expected to have his portrait painted or, at the least, to be observed.

My cousin Thomas was very handsome. He had a well formed face with high cheekbones and beautiful grey eyes. The face was framed in abundant chestnut hair. His body was slender. He carried himself as one that knew his own worth, or, as some might say, arrogantly. He did so now, standing there, one elegant leg thrust a little forward, one hand extended to beckon me towards him. He had the mannerisms of a player, – expansive, studied, flamboyant.

His mother snorted. "Join him then, Giles, and I hope you hear more from him than we have done. I ask myself where lies the pleasure in having a son that travels, since we are told nothing of what passed upon his journeys, and he having been among the savages."

"My mother believes that the Scots at Holyrood paint their faces with woad," Thomas said behind his hand, "and that I was fortunate to escape with my life."

"Come down and dine with us, Giles, when he has told you of his doings," said my aunt. She was inordinately proud of her talented son, but yet bewildered by him. Had they not set him well on his way in order that he might become a lawyer, or a justice like his father, someone to boast about, and visit now and then? He had been to the university in Oxford, he had attended the Inns of Court and done well there; but now he was in the employ of a great man, Sir Robert Cecil, principal Secretary of State, a little hunchbacked fellow, very clever, son of the great Lord Burghley, and the queen's chief adviser. Tom was becoming a stranger to them, mysterious, not telling all he did. Policy, all was policy, and policy meant secrecy and intrigue, and gossip behind the arras, and backstairs trickery and sudden unexplained journeys; and what did we know of such at Bourton-on-the-Hill?

Thomas latched his bedroom door behind us. A small room, this, with a low beam and sturdy uneven floorboards, the latticed window smudged with the dark leaves of the creeping ivy that nestled the sill. A bed, an oaken chest and stool furnished the room.

Thomas slung a great length of cloth about himself and with rapid movements reshaped it into something like a garment, half gown, half cloak, and he stood thus, draped, and plainly pleased with the result.

"What do you think of that?" he said magnificently.

"I think I see you muffled in a blanket."

"There you are wrong. To your untutored and ignorant eye this rare and wondrous apparel might indeed seem not dissimilar to the homely blanket that you know; but to the Scot this is his 'Heelan tertane', and you are amongst the first to behold it in England, cousin Giles. There will be more of it anon, I promise you, when the hordes come south."

"And do they all wear such, north of the Border, instead of ruffs and doublets?" I marvelled.

"Every one," said Thomas solemnly. "And they are bare-legged and hairy chested, with beards down to their waists. I speak now of the women . . ."

I sniggered. He was jesting – was he not?

It occurred to me that for all that I had been to Burford School and knew the sons of country gentry I had never seen a Scot. Was it true then that when the old queen died our country would be peopled by a race of folk in Heelan tertane which, true to my first impression, did indeed resemble a blanket – dusky red and green cloth woven in squares this way and that, and certainly like nothing I had seen before.

"The old queen may not die," I shrugged. "They say she will out-live the sun and the moon."

"Don't stoop, Giles, to trite rustic adages. Of course she will die – probably of boredom now the Earl of Essex is no more. The question is when she will do so. It is also pertinent to wonder whether the transition will be rough or smooth, and whether the more obscure and tiresome of the potential claimants will be kept at bay. Otherwise we shall see an odd little flurry and when the dust has settled we shall find a Spaniard on the throne – or a bookish female recluse. But Cecil has it all in hand and I," he added smugly, "will have played no small part in the business."

I assumed that he wanted me to press for details of his cleverness, for the enjoyment of preserving an enigmatic silence, thereby implying that the toils of policy were too intricate for my understanding. In this assumption he would have been right. I knew that Tom was in the service of Lord Burghley's subtle son and that the work he did was secret, hidden even from the queen. This was because she would not name her successor, and that probable successor was the man Tom had been sent into Scotland to meet, King James VI. I supposed Tom carried letters, spoke to Scottish lords, picked up gossip on the backstairs, formed judgements, received information, brought his findings back to London. Such work would suit him. He had always been a little devi-ous by nature. Myself, burdened by a painful honesty, and assuming honesty in others, tended on the whole to believe what I was told and found Thomas's character a difficult one to fathom. I never knew when to believe or disbelieve; anyone might fool me when they would. I could no more tread the tricky path of diplomacy than fly.

I sat down on the stool.

"Tell me something of the places that you visited," I prompted, confident that returning travellers liked to expound a little on the sub-ject, and maybe even Thomas. "You went, I heard, to Stirling?"

"A castle on a crag," he shrugged.

"Edinburgh?"

"A street."

"The palace of Holyrood?"

"Pretty enough."

"And are there truly blood stains on the floor where Rizzio was murdered?"

"Giles, I had better things to do than squint at floorboards."

"Thomas, you are an exceeding dull traveller. I see what your mother means when she says that you are not forthcoming. But did you see the king?"

Here you would have thought was a straightforward question, requiring affirmative or negative; but Thomas paused as if to weigh up his reply. He half turned away from me and directed his attention to pouring wine into the two glasses on the oaken chest. He handed me one; we drank.

"I did," he said.

"And – ?"

"And what?"

"And what?" I echoed in exasperation. "You must be one of the few folk in the land to have seen the one most like to rule over us after a queen who has been on the throne all my life and for over forty years. What is he like?"

"What he believes himself to be," said Thomas carefully, "is a wise and righteous teacher, an honest good fellow and God's regent upon earth. What he is in actuality is a short self-opinionated man with uncouth habits and a fear of the dark."

"Of the dark?" I said. "Have they no candles in Scotland?"

"I speak symbolically. This is a king who has spent his youth in terror of assassination by those who would have wished his mother back upon the throne; who has been taken prisoner at least twice; who cannot see a naked blade without a shudder; who jumps when he hears a noise for fear it is a blast of gunpowder; who has seen armed men burst into his chamber; and who believes that every woman is at heart a witch."

Thomas laughed at my sober countenance.

"He will do, Giles, he will do. He wants a quiet life. He wants to spend his days in hunting, his evenings in study, his nights in the arms of a pretty boy, and all the time in between in drinking Scottish ale. Under such a regime the clever man may rise all unobserved. However," he continued, with an elaborate yawn, "I did not ask you here to talk of things which will be common knowledge in a month or so. No,

Giles – I brought you here to share with you a strange adventure which
befell me in Scotland. A very strange adventure. It concerns a boy . . ."

CHAPTER TWO

"**P**icture to yourself a banquet at a house in Edinburgh," said Thomas. He sprawled upon the bed, still in the chequered plaid, and beckoned me beside him. We lay there side by side, leaning on our elbows. Even so as boys we had lain in the grass of a summer meadow, overhanging the Evenlode, watching for fish.

"Remember," he continued, "it was springtime when I first went north. Now I have never been the kind to let the season of the year affect my thoughts and my behaviour. But even I could not but be aware of that time of which the poets sing. Sweet air, the song of the birds, the blossom on the bough – you know the kind of thing?"

"Yes; we had springtime here in England too."

"It was at the house of Will Cornwallis, my companion from Queen's. We were drinking. We were very much at our ease. We discussed encounters of the lustful kind."

Boys. Tom had always been a man that liked a pretty lad. I never heard his name coupled with a wench's. But he had told me tales of the bedchamber, snippets of his London triumphs, exploits of his cronies and himself. It seemed a natural way of life. Lately I had become aware that it would be my own.

"And then – ?"

"He said that it was time I fell in love. I ridiculed the notion. He began to tell me the names of young men who might interest me. He said some of them were at the banquet. I said yes, the sexual provender had not escaped my notice. One in particular. And then there came a singer of ballads . . ."

"Your strange adventure?"

"Wait; no; merely its commencement."

"A ballad singer?" I queried dubiously.

"Oh, not your street corner hawker – uncurl your lip, Giles. No, this was a beauty. Not in the truest essence of the word, but beautiful nonetheless. A long-haired lean youth, big-eyed, eyelashes two inches long, the kind who looks as if he never gets enough to eat or warmth enough – the kind you long to take home and place by the fire, the kind that preys upon your nobler emotions and finishes by trading on your weaknesses and causes you to kick him out . . ."

I bowed to Tom's superior knowledge. I had never known one such,

13

but Thomas spoke with feeling.

"The song he sang was one I'd never heard," continued Thomas. "I'm told that there are any number of such, home grown in the Border country, and in particular where the Ettrick and the Yarrow meet. They are rivers, Giles," he added loftily.

"And your ballad singer came from there?"

"He did. And his song was of a lady that picked a rose in Carterhaugh, by Selkirk – there are three rings upon the ground there, where even today grass never grows; and once a man was cutting broom there and fell asleep and awoke in a city which he had never seen before, where the folk were dressed in green and very fair to look upon."

"Do you mean that he was stolen away by the fairies?" I said uncomfortably. Thomas was to my certain knowledge a cynic of the first degree, and now would he have me believe in Robin Goodfellow, like any milkmaid?

"Oh, Giles, Giles," laughed Thomas, rolling on to his back. "I have started you at the wrong end of the story. Dear Giles, you have never been to Scotland – you have not been spellbound by its strangeness and its charms. This is a land of mystery and magic. The trees, the streams, the hills are of the Otherworld. It is the land of Thomas the Rhymer who was led through seas of blood down into the hill of the Fairy Queen's own realm – and of Michael Scott the wizard and astrologer, who cleft the Eildon hills into three, and now lies restless under stone in Melrose Abbey."

Mischievously Thomas quoted: 'The burn of bried/Shall run fow reid' – whose sense, either from Tom's inability to render the Scots tongue or from my own undoubted ignorance, I did not understand.

"The stream of bread shall run full red," said Thomas patiently. "Bannockburn running with blood. You see – Thomas the Rhymer foretold the Battle of Bannockburn. He also foretold that Scotland and England shall have one king."

"They have not, as yet."

"No, but they will have. Giles, don't pick holes in my narrative."

"Did Michael Scott really cleave hills in twain?"

"Of course he did not; don't be so stupid. Now may I continue?" Thomas lay upon one elbow, like a Roman at supper.

"The Borderland between our two countries is a wilderness," said Thomas dreamily. "A land of hill and rock, of ancient forest, of roe and red deer. There are ruined towers and holy springs and streams that glitter and marshes black and deep. Why, King Arthur himself lies buried beneath the hills. The same ones that Michael Scott split," he grinned. "The same hills where Thomas the Rhymer slept on Huntlie Bank. I saw his very tower. I laid my hand upon the stone. I wondered whether he would grant powers to his namesake . . . myself."

"Thomas the Rhymer," I agreed dubiously. "Well, it is true you are a poet." I had read some of Thomas's poems. I found them laboured and pretentious, but he told me they were the writings of a university man and were considered very witty. I accepted this; what did I know? In conversation he was reasonable enough.

"The ballad I heard sung came from this place; from the Forest of Ettrick," said my cousin. "When the lady pulls a rose there, up rises young Tam Lin. He was so beautiful that he was stolen away by the Queen of Elfland. He was out hunting. Pay attention to this, Giles, it is meaningful:

> And ance it fell upon a day,
> A cauld day and a snell,
> When we were frae the hunting come,
> That frae my horse I fell.
>
> The Queen of Elfland she caught me
> In yon green hill to dwell,
> And pleasant is the faery land –
> But eerie tale to tell,
>
> Aye at the end of seven years
> We pay a tiend to Hell.
> I am sae fair and fu' o' flesh
> I'm feared it be mysel'.

"Must the tale be told in that manner of speaking?" I grumbled. "Cauld? Snell? Sae fair and fu' o' flesh?"

"Yes it must," said Thomas firmly. "Giles, the gentleman who is most like to become your liege lord speaks so, and the noblemen whom he will bring along with him speak so – nay, worse! You will have to learn to understand it. Indeed," he added smugly, "I thought my rendition rather fine. Of course, the ballad should by rights be sung, but I will spare you my singing voice."

"Thank you for that at least. They pay a tiend to Hell? The most beautiful are sacrificed?"

"Yes. To save him from this fate the lady must wait by night at the crossroads beside a well on the night of Halloween. The Queen of Elfland will come riding by and all her knights. Amongst them will be Tam Lin on a milk-white steed, his hair all combed and golden. The lady must seize him and hold him fast, whatever may transpire." Thomas paused, stagey as a player, lowering his voice to a whisper. "She waits there. She hears the fairy bridles jingling in the darkness. They approach. She seizes her lover. And in her arms he is changed into a snake. But she holds him fast."

"Brave lady," I said drily.

"Ah, but that was only the start. A snake, then a bear, then a lion, then a burning bar of iron, then a red-hot coal. She flings the coal into the well. And out of the well comes young Tam Lin, naked. Stark naked."

"Well worth the wait then," I quipped.

"Agreed. She wraps him up in her cloak and takes him home." Thomas lay back, the recital done.

I sat up. "As easy as that?"

"What do you mean?"

"The Queen of Elfland stood by and permitted it? She is a personage of some power, is she not? She did not put up a fight to retain this yellow-haired hero, sae fair and fu' o' flesh?" I emphasised the Scots words with some sarcasm.

"Ah, I see your drift," said Thomas. "No, the might of true love, you see. Beside it the Queen of Elfland was powerless. All she could do was curse."

"What did she say?"

"Oh, the usual kind of thing. An ill death for the stealer of her swain; and as for Tam Lin she wished she had put out his eyes."

"I would expect no less. They say a female thwarted is the very devil."

"They do, don't they?" said Tom comfortably.

"You know, this Heelan tertane plaid is very pleasing," I said irrelevantly, picking at it thoughtfully.

"It is," said Thomas. And we thought no more of females, thwarted or otherwise; the matter was not our concern. And how the Fates were laughing then, as our strange destiny began its slow unwinding!

Thomas eased himself up and went to pour more wine. He brought the glasses back to the bed and climbed aboard.

"The reason for my telling you the story of Tam Lin – " said Tom, " – is to prepare me for the story of how you seduced the ballad singer," I responded cheerily.

"It is true that I did so," Tom said placidly. "But no, that is not the reason why. The ballad singer was a lout. All his soul was in his singing. In his own character he was an unwashed vagabond and only after money. No, my tale was but the preface to what came after – better! Giles! I met young Tam Lin himself!"

I snorted. I had after all learnt scepticism from Thomas, no less.

"But wait, Giles," Thomas laughed, accepting my disbelief with equanimity. "Let me explain. I told you that I had observed in particular one young man at the banquet. Our eyes had met. But then the ballad singer cast his magic circle and I was spellbound and so I pursued and gained, and passed the night in his company. In the morning, very weary –" Thomas smirked a little, allowing my imagination rein – "in the morning, bathed and scented, I found the tune of the ballad humming in my head, the words, being simple and rustic, easy to recall –

> She hadna' pulled a rose, a rose,
> A rose but only twa,
> Till up then started young Tam Lin,
> Says: Lady, thou pu's no more.

"Or, as they say up there, nae mae. Into my mind came once again, then many times, the face of the youth whom I had observed at the banquet. After I had eaten, I asked Will Cornwallis to tell me who was the young man. Long fair hair, I said, way past the shoulders. Light coloured eyes, a pale skin, a slender but muscular build. But the hair, I sighed in deep content, to die for! Lovely, yellow as a field of barley in August, rippling as the wheat does in the wind . . .

"'Robbie Kerr', he said without hesitation.

"'Robbie Kerr?' I repeated, savouring the name.

"'The youngest son of the Kerrs of Ferniehirst. Father dead, but a roaring boy in his time – led a gang of reprobates to burn and plunder Jedburgh – shot and killed the Earl of Bedford's son. Warden of the Middle March, peacemaker of a kind. Devoted to Queen Mary of the Scots. A great Border family – any number of branches.'

"'Enough!' I laughed. 'I'm not after his father or his family or the branches, unless they provide a cooling shade under which lovers may lie! No, it's the golden hair that has enraptured me.'

"'Young Robert . . .' My host considered the matter. 'As I say, he's the youngest of many. Born of his father's second marriage. He'll never inherit. No prospects whatsoever. Doomed to obscurity, I feel. Not an ounce of brain between his ears. All muscle and flesh. His only chance of rising would be to trade on his good looks and marry well.'

"My face must have fallen a little.

"'Marry well? Is there no hope for such as I then?'

"'I would not say that, no. What I have heard of Robbie is that either bed will do. Much like the cuckoo pint,' he sniggered, 'you know, lords and ladies . . .'

"'Where is he now?' I enquired, blowing on my finger nails in careless fashion, feigning indifference.

"'He has already left,' said Will. 'If you want him you'll have to go after him.'

"'Where has he gone?'

"'South, to the Forest of Ettrick and Ferniehirst. But you'll never catch him. He has a fair headstart. He could be anywhere. How will you find him?'

"'Oh,' I said, 'I shall pull a rose.'"

CHAPTER THREE

"It was an odd journey," Thomas said, "because it took place on two levels, and I do not mean the terrain. At first I followed the road towards Jedburgh. When I was hungry I ate at a wayside inn; when I wished to sleep, the same. I slept in foul blankets; I drank strange beer. I had a good nag, no trouble to me, and the weather was kind. After all, it was Maytime. You know as well as I do that young lovers and travellers pursue their goals in springtime. There was hawthorn in bloom."

"Was it far? Did you have far to go?"

"Giles, I have no idea. You understand, I was in pursuit of an ideal. Distance and time were irrelevant. I saw the countryside about me – I saw grey-green hills, I saw crags grey-rose in colour. I saw sheep and cattle grazing and heard the strident cries of birds. I saw the lairds' tower houses and I remembered that here men rode out upon desperate ventures – cattle stealers, reivers, men who burned houses, pillaged, slaughtered. Yet it was very peaceful as I rode, and I suspect I saw the whole place with the eyes of one bewitched. Maybe I was in danger. Maybe I was fortunate to escape robbery or violence. I could tell you nothing about the folk on the road. All I could see was him who rode before me."

"You mean that you were not far behind the fellow you were seeking – Robert Kerr?"

"I mean he knew that I was following him, and he played me such a game."

"He saw you?"

"Yes, at some moment early on he saw me and he must have guessed that I was in pursuit. I told you that our glances met, that in a hall of strangers we were bonded briefly, fleetingly, yet memorably. And he led me on. Giles, it was very strange . . ."

"It seems so."

"You see, he rode a milk-white steed, like young Tam Lin."

"Many people ride upon white horses," I remarked, unwilling to see supernatural agents at work here.

"The sun flashed upon the horse's trappings. The sun caught the iron of the horse's shoes. There was gold about the rider. He had golden hair. It streamed behind him as he rode. He looked back over his shoulder. And into my mind all the while came back the ballad song:

The steed that my love rides upon
Is lighter than the wind;
Wi' siller he is shod before,
Wi' burning gowd behind.'

"I wish you would speak in your native tongue," I grumbled and returned our empty glasses to the chest and myself to the bed, where I sat leaning against a bedpost.

"Oh come, you understand me well enough," said Thomas. "Besides, I have very much grown to love the Scots tongue, particularly his," he smiled. "But to be sober, let me say that it will soon be politic for all men to embrace the Scottish way of speaking. Acceptance of the Scot is acceptance of peace and stability and a king of some scholarship and moreover an admirer of male flesh. You and I will have our fortunes made, thanks to King James."

I accepted correction and prepared myself to love the Scottish way of speech.

"Without ever permitting me to draw close," Thomas continued, "young Kerr kept more or less in view – sometimes hidden for hours at a time, sometimes tantalisingly close. He could do so," he explained, "because he knew the lie of the land. It was his home country. There was forest enough, and hill. Why, once he rode around a clump of hills and fetched up behind me, and, riding at speed, overtook me, passing within a hairsbreadth of me, but succeeded in deluding me and shaking me off the scent when I attempted to ride faster. And if I lost him he contrived to reappear, but so far ahead that I could never quite achieve him. I lost him in the dusk of the night I put up at an inn and thought myself a fool for the quest I was upon, but in the morning when I continued on my way he was ahead of me and waiting. The sun shone upon his golden hair. Wretched elf! My rational mind cursed his trickery. Some other part believed that there was magic in it."

"You might have given up and left him to his magic," I observed. "He took a risk there."

"Oh, he knew I would follow," Thomas said ruefully. "They always do, the lads who are too pretty for their own good. Besides," he added with a rapturous sigh, "not for all the world would I have quit my quest. With every mile he was leading me towards the forest of Ettrick, towards Carterhaugh, where he must show himself. And so on we rode."

"Until, as I suppose, you caught him."

"Until he permitted himself to be caught," said Thomas, "in a glade in the Ettrick forest. This is a most ancient place," Tom said. "They say it is King Arthur's forest. Oak, ash and thorn grow there, pagan trees. Silver streams flow, flanked with alders. And there are meres fringed with reeds, where the red deer drink, and rough scrubby bushes and wild grasses, dense thickets of brambles, hazel, rowan. The sun shafts through them all, transparent gold. I saw his white horse tethered in a grove of birch trees. I dismounted and looked about me. Then he dropped down from a bough, straight into my arms."

"You may guess the magnitude of my enchantment," Thomas said, "when I tell you that it was a shock to me to find I held a youth of flesh and blood. I half expected him to fade into insubstantiality in my arms, or to take on the weird and startling shapes recounted in the ballad. Had he become a snake, a bear, a red-hot brand it would have occasioned me no surprise. Of course," he added with a sudden grin, "I would have dropped him instantly had this been so. Fortunately he remained as I had first supposed him – a handsome youth with long yellow hair, and by his amicable demeanour one who welcomed my proximity. We kissed.

"Oh, Giles, the honey of that first embrace! The sweetness of his lips! If I should live a thousand years I never shall forget it!"

Indeed Tom must have been in the grip of passionate emotion so to forget himself as to speak in language so conventional, so typical of the mere commonplace lover. More was to follow.

Lying upon his back, arms behind his head, Tom gave himself up to the remembrance. "I clasped him to me and devoured his lips. I seized hold of his flaxen hair and twined my fingers through its lush abundance. I felt the warmth of his body against mine, pulsating, eager. I flung my cloak upon the ground and we lay down together in the grass."

A pang of envy pricked me, hearing this, for truth to tell I had never in my fifteen years known passion sharp and sudden as that. What was it, this encounter in the Maytime woods – lust? enchantment? Or perhaps, said a peevish voice somewhere at the back of my mind, simple exaggeration . . .

"Carefully and slowly I undressed the beautiful youth," said Thomas. "He lay back on my spread cloak, stretching like a cat before the hearth, turning this way and that to facilitate my work. Plainly this was one who knew himself beautiful and this was not the first time he had been undressed for pleasure's end. Myself I was as some adventurer that chances upon a treasure chest and puts his disbelieving hands amongst the emeralds, rubies and gold, uncovering jewels beyond price, each one richer than the last. In sober fact what I uncovered was a slender body – strong arms – firm muscle – a smooth belly – a crotch of golden hair – an upright prick that glistened at the tip. And here my search ended, for, my mouth being close against this last, I must take it between my lips and kiss it to our mutual satisfaction. I would have believed myself in Heaven – but the preface to my tale being one of the faery kingdom I was obliged to consider myself much like my namesake the Rhymer, who was spirited away to a wondrous land for seven years that passed by in the twinkling of an eye. I was a man bewitched, I own it, and put up no resistance, my will not my own. How long this happy state lasted I have no idea."

"Until his quiver was empty, I daresay," said I, the reluctant voice of reason.

Thomas smiled, nodding. "I daresay. Ah, but Giles, naked he is the most beautiful creature you have ever set eyes upon. But perfect. The neatest firmest arse – round white globes lightly furred with palest gold – and Giles, the thighs, so muscular and strong . . . oh, am I rambling?"

"A little. I am all envy."

"It occurred to me that I could bring him to England," Thomas said. "And when he was settled and at ease I would take him to London. He could meet the great ones of the land and be an ornament at Her Majesty's court. I continued to gaze at him in great delight, my mind awhirl with plans and expectations."

"I assume then that the Queen of Elfland did not arise out of a bush and turn either of you into toads," said I. "And I know that you were not away for seven years because I saw you in the spring before you went away to Scotland, and I see you now upon St Simon and St Jude's Day here at Bourton-on-the-Hill."

As if to verify the same there came a shriek of laughter from downstairs from one of Thomas's sisters, and I heard the opening and closing of the front door and the babble of conversation as a visitor was received below.

"We'll go down later," Thomas grumbled, rolling back into the folds of the plaid. "It's only John Lidcote, courting Mary. He will stop to dine now and he's a monstrous dreary fellow, the kind they call the salt of the earth – reliable, kindly, deadly dull; my father much approves of him. Well," he added, "now we are truly back upon solid ground. As indeed was I, when my young Tam Lin began to speak."

"You had not spoken to each other all that while?" I marvelled.

"No, we conversed in laughter and in grunts and gasps and groans of ecstasy. No words were needed. However," Thomas said, "the acts of pleasure being completed, conscious now of social nicety, I said most politely: 'Thankyou; may I introduce myself? My name is Thomas Overbury; I have travelled here from England and at present I am lodging in Edinburgh.' My golden-haired vision then replied. Now listen to me, Giles, and I will try to replicate exactly what he said. 'A ken wheel who ye are an' a leid ye here tae ken ye baitter.' You look puzzled, Giles, and so was I. Lord, Lord, thought I, staring into the big beautiful eyes, what have I done? I do not understand his speech! Take him to London? He would be as incomprehensible there as one of Sir Walter Raleigh's Indians. Take him to Whitehall? He would be laughed out of doors. My plans and dreams came tumbling round about me like a house of cards.

"The face of an angel – a voice that would make King James sound almost Stratford-atte-Bow, and which could only be described as barbarous and uncouth – and that is to be generous!

"Oh, fool, I told myself, for you are notwithstanding deep in love with him, and foolish that you be, you are wise enough to guess that this will lead you into trouble."

I am glad to say that Thomas never guessed how deeply; nor how very apt was his foreboding.

CHAPTER FOUR

"Now some would say, Tom," I observed, "that you being the foreigner and Robert Kerr a Scot on his own ground, he had a perfect right to speak as he did, and you were much at fault for ridiculing what he said."

"And they'd be right!" exclaimed Thomas cheerfully, sitting up. "But put it thus: the centre of the world in terms of advancement and prosperity is London. If Robert Cecil has his way, King James will slip into his English inheritance as neatly as a boat into a harbour and then it follows that all those who wish to rise will flow with that same tide. And what will they encounter? On the one hand the old nobility, sneering and hostile, and on the other the common man – the sailor who saw off the Spaniard, the yeoman who will punch the face of a passing Frenchman, Dutchman, Welshman, Scot as soon as look at him. So here I am thinking to bring Robbie south and know him better and have constant access to his many charms, and I am fetched up against this obstacle: he will not be able to make himself understood. You see, Giles," he explained, "in Edinburgh there are many gradations of language. There is the Scot who has already been to England and modified his speech accordingly. There are the educated, who through familiarity with Latin, French and Italian, are fast losing any native accent, hardly knowing who they are. And there are the Roberts – handsome, strapping, stalwart, lusty – and dim-witted."

"Oh, now I am sure you wrong him," I protested. "You have made a superficial judgement because you did not understand him. You said he came of a great Border family. Surely he was educated?"

Thomas shrugged. "You forget that I have had much more to do with him since that first primeval encounter. Nothing that I have seen since persuades me that between the pretty ears of Robbie Kerr lies anything but air."

"Then I suppose that in spite of his great beauty, you have now decided to abandon him as unworthy of your interest?" I said drily.

"No," replied Tom loftily. "I have decided to mould him, to improve him. And I shall need your help."

"Me? My – ?" I stuttered startled. "Whatever has this to do with me?"

"Nothing as yet, but I hope otherwise. Giles," said Thomas, eyeing me with a probing stare. "How do you envisage your future?"

"With some gloom," I admitted. "I am supposed to follow in your footsteps; I am to go to Oxford. But you and I both know I have not your ability nor ambition. I am not one given to study, and at the least persuasion I will leave my books and idle away my time. I don't know," I said ruefully, "but I seem to have the makings of a wastrel of the first degree."

"You underrate yourself," said Thomas. "Maybe your path lies elsewhere, and your talents also."

"You sound as if you had some ideas on the subject," I said. It would not have surprised me. Since we were boys Thomas had always had strong opinions on his own and everybody else's life, had led us in our childhood games, had ordered me about.

"Would you like to see a portrait of young Robbie?" Thomas said then, though I had the impression that he was not changing the subject.

"Of course."

Thomas reached out with one hand and returned it with a little oval miniature set in the palm. We perused it thoughtfully.

I saw a young face, a mischievous one, with light-coloured eyes and sandy eyebrows, a very pleasing face, neatly formed, framed by thick golden hair that touched the shoulders. Indeed – or maybe I was influenced by Thomas's narrative – it had an elfin look, a merry look, a half smile lying lightly on the pretty mouth.

"Not the face of a great thinker, eh?" said Thomas affably.

"I am sure you will do enough thinking for you both," I said. "As I guess it, you are already making plots concerning him."

"Plot is not a word to be used carelessly in this day and age," said Tom, mock serious. "But plans I have, yes. Plainly something must be done to prevent this little jewel going awry in the great confusion which is sure to follow. Picture it, Giles. No one knows when the queen will die – a year, a month, three years, six months. This, by the by, is treasonous talk and you will forget I spoke it. Scotland is very fidgety. The Border is like the starting line of a race. Everybody wants to be there when the moment comes, and not out in the Western Isles or visiting an uncle in the north. It will be first come, first served. There will be a southward rush akin to the onslaught of a marauding tribe, and some will be trampled underfoot. It is my intention to see that Robbie goes not under."

"And where is he now?"

"In Edinburgh, I believe. He must go where Earl Dunbar goes; he is one of his pages. As far as I may ascertain the arrangement is an indifferent one – among many lads of similar background he passes the earl his cloak, helps him to the saddle and hands him a goblet now and then. You say he must have been educated – yes, but not as you or I would understand the term. He can read and write, of course, the latter in illegible handwriting, possibly due to his being left-handed, as, curiously, are all his family – why, they even have their spiral staircases built the better to accommodate a left-handed swordthrust! Someone has tried to teach him Latin, but without much success."

"And what does Robbie think upon the matter?" I enquired. "Does he want to go south? Perhaps he is content at home."

"Of course he wants to go south," Tom said firmly. "Of course he wants to seek his fortune – who would not? There's nothing for him in Scotland. He has no chance of inheriting Ferniehirst. Besides, he wants to be with me."

"So you are confident of his affection?"

"Oh yes, there is no doubt of it," Thomas assured me without hesitation. "He is happy to put himself in my hands and allow me to change him for the better."

"The shape shifter," I observed drily.

Thomas laughed. "You could well say so. I shall change him from a rough uncouth reiver lad into – " he paused.

"Into?" I wondered.

"Someone worthy of myself," said Thomas pompously.

Tom spoke the words in all soberness. As so often before, I marvelled at his self-conceit.

"Once, after lovemaking," Tom said, "we lay and talked about the future. We were at Ferniehirst, where, I may say, I was made very welcome by his family. It is a dainty castle, Giles, with turrets and a tower, and everything very new, for it is only latterly rebuilt – one army or another is always knocking it down or setting fire to it; it is no easy matter living in the Borderland. They call it the hidden castle, as it lies in a fold of ground on a wooded slope above the Jed Water. Down beside the river we would wander in the drowsy summer heat – there we would slap the midges from our skin – there, nonetheless, we would lie on a couch of fern, while the sunlight through the branches dappled his bare shoulders. I told him how I planned to rise in my estate.

"'My father is a simple country squire,' I said, 'content enough in his place. But I myself have some ambition. Robert Cecil treats me as a valued emissary. I am engaged upon important work. I have had close converse with King James and when His Majesty becomes monarch of England I shall hold a position of some importance. I hope to be an ambassador – France, perhaps, or the Low Countries. It is only a matter of time. A man who stays close to me will rise as I rise. A man whom I may trust will share a golden future. Robbie, I believe that you will be that man. What do you say? Will you be my companion?'

"He said yes, of course, or to be more precise he said 'Och, aye.' His meaning, however, was clear enough.

"'Then,' says I, 'we must work upon you, Robbie, and you must have a smattering of culture and a familiarity with the Latin and French tongue – a graceful walk – an easiness with the sugared phrase. Here I can help you. Will you put yourself in my hands and accept my guidance?'"

"For answer he entwined himself about me and pulled me to him and so engaged me in a deep-throated kiss that all considerations of a tutelary nature slipped my mind. I fear that the translation of Robbie to a courtier *par excellence* will take a little time. Hear this:

"'Show me,' I said, 'the sights which are considered worthy. What should a traveller behold?' Abbeys, I thought, castles, houses, libraries, holy relics, places where the great have lived or died . . .

"He took me to a meadow. 'When Ferniehirst was captured by the English, it was a bloody time,' he told me. Oh, and Giles, he did not say it in the well-modulated tones I use when I recount the same, but with a deal of hissing and spitting, as is sometimes common in the broad Scots speech. 'And so, when John Kerr drove the English out, it was blood for blood. And in this field they played the ba' game wi' the heads of those they killed.'

While I digested the sense of the above, recoiling somewhat in revulsion, Robbie smiled at me with those lustrous eyes and said with modesty: 'I am no' bad a' the ba' game mysel'.'"

"Not," conceded Thomas, "that he plays the ball game with the severed heads of those inimical to him. I verified as much. No, he plays it with a pig's bladder. And as I understand it, there is nothing in his estimation to equal the excitement of taking part in what to you or I might well seem like Bannockburn re-enacted. Two gangs of ruffians fight one another for the possession of the ball – they break each other's heads, they kick each other's privities, they roll in mud, they charge through rivers, they hurl aside a passing townsman, throw women and children out of their way, trample through churchyards, brawl and bawl; and finally one gang is adjudged victorious, they all become friends and they drink themselves to oblivion in the greatest good humour and consider the time well spent. And Robbie is deemed something of a hero at the ball game. And this is the man that I have undertaken to reform!"

"I would surmise," I said, "that you and he have very little in common. Would it not be more practical to forget the whole business and look for a lover more like yourself?" I added drily in case he should have thought I meant anything other: "Refined, scholarly, competent at court?"

Thomas looked suddenly bewildered, pained. "Of course it would. This is not a friendship based on logic, reason. I scarce comprehend it all myself." He sighed. "Giles, I have always lived my life on a course impelled by the intellect. My previous lovers have been fellow students, and we have conversed in Latin and written love poetry in the style of Petrarch and Ovid. Think what it has done to me to be possessed by Robbie Kerr! Lust, I grant you, drew us together. But that first priapic encounter past, there yet remained a something stronger. A spell cast by the elves of Ettrick? I half think so. Tam Lin and Thomas the Rhymer and the hidden sorcery of the Faery Queen. And yet what nonsense am I talking? There has been no place for foolery of that nature in my life till now."

"Not at Queen's, no, not at the Inns of Court," I agreed. "But consider your roots, Tom. I was thinking even as I came up Bourton Hill about an old fellow who saw a headless lady leaning over a wall, and how the cider must be made before the long dead wayward souls abroad on All Hallows night step in and drink it. Don't we hear the milkmaids say charms over the butter churn? Don't we put rowan about the stable, and as boys did we not watch in the church porch on Saint Mark's Eve to see who would die in the coming year? Why should you not believe in magic – you have grown up with it?"

"I turned my back on old country ways long ago," said Thomas curtly. "For the inexplicable nature of my friendship with young Kerr it pleases me to flirt with notions of the Faery Queen, but I know full well that I jest. It was lust that brought us together and that which shall keep us so is his wish to learn and mine to teach. He understands that he lacks worldly knowledge and that as a result of my own superior education I can help him. I grant you that the desire to teach would have been less fervent had the pupil not possessed an arse to die for . . ." He paused in contemplation of the same, in which vicariously I joined.

"It was a summer of love, Giles," he admitted. "We were often together in Edinburgh. At any other time I might have marvelled at the Royal Mile, along which so many kings and queens have ridden; I might have admired the castle on high; the deer park; the mountain which they call the Chair of Arthur. I might have made my way down Thieves' Row to the insalubrious quarter where stood the house in which the king's father was murdered, and reflected upon the transitory nature of mankind. I should have studied the gun loops and battlements of the tower of Holyrood – I cared nothing for them. The marvels of the famous town centred for me upon the room where Robbie Kerr and I met. When I think of Edinburgh I think of the sun shafting in upon Robbie sleeping. I see him dozily waking, I see his slow half-smile, his open arms all invitation; I see the wondrous curves of his ripe buttocks and the crumpled sheets and strewn clothes; and I taste again his mouth, his skin . . .

"Sometimes, Giles, I went to watch him train with some other youths. Quarterstaff, fist fighting, wrestling, riding – he excels at them all. He can beat any opponent into the ground, whack a fellow black and blue, jump furthest and highest, win any race. And I watch and admire and I congratulate him, and then the chill voice of my intellect says: this is a boy can scarce write his own name, has no conception of how to compose a letter, has small Latin, knows little of the history of England, nothing of policy, nothing of the lands beyond the seas. Our gracious queen is but a name to him – her attributes, her triumphs, her statesmen, her sea discoverers a mystery. Philosophy, astronomy, logic, rhetoric – mere rumours. Fifteen years old – why, *your* age, Giles, and in comparison you are Cicero!"

I gave a modest smirk.

"And yet," said Thomas, "I half suspect that Robbie's very igno-rance is partly what attracts me to him. His is a mind unformed. In the brief time that we were together I was able to give him some hint, some inkling of the wealth of knowledge which might be his. But I was as one that pulled aside a curtain to reveal a promised land, only to let the curtain fall. There was not time . . ."

"If you had spent less time in lovemaking?" I laughed.

"In spite of that," Tom claimed, "I made a good beginning in the gracing of young Robbie. At least he knows his ignorance now. He knows that if he would rise in England he must learn. We went to buy books. I think that he will prove a good pupil. His mind is eager, malle-able. I wish I could devote my entire time to its improvement. But there it is – he knows now that there is a path. And I have set him on the way."

"And how will he fare without your guidance?"

"Well may you doubt him!" Thomas laughed. "You should have seen his face as I piled book after book upon him. 'And must I know this?' he wailed. 'And must I know this more?' 'You must,' says I, im-placable, 'everyone at the English court will know as much and more. Do you want to seem a hammerhead? Why, look at King James. He is a bookish man and he will set the tone of the court. Plutarch, Cicero, Livy, Ronsard, Du Bellay, Froissart, Calvin, Elyot's *Governor* – which you have there – Calepino's *Septilingual Dictionary*, he knows them all, and the Bible from beginning to end. When you come to the English court as my companion it will not be enough for you to boast that you can wrest a pig's bladder from your opponent and run with it for twenty miles! Requirements at the English court are somewhat different, my lad!'

"He grimaced, but he settled down with Elyot. He read Ronsard too, with the aid of a dictionary. In the study of French he sees some purpose – after all, because of Scotland's ties with France there is a strong French influence in Edinburgh. You see Frenchmen walking, riding – you know that they exist, their manners much to be admired. Did you know that the king's most celebrated lover was a Frenchman? Well, Rob knows of it, and of the king's Scots paramours, and thus takes it for granted that men make love to men, which made it simpler for my own case! Rob knows that one picks up pretty ways by studying the French. Sitting there at the window with the sun on him and a French dictionary in his hand, he told me that he intends to go to France . . . Ah, but he's like a child – he wants things. To go to France, to improve himself, to acquire knowledge – all preferably without lifting a finger. Study? – he has no concept of it. Hard work late into the night by candlelight? – that's not his way. Latin? It's too difficult. Elegance of speech? He shrugs indifferently. A graceful bearing? He laughs, and sits there with his knees apart, as if the space between is not wide enough to accommodate his balls." Tom shook his head and looked at me. "Whatever will become of him?"

"What do you think, Tom?" I said, like a good player on cue. I suspected that the information he had passed to me had been to some purpose.

"I think it partly will depend on you, Giles," was my cousin's startling reply.

"Indeed?" I answered guardedly.

"Indeed," said Thomas smoothly. "You see, it is my intention that your future and his be closely intertwined."

CHAPTER FIVE

I have said that Tom was dictatorial and full of self-conceit. It should not have surprised me that he made a remark of such incredible absurdity. Yet it did surprise me. It took me aback. However, I responded with the voice of common sense.

"Tom, your pretty catamite lives in Scotland and I in the Midland shires, and it is my intent to go and study at the university."

"Oh, pish," said Tom dismissively. "I know your heart is not in study any more than Robbie's is. Burford School has given you a grounding and your natural good temper does the rest. The sober truth of it is that you have no idea what you wish to do with your life and stand a fair chance of wasting it. And this is where my plan falls out so neatly. I intend that you shall oversee the fortunes of Robbie Kerr while I am overseas. You see, dear coz, I must pursue my own advancement."

"What do you mean? Where are you going?"

"On the express orders of Robert Cecil himself I am to travel in France, Spain and the Low Countries," Tom said. "I am to familiarise myself with their customs, perfect my grasp of their language, learn all I may, and bring my knowledge home. I am being groomed for the post of an ambassador."

I was properly impressed. I congratulated my cousin on so fair a prospect.

"Yes, 'tis no bad thing," said Thomas complacently. "And I have no doubt as to my fitness for the post. There is, however, the matter of Robbie. I could be away for a long time. I mean more than a year – two years even. I am young yet; there is much to learn."

"You think he will forget you?"

"Of course not," Thomas said scornfully. "Have I not conveyed to you the extent of his dependence upon me? He sees me as his guide and mentor, the one to lead him through the thorny briars of the transition from one reign to another. The difficulty lies in the fact that no one knows just when this same transition will occur. Smooth it is like to be, for Cecil has it all in hand – that is a monstrous underrated fellow, Giles, and is sure to be important in the new reign, and therefore all that follow Cecil will rise high. But Giles, policy is a quagmire. I am Cecil's servant but I will be overseas. If Her Majesty dies while I am far away our family risks being overlooked. This is where you come in, Giles; you must take my place."

"Whatever do you mean?" I said alarmed. "I know nothing of policy. I would probably spoil our chances by some blunder. Whatever can you be thinking of to suggest it?"

"In plain terms – Robbie! For there is something else, Giles, a further pitfall. There is someone at court into whose hands Robbie must not fall."

"And who is that?"

"There is a dangerous man already in touch with King James. A sleek lean cat-faced charmer, a man whom the queen – God bless her – has had the good sense to keep well at arm's length, knowing him for a villain. And part of his essential villainy is that he seems to be the flower of courtesy, with a silver tongue and a deep affection for whomsoever he converses with. But he is all show, all honey. They say he is in league with Spain; he is a great intriguer."

"Who is this monster? He would seem the creation of a playwright's pen."

"Unfortunately he exists beyond the confines of a playhouse; though, as I say, a certain obscurity has been forced upon him through our queen's shrewd judgement. He is Lord Henry Howard, son of that Earl of Surrey who was executed by King Harry, and he is brother to that Duke of Norfolk who was executed for his treachery to the crown some thirty years ago – before your time, Giles, but you know of it. This is a man who has been feeding long on bitterness. He has had no chance to thrive while our good queen yet lives. But now . . ."

"You know him, Tom? You seem so sure of what you say."

"I have spoken with him, yes, and he was all politeness and affability, as he always is to one's face. He's an old man, Giles – why, he must be sixty now. I daresay it is the pleasure which he takes in scheming that has kept him so alert and lively. He relishes it. A little merry smile of innocent delight hovers at the corner of his mouth when he speaks of anyone whom he would sooner see disembowelled. And this man has been working on King James by letter and by messenger. God damn it, I have taken some of the messages myself."

I shifted, secure in the sense of pleasant detachment of someone who hears a tale of wickedness that does not touch him, by the comfort of his own hearthside.

"But will King James be fooled by him?"

"I think he will," Tom answered. "Between them, he and Cecil have already poisoned the king's mind against poor Raleigh, an honourable and reckless fool steeped in the glories of the old days and making no provision for his future. But James is easy meat for Howard insinuation. You see, the Howard family adored his mother. King James bears a heavy burden of guilt for that his mother died and he continued in the pocket of the queen who signed the warrant for her execution. One Howard went to the block for Mary of Scotland, and now there are a swarm of them, Giles, a swarm of Howards, buzzing round, all eager to settle upon the Stuart bloom. Lord Henry Howard is merely one; but he has nephews, cousins, nieces – all voracious, glutinous and grasping. The Howard family will be a mighty force, I fear. But Henry Howard is the poison at the heart of it, and I have no intention that Robbie shall go near him."

"What interest could a homespun page from Scotland have for your wicked old spider spinning webs of intrigue?" I enquired.

"Merely," said Thomas, "that he is a man who loves his fellow men. Intimately."

"Ah," I said. "Very well then, I see that Robbie must be kept out of his clutches."

"I've warned Rob, of course," said Thomas, "but he did not take proper heed. He will surely have forgotten. And Henry Howard is so cunning and unscrupulous it takes a mind of equal deviousness to deal with him."

"It would not do for me," I laughed, "this flirtation with the iniquitous, which you so much enjoy."

"I do enjoy it," Thomas admitted. "But this is because I am confident in my own skills. It is a kind of game. But not one Robbie understands. It requires somewhat more subtlety than the ba' game!" He smiled. "And you, Giles, can remind him of my warning and be sure that he takes heed."

I grimaced. "I'd be no use. What could I do? This is a foolish notion which you have concerning me and Robbie Kerr. I would much sooner not have anything to do with it."

"Now listen, Giles," said Thomas briskly. "All you have to do is this: as soon as you hear that the queen has died, you ride north. You seek out Robbie and accompany him south to London. You see him well lodged. If I am fortunate I may contrive to return. But if not, you write to me and keep me well informed. Get him to London. I'll write to you there and let you know where I am. I have a particular friend there, a playwright, a roaring boy with a brilliant mind. My friend's a married man, which betokens a certain stability – his wife and babes will be there if he is not. He will either be in Newgate gaol or hanged or the most celebrated playwright of our day. You'll have no trouble finding him out, but I'll give you his address."

I enquired the name of this daunting fellow and was told Ben Jonson.

"You'll love London, Giles, since you love plays," Tom enthused. "There's a new playhouse on Bankside and a welter of good plays about. Go see 'em all, and take Robbie to 'em; write and tell me what he says and which he likes and what you think of 'em yourself. I wish I was joining you and not going off to France."

"I know that you do not."

"Now all the while, Giles," Tom said soberly, "comport yourself well, and if you get close to His Majesty stay close and see what may befall. Chance, unfortunately, always plays a large part in the unravelling of events. At least if you are there, our family will not be overlooked."

"This troubles you enormously, does it not, the prospect of being overlooked?" I teased. "Myself I am well content to be so, nay, I would prefer it."

"This is no time for maidenly modesty, Giles," said Thomas impatiently. "You will go north and do as I say. Promise me. I insist you swear it. I cannot be travelling in foreign parts and fretting about what I leave behind. It is heartily selfish of you to imply that you will not do as I say. You have nothing of importance to do instead."

I had no answer to this. Unlike Thomas I had no plans for my life. His own was charted like a sea discoverer's.

"Promise me, Giles." Thomas gripped my arm. "Do as I say – go north, discover Robert. Accompany him south. Ascertain his plans, his movements. See that he writes to me. Be my ambassador. Let me be there in your lively account of me."

I laughed in some bewilderment. "Are you not afraid I might be so much your ambassador that I grow over close with him? Do you not fear to leave us so much together and you hundreds of miles away?"

"Not at all," retorted Thomas. "First of all, I believe him entirely loyal to me; secondly, if he should dally with you it would mean nothing but the toying of an idle moment, which any man may do and be forgiven; and thirdly, when I return I am confident in my ability to win back the errant sheep to the fold of my influence. You are a dear boy, Giles, but you possess no self-esteem, and I when I return will have all the marks of greatness. But I do not foresee this happening – you are both devoted to me and neither of you will wish to cross me. You are both affable and easy going – too much so, a man might say. Both of you," said Thomas brazenly, "are ineffectual without the guidance of a forceful hand – mine. You will flounder without me. I shall return and put all to right."

Thomas plainly believed every word he said. Arrogance, insolence were to mark Tom's passage through life; here were their beginnings.

"It may never happen," I shrugged. "The queen may not die for ten years or more. You may not be away for as long as you suppose. Robert may choose to remain in the north."

"Stow-on-the-Wold may become the most celebrated centre of learning in the known world," agreed Thomas. "But if these things do not take place and all continues as I suppose, do you accept my proposition, Giles? I will of course reimburse you for the cost of your journey. I need to know that my interests are well served in my absence."

"I will do as you say," I answered. "I hope I may prove equal to the task – it is one of some responsibility, shepherding your loved one the length of England. And I have not your skills, Tom. I intend merely to be an observer. The momentous changes must occur without my participation."

"I wish that you were not so self-effacing," Thomas reproved. "You are not bad looking, particularly when you don't slouch. You have the fine eyes of our family and many would give a small fortune to possess hair like yours that curls of its own accord. You ought to learn to strut and swagger. A man must stand on his own feet and speak out boldly in this shifting world. Politeness and gentleness have their place, but Giles, excess of those good qualities can leave a fellow very much forgotten."

"I am phlegmatic," I agreed. "I daresay I will always be so. Fortunate for you. It means that I will always do your bidding. It means that when you propose a ridiculous venture I agree and meekly set off on what is very like to prove a fool's errand. I think at heart you would not wish me otherwise."

Tom laughed. "You could be right. Well," said he, unravelling himself from the plaid, "now that the important has been decided between us, shall we go down? Shall we dine and meet John Lidcote and be gracious?"

"By all means. After all, the whole Scottish notion may come to nothing."

Before the parlour hearth fire we found Tom's younger sisters on their knees, giggling, surrounded by apple parings.

"Join us, Giles – Tom," they invited cheerily. "It is St Simon's Day and we have been throwing apple peel over our shoulders."

"And these are wenches who consider themselves of rational inclination and wish others to believe them so," said Tom in mock disdain.

"Giles? You will not be so haughty?" they persisted. "Try it – you will see the initial letter of your future beloved."

I grinned and knelt down beside them and they watched and encouraged as I cut the apple peel.

"Well done! Look, he has the complete skin. Throw it, Giles, throw it over your shoulder – the left. And do not look behind you."

"I will not; I've no wish to see Tom standing there curling his lip with disapproval."

"You wrong me – I am all benevolence," Tom protested.

"Very well; attend to my throw." Kneeling there on the flagstones I cast my apple peel. The girls scrambled to discover the mysteries of my future.

"S! It's an S, as clear as can be!"

I turned and studied it. Yes, here was no doubt of it; it was an S. I pulled a face and shrugged.

"Susan? Stella?" they prompted.

"I know none of those names," I said.

"As yet!" they chorused gleefully.

"Give me an apple," Tom said, won over. Cries of delight accompanied the peeling of the fruit. And now Tom strode about the room, the peel in his hand, pretending to throw, hesitating, finally flamboyantly tossing the curved shape over his shoulder and retaining his pose of indifference as the girls and I crowded over the apple peel.

"It's an S," we decided – with some disappointment, for here was no variety.

"You will love the same girl?" it was suggested.

"Impossible," said Thomas firmly. I knew why he was so adamant on that score, though I suspect the girls did not. "And have you thought, an apple being the shape it is, the probability of the parings making an S is very high in an unbroken peeling?"

He was shouted down. "We have already had C, M, W, L, and O."

"What?" Tom cried. "Will you take so many husbands? Or lovers?"

The matter being one we could not settle, we abandoned the notion for the serious business of assembling for the meal, which was a merry one, with my aunt presiding and John Lidcote very attentive to Mary. I did not share Thomas's opinion that Lidcote was a dull fellow; he seemed pleasant enough and most polite – but then, I had not Thomas's superior education and for all I knew John Lidcote would have been deemed a country bumpkin by the discerning.

We had mutton with gallandine sauce and several small birds well boiled; and tart of almonds and several kinds of cheese. I was comfortably replete when I set off to return to Moreton-in-Marsh and begin the descent of that steep hill.

Naturally I thought much about Tom's narrative, of his meeting with the beautiful Scot and their subsequent friendship, and of Tom's proposition that I should involve myself in the young man's future. I mulled over the foolish business with the apple peel and could make no sense of it. Tom had scoffed at it, of course, but I had not his total disregard for signs and portents, and thought solemnly about acquaintances we had in common whose names began with S. I had no success. Even Robert Kerr's name did not qualify.

And what of this odd venture I had agreed to undertake, to go to Scotland and find Robert Kerr, to bring him south with the fortune seekers, and to watch over him for Tom? I felt most ill-equipped for such a task and already regretted my reluctant compliance. I would probably make some blunder, offend someone by accident. I wished I had told Thomas I would have nothing to do with the matter. Years of subservience to his leadership, from childhood wrangling to boyish games, had embedded in my character a mild-natured acceptance of my cousin's schemes, and here I went again. I was the Fool in the Tarot, the more so if I embarked upon the unknown journey north.

As I rode past the church to begin my descent of the hill I remembered once again that it was St Simon and St Jude's Day. It occurred to me that I need have no qualms. Any plan made on St Jude's Day – the patron saint of lost causes – would surely come to nothing.

CHAPTER SIX

So there I was upon the road to Scotland . . . It was just over a year since my conversation with Thomas. Thomas had gone overseas, as planned, and I had gone, in desultory fashion, to Oxford, where I had spent an unsucessful sojourn as a student. I pass over a time which proved a disappointment to my family and which was memorable to me only in terms of having fallen in love at least twice – once with a player of female characters in a travelling company that performed at the Bear, and once with a fellow student of higher station than myself. Neither resulted in a happy outcome for me and I retained a somewhat sour opinion of love and wrote some mournful verses on the subject.

I was always short of money – we were not a wealthy family – and I supplemented my meagre store by acting as a kind of valet to the sons of lords, waking them in time for chapel, and folding up their clothes. This was not unpleasing to me, though some – and Thomas certainly – would have considered it menial work.

I had never been so close to taffetas and velvets, and shamelessly relished the pleasure of handling the fine stuffs so frowned upon by the authorities who attempted to forbid the wearing of them in public. For a poor student I lived well then, as there was always a fire in the lordlings' lodgings, glass at the windows, and good food. I was given three fine cast-off cloaks – one velvet with a braided collar – some padded epaulettes and a tall crowned beaver hat with only the smallest of singes where it had been burned by a candle flame.

I studied little and I saw secretly a good number of plays both excellent and wretched, and several times considered running away to London where the best plays were seen first and in playhouses built for the purpose. I heard all about the Globe, with its galleries and tiring house and stage, its Hell beneath, its wardrobe stacked with finery and glass-jewelled crowns and mossy banks, its hidden machinery that made marvels and alarms, its Heavens above. I would have liked to see it for myself.

I somehow contrived – by dint of possessing an honest face, an absent-minded tutor and a certain amount of natural wit – to avoid expulsion from the hallowed halls, and I muddled along, picking up in passing some increase of education

I was sitting one day in the chamber of the young lord upon whom I was currently in attendance. I had a needle in my hand, and thread, and I was grappling with a velvet cloak lined with silk, repairing a rent. A fire burned in the hearth and the small room was well heated, the season being by no means cold. It was the month of March.

I heard running footsteps and shouting on the stairs. I opened the door and demanded to know what was happening.

"Have you not heard?" they cried. "The queen is dead. They have gone hot-foot to Scotland to bring forth King James!"

I turned back into the room and picked up the cloak. I folded it carefully and put it on the chair. In that moment it came to me with clarity that it would occasion me no sorrow to turn my back on the halls of learning and a life to which I was not fitted. The conversation with Thomas, some sixteen months previously and never far from my thoughts, came back to me as clearly as if it had taken place yesterday. I had thought much on the subject of Robert Kerr during that year. It had been as if I had a jewel hidden which from time to time I took out and polished. I had my own image of him, grown from Thomas's account as a flower grows from seed. The fanciful result was now as real to me as my own face, as much part of my day as eating, washing, toying with the pages of a book. The knowledge that I would one day be called upon to see him in the flesh gave stimulus and purpose to my imaginings. I longed for the time when I might turn my mind's pictures into truth and do my cousin's bidding. And so, on hearing that the queen was no more, I showed no hesitation. Confident in my justice uncle's ability to square my departure with the authorities I made my preparations.

Within a week I was on the road north.

The old queen had finally turned her face to the wall on 24th March, St Gabriel's Day, and immediately Sir Robert Carey had set forth to ride at breakneck speed to Scotland, to bring the news to James. Ah, what a ride was there! Horse after horse he rode to near exhaustion, never pausing, impelled by the enormity of his tidings, till, mud-stained, bruised and bleeding, he fetched up at the feet of the Scottish monarch to gasp out – what? The glorious days of Elizabeth are over – the brilliant golden days of sea discoverers, of Spaniard beaters, of silver-tongued poets, of bellowing bombastic players strewing their stages with sheep entrails, of worship of the goddess of the moon! But wait – we had not been so golden of late. It was no secret that the goddess had bad teeth and a bald head; Thomas said so. It was no secret that the Earl of Essex had been able to raise a discontented crew to riot, that since the uprising Her Majesty was sunk in melancholy and could formulate no policy at home nor overseas. If a country might be said to act as one, it might be said the country had been marking time, as I myself had been. This aimlessness was now at an end.

With the new reign something was beginning; but what? What would it mean to us, the arrival of this Scot of middle years and timorous disposition? There would undoubtedly be changes – some would prosper, some would fall. I shrugged. But most would doubtless continue much as before, gathering sloes and seeing Aftermaths among the wispy hedgerows.

As for myself, the choice was made, and I would ride to seek the golden-haired elf. If he was to be a part of the changes I envisaged, I intended to be there with him. For Thomas's sake, of course.

I had already considered myself the Fool in the Tarot. How much more justification had I now for that surmise! I wished more than once that I had the crow's powers for the sight that the old bird must have of the road north. There must have been a constant stream, a strange fluidity of shifting mass and colour, yet contrary to nature, this stream flowed in both directions. Northward rushed all those eager to be first to greet the king and claim his favours. Southward came those sent to prepare for his coming, harbingers preceding the main onslaught. And I, amongst the muddle and confusion, had the task of searching out one man. Fool's errand indeed!

I felt much like an ant that must seek out another ant, possessing nothing of the ant's ingrained knowledge of his own kind. Enquiring as I went, I had ridden up as far as Grantham, where they had told me the bulk of the king's entourage was gathered, before I learnt anything of any relevance to my quest. No one, without exception, had heard of Robert Kerr.

It was now mid April and a curiously warm one. The greenness and freshness of which the poets sing and the farmers make good use was lacking; and in its place the grass was a baleful yellow, withering at the wayside, the violets wan and drooping, the primroses small and shrivelled. The air was dry and caused the sweat to trickle in the collar. More than once I heard the gloomy observation that the wind was from the south and tainted; this, as always, followed by a grim prognosis of all manner of dire events to come.

It seemed that everybody was abroad to catch a glimpse of our new king. King! – the very word was new to us. At every inn where I stopped – sleeping in crowded rooms, dining at crowded tables, drinking in noisy excited huddles – the talk was of little else. We were all aware that we were alive in a momentous time. Those who had seen the king must tell of it, those who had not must ask. Oh yes, the fortunate ones said obligingly, they could describe His Majesty in the very finest details, thus: he was neither tall nor short; he was neither fat nor thin; he was neither fair nor dark; he was neither handsome nor ill-favoured. It was plain enough then that I would have no difficulty picking him out in a crowd, and I hoped that he would have the courtesy to wear his crown, so that I did not make obeisance to the wrong fellow.

However, soon enough I was to see His Majesty, albeit briefly. I had come away from a country inn and had not yet mounted, leading the mare by the bridle.

From out of the trees a hunting party burst and crossed the road at speed, hounds yelping, horses' hooves thudding, the riders very well apparelled, shouting as they went.

The folk who had been drinking ran forward and behaved like

mad things, throwing their caps in the air, kneeling down in the road at great risk to life and limb, and there – I had seen the king, and I can vouchsafe for the truth of it: the man was neither tall nor short, nor fat nor thin, nor comely nor ill-favoured, neither fair nor dark. He rode well and he wore burgundy velvet.

But there was beside him a rider of such dazzling physical splendour that for me His Majesty was entirely overshadowed. Dressed in sumptuous azure velvet the vision had a mane of yellow hair and even at the distance I stood from him, I could judge his eyes as blue as cornflowers. He must have been no more than three and twenty. As he rode past he flashed a brilliant smile. Hardly knowing that I spoke I said in tones of fervent admiration:

"But who is that?"

A fellow who had been kneeling in the dust just at my feet now rose and looked at me in some surprise.

"But that is His Gracious Majesty, no less – how can you ask?"

"No, no, I understand which one was the king. My enquiry concerns the fair-haired gentleman that rode behind him."

"The fair-haired gentleman? That was Sir James Hay, the king's particular companion."

"Sir James Hay?"

"Do you know nothing?" smiled my informant. "I thought that everyone knew the great ones about the king."

"Not I," I assured him. "I know nothing at all. Please have the goodness to instruct me if you know anything of the folk that we have seen. My name is Giles Rawlins and I have travelled up from Oxfordshire."

"I am Gervaise Elwes, at your service." He was a man of good quality, some forty years of age, with a lean pleasant face and mild gentle manner, his face a little lined with furrows of anxiety, as one who considered the world a place of pitfalls where the cautious man trod warily. "I can tell you nothing of Sir James Hay but that he dresses very well and is much admired for the splendour of his apparel."

Extravagant, I thought he would say, but dare not. I was to get no gossip about whether the gorgeous Sir James was the king's bedfellow.

"And the king himself?" I asked. "You have met him?"

"A noble worthy monarch – we are fortunate he comes to rule us," Master Elwes promised me. "They are all great men, our lords and masters. We are living in a blessed time. Our king is a mortal god, England's true joy, a Solomon."

Ah, I thought with Thomas's cynicism, a man determined to rise.

"Are there other noblemen whom you have seen?"

"They are all nearby, the great ones of our age. They are gone to Belvoir castle. There are the great Scots lords the Duke of Lennox, the Earl of Argyll, the Earl of Moray . . . And our own nobility: I have seen Sir John Harrington, Lord Thomas Howard, Sir Robert Cecil, Lord Henry Howard . . ."

Wait now, this name I know. What was it Thomas had said? *A man who loves his fellow men . . . intimately; a sleek cat-faced charmer who loves to scheme and plot; a man into whose hands Robbie must not fall.* And was this monster just nearby?

"Lord Henry Howard?" I enquired in careless tone. "And what do you know of him?"

"A man who loves the poor, a giver of gifts, a collector of fine paintings, a caring gentleman beloved by all who know him, a great family man grown old in the service of the queen and now ready to spend himself in the service of our new master . . ."

Yes, yes . . . I listened with a polite smile.

"And you yourself, Master Elwes, are you from these parts?"

"A Lincolnshire man, yes, young sir, but I'll be going south. They say the king is very liberal with his favours. I hope to bring myself, unworthy though I be, to his attention."

Knighthoods . . . I'd heard it said already in the ale houses – our new king gave out knighthoods like sweetmeats, one for you and one for you . . . The old queen used to squeeze them out like water from a stone. Times had changed.

"Wait – " I said, seeing Master Elwes would be gone. "Have you heard of Robert Kerr?"

"Who?" said Gervaise Elwes.

He was away to Burghley House. He had it on the best authority that the royal party intended staying there. He would be waiting, docile, grateful, sycophantic, palms outspread. But he had not heard of Robert Kerr, nor of the Earl of Dunbar, in whose household Robert might have been a page.

No one had heard of Robert Kerr. He must have been the most anonymous youth in the whole of the crowd that shuffled south. I made enquiries now concerning him of whomsoever I encountered – a group of men-at-arms, a gaggle of pages, a pedlar, a carter, a couple of female whores following the soldiers. To each I gave my name and said that I was Thomas Overbury's cousin. I was as one that cast a die upon a numbered board. But chance would rule the outcome of the throw.

At the little town of Stamford I struck lucky with a suddenness that caused me to marvel at Dame Fortune's careless generosity.

I drank at the same tavern as a group of servants from the Earl of Dunbar's retinue, the first Scots I had seen at close quarters. I sat listening unashamedly to their strange speech, deciphering the meaning with as much attention as the intelligencers in old Walsingham's service had given to the packages from Spain; and when I dared, much fortified by ale, to interrupt them and to wonder if they knew the whereabouts of Robert Kerr I was rewarded with a cheerful guffaw and the information that they did not.

Now it might be supposed that this was no reward at all; not so. After so many blank stares, shrugs and oaths, to find any that knew of his mere existence was akin to finding an emerald in an acre of grass.

"Rabbie is a law unto himsel'," they told me. "Noo here, noo there, and noo," they sniggered, "awa' wi' Bonnie Jamie."

"And where would that be?" I said eagerly.

But they spluttered over their ale and thumped each other in the gut and one fell off a stool in his mirth and I could get no more from them.

"Are you like to see him?" I demanded.

"Wha can say?" they answered helpfully.

"Then if you do," I said, as firm and plain as I could make myself, a little the worse for ale as I now was, "will you tell him I am Thomas Overbury's cousin and I am enquiring for him and am sleeping at the Lion."

In a chamber no bigger than a kennel, with a sloping roof, no window, and a door that hung like a drunkard on its single hinge. Here I repaired in some despondency, setting myself carefully down upon the truckle bed, for sudden movement caused one's head to bang into the roofslope. Excess of ale caused me to fall into a deep slumber.

I was awoken by the bright light of a lanthorn shining in my eyes, and a hand upon me, shaking me from sleep.

Leaping shadows danced upon the walls. A voice beyond the brightness said:

"Wake up. You want me. I am Robbie Kerr."

CHAPTER SEVEN

I guess I had always known that I would fall in love with Robbie. I daresay that the cause of it was my weakness of nature, my being easily led and influenced by Thomas's judgement. All through my childhood if Thomas said a thing was good I believed him; if Thomas said a place was worth a visit, there went I. And now I had been sent to

41

find the most beautiful of elfin Scots and I had found him, or rather he had found me. And lo and behold, he was everything that Tom had promised.

In the glowing darkness of our first encounter I saw very little of the joys to come, but I could tell that he was comely, beardless, with a wealth of golden hair. I sat up with a yelp as my crown and the low beam met, and Robbie laughed and reached out a friendly hand to rub my head.

"I am Giles Rawlins, Thomas Overbury's cousin," I spluttered. "I am most pleased to make your acquaintance, Robbie Kerr."

Robbie eyed me, lifting the lamp.

"Burn me, but you're awfu' young," he observed.

"We are the same age," I protested.

"Aye, but Tom was aulder and I thought that ye wad be the same."

"Tom warned me that you spoke broad Scots." A particularly stupid remark to blurt out to a Scot, I know, and I instantly regretted my boorishness; but believe me, Robbie's speech was hard to decipher for the untutored ear and I had small experience of language beyond the borders of Oxfordshire.

"I thought nothing of it till I came tae England," Rob replied unruffled. "Tom tried tae teach me otherwise but all tae no guid. And why the deil should I change my ways, when the king himsel' gies me example?"

"Indeed; I daresay he will pass a law ordaining the Scots tongue to be the natural way of speaking, and we poor English folk shall come to you for lessons."

"Ah – you think that I could maybe teach you something?"

There was no mistaking the merry glint in his eyes. The eyes glittered in the lanthorn light. Stars, thought I, rapturously, inconsequentially, with total lack of inventive spark.

"I am certain that you could," I said.

"Then it wad mak a change frae Thomas who thought that I had all tae lairn. You'll no' be buying books for me and testing my Latin?"

"Certainly not. You almost certainly know more Latin than I do."

He laughed. "I dinnae' think so and nor, I guess, do you. Well, Tom shall teach us both when he returns. And when, by the by, is that tae be?"

"I don't know, and nor, as I suppose, does he. He is as the driftwood on the stream and he must go or stay as Sir Robert Cecil orders. He will be monstrous learned when he comes back to London, speaking French and Dutch like a native."

"And very useful that will be in London," Rob grinned. "But hae ye messages frae him? And does he yet remember me?"

He sounded of a sudden wistful. I felt a warm affection for him, mingled with surprise. This beautiful boy cared for my self-conceited cousin and believed himself forgotten. I spoke to him of Tom, of how Tom praised his beauty and his eagerness to learn. I told him Tom had not forgotten him and dreamed of him in far-off France, and how, his love being so strong, he had sent me to search for Robbie to tell him of Tom's longing and to care for him on Tom's behalf till Tom came back to care for him himself.

"Och, he was a braw guid handsome man, was Tom," said Robbie, well content. "And he thinks me fair? He said so?"

"Many times and with great passion," I assured him.

"I could not understand why one sae wise should waste his time wi' a simpleton like mysel'. That is an awfu' learned man," said Robbie in a tone of awe.

"Yes, Tom was ever considered so; no one will dispute that," I agreed.

"And bonny. Some that are learned are dry auld sticks, lean-shanked and laidly. But Tam is very handsome."

"That's true. Everyone who sees him admits as much. He has very fine features, very well-formed. I have always admired his good looks."

It occurred to me that now I knew how Tristan must have felt as he pleaded the cause of King Mark to the listening ears of the fair Isolde. It thus came as something of a shock when Rob leaned forward and laid a hand upon my own and said: "But Giles, ye're awfu' bonny too."

This remark stunned me to speechlessness. I hesitated, teetering between elation and amazement, while my friend continued: "Let's no' stay here. Let's noo awa'."

"Awa'?" I stammered. "Where?"

"I ken somewhere better," he explained, "where we may sleep awa' the night."

"But," I began, "I am reluctant to give up this bed – there are so few to be had in Stamford, with all the crowds. Would you not sooner bide here?"

"No, I wouldnae'," Rob said frankly. "Are ye daft? Would ye no' sooner sleep in furs and velvets?"

Lord! Wherever did he mean?

"Come awa' wi' me," said Robbie Kerr, an invitation I could not refuse. I got out of bed, pulled on my shoes, gathered my belongings and followed him and his lanthorn down the stairs.

Pixie-led, I thought, watching the bobbing light!

The night was moonless and the air was mild, again with that unnatural warmth that had permeated the days of this most gentle April. I went with Robbie along streets I did not know, now down an alley, now across a square and past a church and now towards a goodly town house, as so it seemed by lanthorn flame and from the smudges of light at its diamond-paned windows. Robbie went round to a side door through which he let us in, and we went up a back stairway unmolested, unquestioned.

"Rob, whose house is this?" I whispered, fearing at any moment the shout of accusation, the forcible propelling of ourselves out of the door by angry burgesses in night attire.

"I dinnae' ken whose house it is, nor does it matter – it's where I sleep and you may sleep here wi' me, if it please ye, Tom's cousin Giles."

To my astonishment we entered now a large upper chamber that looked out upon the street. I caught a glimpse of the street below through the leaded panes before Rob closed a shutter. He set down the lanthorn and lit candles, moving here and there like some ethereal creature, light-bringer, dispeller of the gloom. I put down my travelling bag and gawped about me.

There was a large bed with four posts and tester, and the rich warm coverings of which my companion had boasted. There was a big carved linen chest with a high-crowned hat upon it, trimmed with plumes; and two great chairs, these also piled up with hats and epaulettes and collars. Along one wall from a wooden rail hung a wealth of sumptuous apparel – doublets and cloaks in satins and velvets, slashed and padded breeches, and beneath, several pairs of shoes adorned with bows.

"Are all these yours?" I marvelled, greatly impressed.

"No, but I may borrow them."

"Whose are they?"

"Bonnie Jamie's."

This was a name that I had heard amongst the drinkers in the alehouse. *Awa' wi' Bonnie Jamie*, they had sniggered.

"I know nothing about anything, Robbie," I said. "Who is Bonnie Jamie?"

"Sir James Hay. We call him Bonnie Jamie. For that he is sae handsome," added Robbie kindly, in case I needed explanation.

"He is that," I agreed.

"You've seen him?"

"Briefly. He was with the king."

"Hunting wi' the king," said Robbie sagely. "Eating wi' the king, drinking wi' the king, fucking wi' . . ."

"I . . . see." I carefully studied the tall crowned hat, turning it over in my hands.

"And that is why I hae the use o' the chamber, for Jamie'll be elsewhere, if he can work it. Puir Jamie – it's no' an easy time for him."

"Why not?"

"Wi' a' the English laddies noo about him, will the king still fancy Jamie? All those earls and knights and younger sons to make their way in the world and mony of them bonnier than Jamie, maybe. And younger. Burn me, everyone talks of nothing else: will the king take an English laddie and if so, who? They are taking bets on it."

"And who is the favourite?"

"Favourite tae be favourite?" laughed Robbie. He had finished lighting the candles now, and stood there poised, surrounded by light. "They say it will be the Earl of Southampton. He that was imprisoned by the auld queen."

"That's right – he joined with the Earl of Essex who is now dead. It was supposed that they were lovers. Men said the Earl of Essex had bewitched him. Southampton doted on him. Thomas said Southampton was not held responsible for his part in the uprising, for that he was very young and easily led."

"And is he very beautiful?"

"The most beautiful creature at court, said Thomas. Long curled hair and a body that poets praised. He was prodigious with his favours, they say. That's how so many sonnets came to be written in his praise – his lovers all turned to rhyme to boast of what they had enjoyed."

"Imprisoned he may well hae been," said Rob, "but the king has set him free. It was one of his first deeds as king of England. He ordered him set free and bid him come hither and bring the Earl of Essex's boy wi' him."

"What boy?"

"The Earl of Essex's son, some brat, twelve years old."

"Yes, I recall there was a son," I said. "Well, as I guess, his fortune is well made, through his being who he is. Tom said that Essex was in close collusion with King James before the old queen died, and wore a picture of the king upon a chain about his neck and a letter containing promises. But then it all came to naught and he was executed. I daresay that the king will wish to pamper the boy and treat him kindly for his father's sake."

"Well, that is no concern of ours," shrugged Robbie; and I daresay that the Fates above were sniggering and rubbing their hands in glee at the irony of Rob's remark. The Earl of Essex's son was to be very much our concern . . . "All I hope," continued Rob, "is that our Jamie stays in favour, for my star is hitched to his."

"It is? In what way?" I carefully replaced the hat upon the chest. I could not believe that Thomas knew of this.

"He said he would look after me," said Robbie, looking innocent as a newborn babe.

I looked at the bed and the beautiful clothes and at Robbie. I tried not to jump to conclusions. There was perhaps a family connection. Maybe Sir James Hay was merely his benefactor. Maybe Robbie was his page and helped him fold his clothes. Maybe nothing – my unworthy suspicions were correct.

"There is no need tae tell Thomas," Robbie said guiltily, a boy caught with his finger in the pie.

"To tell Thomas what?"

"It was only kissing, and wha wouldnae' want tae kiss Jamie?"

"But your first care is for Thomas?" I frowned.

"Och aye; I long tae see him. I can lairn frae him. All I can lairn frae Jamie is how tae dress well."

He laughed, and darted over to the brilliant apparel. "He loves his claes, does Jamie. He's a gorgeous dresser; they call him a peacock. Always blue, tae match his eyes. And he thinks nothing o' spending a' his money on his finery. He says: Spend, spend, and God will send!" He laughed, as one, I thought, who did not entirely agree. He stroked the satins. "Feel that. See how its glisters in the light." Briefly our hands touched. "Would ye like tae meet him?"

"Well, yes – and no," I stuttered stupidly. "I would not know what to say to him. I'm not like Tom, you know, at ease in the company of those whom Gervaise Elwes would call the 'great ones'."

"Gervaise – ?"

"Elwes. A fellow I met on the road, who hopes to get a knighthood. He thinks everybody with a title is a saint, and men whom the world knows to be villains praiseworthy if they be a lord."

"And there are many such as he," Rob agreed. "But you need hae nae fear o' Jamie. He's as merry a man as maybe and a friend to a'. And Giles, why do ye fear so? You are as fair as any. You need never fret about yoursel'. You will be comfortable in high company."

"Never!" I said, uncomfortable merely at the prospect.

"Then I'm sorry for ye," Robbie grinned, "for tomorrow when we meet up wi' Jamie we are like tae meet wi' noblemen and lairds and wi' the king himsel'. How do ye like the sound o' that?"

"Not at all," I answered fervently.

"Och, there's nae need tae fear the king," said Robbie. "He's a braw guid fellow, easy and guid tempered, and can talk o' farts and arses wi' the best o' them."

I was still marvelling over this recommendation concerning the prospective king of England when Robbie looked at me and said: "Are ye weary, cousin o' Thomas? Shall we tae bed? We live in bliss tonight and we even have a velvet padded close stool." He grinned. "Ye shall live weil, Giles, when ye live wi' me!"

He began to undress and I followed suit, hesitantly.

"Och, take off all your claes," he said. "We shall be warm in this bed, not like that puir truckle at the inn. And if you're not, I'll cuddle wi' ye."

We were soon between the sheets, the candles all blown out, the darkness thick about us, and the heavy folds of the rich bedclothes.

"Shall I do ye wi' my hand?" invited Robbie.

The unseen image of Thomas hovered between us. "I think not," I mumbled, knowing Tom would ask for chapter and verse from this encounter.

"Then will ye do sae for mysel'?" continued Rob, incorrigible.

Merely to oblige a friend, I thought; there is no harm in it. I felt for his body. My hands discovered his warm skin, his crotch hair; my fingers closed upon his shifting prick. This golden youth, shining star of Tom's rapturous accounts of journeys into Elfland, now throbbed beside me. I had barely begun when with a grunt of pleasure he erupted into my hand. His moist lips planted a kiss upon my cheek.

"Guid nicht," he said and turned aside to sleep.

"Good night," I said. I brought my fingers to my lips and licked them. Whatever was I about, I wondered dumbly, settling myself, back to back with Thomas's elfin fantasy, in a bed where King James's favourite was wont to lie; and promises of a morrow very different from anything that I had known before. Had this been Thomas's intention when he sent me upon this quest? I did not think so.

Och weil, I thought, it seems that I must make the best of it. And as Rob so justly observed, Thomas isnae' here . . .

CHAPTER EIGHT

Forget that miniature of Robbie painted so much later in his life. The eye of love must admit it: by then he had gone somewhat to fat. Now he was sixteen, and the morning sun that spread its honey over him showed Rob to be as beautiful a young man as could be. I climbed back into bed and lay there on my elbow, looking at him.

The golden hair alone would have drawn the lover, bee-like, to this flower, each strand a gauzy gleaming thread – such, I thought with a brief pang of guilt, as the bird brought from Isolde to King Mark and caused the burgeoning of his desire. This incandescent mesh lay spread about the pillow, half obscuring Robbie's face. He moved a little. I saw then the long gold lashes of his sleeping eyes, his full well-shaped lips, his clear pale skin, the perfect curve of shoulder and the muscled arm, the thick strong neck – a body built for strength and use. I felt a swift lift of the heart as it occurred to me that I must of necessity soon see it in its entirety when he got out of bed. He opened his eyes and smiled. His eyes were a light hazel. In their full stare I felt of a sudden vulnerable, as if my thoughts were written on my face. He reached up to pull my face down to his and kissed me. A persistent obligation of loyalty to Thomas held me back from a response of any intensity, and we drew apart.

Robbie clambered out of bed and pattered across to his clothes. Lazily I watched the firm round buttocks and the muscular thighs. Suddenly he laughed and, naked as he was, made a grab for the mass of swaying velvets that belonged to Jamie Hay. He swirled a cornflower-blue cloak about his shoulders and put on his head a high-crowned hat with an apricot-coloured plume. He turned to me and struck a bold provocative pose.

"What d'ye say, Giles?" he said. "Do they become me, Jamie's claes?"

"Very well," I said, not looking at the clothes.

"They come tae Jamie beggin'," Rob said. "*Ask the king for this, for tha'; I'll make it worth your while.* Gone all simplicity. It's double-dealing, secrets; lightness o' hairt no longer. So awa' wi' velvets, eh?" He flung the cloak from him and found the clothes that he had cast from him last night – good quality and serviceable and not without some frippery. He wore clothes well. He was of middle height, lithe and strong. He stood well, walked well; a man would notice him. A woman also, no doubt.

We breakfasted back at the inn. The streets were full of travellers, and in the air a bustle of excitement, an almost tangible greed, as if the nearness of the king would cause the sky suddenly to rain favours like a windy shower of blossom. It was open knowledge that the king was very free with his bounty – in the first flush of his coming into his own he was like a rich child happy to share out his toys. The cynical supposed this phase would pass, but ah, not yet, please God – a knighthood, a piece of land, a position of some trust, a benefice, a grant . . . All one had to do was to be in the right place at the right time and say the right thing. I thought once more of Gervaise Elwes and I wondered how he fared.

The royal party was now at Burghley House, the seat of Thomas

Cecil, second Lord Burghley, Sir Robert Cecil's half-brother. All the followers might encamp where they could. Dozens of tents were raised about the grounds and all along the road, colourful pavilions beside which horses milled about and servants hurried to and fro and pedlars sold their wares, while street musicians sang their ballads, banged their drums and played their pipes.

Whereas yesterday I would have loitered there, unsure of myself and my part in the melée, now in Robbie's company it was a very different matter. Secure in the affection of Sir James Hay he went boldly anywhere, and thus we rode in through the gates with the best of them, myself in greatest apprehension, Robbie waving cheerily and exchanging quips and pleasantries with men of Scottish origin, of which there were, it seemed to me, several hundred.

"Your people have come south in some force," I observed.

"My people they are lovely," Robbie laughed.

"Your people they are many!"

It was only at the very door of Burghley House that we were challenged.

"Robert Kerr of Ferniehirst, companion tae Sir James Hay. And this gentleman is even more important – he is the cousin of Thomas Overbury, Sir Robert Cecil's special emissary to the Low Countries and France." They let us pass.

We now found ourselves in a throng of well-dressed folk, all talking loudly, brightly, every sinew strained to appear most natural while yet listening and waiting for the king's arrival.

It is still with astonishment that I recall the complete unremarkableness of the entrance of the king. I do not know what I had been expecting, but as a child I had seen the old queen's majesty at Oxford and had felt a shiver down my spine as if a magical being had passed by; and I had been lifted shoulder-high to wave my cap. Almost drunk upon the heady tide of passionate and fervent loyalty, my ears reverberating with the bellowing of cheers, I had squeaked 'God save the queen!' in childish treble with the best of them. And now a group came shuffling down the stairs. Amongst them I saw Sir James Hay, big and broad with yellow hair, and next to him and leaning on his shoulder James of Scotland, uncrowned king of England. He was smiling, affable and jovial. He had fairish hair, a longish beard, a portly build and a pleasant face. The crowds about him bowed. He gestured with the hand that was unattached to Jamie.

"Nae ceremony!" he called. "All friends here."

And as if to prove the point he raised folk up and patted them and squeezed a shoulder here, acknowledged others with a gesture of benignity there; and stopped and spoke to others. He had gone by when it occurred to me with disbelief that I had had my shoulder patted by the king. I put my hand upon the place in wonderment and when I brought my hand away I half expected to see a rose petal, a flame, a glowing thumbprint at the very least.

Robbie, who had seen the king before and had stepped back behind me to allow me better view, grinned. "There, Giles, you hae been close tae His Majesty this day. Something tae write and tell your cousin!"

I smiled. I thought I would not. Perhaps if I had had my wits about me I might have gained myself an earldom! I could hear Tom's scornful tones: 'And you just gawped?'

"D'ye see the others wi' him?" Robbie asked, taking upon himself the role of guide and mentor to the rustic visitor. No doubt as a result of Tom's influence he had now familiarised himself a little more thoroughly with the scene of policy.

"I do. Who are they?"

"The Howards," Robbie muttered in my ear. "A very celebrated family. Auld gentry. Jamie says they're like tae rise." He jerked a thumb towards the passing nobles. "In the brown velvet and plumed hat and wi' the big nose and dark beard Lord Thomas Howard, an admiral who fought against the Spaniard; beside him his wife, who rules him, as is said. The wizened auld man is Lord Howard of Effingham, Lord High Admiral . . ."

I knew their names of course, heroes of my boyhood, the sea captains who had repelled the Armada and had fought in the Azores and at Cadiz.

" . . .Lord Henry Howard," Rob continued, "who helped the king tae his inheritance. But I daresay he's too auld tae be o' any use – he mun be over sixty. Nae doubt the king will gie him his reward and put him out tae grass!"

Lord Henry Howard! My ears pricked at the name. Elderly and useless – this was not the opinion Tom had formed of him. A man that loves his own kind . . . an intriguer . . . a man into whose clutches Robbie must not fall. Was this the moment to warn Robbie? No; but soon – soon as occasion presented itself.

Watching the tall crowned hat of Lord Henry Howard pass into the crowd, my eye was caught by a figure that needed no introduction to me. I knew instantly this was Sir Walter Raleigh. Head and shoulders above the common folk, the handsomest man in the room, with his noble brow, exquisite features, jet-black hair. I stared in awe and adoration. I would have liked to push my way through the throng to tell the great man how I had admired him all my life. But as far as I could tell, the king paused only very briefly as he drew level with him; so brief, thought I, as to be curt and dismissive. I could scarce credit it – this admirable man should be treated with respect, a radiant sun in a court of inconsequential stars.

"Let's be awa'," said Robbie. "There's games outside."

Still that same oppressive warmth, the air heavy, possessing none of the sharp freshness and showers of other Aprils. The lawns looked pale and withered. Over towards the trees where a track led away towards a wood, a cart laden with timber had been waylaid by a merry gang of Scots, and with much laughter they had seized the felled trees, rolled them to the ground, and were about a game of which I had not seen the like. Lifting a tree by one end of it they ran with it and hurled it forward, seeing who could toss the tree the furthest.

"Join us, Rob – ye hae the muscle!"

"Help me off wi' this, Giles."

I picked at the tiny buttons of Robbie's doublet and helped him to his shirt and breeches. He bent to take hold of a fallen tree. I joined the watchers; we ran to and fro accompanying the players, yelling as the tree hit the ground, darting clear as it fell. I remembered Tom's account of the ba' game at which Rob excelled. Rob and his compatriots were lost to the world, heaving trees, bawling advice and derision, risking life and limb in cheerful bravado and we ran with them. What a rabble we must have looked!

None of us saw the approach of the strangers. It all happened so quickly. Rob's tree landed with a thud, embedded in the grass. A horse reared and a rider tumbled to the ground.

We all turned to stare at this diversion.

It was a small party of riders which had come in through the gate, making its slow way towards the house. Our raucous reckless game had brought us right across their path. The tree which Rob had hurled had come too close to them and startled the horse. Its rider was a boy. He scrambled to his feet, white-faced and seething, a monstrous angry boy some twelve years old. A plain-favoured lad, with straight brown hair and, I thought, a sour pinched face; but then, I was not seeing him at his best, and anyone may look aggrieved when he has landed on his arse amongst a merry crew of guffawing spectators.

Rob, crimson-faced with exertion, sweat dropping from him, his golden hair stained dark with the same, his shirt plastered to his body, now ran forward to help the boy and gasp out his apologies.

"Forgive me! Och, I might hae kilt ye! Did ye no' see me wi' the tree? Could ye no' turn aside? Praise be y'are no' hurt."

The lad was so enraged that he could barely speak. He glowered at

51

Robbie. His venomous gaze would have cracked a nut from ten paces. At last he summoned wit enough to say: "You stupid uncouth lout!"

Rob blinked, still breathing hard, astonished at this rebuff to his gesture of appeasement. "Uncouth, is it, tae gie ye my apologies?"

"Uncouth it surely is to blunder into the path of noblemen with your rowdy rioting. Yes, I think uncouth is apt."

"Och well, maybe you're right," said Robbie with a grin. "Although if ye could hae held your horse better ye wadna' hae fallen off. I'm hairtily sorry for your misadventure. I hope we part friends."

"You fool," said the boy in icy tones. "Do you know to whom you speak?"

"It seems I speak tae an ill-mannered brat and one who is unworthy o' my guid will," said Robbie, calm enough now, and his fellow players, seeing Scottish insult in the offing, gathered about Robbie, loud in their support.

The gentleman on horseback accompanying the outraged boy now leaned forward.

"You speak to Robert Devereux, the son of the Earl of Essex," he said smoothly. "Now let there be an end of it." Turning to the boy he said: "Mount up, lad, and have done."

I looked anew at Devereux's companion. He was a handsome man, some thirty years of age. I admired his finely formed features and noble bearing, his grey eyes, high cheekbones and well-arched brows. This must surely be Southampton, darling of the young boy's father, he that the poets praised – and lay with? I noticed then his strained and sober mien. I knew this was a man now stranger to lightheartedness. His lover slain, himself a prisoner in the Tower these past two years, his fate uncertain. In my heart I wished him well and hoped James would be kind to him.

"But this foul Scot has insulted me," Devereux was saying, "and he must pay for it."

And there and then he drew his sword. Robbie stepped back alarmed, fell over the fallen tree and landed sprawled upon his back. Somewhat appeased and with something of a leer, young Devereux lowered his weapon.

"Put it up, Robert," said Southampton, touching his shoulder. "This fellow is not worth your anger."

Robbie sat up with his legs splayed out across the tree, like someone in the stocks.

"You are right, my lord," said Devereux loudly. "It seems that in His Majesty's wake came all the riff-raff of the ratcastle."

He mounted very neatly and with excellent control manoeuvred his horse clear of the sullen Scots and well out of the range of their muttered oaths against him. They gathered around Robbie, lifting him, rubbing him, voicing noisy sympathy.

"I'm well enough; nay, leave it – there's an end," he said. "Burn me, I'd like tae clout the little bugger's heid for him."

We agreed, possessed by communal and righteous indignation. We looked after the retreating party making its now dignified way towards the house.

Now in Robert Devereux we see personified the old nobility, the kind, warned Tom, that would not take kindly to the encroachment of the Scots. This was a family that came over with William the Conqueror, a family of ancient lineage, the d'Evereux. And young Robert was a lad who from birth had been known as Viscount Hereford; he could have claimed a seat in the House of Lords, led troops in battle, and in peacetime taken position of precedence near the monarch. That is, until his father's fall. Now his blood was deemed tainted, he was become the son of a traitor, with loss of all rights and privileges, including the earldom of Essex and the family estates. No wonder this was a thin-skinned querulous tetchy youth. But there was about to be a change for the better for the son of the earl of Essex.

"Did you hear his name is Robert?" I remarked with a smile. "The same as yours."

"It's a fair enough name," shrugged Robbie, "and anyone may grab it."

Across the lawn the party dismounted. Out through the door of the house came the king. He opened wide his arms. Southampton led the boy towards the king, bowed and stood back. The king clasped Robert Devereux against his breast and swore to love him as a father loves his son, to restore his birthright and to cherish and protect him all his life.

Yes, I thought morosely, much as I supposed – this was not a good person for Robbie to have offended.

I wondered fleetingly if anything untoward would come of it.

CHAPTER NINE

His encounter with the future Earl of Essex had left Robbie thoughtful. Now in another this thoughtfulness might have manifested itself in a preoccupied silence, the chin resting on the hand. In Robbie's case it showed in a serious consideration of the necessity for ear piercing.

"But did ye see him?" he marvelled as we wandered across the level lawns. "So young and already master o' the withering glance. They look at you as if y'are a dog turd. I think it comes wi' breeding."

"I think it comes with an unpleasant nature. You yourself are far too agreeable to stare at anyone so."

"As y'are yoursel', Giles. The plain truth is we are no' blessed wi' elegance o' manner."

"We don't know how to slay a person with a glance," I agreed.

"I think I would be more personally superb," said Robbie, "if I had my ear pierced."

"I don't recall that Devereux wore an ear ring?"

"No, I was thinking then o' the bonny Southampton," said Rob. "He had an ear ring – a wee pearl on a thread o' gold. Did ye see the way he leaned forward, sae dignified? I see what Tom was telling me. I see what Thomas meant when he said it was no' enough tae excel at the ba' game."

I could not help but laugh. "I fear it may be too late, Rob. It begins at birth, and then they go to a fine school and mingle with the sons of noblemen. Look at poor Robert Dudley, the favourite of Queen Elizabeth – all dressed in silks and riding the finest horses, and yet the old nobility always considered him an upstart."

"I come o' guid stock," Rob growled. "I am not some nobody."

"I know it," I assured him peaceably. "But there will always be some folk at court who consider the Scots barbarian."

"Unless we go tae France and pick up excellence."

"Why? Who has gone to France?"

"Well, Jamie Hay for one, and he wears an ear ring – a ruby on a little chain. He learnt his dressing and his courtly ways in Paris. In Edinburgh the flower o' excellence was considered to be Esmé Stuart, the king's great love – a Frenchman. He wore an ear ring," added Robbie. "Giles, I'll hae an ear ring and you shall make the hole for me."

"I – ?" I blanched.

"We could go tae Jamie's room . . ."

This most marvellous of dwellings, home of Lord Burghley and of its kind the very pinnacle of perfection, had taken on for the duration of the royal visit something of the quality of an extremely well-appointed hostelry with a superior breed of inmates. We could wander more or less at will once known to guards and servants. Robbie's connection with Sir James permitted us then to cross the hall, to climb the staircase and wind our way along the panelled passageways until we reached the chamber where the king's Scottish favourite was supposed to sleep.

It was there that Bonnie Jamie discovered us, Rob in a chair, myself leaning over him, a bowl of salty water at my elbow and a needle in one hand, the cork heel of a shoe in the other. Pressed between these two last was Robbie's ear. Slowly and surely my needle penetrated the soft cork, taking in the thickness of the lobe as I applied pressure.

"Quick – the ring!" gasped Robbie.

"What, is this a marriage?" Jamie teased.

"Rob is working to gain excellence," I answered, "and I am the means."

"I have seen excellence more aptly personified," said Jamie. "Rob appears to be in no little pain."

"Not at all," Rob winced.

Having inserted the gold circle in the lobe I stood back and surveyed my handiwork.

"Perhaps, Sir James," I said, "you could give us the benefit of your advice. Is it well done?"

"Advice, aye, and also the latest news concerning His Majesty's most intimate concerns, which, by the bye, is of no small relief to myself", said Jamie bending over Robbie's ear. "Bathe it well and be sure to keep the puncture open. It seems clean enough to me. Turn the ring constantly, Rob."

"And the news, Sir James?"

"The new English favourite is not to be Southampton," Jamie chuckled. "He is too old."

"How old is he?"

"Thirty. As you see, of an age to qualify for the position of elder statesman rather than His Majesty's companion."

Jamie was twenty-three. He was good, then, for the next seven years. Both Rob and I were too polite to say so.

"Do you think Southampton expected to be favourite?" I wondered then. I knew nothing, of course, but the handsome earl had looked of sober mien, as if playing down his undoubted good looks rather than accentuating them. It has sometimes crossed my mind, in the intervening years, that maybe the situation was the other way around – that Southampton had been asked for his favours by the king and had refused; this would certainly explain James's continual hostility towards him in the days to come.

"It must have crossed his mind," said Jamie. "He's no' bad-looking, for an older man, and everybody knows he slept wi' Essex and half the army in Ireland. But I know what you mean. That is a man who could have died along wi' Essex, if the queen had willed it; and I daresay his months in the grim fortress have given him cause for thought. They say he was not well. They say he has lost something of his nonchalance."

"And being imprisoned in the Tower could do it," Robbie laughed.

We agreed, with shrugs of affable indifference. It did not seem a problem with which we needed to concern ourselves.

"Here, Rob," Jamie said, with careless magnanimity, "here's something to plug that pinprick."

A pendant pearl set on a thread of gold as fine as gossamer! Robbie took it carefully and his eyes widened.

"Och, Jamie! You're a guid guid man!"

Jamie inclined his head in becoming and unconvincing modesty.

"Och, and Jamie, may we hae the room tonight?"

"You may," said Jamie, high on the crest of the certainty of the king's continued affection. "But don't forget your search for excellence. Make use of the sights you see around you. Study this dwelling – it's very fine. Peruse the paintings and the tapestries, and the beauties of the chapel. And while you are there, ask the good Lord for virtue and sobriety. In your search for excellence you may find that a pierced ear might not be enough!"

Rob grinned a little sheepishly and watched the lovely Jamie swirl away, a vision in blue satin.

We did indeed admire the magnificence of the dwelling. We did indeed enter the chapel. We had scarcely been there a moment when I became aware that we were observed. There was a small embrasure high up in the wall, a window niche where persons unable to descend to pray might watch the service from this vantage point. There would be a little room there and a good view of the chapel beneath. Someone was watching us.

Robbie had his back to the intrusion. I looked beyond his shoulder. I could see a young girl and behind her a woman in a green gown. The girl at once caught my eye and smiled. I thought her about thirteen years of age. I was mistaken; she was younger, ten or eleven years old, but painted cheeks and natural precocity contrived to make her seem older than she was. Her hair was long and loose. It was the colour of honey.

I turned away. I found it irritating to be watched. My lack of interest did not please her. She called out: "You down there – look at me!"

"Don't look," I muttered to Robbie, who was just about to turn. "It is a brat – a girl. She has been watching us."

"A girl?"

"Don't excite yourself; she is a child. Her nurse is with her."

"Pretty?"

"Fair enough," I said unwillingly.

"I tell you – look at me!" the young shrill voice declaimed imperiously.

"In your search for excellence, Rob," I murmured, "you do not turn your head to stare at some rich man's infant when she orders it; you preserve a dignified silence and ignore her."

"You down there! You with the yellow hair! Turn round and look at me!"

I looked; I was not in pursuit of excellence. How puce she had become in her frustration! She was leaning forward, looking down.

"Tell him to look at me," she ordered.

"I am sure that Robert Devereux would not turn round and gawp," I said to Rob severely. "Are you at her beck and call?"

"No, but – ," Rob said wrily, "by forbidding me you make her seem the more enticing."

"Heaven forfend," I shrugged. "It is all one to me. Stare if you must. It is of no consequence."

Robbie turned around.

"H'm," said the maiden brazenly. "You're pretty."

"And are you well content now?" I said to Rob out of the corner of my mouth. "You have been inspected and adjudged like a bull calf in a market. She will descend in a moment and expect to prod your buttocks."

"I would she might!" Rob answered shamelessly. "A child!" he teased. "She's of an age tae be bedded! And what was that about a nurse? The other one is a dame-in-waiting."

The dame in question leaned forward. Now she spoke to her charge. We heard her voice, carrying, disdainful, carelessly indifferent.

"See, child – they all turn around sooner or later. Men are so gullible. They do anything we ask."

We heard them laughing as they withdrew.

I felt vexed on Rob's behalf. I wished he had not turned at the maid's insistence and proved himself to be like any other. He was nettled by the encounter; it had come too close upon the heels of his brush with the boy Essex. One may rapidly have enough of being bested by the nobility.

"I never hae an answer ready," Rob said ruefully. "I hae nor wit nor poetic skill, nor way wi' words; and my written hand is unreadable. I daresay I shall pass my days in the wrong place at the wrong time and shall be overlooked and passed by. If it wasnae' for acquaintanceship wi' Jamie I would be one o' the crowd, sleeping where I could, waiting at table for a Scots laird that an English laird looks down upon."

"I have thought much the same about myself," I admitted. "I grew up in the shadow of a successful cousin. Thomas has wit and beauty and has already risen by his own skill. He mingles with the great, he travels overseas. My parents look at him and shake their heads about me – *why could not he be as Thomas? What will become of him?* You at least, Rob, are very beautiful; the beautiful have an easier passage, I believe."

"You think that I should marry money then?" said Rob in all soberness.

"No!" I said, startling myself by the vehemence of my response. "No, I did not mean that at all."

"It is a way tae rise," Rob said. "After all, I wadnae' need tae love the heiress. That is the way of it in this wicked world! You heard," he added caustically, "the maiden has pronounced me pretty. I should find out who she is; perhaps she'll hae me."

"You are much too young to wed," I said alarmed. What business was it of mine? Why did I find the notion so repellent? A burning jealousy arose within me, a jealousy of the possible bride, the nameless woman who might lay claim to Rob's affection and bind him to her by the ties of the marriage bed.

"And what would Tom say?" I persisted. "I am sure it would not please him if you wed. Let's hear no more of this. Remain a free man – revel in your liberty."

"I will, Giles, never fear," he laughed. "And Giles, I am no' the only one of us that has the looks; I wish ye wouldnae' underestimate your own."

A pleasant glow suffused me at his compliment. We went outside. All afternoon and evening in the fringes of the wood a group of Scots showed off their prowess – running races, throwing the javelin, fighting with quarterstaves. Rob bested every one. I swear that he won every race, jumped furthest and highest, beat down his opponent and hurled the javelin such a distance that the eye could not tell where it fell.

Later, the king came riding by, with a small retinue. He stopped to admire the participants. He watched them at their game.

But Robbie was not there; he had retired to James Hay's bedroom and lay moaning on the sheets while I bathed his ear and wiped the pus that oozed from the infected lobe. It seemed that more had been required than a needle and a piece of cork in the skill of ear-piercing.

If the king had come by earlier he would have seen Rob in his glory, half-naked, glistening with sweat, his muscles rippling, and his long hair golden in the rays of the setting sun. But the king came by later, paused, observed, saw nothing there to take his fancy; and rode on.

CHAPTER TEN

In so far as Robbie gave any thought to the future at that stage it was merely in terms of his own immediate self-improvement. It had been his encounter with Thomas that had brought home to him his shortcomings, of which previously he had been generally unaware. As a result of Thomas's suggestions he had applied himself with difficulty to a study of the French language, and with even more of a struggle, to Latin. A nodding acquaintance with the scions of the English nobility now engraved upon his burgeoning sensibilities the realisation that his gracing had some way to go before he would appear to the censorious anything other than a rough and ready Border reiver. In physical strength and beauty, however, he surpassed all those about him. All those about him? – other pages, men-at-arms, the flocks of country folk that lined the waysides and pressed about to gaze. We did not associate with the English nobility, nor did we wish to, both being of a self-effacing nature and no credit at all to our celebrated friend and cousin whose name we might have used to push ourselves forward into more discerning company.

Yet our part was an ambivalent one, for, knowing James Hay, we slept time and again in the bedroom offered officially for his use, he being elsewhere and returning only in the early morning, his status with the monarch still intact, though, we suspected, precarious. And thus it happened that we often found ourselves close to figures of note, and sometimes, in that atmosphere of both camaraderie and caution, to the king himself.

The unwieldy royal procession was now at Theobalds, the home of Sir Robert Cecil, whose skill and diplomacy alone, said Thomas, had ensured a peaceful succession.

It was early May. From waysides white with hawthorn blossom and tracks of dry-baked rutted mud we turned into a tree-lined avenue and saw a million glints of sun on glass – the many-windowed frontage of the stately house. The little hunch-backed figure of Sir Robert now came forth to greet the king. It was the first time I had seen Thomas's employer. So little he was, his face in repose a thin and troubled one; no doubt it had not been an easy matter to save the realm from civil dissent and gently to show a sad-eyed and undignified Scot in a quilted waistcoat how to succeed the goddess of the moon. Sir Robert led the king and his entourage within and those of us less privileged grouped about and marvelled at the magnificence of the building with its towers and turrets, golden weather vanes and rose-red brick. And yet because of

Robbie's understanding with James Hay, it was ourselves who lay that night in this beautiful mansion and slept in an ornate bed with scented sheets beneath a coverlet of gold-threaded brocade. I wonder that we were not found out, ejected and hanged from those great elms that flanked the approach to the entrance.

It was a house of marvels – a hall with a ceiling made into the starry heavens, walls composed of tree bark and branches whereon real birds perched; elsewhere an entire map of England spread across the walls and ceiling; now a great gallery displaying foreign wonders; and here again an indoor fountain. Thomas was on familiar terms with Cecil and had been to Theobalds; all this would be commonplace to Tom. I was a country bumpkin, marvelling at it all. A man who had attained the excellence we sought would be at ease among these marvels; we had some way to go before we acquired such worldliness. Glancing at Robbie I saw that he had grown reflective.

"Our nobles live in small square towers," he said ruefully, "and think themselves as kings."

He disappeared for the rest of the afternoon, playing at the ba' game with his Scots cronies in a meadow some way off. When night fell and we settled into the splendid bed I took it upon myself to act on Tom's behalf and spoke severely.

"Robbie, that is not the answer. You excell at the ball game and you have reminded yourself of it, but of what use will it be to you at the English court?"

"Who says I'm going there?" he replied ungraciously.

"I thought that was the general intent. Why else are we going south?"

"Och, I grant you, when we started out . . ." he shrugged. "I thought I'd take my chance along wi' the others. But I'm no' stupid, though you may suppose me so. I stand no chance wi'out Tom. Leave it tae me, he said, I'll see ye thrive. But wi'out him tae gie me guidance I'm an unco' blunderer hacking my way through briars. One more fly about the honeypot. And it's all push and shove and grab – that's no' my way. Tom said he'd make it all right for me; but he's no' here."

"He will be. He'll be back from France and when he returns . . ."

"D'ye see the pretty ways that Bonnie Jamie has? He learnt them in France. It's the French I should be studying. You'll try me, Giles, wi' the words I know."

Tom would have laughed to see us there by candlelight in the lovely room at Theobalds, I reading out a word, Rob giving me its French equivalent. I was not a traveller myself but I had the uncomfortable feeling that the French themselves did not pronounce the words as Robbie did. We persevered at this task long into the night, and the candlelight played upon the gorgeous limbs and golden hair of Robbie and cast shadows on his beautiful preoccupied face.

"Tom says that the way to rise is to bring yourself to the attention of the king," I said. "I rather think he hopes I might do so myself and increase our family's fortunes thereby."

"Aye, but ye mun hae skills beside," said Rob. "Otherwise it's like offering His Majesty the front of a house and nae chambers behind it."

"Agreed. But even with such a free and easy monarch as ours, who seems to count every man his brother in the first flush of his coming into his own, I do not think one could simply drop into his path and say: I am a man worth knowing, therefore know me."

"It was a' very well forTom," said Robbie. "He was learned and well-spoken and had the ear o' Robert Cecil."

"But have you never met the king yourself, in Scotland?"

"Och aye," said Robbie with a grin. "When I was a lad they chose me frae amongst the other pages tae read out the Latin grace at table. Easter time it was, and His Majesty gracing us wi' his presence. But ye ken, Latin and mysel' . . ." he grimaced.

"Why? What did you do?"

"I couldnae' read it. I fell over the words. *Celicole* was the word. I never forgot it – it means *O ye dwellers in the heavens.* What did I say? Coley caley or something – at any rate it wasnae' what I should hae' said, and once the mistake was made I went frae bad tae worse; you would hae thought my tongue was made o' leather and two sizes too large. His majesty is awfu' learned. He told someone tae tell me tae sit down and leave off murthering the Latin tongue. He couldnae' see me – I was awfu' sma', and hidden by the lectern. I never hae been in any great hurry tae meet wi' His Majesty – it could well be he remembers me. Och, he will say, are ye no' the lad who couldnae' read the Latin?"

"A blot indeed," I laughed. "But it was long ago."

"I still can read nae Latin – there will be nae place at court for me, not wi'out Tom who can direct me and tell me what tae say. Truly, Giles, I was counting on Tom being there when we arrived in London. Bring mysel' tae the attention o' the king? I would sooner hide behind the arras!"

"Ah, Rob," I sighed. "You are so dazzlingly fair that golden beams from your glistering hair would spread out like the sun's rays and give you away."

Robbie grinned. "Would they so? You're kind tae me, Giles. Come close and let's cast awa' the French lesson – it was a' tae nae purpose."

On the night that Robbie said he wished never to bring himself to the attention of the king, I made love to him in the beautiful bed in the chamber at Theobalds. In another part of the wondrous house the king lay with Bonnie Jamie; and in another part again lay Robert Cecil, content for once maybe, for that his plans were safely come to fruition; while somewhere else lay the lad soon to be restored to the earldom of Essex, dreaming of golden days to come, secure in the afterglow of his father's good name; and handsome Southampton, too old to be the first English favourite; and cunning Henry Howard into whose hands Robbie must not fall; and Thomas Howard and his scheming wife. Somewhere here in scented sheets slept the lady in green and the imperious maiden with the honey-coloured hair. Further off, his great ambition satisfied now, Gervaise Elwes, knighted at Theobalds, his sycophancy towards the great ones rewarded; and wherever Sir Walter Raleigh found rest that night, the wheel of fortune was for him upon a downward turn. Here, on this May night, the world hung in balance. All the characters in our play were there, save one, caught in a moment of time, players awaiting the cue to step forth upon the stage; and all of us unknowing of the way our destinies were to be intertwined, to no one's good.

The room was warm and Rob and I lay naked in the silken sheets. I kissed my way about his perfect body; this way and that I moved him, lifting his arm, toying with his golden hair, tasting the flavour of his skin, tracing my fingertip along the luscious curves of his arse, the hard firm lines of his shoulder blades, the warm power of his resting muscle. I kissed his lips and savoured the intensity of his response. I don't believe that either of us felt disloyal to our friend and cousin. I'm sure it was understood between us that Tom had first claim on Robbie and that if Tom had been here I would have been elswhere. But as we had both remarked, Tom was not here.

"I think I love you, Rob," I said. I could not help it. Poor fool, I thought, for it surely was a love destined to come to nothing. Tom would return to claim Robbie and I would be left with a sense of loss. Who else might I love after having loved perfection? Rob held me close, ruffling my hair, and thinking, as I supposed, of Thomas, and in response to my mumbled declaration he said nothing. Soon after that we slept.

However, I slept well, and being of a reasoned and phlegmatic nature, I wasted no time in displays of anguish, poesy or loss of appetite; after all, I had passed an excellent night.

In the morning Rob went riding with Scottish friends and I remained about the house and gardens, my idea being to make some observations for Tom's benefit concerning the glittering folk all gathered under one roof at this piquant moment in our nation's history.

It took no seer to prophesy that Sir Walter Raleigh was a man well out of favour. I had grown up to venerate him as a brave man, a man high in the old queen's favour. Now it was not so. A new wind was blowing and some would be swept away. But who would rise? Possibly Francis Bacon the lawyer. Or Philip Herbert the brash good-looking brother of the Earl of Pembroke? Certainly the Howards. Suddenly there seemed very many of them. They and their retainers were much in evidence, strolling in the parkland, loitering on the stairs, talking in loud voices, confident, assured.

With a deviousness of which I believed Tom would have been proud I contrived to make myself seem about some business or other, as if sent by an important person upon an errand of some urgency, and I went about the halls and galleries or studied the brilliant stones at the fountain's base and listened as I went. However, I found myself too easily distracted by a painting or a fine ornament or a view from a window or the wondrous gems worn by the rich or the startling widths of the women's skirts. I did hear it said that there was plague in London but, my mind being much on Robbie and the night that I had spent, I put such gloomy notions to one side.

A great many of the guests were in the gardens and I made my way there, past the semi-circle of white marble Roman emperors, keeping to the green alleys which, set with holly and bays, were thickly hedged and private. Here I was somewhat taken aback in turning a neatly trimmed hedge corner to encounter sitting in an embrasure the lady in the green gown and her charge, the honey-haired maiden. Their heads were bent over some book. I had heard conversation but I had not guessed the speakers to be so near. I almost fell over them. I could not in politeness withdraw without a word. I stuttered something.

"No, please, don't dart away," the lady said. "We have already met; we are no strangers to each other."

I was not much put at my ease by her reference to our previous encounter. *Men are so gullible . . . they do anything we ask.* She was attractive; not yet thirty, I thought, and not a great beauty, but with a great vivacity of countenance and very lively eyes. These now regarded me, and very much mocking, if I was not mistaken.

I thought that Rob would be amused by my blundering into them, and so, rather than pursue my own inclinations and depart, I lied and said that I was happy to renew their acquaintance. I told them my name.

"My cousin is Thomas Overbury," I boasted. "He is in the service of Sir Robert Cecil and is at present engaged in business for him overseas."

"Indeed?" said the lady smoothly. "We have not heard of him."
Her name was Mistress Anne Turner.

"And this fair creature," she indicated the young girl, "of course
you know."

"Indeed I have not that privilege," I said, pleased for Thomas's
sake to be able to match ignorance with ignorance.

"Not know – ? My dear young man, where have you been living?
In the moon? This is the Lady Frances Howard."

Ah – one more of the huge Howard family – though where she
fitted in I had no idea. The maiden murmured: "Lord Henry Howard is
my great-uncle."

It was odd, but somehow the simple statement carried a curious
overtone of menace and complacency, as if enough had been said, and
as much left unsaid. What? *So do not tangle with me . . . this is where the
source of power lies . . . I will be well protected in all I do . . . look to yourself
. . .*

"And where is your friend with the golden hair?" said Mistress
Anne lightly.

"He has gone riding."

"Not too far away, I hope?" teased Anne. "We very much fancied
his golden locks." Her next remark surprised me. "Under what sign
were you born, Giles? We are reading a book upon the subject. I will
explain your character."

"Taurus is my sign."

"I knew it!" Anne decided.

"I wonder at that," I said.

"You have strong shoulders and curly brown hair," was her reply,
"and it does not please you to give away the information. You are a
pleasant-natured man, not given to quarrelling; of easy-going ways, given
to laziness and a pleasure in stage plays?"

I laughed and said nothing.

"It's all here in this book," she declared; and I caught a glimpse
upon the page of a horned hooved creature with a fatuous smile and
starry circles about it.

"Frances here was born under Gemini," she said then. "It will be
her birthday on the last day of this month."

Frances lolled in the crook of Anne's arm, saying nothing; but it
was a marvellous expressive silence. Her lips parted and her little pink
tongue played there, a display I found disagreeable in one of her young
years.

"An excellent disputant," Anne said proudly. "And so she is, for
she always achieves her desired ends. Eager to learn . . . sharp and witty

. . . learning easily . . ."

"And that?" said Frances languidly, pointing a finger at the page upon which Gemini was portrayed.

"Which, dear?"

"That long word, next to wicked arts and ungodly knowledge. *Given to wicked arts and nec-ro-mancy.* What does that mean, Anne?"

Anne snapped the book shut suddenly. She turned to me and said in a high shrill voice: "Well – we cannot be blamed for what the book says. Can we? We cannot be blamed."

I had the strange sensation that she was asking for my collusion in keeping secret the foolish incident. A reference to necromancy? Was her fear that I might go and tell the king, who was reputed to possess an unnatural dread of the same? The whole thing was too trivial for further consideration.

"No, madam, you cannot be blamed," I said, which seemed to be what was required of me. "I take my leave of you then," I said abruptly, and Anne murmured some politenesses. I hurried away, glad to be out of their company. I thought Mistress Anne a marvellous silly female, and her charge a mischief maker.

I made my way to the avenue of elms to join those who awaited the return of those who had been riding.

A few small drops of rain began to fall.

This would of course in ordinary circumstance occasion no surprise; but we had had a spring of curious warmth and aridity. Cries of delight and astonishment abounded. Some ran indoors; some danced and held their hands out to the rain. About this time came Robbie riding back, waving as he caught sight of me. My heart welled up with pleasure as I saw him. His face was ruddy from the open air, his gold hair clustered about his brow, moist from the rain. I accompanied him to the stables, then back into the house.

As we prepared to mount the stairs we heard the king's party returning from the hunt and we stood back respectfully to let them pass. We bowed and stared. His Majesty looked at us, smiled and went on.

We went to Jamie's room and Rob took off his boots. I had commandeered a manservant to bring a tub of water and I helped Rob from his clothes. Into this bath now Robbie stepped and I began to scrub him, cheerily, for it was work much to my liking.

Into the room came Bonnie Jamie unannounced, unceremoniously, slamming shut the door. He looked down at Rob who grinned winsomely from amongst the suds, his chest and knees glistening, his hair well plastered to his head. Jamie stared at him. Venom was in that gaze.

"Out!" he said.

"Wha – ?" spluttered Robbie.

"Out!"

"Out? Out o' the tub?"

"Out o' the tub, the room, the bed, out – of – my – life!" said Jamie. He then strode about the room, kicking at Robbie's clothes – and mine – throwing the bedcovers awry, and finishing with legs apart and hands on hips in the manner of the portraits of King Henry.

"What for?" said Rob in the tub, his face a grimace of disbelief. "Where shall I go? Do ye mean I am tae go into another room?"

"I mean that you will leave this house," said Jamie. "My regard for you, Robbie, is as strong as heretofore. But this is not the time for fond affection. I am fighting all contenders. I have enough to do to keep His Majesty from Philip Herbert; and there are others." Stressed, Jamie's veneer slipped. He cried: "Och, I hae mysel' tae think about. Rob, I dinnae wish tae see you here again and if I do I swear I will make trouble for you. So go your ways, and you, Giles, see he stays away or I'll not answer for his safety."

"Jamie!" Robbie blanched. "But why?"

"But why?" said Jamie. "A simple matter. When His Majesty passed by and saw you as you waited at the stairs, he asked me who you were."

CHAPTER ELEVEN

A man more self-seeking, more politically astute than Robbie, might have gone directly to the king and thrust himself upon His Majesty's attention, following such an open invitation, and to Hell with Bonnie Jamie.

Rob, however, was of an honourable disposition: Jamie was his benefactor and Rob owed his wishes some respect. Therefore Rob did as he was bid, and our sojourn among the mighty came to an abrupt end. We slept that night in one of the tented pavilions with many others and counted ourselves fortunate, for all the inns were full, and the roads taken up with the encampments of those that had made temporary abode as near to the king as they might.

Now that the king was so near to London, folk flocked in their hundreds to catch sight of His Majesty. We had thought the waysides thick with crowds before, but that was nothing compared with that we witnessed now. People were trampled underfoot and carts wrecked in the excitement. It continued thus all the way south. A choir of singing children placed in neat rows to praise His Majesty was knocked over by the multitude, but their singing had not been heard anyway, being drowned in the raucous clamour.

Rob had suggested that he and I should ride direct to London and find ourselves a lodging and be there in readiness when the royal party finally arrived, and so with no little difficulty we went against the flow and made our way towards the city.

"London?" said one man to us in scorn. "There's plague in London. Half of this mob you now see are fleeing the grim reaper, with the king a mere excuse. You don't want to go to London! Nor does His Majesty if he has any sense. Thirty or forty have already died and they say it's only the beginning."

It was the hot spring, they said, the cause of it. But folk always love tales of gloom and terror. These reports of plague were surely exaggerated.

As we drew nearer to the famed goal of our journey we encountered any number of families setting out in the opposite direction. Carts laden down with household goods, rattling pots and pans, and yowling brats plodding on foot beside. In every instance the explanation was the same.

"We're quitting London and if you were wise you'd do the same. There were three deaths in our street and now they're putting up the red crosses on the doors. We're away northward. I'd advise you to do the same." But they directed us to Cripplegate where lived that friend of Tom's and where we hoped to find his letters waiting. St Giles' church was our landmark as the tall timbered houses closed about us.

As we were about to turn a corner a woman bawled at us: "Are you mad? The sickness is down there!" We caught a glimpse of doors nailed up with red crosses, a deserted silent street. About us buzzed street waifs, like flies.

"Buy a bunch of rosemary, the only safeguard, six shillings a bunch!"

Such was our introduction to London. We picked our nervous way between the houses. Still that ugly and oppressive warmth. It hung about the streets, picking up the foul town scents, enlarging them – the gutter offal, the horse dung dry and thick with flies, and at shutter windows where we asked our way, the smell of sweat and fusty garments, woodsmoke, beer, roasting meat and rotting fruit. Rats scurried in the shadows by the walls and prowling dogs rooted for food scraps. The stench in the heavy air seemed to waft like shifting smoke, tangible, as if it was not air we breathed but a distillation of all we saw about us.

I turned to Robbie, hesitating. "What if we left Tom's letters well alone?"

"I cannae' do that; I must hear frae Tom. He will be advising me what tae do."

"He would advise you to turn back," I answered tartly.

"You may turn back, Giles, but I shall go ahead."

"After all," I agreed reluctantly, "Cripplegate is on the outskirts. We need go no father in. We'll find this Ben Jonson and retreat."

It turned out that Ben Jonson was well known, a figure famed for his irascibility and his great learning and because he numbered lawyers and scholars among his acquaintance. But, we also learned, he was from home, gone into the country, staying at the house of a lord, as it was understood. His wife was left at home, his infants also, but . . . the sickness was about, you know, and infants first to go . . .. there was some sympathy for the wife here, for all that she was shrewish. We were directed to his house.

"Wise fellow," I muttered. "Gone into the country."

"His wife will hae the letters."

"It is as well you came to claim them," said Ben Jonson's wife in her doorway, infants at her knee. "Another few days and I would have burned them. Useless clutter. Take them and be off, and if you have somewhere to go, out of the town, then go there."

Heaps of soiled bed linen lay piled against a wall in the street. A dung heap shifted and a rat emerged, blinked, scuttled out of sight.

"Rob, this is an unwholesome place," I urged.

Rob nodded. We turned our horses.

"Lucky you don't have to live here," called Ben Jonson's wife to our retreating backs.

As we turned the corner of the street we were obliged suddenly to draw rein. A coach was coming at speed, bouncing horribly on the cobbles, clattering noisily north. We stared at it as at a phantom coach. You have never seen a coach the like of that same coach, those horses. Every part was bound about with leaves – herbs, we thought as it came past us, herbs whose property is to ward off infection. The two horses, the shafts of the coach, the wheel spokes, all were twined about with leaves. The windows were entirely covered; no one might see the protected one within. All that could be surmised about the occupant was that he owned a big herb garden and was in a hurry to quit London. But what a sight! You would have said it was a coach from Faery.

Ourselves were not far behind that elfin coach. We rode onwards at a smart pace, out towards the green meadows, and by a common consent put a fair distance between ourselves and the contaminated city.

The sickness! They said it fell in droplets from the air. They said dogs carried it. They said the south wind brought it. I felt as if my clothes, my hair, my skin, were touched with it, smeared with its taint. The air that fuelled those grim streets was on my lips. I shuddered. Into my mind tumbled the lurid pictures I had heard about – the black bulbous pustules, the fetid carbuncles, the fever. Its swiftness – you could be one minute hale, the next gone . . . the woman who promised on her wedding day to love to life's end, and life's end was the morrow . . . the woman who on her deathbed confessed to adultery with many – all neighbours – and then recovered. Recovered! Ah, so it was not always fatal then . . . we might survive. But I might and not Rob – then Tom would slay me. *How could you permit him to enter the infected town? How could you be so careless of his welfare?*

"Rob, how fare you?" I asked nervously.

"Very well."

But *within moments* , they said . . . I eyed him cautiously. "We had better find a lodging."

We took a room at a wayside inn near some small village surrounded by meadows. Here we read Tom's letters, seven of 'em, all about the wonders of Paris and the sights to be seen – the chambers of the Louvre, the Bastille and its cannon, the chateau where the Duke of Guise was murdered, the Crown of Thorns in the Sainte Chapelle, the piece of the True Cross in the cathedral of Notre Dame, a paten engraved with a love scene between Achilles and Patroclus and used by King Henri III, a missal-holder in the shape of a naked Dionysus in solid gold. An entire letter was devoted to his meeting with King Henri IV. Apart from general good wishes for our health, there were no particular instructions concerning Robbie or clues as to how we should next proceed. They were the letters of one who was very much enjoying his present situation.

By comparison our own seemed somewhat dull and dire. I remembered Thomas tempting me with promises of how much I would love London – always something going on, so many playhouses and any number of good plays. Well! The playhouses had been closed since the old queen died, and now were not like to open as long as the sickness smouldered in the city. And what pleasure was there in venturing within, with a daily increase in the number of the dying, and rumour rife, and fear. The tankard in the tavern touched by the lips of one about to discover a black boil in his armpit – the bite of a dog that carried contagion in its jaws – the venomous vapour – the rancid dust that settled on the vittals sold in the streets, all invisible carriers of doom . . .

Like an army of ants that straggles blindly but purposefully onwards before fetching up against an obstacle and dividing right and left, the unwieldy procession that had made its way south now paused and divided in the face of the inhospitable nature of the insalubrious city. It would have served no useful purpose for His Majesty to enter it in triumph only to perish within the week; therefore he waited. He was first at Charterhouse, the home of Lord Thomas Howard, later at Windsor, and at the Tower, at Greenwich and at Hampton Court, circling about his new possession like a child with a new toy that he may look at but not touch, and gazing on the town from a boat upon the river. We heard that he had ordered Sir Walter Raleigh to give up his home, Durham House, and vacate it within a few days – hurriedly, as if he were a nobody. Plainly the old days were over when a hero could be treated so.

There was to be a crowning, we were told, upon Saint James' Day, which was in late July, but it was forecast that it would be a poor affair, a rushed thing, with no pomp and ceremony other than was needed to make James our lawful king and so enable the good government of the realm.

His wife had come south now, and some of his children. The eldest son Prince Henry was to have as his companion that pompous young earl of Essex – the brat's future was secure now, pains and sorrows past.

Philip Herbert was become the first English favourite and, as it was said, like to oust Jamie Hay, though, as with an old war horse, old favourites were never abandoned and cast out, but, as long as they behaved themselves and took displacement with serenity, their situation at court was assured for as long as they wished it, in the gentle sunshine of a pleasant obscurity.

And Rob and I, like Troilus looking towards the Grecian camp where Cressida lay, watched London from without, kicking our heels. London – a treasure house of forbidden wealth: palaces, playhouses, pleasures, lying dormant – a luxurious and decomposing flower, with honey at its heart.

At night we saw the burning of its lamps in the summer dusk, the sudden flare of torches, the fires that burned in slow-rising pyres, and the white moon like a sliver of bone in the throbbing sky. Sometimes Rob and I rode close enough to hear the awful sounds within. In that great stillness in the festering air we could hear the wails and groans of the tormented, we could hear the tolling of the bells, the sound of running feet, the hammering of nails into the coffins, the echo of that hammering as nails were driven into the doors and windows of the houses of the dying, the scuffles as the incarcerated live ones tried to break outside and were thrust back in by those who feared they brought the sickness with them. In the rustling of the breeze the useless herbal flower petals strewn about the streets would be shifting, speckling the slithering dung heaps with their withered blossom, and bright-eyed rats twitching in the discarded bed linen, and mangy dogs sniffing at the limbs of the dead.

"I think I shall go back tae Scotland," Robbie said abruptly one day.

"I think you should not," I replied. "You owe it to Thomas to be here when he returns."

"But this," Rob gestured wildly, "could go on all summer." There was no denying this and I did not so.

Every day at the inn it seemed someone had heard of a new cure for the plague – angelica roots and vinegar inhaled – sulphur fumes – a vomit of treacle – male flesh cut into small pieces, mixed with wine – the brains of any that had died a violent death, mixed with the pith of the backbone, in wine.

"It doesnae suit my nature," Rob said, "waiting here and hearing tales o' gloom."

I thought the remark somewhat unnecessary. "Tell me the fool whose nature it might suit," I answered sourly, and he scowled. I noticed with resignation that even scowling he was beautiful.

A pedlar came by one day and I bought a flute from him. I passed my days of waiting either in the upper chamber of the inn, writing lengthy epistles to Tom with all the information, rumour and gossip I could lay my hands upon, or practising the flute in the fields and woods like some Arcadian shepherd. Robbie hovered around the edge of the sphere of what Sir Gervaise Elwes called 'the great ones', riding off to Hampton Court, performing the duties of a household page from time to time. He was sometimes with me at night, more often not; and such closeness as there had been between us diminished in the boredom and uncertainty.

I came back once from playing the flute to find Robbie in our bedroom with a woman. She was sitting up in our bed as bold as brass, a coarse wench with a freckled face and a mane of reddish hair, so much at ease that I was obliged to assume that Rob had given her good cause to be so. Rob, dressed, but much in disarray, laughed, slung his arm about the girl and said: "Come join us, Giles, and dinnae play the preacher. Your face would turn the milk sour."

I slammed shut the door, fetched my horse, and rode the meadow tracks until my anger cooled. That evening Rob and I supped sullenly and argued in low voices in the corner of the inn parlour.

"I may take a wench if I will. Burn me, it is the way of man."

"What about Thomas? What would he say?"

"Thomas need never know. She was nothing tae me, Giles, nor I tae her. There is nae more tae say."

"This I dispute. So you would go with women, Rob, no man being by?"

"Why no'? It's no' the first time. Besides," he added, "she was desperate for me; I couldnae' refuse her pleas and tears."

"But did you desire her? The breasts and all?" I marvelled, curious in spite of myself.

"I thought each breast a bonny handful," he said defiantly. "You should try a woman, Giles, and see if you do not agree."

"There will be no chance of that," I answered loftily.

"Ah, Giles, let's no' wrangle," Rob said winsomely. "You are my dear dear friend and bedfellow. I was unkind. I had bad news today while I was out."

I waited.

"I am dismissed," he said, "an' a' the pages who came south frae Scotland. We are no' wanted. We are no' a' fault," he explained. "It is something tae do wi' new brooms sweeping clean and a' that. We hae some reward and now we are on our own tae make what shift we may. I was angry when I heard, but now I wonder if it isnae' for the best."

"I see," I murmured. "You believe there is no place for you at court."

"Och, the court," he shrugged. "I am no' even sure I care for it. I heard that it might be worth my while tae come back later but I didnae' believe it. I gave the matter thought – I shall go back tae Scotland."

"But there is nothing for you there," I protested.

"Or anywhere," he said; but it was his despondency that spoke.

The weather that July which had been so dry now broke and gave us rain. Maybe it was adjudged that this intemperance would wash away the sources of infection, for King James went to his crowning; but hurriedly, and without all the ceremonies which he would hold later, when the plague had gone.

Robbie and I went in the rain to see the procession; but we could not see it – the populace was ordered to stay clear and was kept back from Westminster Abbey for fear that we might breathe upon the king. Beyond the men-at-arms we caught a glimpse of the banners, we saw the gold tips of the palanquin, passing like a great four-poster bed, the king beneath it no doubt dry, unlike ourselves drenched in the cause of loyalty and curiosity. We heard the drummers and the trumpeters and we heard the guards telling onlookers to keep back. The rain poured down steadily and I saw a sodden garland lying in a puddle. Into the portals of Westminster Abbey went the procession, and thus was our new king made, in a half empty building, in the rain.

"So, 'tis done," I said. "Long live the king."

"Aye, may he do so," Robbie said, "but I think I'll no' stay here tae see it."

Rain trickled down his cheeks and glistened on his eyelashes and mouth. A gold ear ring gleamed in the well-established pinpoint in the lobe. I looked at him, so lustrous and bedraggled, so shimmering and so waterlogged, and a sudden ache of love pained my heart.

The king had been within some hundred yards of us, but what of that? He had not seen us nor we him. It seemed that the momentous moments of the age were like to pass us by.

"Where will you go?" I said.

"I shall go overseas and seek my fortune."

"Overseas?" I blanched in sudden desolation.

"Aye," Rob grinned. "They say that Paris is a sight tae see. I'll go in search o' Tom."

It was to be four years before I saw Robbie Kerr again, when he came to the attention of the world in breathtakingly spectacular circumstances.

CHAPTER TWELVE

In that quiet time before events precipitated us upon the world's stage I passed my days in an equanimity I should by rights have savoured, had I but known how soon it was to end.

I spent the year in Oxfordshire, partly at home, partly in Oxford, where I devoted my time to mastering to some degree the musician's craft, so that within the twelvemonth I could play, as well as the flute, the cornemuse, hautboy and crumhorn, indeed any instrument that one might blow.

In the autumn of 1604 I set off once more to London where I was lucky enough to join the group of musicians that worked at the Fortune playhouse in the northern suburbs; and there would I be still, were it not for my cousin Thomas's friendship with Ben Jonson, and Ben Jonson's having risen to fame.

When I came again to London I had no idea that Tom's friend Ben, whose wife had kept Tom's letters for us, had become so celebrated. But then, many things had happened in the flower of cities since I had paid my nervous visit there some fifteen months ago.

Lord Henry Howard had become a privy councillor, Lord Warden of the Cinque Ports and Earl of Northampton. That handsome lout Philip Herbert, our first English favourite, was made Earl Montgomery and was to marry Lady Susan Vere, the daughter of the Earl of Oxford; this same earl died, the two events not necessarily connected. Sir Walter Raleigh had been condemned to perpetual imprisonment and was locked up in the Tower of London. The Earl of Southampton had been praised for his skill at tilting at the Barriers – the ceremonial joust – and arrested for plotting to slay certain Scots about the king; and then released.

An Act of Parliament had been passed against witchcraft. Of course I had at that time no suspicion that the same would ever become of interest to myself within so short a time.

"If any person shall use, practise or exercise any invocation or conjuration of an evil and wicked spirit or shall consult, covenant, entertain, employ, feed or reward any evil and wicked spirit to and for any intent or purpose, or shall practise or exercise any witchcraft, enchantment, charm or sorcery, whereby any person shall be killed, destroyed, wasted, consumed, pined or lamed in his or her body or any part thereof, being lawfully convicted, shall suffer pains of death as felon, and if any take upon them by witchcraft, enchantment, charm or sorcery to the intent to provoke any person to unlawful love . . ."

And in that year King James had had his coronation procession of which he had been deprived the year before. Triumphal arches were decorated with living figures. Edward Alleyn the great actor played the Genius of the City in purple buskins and a long white wig. A boy from the Blackfriars company stretched out on one elbow, reciting poesy and clad in a flesh-coloured skin-tight costume with a garland of sedge and water lilies on his head, played the River Thames, shivering in the winds of March. The king admired the boy but fidgeted at the Genius of the City whose speeches went on too long. And who was it that prepared this marvel but Tom's friend Ben Jonson!

Master Jonson had acquired a patroness, Lucy Harrington, Countess of Bedford, now Queen Anne's favourite lady-in-waiting, and a friend to poets. He had already written an entertainment for the queen; and several plays. He was high in the king's favour for his book learning. And now he was working with one Inigo Jones to produce the Twelfth Night masque at court, which was now in rehearsal. All this I did not know as I set out for his house to see if there were any letters from Tom awaiting my collection.

I was extremely fortunate to find Master Jonson at home; he was then living apart from his wife but sometimes visiting the house in Cripplegate. He was a big man, corpulent, some thirty years of age, with short brown hair and a small beard. On hearing of my connection with Tom he clapped me on the back and made me welcome, and there being indeed letters from Tom in Paris, poured me some wine while I sat down to read them.

Master Jonson was as eager for news of Tom as I, and I passed the letters to him after I had read them. After all, they contained no secrets; indeed they were dull enough. I fear Tom wrote a learned kind of letter, with plenty of Latin asides, which Master Jonson was able to translate. They were addressed from a lodging on the left bank of the river near the Pont St Michel. They contained many pleas for me to send him news of court.

"'P. S. Robbie Kerr is with me?'" Master Jonson asked. "Do you know who that is?"

"Yes. He is a Scot."

"Oh," grumbled Master Jonson. "Better in Paris than here."

I looked surprised.

"You don't know the court then?" he asked.

"Indeed I do not. I have been living in the country this past year."

"My meaning was that we have more than enough of the Scottish kind at court; that's all."

"I see. I have to inform you then that Robbie Kerr would be an ornament to any court, and therefore I cannot truly wish him elsewhere."

"An ornament? We have plenty of those also. No, I stick to my original pronouncement. One more Scot, even a pretty one, would be superfluous. Let him remain in Paris. But Tom I'd like to see again. When is he coming home?"

"I wish I knew. I don't believe that he himself knows. He must await a summons from Sir Robert Cecil, who pays his wages."

"And you, what do you in London?"

"I drift somewhat; but in between, I play the flute and the crumhorn at the Fortune."

"Have you spare time? That is, if you would like to know more of the court, for Tom? I'd be well content to give Tom's cousin opportunity and you would be a help to me . . ."

I needed no persuasion; and it was thus that I became – no, not the leading musician in the masque (the music of the masque was performed by professional musicians) but Master Ben Jonson's assistant; which meant in plain terms that I worked the crank that moved the wave machine.

And so as the year drew to an end I therefore found myself at the palace of Whitehall almost every day – a situation which by rights should have astonished and overwhelmed me. The palace of the king, no less! That it did not was for two reasons. One was that the palace of Whitehall was not particularly impressive. It sprawled along Thames bank haphazard and illogical, covering more than twenty acres of ground like a small town, and split through by a thoroughfare between King Street Gate and Holbein Gate, through which anyone might pass, and did. I believe that there are palaces hidden away in parkland, approached by marble stairs, with pillars stretching upward, causing a frisson of awe in the beholder. Whitehall was not one such – it crept upon one intimately, like one that would sell you a lewd picture secretly. The Banqueting House, where the rehearsals for the masque took place, an old and ricketty building opposite the tilt yard, was at the very edge, along the outer wall, and therefore could be reached without seeing any of the royal apartments and rooms of state; and so my first impression of Whitehall was that it differed little from a playhouse, but one wherein the players were exceptionally well-dressed.

The second reason was the character of Ben Jonson, who had scant regard for those whom Sir Gervaise Elwes termed 'the great ones', and spoke out openly to me of his worthy employers with scorn. Before their faces he was pleasant and polite, smooth-tongued, obliging. To me he said: "Lord save us, they are folk just like ourselves, clad in rich clothes, and most of them lead a life at which the common man would blanch, did he but know the half. Double dealers all, deceivers and betrayers. I would offer no man respect for nobility of birth – that which comes to him through no devices of his own. Nobility of mind is all. But we are not here to pass judgement. All we need to do is make sure that my masque's a triumph."

The Masque of Blackness ! It was a name which I found laced with meaning.

In plain terms it was a monstrous silly story. Oceanus – with hoary grey locks and a trident in his hand – asks the River Niger – with curled blue-black hair and bracelets of pearl – why he has flowed as far as Britain. Niger replies in rhythmic couplets that his daughters have come in search of the light that makes all beautiful, namely King James. Niger has twelve daughters. They were all played by ladies of the court, with blackened faces. It was Queen Anne's idea. Her Majesty believed that the African woman was a symbol of power, and to blacken their faces and assume that role was to challenge the authority of the male. A piquant conception! And therefore ladies of high degree were to be found wandering about with black faces and arms and revealing a good deal of their ample forms in robes of azure and silver gauze. One of the ladies was the queen herself, one was Lady Bedford and one was the countess of Suffolk, Frances Howard's mother; and as Lord Chamberlain the Earl of Suffolk her father was in ultimate control.

There was a good deal to rehearse, not merely the speech and song, but in particular the wonderful mechanism and effects. The stage was a great edifice on wheels, some four feet above ground level to house the machinery beneath. There was an artificial sea with waves that tossed and billowed as a result of moving cylinders covered in blue, black and silver cloth. There was a painted curtain, and a moon upon a silver throne in a blue silk heaven. The lady masquers sat in a great concave shell which rose and fell with the sea. There were woods and hills and two great sea horses. There were torchbearers wearing green, gold and silver, with garlands of sea weeds in their hair. There were musicians and any number of folk like myself who worked behind the scenes in half light, working the machinery, tripping over lighted candles, making sure the marvels properly astonished. And there were the light effects, the positioning of candelabra to illumine the great shell into translucent pearl and to make the ladies' dresses glisten like the moon upon the water, to create illusion.

The Howard family were everywhere – my lord of Suffolk giving orders, his glamorous lady wife with her strident voice, one of her daughters, who like herself, played one of the rivers; and that other of her daughters Lady Frances, her spoilt and pampered darling; and Lady Frances's fair-haired companion Mistress Anne.

Some twelve years old she was then, Frances, and precocious, as one who saw at first hand the mysterious delights available to the rich, and therefore must make haste to grow, like some exotic blossom unnaturally brought to fruition. She could come and go where she pleased. Unfortunately she remembered me.

"Giles Rawlins! Where's your pretty friend? So you are helping with our festivities! You turn the machinery – what a position of power! For all that the ladies think they are so magnificent, the greatest power is yours. One flick of your wrist and you could upend the shell and tip the ladies into the sea!"

"Indeed, I would do no such thing."

"Would you not? I would."

Chortling with amusement she danced away to leave me to perfect the handling of the mechanism and to pray that by some mischance I did not inadvertently indeed cause the shell to tip and the great ones to tumble out. A grave offence, no doubt. I shuddered. One might secretly think little of the nobility, but it remained a fact that they had the power of life and death over we lesser mortals should they choose to wield it.

All around us now there was hammering and bustle as the scaffolding was set in place for the seating, and a great chair for the king.

Carpets were laid for the dancing. Wires were strung about the roof and walls to hold innumerable candles. Music wafted – lutes and violins, cornets and harpsichord, the pretty singing of the boy seamaids, the resonant tenor of the Triton with the long blue hair. The curtain was drawn time and again to test its smoothness. The moon's throne was adjusted. They said the masque cost £3000. It was to celebrate little Prince Charles becoming Duke of York. If it proved successful, Ben Jonson's reputation would be made – if he kept out of trouble.

"Look at them," muttered he to me, as the court ladies practised their dancing, with their blackened faces and arms, their blue gowns, their golden shoes, their plumes. "*She* has left her husband to live openly with her lover . . . *she* was one of Essex's lovers in her youth . . . *she* and *she* are both Sir Robert Cecil's doxies . . . *she* is a self-seeking opportunist . . . *she* is a shrew . . . and *she* – well, it was always my belief that it was she who had Kit Marlowe murdered in revenge for him fucking her husband. And how they do smile! And why not – no one will challenge or accuse them. As for Her Majesty, she has half the brain of a gnat. And I must speak her very fair, for she loves masques to very distraction and will have others." And then he added: "And what about the honey-haired brat? How she does weave amongst the dancing! They permit her to do all she will. If she were mine I'd clout her. She cannot wait to be one of them. I pity he that weds her; he must needs be strong."

We performed the *Masque of Blackness* on Twelfth Night, and it was breathtakingly beautiful.

> When torchlight made an artificial noon
> About the court, some courtiers in the masque
> Putting on better faces than their own,
> Being full of fraud and flattery . . .

Moonlight on water, torchlight on mother-of-pearl, candlelight on gossamer . . . ethereal music . . . silver and shadow . . .

But it was the *Masque of Blackness*; and in recalling it blackness is what I recollect. The blackness of shadows. Because it was a night in the depth of winter? Because the ladies painted their pale faces and limbs to the colour of the Ethiop? Because they all had secrets, hidden from the sun? No – it was because *she* was present – Frances. She was the blackness at the heart of it.

She came and stood beside me when the play was over, when the ladies had descended to take partners for the dancing. She was so quiet that I had not noticed she was there. She slipped her hand in mine.

"Dance with me, Giles."

"I am not dancing – watching, merely."

"Shame on you! If there are watchers and dancers, would you not rather be a dancer?"

"Let others dance who have the skill."

"Many men would be honoured to partner me . . ."

I looked down at her. She had blacked her face like the dancers, and her throat, about which hung a rope of pearl. Her pale hair looked incongruous, her teeth unnaturally white. She smiled.

"Am I the only one to notice?" she said. "Niger's daughters are still black."

"And so?"

"They came to Britannia for the bright sun of King James to bleach their blackness. But he has not the strength."

"It is only a story," I said.

"The women have their power still," she said and laughed. "I go to find a dancer."

Where she had held my hand my palm was stained with blackness. Excessive, glutinous, it left a mark on everything I touched.

Chapter Thirteen

A year later to the day, in the capacity of Ben's assistant I attended a masque to celebrate an occasion of some significance – the Lady Frances Howard's marriage. And to whom? To that haughty brat the Earl of Essex, the little cull that once called Robbie Kerr uncouth.

It had been a year not without event. In my own life nothing untoward: I lived in lodgings near the Fortune; I formed an intimacy with a player, one moreover who had great difficulty learning his lines, and therefore any lovemaking was heavily interspersed with hearing him speak his part. I wrote to Thomas and received some dull replies. Tom seemed to think a letter from across the seas must needs contain Tom's thoughts upon the nature of the people, culture and terrain, and I, poor insular fool, would have preferred some news of Robbie.

Ben Jonson's twelvemonth was a sight more eventful. Imprisoned for a play he writ – for that it had some stinging jests about the Scots at court – he would have had his ears and nose cut off if they had found him guilty. Released intact he gave a feast in the autumn. Some friends invited him to dine at a house in the Strand. The company was agreeable and Ben came away thinking no more on it. A month later it transpired that amongst the guests were most of the chief conspirators in the Powder Plot. Sitting about the table so convivial were the very ones who intended to destroy the king and Parliament with gunpowder. Poor Ben was called before the Privy Council, but he extricated himself from the unpleasantness with aplomb and was as high as ever in the royal favour. In a court still reeling from its brush with sudden precipitation towards eternity he provided the entertainment for Frances Howard's wedding, *The Masque of Hymen*.

King James, already known as Jacobus Pacificus, albeit with something of a sneer by those who would have sooner gone to war, decided to bring harmony betwixt Devereux and Howard. What though the Howards had helped Essex to the block? – all was now forgive and forget, and Essex's son must learn to love the Howards.

How rampant they were now – how settled in the king's affections! The Earl of Suffolk, Frances's father, the sailor hero, now bluff and hearty in peacetime and all his energies directed to the amassing of a fortune and the building of a great mansion, Audley End; Lord Howard of Effingham, Lord High Admiral, who had put down Essex's rebellion and now settled to a life of ease and dotage in the bland new reign; Thomas Earl of Arundel, Frances's cousin, a sober-visaged young man with large black piercing eyes and warts upon his face, shortly to marry a rich heiress; Lord Henry Howard, Earl of Northampton, smiling much and plainly relishing the sunshine of success after so many years in the shadows. He seemed to dote upon his great-niece, his manner to her sweet as honey. He watched where she went and looked after her thoughtfully, stroking his chin. Then there was the Countess of Suffolk, Frances's mother, loud and fulsome in a headdress of heron's feathers, always at Frances's side, kissing her, calling her 'my baby' in a screech of a voice, so that everyone knew who was the mother of the bride.

"The countess's mother," Ben said in a voice he barely took the trouble to lower, "came from a family of clothiers – the Stumpes of Malmesbury! It is the countess that takes the young men whom the king fancies and has their hair curled – he likes curly hair, Giles, take care! – and teaches them to sweeten their breath."

The wedding of the happy pair took place in the Chapel Royal before the whole court. The king gave the bride away. The masque that followed was written to portray the sacredness of marriage. There was Hymen the goddess in a saffron robe wearing a crown of roses, and Juno heavily bejewelled, in a long veil set with lilies, carrying a sceptre. There were gentlemen masquers in crimson, portraying the disruptive Humours and Affections; there were lady masquers in white, drenched with jewels, descending from a framework of clouds. There was venerable Reason with long white hair and a crown of burning tapers, wearing a blue robe covered with stars, in one hand a lamp and in the other a sword – Reason's voice alone could still the wayward passions and bring unity – and there was beautiful music. There was a globe that hung and turned, twelve feet in diameter, eight men within; a sea with silver waves, clouds that opened and closed. Machines worked it, and Ben and I worked the winch for turning the machinery.

In the leaping light of many candles, my attention mostly kept to the careful adjustment of the mechanism working wonder and delight, I could yet glimpse the vibrant scene within the hall. His Majesty looked well content, a benign father-overlord, encouraging the happiness of dearly beloved children. I saw the Earl of Southampton in the shadows, sober and preoccupied. Is this what Essex would have wanted for his son, he must have asked himself? The bridegroom then, fourteen years old, dark-haired and pale, grave and dignified. A dancer? *I go find myself a dancer*, she had said to me; and I guessed that by that definition she meant one that was at home upon the stage of Whitehall, one that folk admired, a man of moment, a beauty, a man who made things happen. Essex? Where was she then, the lovely bride? Not with her young husband. She was dancing with Prince Harry.

The king's eldest son. Twelve years old, but tall and gorgeous. Eyes of cornflower blue, hair red-gold, and a very gracious smile; smiling now at Frances.

How odd and false it was, this business of dynastic marriage! The youthful bride and groom would not share one another's bed that night. Frances would return to her mother, but now a wife; and Devereux would go beyond the seas to complete his education. But they were married, and when he returned they would set up house together. To-night they barely smiled at one another. An observer who knew nothing of the match would swear that her affianced was Prince Harry. He was the one upon whom she lavished her attention. I saw her dimpling, arching her throat, laughing behind her hand. She was very pretty, even I have to admit who think of her with loathing.

Another watched them, Anne her friend, the fair-haired lady with the knowing air and the astrology book. She caught my eye and smiled at me. I returned the smile reluctantly; it seemed to implicate me in some mysterious collusion which I had no desire to share. I wished I had not had the misfortune to come to their attention. I turned away and watched instead the glamorous figure of James, now Lord Hay, among the dancers – very graceful and proving that there was life after the arrival of a newer favourite.

Throughout the rehearsals Jamie had treated me with his expansive bonhomie, as if we were old friends. Now he came over to me, where I sat beside the winch that turned the globe.

"Divine power is yours tonight then, Giles."

"It is?"

He laughed. "You turn the world itself."

"Ah . . . it was mostly Master Jonson."

Florid and over-heated Jamie was a little gone to seed. Close to, one saw the jaw blurred by rather too much flesh. Good living put a gloss upon a man. He was breathing heavily from the dancing.

"Your globe turns well," said Jamie. "I would the world were in so fine a balance."

"This is a night of unity, as I understand," I said. "Howard and Devereux; man and woman; king and people; Scotland and England."

"Aye," said Jamie, "but you and I know it to be other. Men and men; England more than Scotland; and an excess of Howards."

We heard Frances laugh. She curtseyed to her partner the heir to the throne and tossed her hair. She wore her long hair loose, and a white gown glistening with jewels. Where the torchlight caught her she was irridescent.

"Poor young Devereux," said Jamie. "She'll take some handling. But that's all one; what's it tae me? But I could wish less Howard and more Scot. Tell me," he continued, still watching the dancers, and *à propos* of nothing, as it seemed, "when does Robbie Kerr come back?"

I jumped. "Robbie? I have no idea."

"Do ye no' write tae him?"

"No."

"Why ever not? You were such good friends."

"Not really. My cousin Thomas is his friend. They are both overseas and, I assume, together. I don't ask."

"You should. You should ask." Jamie looked me squarely in the eyes. "Ask. Ask Robbie when he's coming home. Tell him Jamie Hay was asking for him. Say I'll see he fares well. He'll no' regret it, tell him. Will ye do this for me?"

I shrugged, astonished. "I will."

"Remember!"

And he bounded away, pausing only to look back at me over his shoulder, pointing. I grinned. All very well for Jamie to behave like a retreating Ghost, but substantial as he was, and red-faced in the glow of torches, the effect was merely humorous.

Would I write to Robbie? Why should I? He had gone off to France without a backward glance and no doubt had been living happily with Thomas and no thought of me. I did not need him. I had done well enough without him. I had had lovers. I was doing well. Why disturb their idyll? If they wanted to remain in Paris or wherever it was they now resided, what was it to me? Let them go their ways. Ties of blood would always bind me to Thomas – no doubt we would always meet at Yuletide, a family wedding, a family death. But as for myself and Robbie Kerr there was nothing to bind us. The journey south three years ago seemed far distant, as if it had happened to somebody else. I wondered why Lord Hay should mention Robbie's name at this juncture. Robbie must have meant something to him then? Lumpkin that I was, I had no notion of the true purpose of his asking. Tom would have known. Tom would have sensed his meaning instantly. And that was why Tom was a diplomat in the service of Robert Cecil, Earl of Salisbury; and I was turning cranks and handles.

The next day when I wrote to Tom I said: "I believe you spoke of Robbie Kerr in a previous letter. Lord Hay who knew him in Scotland was enquiring after him. Is there any news of Kerr for me to pass on to the gentleman? I believe you are together?"

Because Thomas was no longer at his former address in Paris and because of the vagaries of the passage of letters it was not until autumn that I received a reply. Amongst a detailed account of the faults and virtues of the Dutch, came a brief reply to my question.

"Although Robert Kerr was with me in Paris, we parted company several months ago. I understood that he was on his way to England. If he is and if you encounter him, you might tell him to write to me – he is a damned poor scrivener."

On his way to England? When? Ridiculous the sudden pounding of my heart. Why, this was written weeks ago from Antwerp. Rob could be in England already – in London maybe? In Scotland? Would he visit his family in the hidden castle by the glittering Jed Water by the birch glades where Thomas the Rhymer saw the Queen of Elfland?

I put the thought from me. I was no lovesick fool, and Elfland was for the witless. That which was real was my lodging in Wood Street, the motley collection of musical instruments I shared, and my intermittent employment at the Fortune. More, there was my burgeoning acquaintance with Simon Trenchard, a new young player who had promised to spend some time with me when the afternoon's performance was over. I finished tidying the room. I punched the bedding and strewed some herbs and blew away some dust. I went out to buy some wine. I could not have been gone more than half an hour.

When I came back, my head full of the hopes and expectations for the coming night, I found a stranger waiting in my chamber. He had his back to me, and all I saw in that first moment was a claret velvet cloak and a plumed hat and a jewel of some worth hanging from the half-obscured lobe of his ear. Even when he turned round there was a moment when I did not recognise him, before I gasped and said in a tone of wonder: "Robbie!"

He grinned, pleased to have surprised me. "Well, Giles, and how are you keeping?" he enquired.

The emotion uppermost in my mind was anger – inappropriate, stupid, self-defeating. I could not believe how angry I was – I had not even known that I was angry. How dare he? How dare he suddenly appear like this after a three-year silence during which he had certainly been living with my cousin, and expect me to be pleased to see him? The smug self-satisfied smile upon his face grated upon my sensibilities. I would have liked to take him by the throat and shake him. And how extraordinarily beautiful he was!

"Who let you in?" I said ungraciously.

"Who else? Mistress Bell, whose house this is."

I now felt vexed at having asked so dull-witted a question. Here came another.

"Why are you here?"

"Tae see you," he replied astonished. "Are ye no' pleased tae see me?"

I had no words. His outward appearance had changed somewhat from that which I remembered. His hair was well cut – shorter, though every whit as golden. There was a pendant ruby in his ear. His clothes were very fine, well-tailored, elegant – Parisian, no doubt. Yes, he had acquired polish, and it became him well. But the voice . . .

"You still speak Scots then," I observed.

"I see nae reason not to."

"But in France – "

"Aye, I spoke French. I speak it fine. Wad ye like tae hear me speaking French?"

"I would not. Why do you suppose that would be a treat for me?"

"How sour ye hae become! I thought ye would be awfu' glad tae see me."

"Why should you think that?"

"Och well, if it isnae' so," he said, becoming nettled in his turn.

"The truth is, Robbie, I am awaiting somebody and your presence is an inconvenience. If you would come back tomorrow, when I have time . . ."

Even then I hoped that he would not. Simon Trenchard had raven-black hair and violet eyes and I had hopes to see him naked. If I was fortunate he would not leave at daybreak. We might spend all morning in the very bed where Robbie's beautiful gloves and hat lay strewn. How dare Rob glide back thus, so confident of his welcome? How dare he assume I had nothing better to do than put myself at his disposal?

"Och, very well then, I'll no' burden you wi' my company." He picked up gloves and hat.

I felt of a sudden sick. I knew that what I was doing was the silliest thing I had ever done and that I would regret it later. Later? I would regret it the moment that Rob left the room and where he now stood in magnificence would be a void.

"H-how is Thomas?" I stuttered, reaching for some middle ground that would keep him here discussing pleasantries.

"Thomas? He was well when I last saw him," Robbie shrugged.

"And is he coming home?"

"I believe he wishes it. But he has no' been sent for. They want him tae spend some time in Spain."

"Ah . . ."

"Is this your friend?" Rob at the window caught a glimpse of someone coming to the house.

"What does he look like?"

"Black-haired and handsome. He has just glanced up at your window. *Mes félicitations* – you will have a merry night."

"If you could come back another time, Rob . . ." I said, sounding, to my fury, humble, pleading; and very much repenting my ungraciousness.

"Maybe," Rob said, affably enough. "I am not sure what I shall be doing." Standing in the doorway he turned back to me. There was a world of accusation and reproach in what he said. It caused his words to stumble.

"I came here frae France. You were the first I thought tae visit, Giles. I came straight tae you. Remember that."

CHAPTER FOURTEEN

Remember – aye, countless times I did so, as I cursed the idiot stance that I had taken. I had more or less thrown Robbie out, one who had travelled over land and sea and, if he was to be believed, had come to me before all others. I had exchanged the possibility of the reawakening of our friendship for the chance of a night of passion with an unknown, and I soon lived to regret that, for Simon Trenchard proved something of a disappointment and it was probably my own fault; for as soon as Rob had gone out of the door I knew that it had been my mistake to let him go.

And now I had no idea where he had gone. I looked for him of course. No street I walked along but I half expected to bump into him, no playhouse did I visit but I scanned the faces of the crowd, no tavern where I ate or drank but I watched the door for his entrance.

I wondered whether he had gone to Jamie Hay, but I had no way of knowing this. Lord Hay was out of my sphere unless I had a role to play at court, and I did not go to Whitehall that Christmastide. This was because I had now lost touch with Master Jonson – it may well have been something to do with the fact that when I saw *Volpone* at the Globe I happened to remark that I thought it pedantic to name the characters after Vices and Italian ones at that, and this I know was passed to Ben, who always got into a fury if his work was not treated with respect. No doubt I was now considered one of the 'rude and beastly multitude'.

I went instead to Bourton for the festivities. Here amid the mirth of the occasion my relations gave me the gift of a lute, considering it more melodious than the noisy instruments they had heard me play. They considered the crumhorn no better than a shepherd's crook distended and its sound akin to the meadow bull; this can be so in the hands of the unskilful – the secret lies in breath control.

Lidcote was there. Unlike Tom who thought him crass and dull, I found Lidcote marvellous agreeable, and the more so now, as I applied myself to chords and frets.

Fretting was indeed close to my heart that day in March when I sat alone in my London lodgings toying with the lute. Like many a young man of twenty I had endured on my visit home for Christmas innumerable hints and threats, queries and warnings upon the subject of my future – namely, how did I propose to spend it and did I not think lurking about London in the company of players an unhappy choice and one likely to lead to poverty and disillusion?

I had no particular answer to offer and so I sat and strummed – with one good result, that I could play all the tunes of the day with a fair skill. It was a Dowland song 'When Phoebus first did Daphne love' that I was playing when the door opened and one entered.

"Robbie . . ." This time he could have been in no doubt of his welcome. I ran to him, lute and all, and hugged and kissed him. His clothes were damp with rain.

"Where have you come from?" I said, half expecting him to have ridden from the ends of the earth. He looked big and splendid in the little room. I began to notice that he was well-dressed. The doublet I was hugging was of a very good velvet, the colour of holly leaves, with padded epaulettes. The short cape was slung carelessly over one shoulder. The hat was tall-crowned and wide-brimmed, the brim tilted at the left side and trimmed with a feather. The breeches too were velvet – padded, as the fashion was. An odd style, it accentuated the arse, which, as I recalled, in Rob's case hardly needed doing.

"Where have I come frae? I have come frae Whitehall."

"How?" I was completely baffled. "That is, what are you doing there? Have you been there all this time?"

"No, no, I've been tae Ferniehirst; I went there after I left you. And by the by, how is the dark-haired charmer? Any assignations for tonight?"

"Not one; and he is long since parted from me. I am all yours, Rob. Have you eaten – drank? Shall we go out? Stay in? Whatever you want."

"Pour me some wine and I will tell you the purpose of my visit."

We sat down on the bed and drank. His hair glistened from the rain, long, lying like spun flax on his shoulders. He was clean-shaven, fresh-faced, boyish. He was twenty, the same age as myself.

"I went tae see Jamie Hay. You said he had been asking after me. Lord Hay, as he now is, and well set up. He seemed pleased tae see me. He found a room for me. Whitehall has more chambers than a beehive. He said I should be groomed."

"What, are you a horse? What a thing to say to you!"

"He says I hae some rough corners yet."

"You seem elegant to me."

"I do, don't I?" he grinned. "But it's the claes – they're bonny, are they not? I was measured for them. Jamie got them for me."

"Yes, they become you very well."

"I hae been much wi' Jamie. Jamie has time tae spare now. It's no' as it was when we came south. Jamie often sleeps in his own room."

"And you with him?" I demanded accusingly.

"Are ye jealous? There's nae need. You are special tae me, Giles, and doubly so for that y'are of Thomas' family. Let's no' wrangle. So I am Jamie's page. And I consider mysel' fortunate, for Jamie's awfu' generous. He gives and gives."

"Aye, I remember – *spend, spend, and God will send*!" I said sourly.

"Is there anything ye lack? I'll get it for ye. Lute music? The new songs at court?"

I had to smile. "Are we all so easily won?"

Rob looked about the room. "And that's no' a' that ye could do wi', Giles. Ye'll no' lack, and nor will I, wi' Jamie as our friend."

I ignored that. I felt sure that hand-outs to such as myself had no place in Bonnie Jamie's plans.

"So my lord Hay has taken you under his wing?" I mused.

"Aye, he has made me page and I am well content. He will be a guid master. And he is sae pleased wi' me that I'm tae bear his shield at the tilting. At the Barriers."

I must have looked surprised. Rob said disbelievingly: "Ye sairly ken the Barriers? Ye ken the tiltyard?"

"Yes, it's near the Banqueting House."

"In three days' time they hold the tilting for the ceremony that celebrates the king's accession. I'm tae hold Jamie's shield. I ride up tae the king and show the shield. It's a very great honour," he explained.

"Indeed it is. I'm very pleased for you."

"Aye . . ." Rob hesitated.

"But – ?" I suggested.

"I wondered, Giles, if ye would be wi' me?"

"Be with you? In what capacity?"

"I thought that ye might like tae hold my horse. Or stand beside me." He turned exquisite beseeching eyes on me. "Or anything, Giles, anything you like," he said in desperation. "I'm sae fearful I cannae' think straight."

"Fearful? I can't believe it. I've seen you ride hard and fast and fight and wrestle and hurl yourself over ditches twelve feet deep and six feet wide; and you have the blood of the Borderers in your veins – whatever can you be afraid of?"

"Of the king," he admitted, "and a' the people watching me."

"What can they do?" I shrugged.

"Well, the king might look at me and remember how I couldnae' speak the Latin. He may turn and say: Who brought this lummock here? And a' the crowds will say: Who's that? Och, one more Scot – have we no' enough o' them already? And is he Lord Hay's protégé? – well, he has a deal tae learn before he's ready for Whitehall – all brawn and nae brain . . . I hear them say it. And I ken fu' well I'll drop the shield and prove them right. Aye and I daresay Essex will be there and laugh and say I told you so."

"No, no, he's travelling abroad," I said. "That is one less bugbear for you to dread."

"That leaves the others," Rob said sulkily. "And it's no' sae droll, so leave your smiling."

"Forgive me," I said penitently, smiling still.

"I know sae few at court," said Rob. "I thought if you were there it would be one face that I knew, one friend who wished me well."

"Of course I'll come and hold your horse, buffoon," I said. "But you'll not need me. You'll see, when you ride up to the king you'll be serene and gracious and break all the ladies' hearts."

He grinned. "I sairly hope not. I would not know what tae say tae the English ladies."

"I hope you never will," I said. "Ah, but Rob," I said and hugged him, "stay now. Tell me all you've done and seen and where you've been. How was Paris? How was Tom? When is he coming home?"

We talked long into the night. I lit the candles. How beautiful he looked by the light of the dancing flame, how gold his hair, how bright his lovely eyes! He caught me looking at him.

"Does Mistress Bell ever come up here?" he asked.

"Never," I assured him firmly. "And she has no prejudices; so think not of her. Rob, it's hardly worth your going home, wherever that may be. Will you come to bed? It is just wide enough for two."

"There's nothing I'd like better," he replied. He reached for me and pulled me to him. He kissed me. I was startled by the passion of that kiss; I thought he really seemed to need me. An explanation then presented itself. "Oh, Giles," he murmured, "you are sae warm and familiar and safe. If only there was you and me and nothing else!"

I stifled my irritation with the compliment which made me sound like a trusty old hound. After all, he was in my arms; I must be content with that.

"It could be thus," I said with reason. "Why should it not be so? Who decrees it otherwise? You don't have to go back to Jamie. Of course, he has somewhat more to offer." I was very conscious that my room was cold and shabby, and Rob had come from court.

"Och, no, it isnae' that," said Rob indignantly. "I like well your room here and there's no one I would rather spend the night with than you. Look at us – three years apart but we take up our friendship as if we pairted yesterday. And do ye think I sleep wi' Jamie? I do not. At least," he added, "just the once the other night, but that was because he was unhappy. His good looks are going and the king is no sae warm tae him as once he was."

"I don't want to talk about Jamie," I mumbled in his ear.

"Then we shall not," he answered readily. "And I'll not ask you about your companions of the night and I am sure there have been some. You are too bonny, Giles, tae have been much alone."

"So we have both known other men," I agreed, "and women too, maybe, for you. But that's now in the past. We might begin again from this moment."

"Here's tae that," said Robbie. "Here's tae our friendship which begins anew tonight. And may it last for ever!"

"May it so indeed!"

The bed invited; we undressed quickly. We were soon between the sheets and wrapped ourselves about each other. Kisses . . . honeyed words . . . the warmth of flesh on flesh . . . a little sleep . . . how rapidly the night passed! I savoured the strength of his body – the hard muscle, the firm curves of his arse, the lithe build of him, the taste of him, the scent of his skin, his hair. I must have murmured fifty times over that I loved him; he hugged me in return. I could hardly believe that he was here with me, after so long away. I felt his body welded the length of my own and held him to me, trying to retain the imprint on my skin. I kissed him deeply, my fingers twined in his golden hair. Time . . . how could I halt its inexorable progress, how keep this moment fixed and still?

Grey daylight came. Dishevelled and hungry we emerged and sought our clothes, strewn carelessly about the room – my homespun cloth, his glossy green velvets.

"I suppose you must go back?" I asked with studied nonchalance.

"I must," he answered. "I owe it tae Jamie. He has declared me his shield-bearer. I cannae' let him down."

Well, I thought – and oh how wrong I was in such a thought! – what does it signify? We shall be close now and meet often, and this night will be the first of many such.

And so I bade him farewell with a cheerful countenance and with no conception of the strange twist of fate that awaited him – nor could I have guessed that I was sending him forth into the chronicles of our time. I was even a little sorry for him, for he was full of fear about his forthcoming public brush with royalty. But I thought that I had comforted him somewhat and I hoped my presence at the tiltyard would a little ease his misgivings.

So, three days later I was with him at Whitehall. I must admit that I was not a little overawed myself. On this occasion the nobility of the land comport themselves much as the court of Camelot. King James becomes King Arthur, though our affable and plump Queen Anne is not precisely how one pictures radiant enigmatic Guinevere. We have shields and lances, we have barriers and lists, we have noblemen in armour, and fierce restive horses caparisoned in bright colours. Moreover, there is some savagery in the sport – men have been known to wound each other – there would be blood and bruises before the end of the day.

Lord Hay, one of the combatants, looked magnificent in his armour – big and strutting, giving his directives to Robbie who was all in blue, the colour Jamie most affected.

It was a dull March day and Robbie's hair shone like a field of buttercups; but he was tense and ill at ease. The great horse he was to ride must have sensed his apprehension. I had some difficulty holding the beast steady; his head twisted this way and that, the nostrils flared and snorting.

Robbie mounted, white as a ghost, and Jamie handed him the shield. The trumpets blared. The horse held back, then started forward suddenly and clattered clumsily towards the dais where His Majesty and 'the great ones' sat. I could see that Rob was having trouble handling the horse and keeping steady the shield. My heart went up into my mouth – I feared that Robbie's prophesies would come true, that he would make some kind of a fool of himself and earn the scornful reputation of a man that could not hold a horse in check, and this before His Majesty.

As Rob drew level with the dais, just in front of the king, the horse reared up. The shield thudded to the ground. The horse bucked and reared again. Robbie was thrown into the air and down upon the ground, with just wit enough to roll clear of the flying hooves. I heard the gasp of the spectators, like a sharp gush of wind. I and Jamie and some half dozen others all ran forward, and the bridle of the horse was caught; but having done his worst, the beast was threat no longer, and stood panting, quiet now, ready to be soothed.

I flung myself down beside Rob, who lay upon his back, eyes closed, one leg twisted under him.

"Rob – Rob – " I gasped, my face close to his own, the which was deathly white.

"My leg!" he said between his teeth, and fainted clean away. I loosened his collar and unlaced his doublet, ripping the shirt open in my haste.

Rob groaned, shifted, and opened his eyes, his face contorted, his teeth clenched. "Giles!" he said. "Help me!"

I raised my eyes, appalled, and found that I was looking straight into the eyes of James the First of England, Sixth of Scotland, God's Annointed. He was kneeling there, the other side of Robbie, backed by an anxious group of courtiers who were fussing round him. It was the first time I had ever seen him clearly as a man. I saw the shrewd blue eyes, the well-defined brows, the small mouth, the square-cut reddish beard. I saw the odd expression on his face. I could not place it at the time. I only know I had the impression that it was not appropriate.

His Majesty had risen to his feet, his hand upon his heart, his lips apart, his entire being seemingly centred on the sight before him.

The sight before him? Robbie, lying supine, writhing in agony, his head thrown back, his throat arched, his golden hair spread out upon the ground; and now, thanks to my inept and eager ministrations, half naked to the belly.

His Majesty was all eyes. I think no one could deny it: Robbie had brought himself to the king's attention.

CHAPTER FIFTEEN

"This may well have fallen out much to our advantage," murmured Jamie Hay to me out of the corner of his mouth as we accompanied the stretcher out of the tiltyard.

"Advantage? He could die of it!" I said.

"Not he," said Jamie comfortably. "Rob has the constitution of a young ox. Well, I'll leave it to you, Giles. I still have to joust. Good luck – take care o' our wee laddie, until," he added pointedly, "others do."

I broke away from him, angry at his callousness, and hurried to be by Rob's side.

"Where are they taking me? Stay wi' me, Giles!" Rob said alarmed and much in pain as the stretcher bearers circumnavigated the corner of the street and brought us to the nearby hospice at Charing Cross.

I had feared to find ourselves in a vast infirmary much as I had seen in books about the monks, where from serried ranks of paliasses the groans of the dying and the intricacies of many unwholesome diseases would go on around us – a prospect which filled me with dread; but to my surprise we were taken to a private room and were received by more than one physician bustling about in most obsequious fashion.

Dr. Paull introduced himself, a neat middle-aged man with a round face and snub nose; and it was he that supervised the shifting of Robbie from the stretcher to the bed and poured some liquid anodyne down his throat.

"Are you his manservant?" he asked me in a lull between Rob's groans.

"Yes," I answered.

"Undress him."

I worked to free Rob from his clothes. I was obliged to cut the breeches from him, for the leg would admit no touching and had taken on an oddish hue and showed an ugly swelling.

Seemingly immune to the beauty laid bare before him, Dr. Paull put his hands about the leg. Rob screamed.

"Yes; broken," said our physician placidly, "but not, I think, badly. I will know more when I have examined further. Fetch me the splint." This to the man beside him, who darted off.

"Who did you say he was?" said Dr. Paull to me as he covered Rob's naked form with blankets.

"I didn't, but his name is Robert Kerr."

Dr. Paull looked puzzled. "Should I have heard of him?"

"How should I know?" I was more concerned about my friend than my lack of politeness. His face was bathed in sweat, his hair drenched with the same to the colour of wet barley. He was drifting in and out of consciousness. I feared for him.

Dr. Paull patted me. "We'll soon have him to rights. He's young and strong. I was told to put him in a private room. This is unusual. A courtier, perhaps?"

"I know nothing of this," I said, "but please do all you can."

Our attention was now caught by a disturbance in the doorway. Other people entered, at their head a man in black, corpulent and unwieldy, with a self-important manner. A medicine chest was placed upon a table by a servant. The man began to speak to us – in French.

"This is le docteur Theodore Turquet de Mayerne," explained his attendant. "He will attend the patient."

Dr. Paull protested. Dr. Mayerne spoke again in French.

"Who is this man?" spluttered Dr. Paull. "What are his qualifications? By what authority does he intrude upon my sick room?"

"Who is he?" gasped the attendant. "This is the physician to his majesty King Henri Quatre of France. He has studied medicine at Heidelberg and Montpelier. He is a doctor of physic at the University of Montpelier. Qualifications? He has them all. And by what authority does he intrude? By the authority of His Majesty King James!"

Dr. Paull and I stared in astonishment.

"I am sent by the king," said Dr. Mayerne in slow careful English and a strong foreign accent. "Believe me, I know what I do. Please give me all assistance, yes?"

"Very well," said Dr. Paull tight-lipped. "But truly we are well prepared here. It is a simple fracture of the leg. We have prepared splints."

"Show me the leg."

You would have thought it an unattached accessory to hear him talk. We grouped about the bed. I pulled the blankets back. Now Dr. Mayerne had his hands upon Rob's broken limb. I winced in sympathy as Rob cried out.

"You are correct. A fracture simple." Dr. Mayerne nodded approval at Dr. Paull. Then he spoke again, in French. He turned to Dr. Paull.

"Excuse me?" Dr. Paull said helplessly. He looked at me. "What does he say?"

"He says will you find something tae put between my teeth while he sets the bone!" Rob shouted. "And for Christ's sake do it – now!"

We stared at him as if the bed had spoken; and suddenly all was action. I had completely forgotten that he had acquired some fluency in French and understood Dr. Mayerne's commands. Everybody moved. The splints arrived, a tray of potions; cloths, stoppered bottles, pestle and mortar, and I know not what.

Within some half an hour or so the leg was strapped from knee to ankle, Robbie was dosed with possets, bathed about the face, and seeming greatly eased. I, sitting at his pillow, felt almost as drained as he, as I sat and sipped medicinal wine, and would have clasped the doctor by the hand and offered profuse gratitude, were it not that I remembered I was here as manservant and should know my place.

I watched the worthy doctor tidy up his medicines. Dr. Mayerne! Born in Geneva, now some thirty years of age, visiting England fresh from the French court, and so esteemed by King James that he would soon ask him to be one of his own physicians. At that moment I thought him a hero. I would have kissed his hands if such had been required, overcoming my natural distrust of one that spoke in French.

But little then did I know the rumours that abounded concerning him. I had not heard that he was well versed in the secret state poisonings of the French capital. I did not know that the physicians of Paris considered him unskilful, rash and useless. Nor did I know his receipt for gout was 'raspings of the human skull, unburied', that his receipt for an unguent for hypochondria was balsam of bats, that he used for his lotions and potions adder skin, sucking whelps, earthworms and the mashed thighbones of oxen. But would I have cared, had I known? Perhaps not – he mended Rob's broken leg, and nature and Rob's healthy constitution did the rest.

But what do I know? That Rob recovered, that his bones knitted, that his leg grew straight and that he never after walked with a limp may have been due entirely to the Oil of Swallows which Dr. Mayerne rubbed upon the break after it had been set. Twenty-one herbs, he said, were in that jar, along with neatsfoot oil, cloves, wax and butter, and twenty live swallows all beaten together – presumably last summer. Our age is very ready to make use of the leavings of beasts in its cures. Frogs' spawn, fried horse dung, woodlice in wine, baked and powdered toadsflesh – all are regularly used to treat our illnesses.

Having always been fortunate in health I may not be the best judge of the same, but in my country upbringing we found everything might be worked by herbs alone, gathered at the right time of the moon. Old-fashioned, yes, I suppose we were. My mother would have used briony root, comfrey root, fern water, bruised scabious and St John's Wort upon a broken bone. These would be followed by all the benefits of distilled rosemary, of garlic in milk, of honey, nettle, poppy, tansy, feverfew, sage and cowslip – all of which are wholesome and cause not that natural revulsion which the leavings of beasts do when applied to face and skin. But as I say, I never broke a leg, and had I done so, one could have pressed a hundred swallows mashed in oil about me, I daresay, and got my thanks.

I had a trundle bed made up near Rob's own and stayed with him for his recovery. Ours was a plain and simple chamber on the ground floor of the hospice. Painted upon the wall was a great nude man, his body covered with the astrological symbols for each body part. That is, a ram sat on his head, and about his neck a bull; a lion lay across his heart, a crab on his stomach and a scorpion about his privities. A naked youth poured a jug of water on his ankle, a goat smirked upon his knee, a satyr leapt over the goat, and a pair of scales balanced across his hips. A smiling female blossomed from his belly and two nude children crawled up his arms. He stood upon two fishes. His obvious discomfort caused us many moments of mirth as we sat waiting for the days to pass.

The days, however, were very far indeed from dull.

At first, Rob's recovery followed what I would suppose the usual course of convalescence. Much of sleeping, of medicinal possets, bed-pans, the shaving of the chin, the spongeing of the body and the combing of the hair; brief fevers swiftly abating, the irritation of an active man confined to bed, the soothing of the brow and spirit.

Dr. Paull was in daily attendance, and to Robbie's anxious queries answered: "You have no cause for despair. We could feel the fracture beneath the skin, but the skin was not broken. The bone is knitting itself unseen. A blood clot will have formed, and then a spongey thickening – soft at first, then hardening. New bone will grow and bridge the fissure. Then you will see a swelling; this will show that all is healing as it should. Later this will diminish. It will take time."

"How long?" groaned Rob.

Dr. Paull shrugged. "Each case is different. The lower limbs are slower to unite because they bear a heavier weight. In two months – three months – the bone will be firm but not always strong enough to do what you ask it. You will be walking with a crutch by summer. You will be walking comfortably by Christmas."

"Christmas?" Rob blanched.

"You are a very fortunate young man. And you will heal the quicker if you are patient."

Our first visitor was Lord Hay.

"Och, Jamie," Rob wailed. "I dropped your shield – what must you think?"

"I think it is of no importance," Jamie laughed.

"But before His Majesty – he mun be sae angry – and a' the court –"

"Now, foolish child, have done. The king is not displeased at all – how little ye ken His Majesty! He is all care and asks after you daily. He is only waiting till he is sure you are well enough to receive him and then he means to visit you."

"Tae tell me what a lummock I was? I could no' hae made a greater fool o' myself if I had tried. To be thrown! And I thought I could handle a horse. I am fit for nothing. I can never go among folk again. As soon as I can walk I'm leaving England."

"Yes, yes," Jamie agreed placidly, and let Rob ramble on and tell us all again that he was every kind of buffoon, no earthly good and better dead.

"Prepare yourself, my laddie," said Jamie one bright morning, "for this afternoon the king will visit."

"Och Jamie, no!" cried Robbie in a panic. "Not here – not in my bed o' sickness – comb my hair, Giles, quickly! And is the chamber pot awa'?"

"Enough!" protested Jamie laughing. "His Majesty kens that ye piss."

I set about to prepare Rob for the royal visit. I washed him, I rubbed perfumed unguents into his skin. I put him into a clean shirt and I combed his golden hair till it gleamed.

"Curl it a little if you can," said Robbie, squinting in his hand mirror.

I cuffed his ear for his vanity and set his golden locks about my fingers.

Now I partly expected drums and trumpets and a herald to announce the appearance of His Majesty. The entrance of the man who came in unannounced took me completely by surprise. I knew it was the king, because we were expecting him, and because the shuffling and bowing of the physicians in the doorway gave us something of a clue. The first thing that occurred to me, beside the fact that he was curiously ordinary in his appearance, was that he was, in his way, a handsome man, and as I bowed and backed away I was of a sudden overcome with fear for that I was four feet from the king of England and I had no idea how to behave.

He was, however, kind, and to my great relief spelled out at once the fashion of visit he intended.

"Be easy, Giles," he said. "I shall not disturb your patient. Ye may stay or go as ye think fit – I give nae orders. I have heard about the loving care ye gie your master and I thank ye for it; the physicians say that it has aided Master Kerr's recovery, and that is very dear to my hairt."

"Stay!" Robbie mouthed at me, wild-eyed. A trapped animal did not look more terrified than he.

"Your Majesty is very gracious," I murmured ineptly, and sat down upon a stool in a far corner. I was impressed that he had found out my name and used it as a friend might well do, though I still smarted at hearing Robbie called my master.

The king sat down beside the bed.

"Now, Robbie Kerr," he said. "How fare ye?"

Poor Rob could barely speak. His stuttering humility was curiously becoming. Fresh-faced and youthful, with his natural beauty enhanced by a startling cleanliness and a cascade of hair like beaten gold tumbling about his shoulder, he was a vision calculated to touch the heart of the susceptible. And such a one was there at his bedside.

King James was then about forty years of age. He was homely in appearance, clad in simple russet. He was of medium stature with broad shoulders, though slender at the waist and somewhat skinny of shank. His hair was short, brown, his beard more ginger. He had a friendly face, with sad heavy-lidded blue eyes. In repose the face looked secretive; but it was rarely in repose – he laughed easily and loudly and his face creased into lines of merriment.

We had been accustomed to a queen, a queen of pageantry and splendour, a goddess of the moon. I still remembered my childhood sight of her; it was as if an angel had come down to earth, the clouds parting to give her path. Naturally it takes a while to grow to understand the contrast that our present king presented. But I believed that now, four years after his accession, the country had settled down to it with some relief. It was easier to have a king – a family man, a peacemaker – to oversee us than to have a goddess who must be placated, wooed, adored, and this plainly when she was ageing, truculent and waspish. As I understood it, men were building houses now in places of their choice, tending their lands free from the threat of war and with a serene involvement in the carving of wood. The oak that our forebears turned into sailing ships we turn into staircases. Enjoyment is the way of it – horse and hound and playhouses and pleasures, eating and drinking, masques by torchlight. And a king that spoke broad Scots and did not stand on ceremony.

"I pray that ye will forgive me, sire," Rob was now saying earnestly. "I am sair ashamed. I was not worthy of Lord Hay . . . I brought disgrace upon the ceremony of your great day. I canna' even look Your Majesty in the eye for grief." (A lie – his eyes were very prettily directed at the king.)

King James took Robbie's hand in his own. "Och no, you do yoursel' wrong. Anyone may tumble – I hae done so mysel'. Landed wi' a crack. I can still feel the pain of it. No, no, ye're no' tae blame, my dear, ye munna' think it. I canna' bear these perfect knights that never put a foot wrong. I hae nae time for Lancelot. Gie me Arthur every time. A king, aye, but a mon for a' that!"

"I am no' worth your kindness," Robbie said huskily, and honestly, I thought. He truly was awash with misery for his performance in the tiltyard.

"Let me be the judge o' that," said James in a firm tone. "Now Robbie Kerr, tell me a' about yoursel' and where you've been and how ye came tae court. I knew your dad, of course, God rest his soul; my family have great cause tae be grateful to him. It seems tae me only right and proper that I should care for his son."

"I never knew my father," Robbie said poignantly. "He died when I was a bairn."

Oh! It was a scene to tug the heartstrings. I shifted in my corner. No one noticed me.

"My puir wee lad," said James patting the hand he held and, I swear, a lump in his throat. "I ken fu' well what it is tae lose a father. Och, Robbie, never fear – your days of grief are over." He gave a nod, a small bleak smile. "Someone cares for ye now. Someone will look after ye. Aye, Rob, aye," he added reassuringly and almost to himself, "I shall be very guid tae ye."

CHAPTER SIXTEEN

"Think of me," said the king, "as a kindly enquirer after your health. Think of me as one of your kin, one who would visit you if he were in London. An uncle. Aye, an uncle. Think of me as an uncle."

He brought with him sweetmeats – marchpane, wafer cakes, sugar flowers, iced cream. He enquired about the hospice food. He feared that Robbie might not be eating enough. He sent dishes from Whitehall. Fortunately (since his favourite meal was reputed to be sheeps' head boiled in the wool – flesh removed and served with butter) not always of his own choosing, but always excellent, and speaking for myself I did full well by Rob's misfortune and ate better than I ever had before.

The promised intention of His Majesty to prove good to Robbie produced in its train one particular change of our circumstance: we were inundated with a stream of noble visitors. Now suddenly it seemed that half the court must flock to see us. We were more stared upon than the great whale that came up the Thames last January.

The chief minister of our day Robert Cecil, Earl of Salisbury, in whose service Tom worked so assiduously, visited us, and sat there, small and bent and pale, with pursed mouth and exquisite hands. You could almost see the brain at work, assessing Robbie. *Threat or ally? Use thus . . .*

Sir Francis Bacon the Solicitor-General visited, a man in his forties, monstrous learned and extremely personable. This was a man who having writ a great work upon the subject of knowledge said modestly that 'twas not much better than that noise or sound which musicians make while they are tuning their instruments – 'so have I been content to tune the instruments of the Muses that they may play that have better hands.' His great work having had the misfortune to be published about the time of the Powder Plot he got no glory, for men would rather talk of scandal, death, torture and hanging than the Advancement of Learning. Tom said Sir Francis was the greatest thinker of our time. Be that as it may, with Robbie he was very sweet and gentle. We knew a thing or two about Sir Francis. We knew that although he was but lately wed to a very young wife, his particular friend was one Tobie Matthew, a young man of twenty-nine, with whom he had been close for many years. And here was Robbie sitting up in bed in his nightshirt and his golden hair awry about his shoulders and Sir Francis being very kind to him.

"Remember, Master Kerr," said he, "I am your friend and was so from the very first."

"I shall, sir; thankyou," answered Rob devoutly, neither of them knowing the strange and tortuous circumstances that one day would bind them in a most reluctant proximity, when life and death would hang in the balance.

And who else do you suppose now honoured us? – none other than Lord Henry Howard, Earl of Northampton! What could I do? How might I brush this nobleman aside and find the words to say: my cousin says you are a scoundrel, sir, and Robbie must not fall into your hands! The plain truth is that I could not, and therefore bowed most graciously and ushered him within.

"My dear!" says he to Robbie, holding out both his hands, advancing like an old acquaintance, sitting down beside the bed and taking

Robbie's hands in his. "My dear young man – we have all been so distressed at your misfortune!"

It was the first time I had seen him close at hand, this supposed ogre of Tom's imagination. That scene so long ago at Bourton-on-the-Hill came to my mind – Tom lying on the bed, downstairs his sisters casting apple peel to foresee their future husbands. *A little merry smile of innocent delight hovers at the corner of his mouth when he speaks of anyone whom he would sooner see disembowelled . . . a man who has been feeding long on bitterness, a sleek lean cat-faced charmer . . .*

He was not far off his seventieth year, Lord Henry. He was very neat and trim. He had a narrow clever face full of sardonic amusement, so worldly wise that one doubted he could ever have been a boy. He had a small well-trimmed beard and a great moustache; a big hooky nose. He had dark eyebrows and pointed goblin ears. I thought there was a bitter twist to the mouth as he smiled – not exactly a sneer, no, it was too controlled for that. He wore a wide-rimmed hat – to cast a shadow and conceal his expression? And he had the saddest eyes.

Sitting in my corner, obscured by shadow and inferiority, I had leisure to observe and marvel. This old man had known all the heroes of my childhood, had been young in the glorious days of Queen Elizabeth before it all went sour and tired; a misfit amongst the splendid ones, a watcher rather than a dancer, a mischief-maker, suspect and unpopular. A man of papist leanings, an admirer of the Scottish queen, a sodomite, it could have been no rose garden for him amongst the robust and Protestant swaggerers at the Virgin Queen's court. This man had accompanied Essex and Southampton when they took the road to Ireland. What had they promised him if they came back successful and Essex made his bold bid for the throne? But they had not been successful, and the cast for the throne had gone wide of the mark. And so Lord Henry turned his eyes northward and worked for James's accession and all had gone very well for him at last. Could he sleep easy now? After a lifetime of intrigue and disillusion, was the habit of perpetual deviousness one that a man might break, or did it cling about him still, like a snake skin that when its outer case is shed reforms and grows again its scales?

"I have known sorrow," he was saying, leaning close to Robbie. "I am comfortable now but I have not always been so. My family are valued by His Majesty for their loyalty and devotion and I am grateful that he understands the magnitude of my own devotion. But I have known lean times. I understand the vulnerability of a young man far from home, a man who has not yet made friends and knows not whom to trust. The world holds many pitfalls. I am an experienced traveller in its boggy mires. If I can extend a helping hand, Robbie, I will do so with all my heart. Reach out and take it – fold it to thy bosom – think of me entirely as your friend."

"I do, and am most grateful," Robbie stammered, moist and pink and scented, and holding the very hand of which Northampton spoke between his own. It was pale and thin and speckled with brown liver spots; it bore a ruby ring big as a cherry, which set me thinking about those rings that come from Italy and carry a secret compartment where a man puts poison and he drops it in a glass and it becomes one with the wine . . .

I jumped, appalled at my own fancies. Too much of Thomas's influence and a man grows over wary.

"I will not weary thee," his lordship said, and rose slowly to his feet. "But call on me, my dear, when you have need. I was ever a slave to beauty."

His face was very close to Rob's. And then he leaned a little further forward and held Robbie gently by the chin and kissed him lightly on the brow. Then out he glided, gracious to the last.

"What a kind auld man!" said Robbie warmly.

I looked at Robbie, seeking for a trace of irony in his observation; there was none. There was a certain innocence in Rob, not of a physical nature, no, but of that quality of trust which generally believes what it is told. But I had some kind of responsibility towards him, and still surely some towards Thomas, who had entrusted Rob's welfare to my charge.

"Do you think perhaps that Lord Henry Howard has an eye to the main chance?" I asked in the cautious tone of one that broaches a subject of doubtful taste. "Might it not be possible that he sees the king's affection for you and supposes that a friendship with you might be no bad thing for himself?"

"I dinnae' see why," Robbie shrugged. "A' the king has done is ask about my health."

If Robbie understood that to be the case, there were others that understood it differently. Our next visitor was the Countess of Suffolk, Thomas Howard's wife, Frances Devereux's mother – a good-looking woman, very finely dressed. *When the king sets eyes on a young man it is she that seeks him out, curls his hair and sweetens his breath . . .*

"Robert . . . I would like to know you better. Tell me all about yourself. Robert . . . or do they call you Robbie? Which do you prefer? What I would suggest, dear, is Robin. It sounds so English and," she added with a little arch smile, "there is a precedent. Robin. 'Bonny Sweet Robin is all my joy' . . . you know the song. And Robin, dear, the other name, the Scottish name, your family name – how do you say it

101

and how do you spell it?"

Rob replied politely with the information she requested.

"Kerr," she said, and laughed. "It sounds like the noise a crow makes!"

Understandably Robbie did not join in her merriment; but still remained polite.

"I understand, dear," she cooed, patting him. "You do not wish to change your name."

"Of course I dinnae'," Robbie said. Was it necessary to point out to this interfering but well-meaning female that she was speaking of the most venerable name of the Scottish Borderland?

"Then soften it, dear. If you decided to spell it C-A-R-R it would sound more acceptable. It would even sound English. Think about it. Well, enough of that. You have the most wondrous hair! So beautiful on a man, that spun gold. My poor Frankie will be so envious. What do you use – chamomile?"

I have to assume that Robbie was bemused. He answered all her questions and they sat discussing distillations and concoctions like two hedge crones in a meadow. Their conversation ended much as the other ones had done.

"I'll leave you now, dear, so that you may rest. Best not overtire yourself with talking. Remember my interest in you. Your welfare is my greatest concern. All my family want nothing more than the king's happiness. And the king loves to have his dear ones close about him. I have observed His Majesty; I know a little about his likes and dislikes. If I can help you, Robin, in any way, just ask me. If you need my opinion or advice . . . the best way to wear your hair, the colours which most flatter you – I have some knowledge of these things. The ways of the English court . . . these will seem strange to you and I can help you here. Remember my kindness. Remember it was I who helped you first. Remember this when you settle at Whitehall . . ."

"When I – ?" frowned Rob.

But she smiled and departed, and a flock of courtiers hurried in to take her place, settling in their finery about the room, like butterflies upon a bush. They told us their names; some we forgot and some remembered. Some were agreeable, some merely curious. One whom we particularly remarked was Philip Herbert, the Earl of Montgomery. How could we not, especially as he brought his two greyhounds with him?

"Sit!" he commanded, and they did so, watching us with bright alert eyes. Handsome, elegant, perfumed like a summer garden, Montgomery breezed in as if his presence here was the most natural thing in the world. We would have known who he was, of course, even if his manservant had not announced him. King James's first English favourite, supreme these four years, though not unrivalled, for the king was very prodigal with his favours. There he stood and surveyed Rob and eyed him carefully and smiled. He did not say as the others had said: *remember, I shall be your friend.* He said:

"H'm, well – you run true to form. I cannot say that I'm surprised. You're pretty, I'll say that for you. It seems I have no choice then but to wish you luck. Be glad I do, Kerr, for your rise would be more difficult with my enmity. That I feel none, count yourself fortunate." He paused. His eyes ran over Robbie thoughtfully, assessingly. He said: "I wonder if you'll remember this moment when you stand where I do now. And be as magnanimous?"

I believe that Rob had not the least idea of what he meant. Rob thanked him. He thanked everybody. Everybody thought him affable and pleasant – which indeed he was – and went away content. It was plain enough – you could see them thinking that here was no threat; young Kerr was none too clever and would be easy to manipulate. Time and again Jamie Hay clapped Robbie on the shoulder and beamed at him.

"Wonderful!" he said. "They like you! Everybody likes you! It's going very well. Aye, so very very well!"

Meanwhile, in quiet moments I read to Robbie. He liked Nashe's *Unfortunate Traveller* and Deloney's *Jack of Newbury*. When he was fretful I twanged him to sleep with some airs upon the lute and our days passed well enough.

When Robbie put his first faltering foot upon the floor and with the aid of a crutch hobbled a yard or so, Dr. Paull pronounced himself satisfied, and with Robbie once more stretched upon the bed, white with exertion, declared: "Well, I have done with you, young man, and am no longer needed. I will examine you once more and then you pass out of my care."

He pulled back the sheets and gave Rob a swift and peremptory handling. He was in no way gentle. I watched in some surprise.

"You believe him ready to enter the everyday world?" I queried doubtfully. "He scarce can walk and tires when standing."

"Well, I daresay he will not do much of that where he is going," Dr. Paull responded darkly.

"And where is that?" I said.

"The less said of the same the better," answered Dr. Paull. "And it's not for me to give opinion on the subject."

But he plainly intended to, and showed that the opinion was adverse by his kneading and his pummelling. Every gesture betokened disapproval and hostility. "Little did I think, Robert," said he, "when I first took you in, what I would be required to do. It is like the fattening of the chicken for the table. And fine indeed you'll look upon the golden dish, my boy, with herbs about your nostrils and up your arse." He slapped the offending portion of anatomy. "Ah, Robert, Robert, would you not sooner be a soldier and fight in foreign parts, as men do? Have you given thought as to what you are about? What would your father say?"

"He would say that a good physician knows his place," said Robbie sharply, "and confines his talents tae bone setting."

"And he'd be right," said Dr. Paull morosely. "Then get your things together – here come your coachmen." Two servants from the palace stood outside the open door. They had come to take Robbie to White-hall where he would complete his recovery under the loving care of the king.

"Dress him, Giles," said Dr. Paull. "The golden platter and the seasoning herbs are waiting for the chicken."

CHAPTER SEVENTEEN

A sumptuous chamber was put at our disposal. It overlooked the river and lay near the orchard at the west of the palace. Robbie's bed was a fine carved four-poster, mine a serviceable trundle, as befits a serving man. In both cases the linen was excellent and Rob's bed had an embroidered coverlet whereon fantastic birds sported in some potentate's garden with much of crimson feather and tail. An uphol-stered chair stood by the bed, and very comfortable it was to one used to oaken settles. And this was not all, for the close stool was upholstered also – a most pleasing luxury.

Rob's meals were placed upon a small oak table; there was also a writing desk with quill, ink and paper; and on the floor a Turkey foot carpet.

A twisty passageway led to this room (in Whitehall every room seemed to be reached via a twisty passageway) while a further equally sinuous passage led away eastward to the courtiers' lodgings. Such a one might never be used by a fashionable lady, for no farthingale might pass along it. If His Majesty wished to visit, all he had to do was leave his privy chamber, walk along the Stone Gallery and enter that same twisty passageway, and after winding his way along its narrow turns he would find our door and Robbie perforce, since as yet he could not hobble far, waiting.

And visit he did, almost every day. At first he did not stay long. After all, there was no hurry – Robbie would be here tomorrow and tomorrow. I was a little reminded of a miser and his gold, of a man just peeping to make sure his treasure was still where he had left it. He would sit upon the upholstered chair discoursing eagerly and pleasantly. Dogs and horses were his favourite subjects. Also he talked much of Scotland, thinking maybe to put Robbie at his ease. Places which they had in common, names familiar to both – Jedburgh, Hermitage, Smailholm Tower, Edinburgh, the hills of Eildon, the Forest of Ettrick . . .

"And remember, I dinnae' stand on ceremony," said the king. "I cannae' bear tae see ye fearful o' my station. Alone as we are now" (he did not look in my direction; a serving man does not count, as anyone knows) "call me by pleasant homely names. Think of me, as I said before, as something like an uncle. Aye," he said complacently, "Uncle will do very well."

"Rob," I said once, when his new-found uncle was gone from us, "had you not better consider exactly what it is you are about?"

I think I had not seen Rob blush before, but he did so now. He looked hot and uncomfortable, even shifty.

"His Majesty's kindness tae me . . ." he mumbled.

"Yes indeed, His Majesty's kindness," I said briskly. "I think you will find that sooner or later His Majesty will expect something in return."

"He has never said anything of that nature tae me," Robbie said.

"No. Up till now you have been on your bed of pain and passers by were at the door."

"I am still abed," he protested.

"Yes, but now you are recovering, and rather than appear infirm you appear inviting."

"Do I? I dinnae' mean tae." He looked down at himself.

"I have never seen a nightshirt so provocatively filled," I said. "The sight before him is not lost upon His Majesty. The Earl of Montgomery plainly expects that you will be his successor and Dr. Paull was certainly comparing himself to whoever it was that prepared the virgins for King David. Listen to me. You can walk, Robbie – just. You have the strength to get out of your bed and hobble from Whitehall. More, I'd steal a horse for you if such was your desire, and set you on your way to France or Italy or somewhere equally delightful and far from London. It is all very well to sit simpering and smiling and receiving compliments and healing. But gorgeous as you are, Rob, you have never been blessed with great imagination. You have seen King James. He is not young.

105

True, he is not old. He is not," I lowered my voice, "excessively fastidious about his person. He scratches at his privities and his nose often dribbles. I don't deny his good qualities. I don't find him bad looking; though his legs are skinny. But he is no Adonis. He has food crumbs in his beard, his breath smells of drink and sometimes he slobbers in his speech. And you must ask yourself now, Rob, in honesty: do you desire that mouth on yours, that tongue in your ear, and," I added carefully, "that prick in your arse?"

"How do you know whether he does that?" retorted Robbie huffily.

"Does what?"

"Fucks. He may not. He may like tae kiss and hold."

"Indeed he may. But on the chance that when and if you ever lie naked in his bed he reasonably expects to use all you provide, you might perhaps consider whether his wishes accord with your own."

"And then again I might not."

"What do you mean?"

"I mean I'll wait and see," said Rob. "I always have done. I never think ahead. I live in the minute."

I groaned.

"But I understand you, Giles," he continued. "Your care o' me. Do I understand what is entailed if I should be sae fortunate as tae gain His Majesty's goodwill? No I dinnae'. And it's no' the bedroom that alarms me – I ken well how tae fuck. No, what alarms me is the politics. When you take a place o' favour they come talkin' tae ye – lords and churchmen and ambassadors – they ask ye things – they ask tae pass on messages tae the king – they ask ye wha' ye think o' this and that. They expect ye tae hae opinion on wha' goes on in France, in Spain. They play you off against another; they gie ye bribes. It fair frightens me. Compared tae that, whether His Majesty likes fucks or kisses seems tae me nae problem. Nae problem at a'." He grinned. "And anyway he hasnae asked me."

The very next day when His Majesty came calling he took me privily aside.

"Shall ye go awa', Giles?" he said. "Shall ye wander in the garden? Shall ye wait there until I come frae here? Good lad." And off I went obediently and closed the door behind me.

It was a day in early summer and the roses were budding and blooming in the Privy Garden. The sky was blue. I reflected much upon the oddness of the situation as I ambled to and fro amongst the sweet-smelling leafy arbours. We were in deep waters now; how carelessly we had embarked upon the voyage! Whatever would become of us? I tried to consider what I knew of the situation of the royal favourite, particularly when the favourite was male. I vaguely remembered that in France King Henri III had had his mignons and that most of them had been killed by jealous nobles. But Henri III had been outrageous, had he not, a painted mincing slightly sinister creation? It was different in England. King James was so stunningly ordinary, so agreeable, good-humoured and sagacious, passionate for dogs and hunting. And Jamie Hay was no mignon and nor was Philip Herbert, both robust and hearty – there was no shame in following such as these. Thomas – long ago, it seemed now – had told me to look after Robbie. Surely he could place no objection to seeing his protégé commence an ascent to such dizzying heights? If Rob became the favourite of the king he would become one of the most important personages in the land, and his friends likewise. Suddenly, in the sunshine, I shivered.

When His Majesty quit Robbie's chamber I hurried back inside. I found Rob sitting up in bed, hands clasped about his knees, and looking deep in thought.

"And so?" I said.

"His Majesty has given me tae understand . . ." said Rob.

"Yes? That what?"

"That he cannae' do wi'out me."

I was impressed. It is not every day that a monarch admits as much to one's companion.

"He hopes that I may grow tae care for him," continued Rob. "If so, there will be titles, honours, manors, gifts frae a grateful heart. And I will live at court, and he will form me."

"Form you? What does he mean by that?"

"Create me. Make me intae what he wants. He says I hae an untouched mind."

I sniggered nervously. "That isn't true, Rob. If he thinks that, he will have a surprise."

"He's about tae teach me Latin."

"What for?"

"He likes tae teach and I will be beholden tae him. It is something he may do tae pass the time until I am recovered."

"And then you move towards your golden future, able to construe and parse," I observed caustically.

"Aye, and he agrees wi' Lady Suffolk that I should anglicise the name. You see, I am tae be recreated, the better tae take my place at court."

"Is it what you want, Rob?" I said urgently.

"I would be a fool if I did not."

"Do you think that we perhaps should write to Thomas?"

"When did ye last?"

"I told him about your broken leg and that you were on the mend."

"Nothing since?" he said uncomfortably

"No. Of course, you might write to him yourself," I said not without sarcasm.

Rob wriggled. "You write, Giles. I wouldnae' ken what tae say."

"What shall I say?"

"Why, that the king has asked me tae be his – " He paused.

"Paramour? Bedfellow? Catamite?" I suggested ironically.

"I dinnae' like those words," Rob muttered.

"You ought to face them nonetheless. Other people will use them of you."

"People generally say 'favourite'."

"They do, but they say that of horses, cloaks, colours. It is a nebulous term."

"Nevertheless it is the one that people use," Rob said growing more defensive with each remark. "But His Majesty only spoke of affection. He said he only wants my happiness. He asked whether I could grow tae care for him. And I said that I could. And you may tell Thomas that."

I did not write to Thomas. Up till now I had entrusted such meagre correspondence as I had writ to travellers at the Deptford quayside about to embark for France, men of some quality. My letters were dull for all that Tom wanted gossip, for I feared to write about the great. Letters were often opened, and the jaws of Newgate gaped all too readily for the indiscreet. I simply dared not write about the private life of the king. Tom would have to find out from some other source.

That night when I prepared Rob for bed he said: "Lie wi' me tonight, Giles."

I needed no second invitation. We lay warm enwrapt about each other. Rob twisted about; I thought his leg pained him.

"Giles, it's not wrong, is it?"

"Wrong?"

"What I am about. Will I be no better than a whore?"

"No, it is not wrong," I said. What did I know? I had no business to pontificate on morality. I wanted Rob to be easy in his mind. What could I say? "Our king is a very learned righteous man," I said. "And I am sure that anyone who cares so much about Holy Scripture will be very comfortable in his heart about the ordering of his daily life."

"Aye," said Rob, "I would say so. I know sae little; he's right tae teach me. I need all the guidance I can get."

"No one questions King James's wisdom," I said feeling on safer ground here. "He's well learned and speaks Latin, Greek and French. They call him Solomon. He will be an excellent teacher for you."

"Aye," said Robbie sounding more at ease. "Giles, there is something more . . ."

"There is?"

"It's this: King James believes you are my manservant; I never have disillusioned him. But you are a gentleman's son and Thomas's cousin and your uncle is a squire and country justice. Can I presume upon our friendship and hope you'll stay wi' me? All I can say is that whatever rewards fall tae me you'll hae your share and never go wi'out. What do you say, Giles? If you refuse me I shall never dare go through wi' this."

"You know I'll stay with you, Rob. I don't even need to consider it."

"Giles, I wish you would consider it. I want you tae consider all it means and no' answer me lightly. It means that you will be bound tae me, what I do and where I go. If my fortunes rise or fall. You will be with me."

"There's nothing I'd like more," I answered warmly, rash fool that I was. "I'll be your man – who better? I've been looking after you since March and I do it well. I know a little, moreover, about the handling of silks and satins from my time at Oxford when I sometimes waited on the gentry. And Rob, let us be honest – I have no other plan. I might as well be living with you in glory than return to the music of the street in Cripplegate."

"Whatever your reason, I'm glad. Ye cannae' ken – I mean you cannot know how glad I am I'll hae a friend wi' me in what lies ahead."

There was that about Rob's speech that savoured of foreboding; it seemed entirely inappropriate. But as I recall it now, it had something of the flavour of the Duchess of Malfi's words:

Wish me good speed
For I am going into a wilderness
Where I shall find nor path nor friendly clue
To be my guide.

"Good cheer, Rob," I laughed hugging him. "You are about to become the king's beloved – this is a matter of some celebration, not a cause of dismay."

"Aye," he answered sheepishly. "So kiss me, Giles, and make me merry."

We kissed. A long slow kiss, a kiss of farewell. We understood it – we would be together – I would see him every day – but he would be the king's. We clung together. Desire grew strong. I would have liked to fling him on his belly and stake my prior claim; but I was as always wretchedly considerate with him, fearful of hurting the mending limb. I merely held his prick, stroked it, gently brought him to his pleasure kissing him the while. When all was done I murmured: "I forget sometimes how much I love you. I suppose I have grown used to it, as I have to my fingers and thumbs. Of course I must stay with you, Rob; I could do no other."

"Whatever your reason, Giles, I thank you with all my heart."

In the morning when I opened the window and the river noise came up to us with its watermen's cries, its snatches of music, of oaths, of splashing oars, Rob's mood was other than the apprehension of the night. He was ebullient, excited. He was ready for all the day might bring.

The day brought the eager royal lover, as did the morrow and the morrow. At first I would withdraw. I grew to know the Privy Garden very well, and the Stone Gallery where everyone walked to pass the time and meet. But soon, it seemed, it did not matter whether I was there or not – the two grew rapidly close and did not care who knew it. In that chamber and with Rob still incapacitated, the tenor of the visits was, while superficially didactic, rampant with unsatisfied lust.

The king had come to instruct Robbie in the Latin tongue. Now this is how he did it: the days being warm and the sunlight shining in upon the bed, all for Robbie's comfort the king suggested that he should not overheat himself with the constraint of clothes but remain in his nightshirt; not, however, underneath the coverlet – which would be too hot and cumbersome – but lying on the same coverlet, bare limbed to let the air about his leg. The king would pace about the room declaiming, Rob repeating all that was required. It soon grew plain enough that Rob was not the best of pupils. He would forget, he would grow muddled, he would confuse his tenses and his authors; he was not a Latin scholar. And so the king brought along a little birch switch which he flexed as he walked about. And when Robbie made an error his teacher lightly corrected him, at first upon the hand, and Robbie meekly extended his palm for the chastisement. But as the days progressed and merriment progressed alongside, and the pupil grew no more skilled and the teacher grew more masterful, the pupil was instructed to stretch out upon his belly, leaning on his elbows; and when he made a mistake the nightshirt was lifted and with a flick of the birch the implement of chastisement descended upon the full round globes laid bare.

I believe I have remarked before upon the perfection of Robbie's arse. Have I not? Each well-rounded cheek was furred with golden hair, downy soft to the touch, now gleaming in the bright rays of the sun.

The muscular thighs were also golden-haired. Spread they caused a little well of shadow to form from the crevice of the arse down to the place beneath.

I have no doubt that great would have been the royal disappointment if Rob had learnt his lessons faultlessly. However, he could be relied upon to give his teacher cause to correct his errors and there were many – so much so that I suspected Rob of guessing the pleasure which his teacher enjoyed in chastising him and ensuring that such pleasure was well indulged. It even seemed to me that the birch was very active whether there were errors or no. And so down came the birch upon the bum, not heavily, but sharp enough to sting. The lovely globes twitched and the lesson sounded so: "Immanitati autem consentaneum est – *ouch* – opponere eam – *ouch* – quae supra humanitatem est – *ouch* – heroicam sive divinam – *ouch* – virtutem." And then after expressing regret that the pupil needed so much necessary correction the magister would bend and kiss the abused posterior to heal the hurt. What this way of instruction did for the two concerned I may not say, but on those occasions when I was witness to the same my own prick hardened painfully.

I was in the Garden one day strumming in an arbour when I saw pass by Lord Thomas Howard the Lord Chamberlain and a bunch of his cronies. I heard what they said, for my lord was a loud gruff speaker and took no pains to lower his voice.

" . . .teaches young Carr Latin, aye, that's what they are about. Teaches him Latin! But have you heard the way Carr speaks? Broad Scots! Somebody ought to teach him English, what?" Much guffawing. "Latin? No, I never got the hang of it myself. I'll tell you the kind of language I best understand – it's this: Come dine with me!"

The study of Latin, however, in a crumpled nightshirt, was the way to the king's heart. By the end of the year at the age of twenty-one Robbie had become Sir Robert Carr and a Gentleman of the Royal Bedchamber; and with a well-healed leg was very much in evidence in a suit of amber satin and shoes garnished with silk roses, and installed in his own chambers in the palace.

That winter I was traversing the Stone Gallery in a press of people when I came face to face with Thomas. Bumped straight into him. My cousin Thomas Overbury whom I still believed to be in Spain.

Astonishment made me speechless. Not so Thomas, though first he gripped me by the shoulders and he shook me. He was quite pale with rage and the effort of controlling it.

"Cousin Giles!" he said – but it was more of a hiss. "I think that I am owed an explanation. Your letters ceased. I had to learn of your

111

change of fortune from another source." He spat his words out between gritted teeth and there being a deal of sibilants in what he said I was the worse for it. "Now tell me – and this I think I have a right to know – what the devil is Robbie playing at?"

CHAPTER EIGHTEEN

It was six years since I had seen my cousin Thomas. He was now about six-and-twenty, lean and rangy, and very handsome with his fine thoughtful eyes, broad brow and beautiful mouth, his dark hair, neat beard and moustache, and his elegant grey velvet clothes. I was not entirely surprised to see him, since my aunt had writ that he was expected to be back in England soon, but I was taken aback to encounter him so suddenly at Whitehall. I brought him back to Rob's apartment – two rooms, larger than our first, but, like that one, over-looking the river and most agreeably furnished. A servant brought wine and I sent him off to seek out Robbie. Tom sat back in the great chair and looked about him.

"Well! You have fallen on your feet," he said.

"Have you spoken to Robbie yet?" I said embarrassed.

"No. You had better give an account of his rapid rise to promi-nence. Although I have been informed of his change in station I would like to hear your version, Giles."

"Yes, no doubt . . .Well, we were, so to speak, swept along by events. His Majesty was much moved by Rob's suffering and came to enquire about his health. I told you that he broke his leg falling from the horse . . . With Robbie looking somewhat appealing in his night-shirt and his distress, His Majesty was moved to fall in love with him."

"And moved him to Whitehall, since moves are the way of it!"

"What could we do? It is a great honour for Robbie. He's still in a daze at his good fortune."

"And James Hay and Philip Herbert – what do they think of it?"

"It was Jamie Hay's idea – something about counterbalancing the influence of the Howards and promoting the Scottish element. As for the Earl of Montgomery, he wished Robbie good luck."

"A shrewd move for a fellow not famed for his wisdom," observed Thomas. "King James has no use for discarded favourites who take their replacement sullenly. It must be all one big happy family at court."

"Well," I smiled, "Robbie is now very much the new bright star. He can do no wrong. I thought the king might find his lack of intellec-tual prowess tiresome but no, quite the reverse. His Majesty delights in what he perceives as native artlessness and has undertaken to shape him as a potter shapes a pot. First there was Latin, then a smattering of policy. Robbie, conscious of his own inadequacy, behaves with utmost deference, humility and gratitude, and His Majesty is highly pleased with his new creation and has made him a Gentleman of the Bedchamber and a knight. And, by the by, he now spells his family name with a C."

"And Robbie . . . ?" Tom said reflectively. "Is he content?"

I hesitated. "He is so when he is with the king. I rather think he looks upon James as a kind of father – you know that Robbie never knew his own. But paternal though His Majesty loves to be, and much as he encourages Rob to consider him as a mentor, it is not of course that simple."

"You mean that they are lovers."

"Oh yes."

"But however does Rob deal with that?" said Tom pettishly. "It cannot be conducive to intimacy if one must call one's bedfellow 'Your Majesty'!"

I said with a little twitch of the mouth: "The king likes Rob to call him Uncle."

"But how ludicrously droll!" exclaimed Tom with a cynical snort. "And not a little incestuous. But perhaps that adds to the excitement?"

I fidgeted. "Whatever it means," I said, "they have now been together for some six months and seem well content. He calls him Robin."

Thomas digested this information. He must have been monstrous vexed at the turn of events. He must surely have been looking forward to coming home and finding Robbie waiting for him untouched and eager to take up their friendship. He showed no emotion. However, his next remark was somewhat waspish.

"I would think him an uncouth lover, James; would not you?" he said. "Rank about the armpits and crotch?"

"You are speaking of my benefactor," I reproved.

"Why not? I am not afraid to say that mine is a hunchback. I merely state facts. I don't envy Robbie if regular fellatio is the way of it, do you?"

"Thomas! Walls have ears!"

He grinned. "Still timid, Giles? Very well, we'll draw a veil over Robbie's antics in the royal sheets. You seemed dubious when I asked about Rob's happiness. Why was that?"

"Only that I know Rob feels out of his depth at court. He has the favour of the king, but he is not at ease with seasoned courtiers. Rob is a simple honest man, and for all that he has been to Paris and picked up pleasing manners there, he remains at heart a somewhat baffled Borderer."

"Yes," Tom said slowly. "Yes, I must admit I never foresaw this. My mistake. It never crossed my mind that Rob would catch the eye of the king. Stupid of me, considering Rob's exceptional good looks." He laughed. "I merely saw him as some kind of appendage to myself! This is a chastening lesson to me; I hope I profit by it. Never underestimate Robbie! Without guile and without knowing it he has played exactly the correct part. How better could he have attracted the king than to be pretty, grateful and slow-witted! I have to congratulate him. I was astonished when I heard . . . even appalled . . . possibly amused. But now I begin to suspect it may be the best thing that has ever happened to me."

I felt as slow-witted as he believed Rob to be. "Why?" I asked bluntly.

"It's obvious, Giles. Who rules the king's favourite rules the king."

I shook my head. "Be careful, Tom. It isn't wise to play games with people and events that have their own separate existence."

"What do you know about it?" said Thomas with affectionate contempt. "When have you ever tried it? You forget that I am not unfamiliar with the workings of diplomacy. I know what I am about."

"How did you know about Rob's change of fortune?"

"Luckily I was not obliged to place reliance only upon your inadequate letters, Giles! You may well suppose that those of us engaged upon our country's business overseas have many sources of information at our disposal. A vast net stretches across the civilised world, pinned down at those centres where the exchange and filtering and assessing of news takes place. No detail is too small to be weighed and considered. An obscure Scot breaks his leg in a tilting match in a certain northern kingdom whose monarch then hurries to his bedside, and they know about it in Madrid and Copenhagen. And what has Robbie done already to consolidate his position?"

I looked blank.

"What changes has he made?"

"Well, as I say, he has changed his name from Kerr to Carr."

"Yes; minimal as that may be it was a wise move."

"The Countess of Suffolk suggested it."

"So, she thinks it worth her while to take an interest in him?"

"Oh yes, she was amongst the first."

"May we suppose the Howards mean to close in? That surprises me; and then again it does not."

I ignored this shining example of political comment. "It still does not make him the man the apple peel foretold."

"Whatever do you mean by that inane remark?" frowned Thomas.

"The apple peel; you remember – we were foretold we would both love one whose name began with S."

"I do remember now that you remind me; but I strongly advise you to pay no heed to an omen of such a ridiculous nature."

"Your sister married John Lidcote," I said, "and she cast an L."

"Oh have done!" said Thomas scornfully. "You are worse than an old hedge witch." He shook his head and eyed me thoughtfully. "And you, Giles, what do you here, looking so comfortably at home in this royal but decrepid palace, home to the succulent deviousness of lust and the absorbing and rancorous struggles for advancement?"

"I am Robbie's man. I look after him."

"This is taking cousinly duty to exceptional lengths!" Thomas remarked. "I know I asked you to supervise his translation from Scotland to England; but to sacrifice your own expectations . . ."

"If you really believe me so subservient to your wishes you possess even more self-conceit than I supposed!" I answered stoutly. " I am here because I wish to be; it suits me very well."

"What – to fold his clothes and brush his hair?" said Thomas with a curl of the lip. "Limited ambitions, would you not say, Giles?"

"I daresay that it compares poorly with your plan to become an ambassador . . ."

"Peace, Giles," Tom laughed. "It's of no matter to me what you do. You live in splendour here – I envy you. I have had my share of some vile and rat-infested chambers in my travels on the underbelly of the beast of policy, believe me. Now pray, how is your aunt, my mother?"

"Thomas! Have you not been home since your return to England?"

"Of course not; what would I there?"

"Well then, your parents are both in good health."

"I'm glad of it. And now, where is our own sweet boy? I long to see him. Is he still as winsome as ever he was?"

"More so. You will not be disappointed."

Like some player at his cue Robbie chose this very moment to make entrance. Habituated as I was to his beauty I saw him now through Thomas's eyes and marvelled anew. Of course he was gorgeously dressed and the clothes he wore on their own account would have turned the eye of the careless observer – the amber velvet wasp-waisted doublet sewn with gold thread, the hugely padded breeches, the white stockings, the prinked leather shoes garnished with rosettes, the lace-edged wing collar which set off his handsome face. But these were merely the rich elaborate frame for the portrait within. At twenty-one Robbie must have been an embodiment of male perfection. His body was beautifully formed, not tall, but toughly built and in good proportion. His shoulders were broad, his limbs straight and firm, his bearing upright. His face was lovely, with his large hazel eyes and generous mouth, his smooth clear skin and the wondrous golden hair. Astonishingly, he had little personal vanity and carried himself with unassuming grace and an affable easy-going manner. In those early months at court when he was unsure of himself and touchingly grateful for King James's munificence there was about him such an appeal that it would have been difficult to dislike him, except out of that envy which resents the excellent. I watched Tom's face. It was a mask. I could only guess at his emotions. Those which I considered proper for the moment were quite lacking. His face now showed merely a mild pleasure. You would have thought that they had parted yesternight.

Rob on the other hand was wreathed in smiles. There was no disguising his delight. He ran to Tom and flung his arms about him, hugging him close.

"Och, Tom," he breathed. "And are ye home for good?"

"I hope so," said Tom gently disengaging himself. "Come now, Rob, where is your dignity? Must you rush at me like a puppy? You'll be licking my ear next."

"Ah, so that's your pleasure these days?" Robbie grinned, and did so.

I was startled by the stab of envy that ran through me at the sight of Robbie's blatant admiration for my cousin. I believed it should have been the other way about. But there it was – Tom stood there lordly and self-composed and Rob gazed on adoringly as if Tom was something special and Rob privileged to know him.

"Now how long have you been at court, Rob?" Tom said.

"About six or seven months."

"And what have you learned in that time?"

"How tae please the king," Rob answered instantly.

"Yes," said Tom reprovingly. "I did not mean to ask for the secrets of the bedchamber."

"Maybe no', but I'll wager you will ask for them sooner or later," said Rob unrepentantly. "Most people would."

"The vulgar, perhaps, and I hope that I shall not show prurient curiosity," said Tom loftily. "I meant what have you learnt about the intricacies of policy?"

Rob grimaced. "I keep mysel' awa' frae all that. His Majesty doesnae' want tae bring his work intae his loving."

"Heaven save us," groaned Tom. "That is precisely the time to ask for his favours."

"I don't need tae ask; I have favours enough."

"Rob," said Thomas carefully, "has it not occurred to you that you are in a position to shape the destiny of England?"

"No. My lord of Salisbury does that."

"But has no one or other taken you privily aside and spoken to you about matters dear to their heart and asked you to take the subject to the king?"

"Aye, once or twice; but I have not."

"You must not waste this amazing opportunity!" Tom said. "The court is awash with undercurrents; don't tell me you are not aware of them."

"Which ones do you mean?"

"Lord give me strength. Have you at least worked out that there are two main factions? One is the Howards, who are for popery and Spain and against the powers of Parliament because the House of Commons would use its influence to whittle down theirs; and against the Protestant lords who are *ipso facto* against popery and Spain – name them."

"Everybody who is not a Howard?" suggested Robbie.

"In particular?" persisted Tom.

"Um – "

"In particular," continued Tom briskly, "the Earl of Pembroke, William Herbert, the older brother of your predecessor in the king's affections. Pembroke is still a young man – well bred, affable, easy going – no figurehead. Then there is George Abbot, an Oxford man, chaplain to the Earl of Dunbar – watch him; much is expected of him. And who else?"

"Um – "

"With whom is Pembroke friendly?"

"With the Earl of Southampton, I suppose."

"Good," Thomas beamed. "Now you must make Southampton your ally."

"He doesnae' like me," Rob replied. "I once offended his protégé, the boy Essex."

"Then you must put yourself out to make him like you; you are personable enough," Tom said relentlessly. "Southampton favours the Protestant cause and is no friend to Spain. Forget all you have heard about the pretty wayward youth of our old queen's reign – lover of poets and soldiers, the shadow of the glamorous and foolish Essex. He's a family man now, our Southampton, and monstrous well liked. I believe

117

he carries forward the virtues of the old days – bravery, courtesy – and on the whole he's honest. You must acquire him; it would be a coup to disentangle him from Pembroke. And this is possible. King James is not comfortable with him. He prefers Pembroke. This will cause some irritation between them, because Southampton will feel slighted. I wonder what it is about him that causes His Majesty unease? Something akin to Sir Walter Raleigh perhaps – a figure of beauty and strength, who ill fits into our artificial and corruptible court, a man of action in a time of peace? Or guilt, because he did not take him as a lover? Or hatred, because he wished to take him as a lover and was spurned? Or jealousy, because he was close to Essex? Who can penetrate the king's darker thoughts?"

"Well, I can," said Rob robustly.

For a moment Thomas looked somewhat taken aback, as if he had been thinking aloud and rhetorically and was now brought back to earth. He chose, however, to ignore Rob's interruption.

"Across these currents cut Northampton's dislike of Salisbury because of his undeniable ability and skills, and Northampton's own devices and desires, which are kept well hidden. Then there is Salisbury's distrust of Southampton, which may be the check to that gentleman's progress; and Her Majesty the queen's malevolence towards those she takes against. And then there is someone else we have not yet spoken of, a key figure in our chessboard. To whom do I refer, Rob? Who is a person of great import, whom you must make your friend?"

"Tom!" I protested laughing. "This is your first meeting after – how long? And you catechise the poor lad as if you were a schoolmaster!"

"If you mean Sir Francis Bacon," said Rob, "he is favourable to me."

"I do not; but well done in respect of that!"

"Who then?"

"Come now, it's obvious – I mean Prince Harry."

Rob snorted. "I know he doesnae' like me. Whyever should he? He's fourteen years old, he's a pure and upright youth of good character and I am sleeping wi' his dad!"

"I agree that there you have a small challenge." A flicker of a smile touched Tom's lips. "But your security is dependent upon the affection in which you are held by a mortal monarch. You will be sure the world will turn another way when Harry takes command. He will instantly release Sir Walter Raleigh from the Tower and make him Admiral of the Fleet and go to war with Spain. Where will you be then?"

"In Sir Walter Raleigh's place, nae doubt," said Robbie wrily.

"So prepare the ground now," said Thomas, "in this instance and the others. You have much to do, Rob. It must not be all gifts and velvets and offering up sweetness and docility to a grateful paramour. You are at the centre of a whirlpool where many vessels vye for anchorage. It is my intention that you steer a middle course and play off one against another."

Robbie's face was a picture of dismay. "Och, Tom, I cannae'. I would not know how tae do it; I have not the skill."

"No," said Tom complacently. "You have not. But I have and I am here to help you and show you the way."

"But why should I want tae behave so," Robbie frowned, "and cause such mischief?"

"It is my intention to curtail the power of those rank and odious Howards," said Thomas. "They have held sway for long enough. I am ashamed for the king that they hold him in thrall. They are like a poisonous plant with roots and tendrils; they must be cropped. Others will then fill the void which their removal and disgrace will leave. This might well mean great power and wealth for . . . whoever that might be. I certainly intend we two, Rob, to be beneficiaries; and Giles, you shall not lack. It will be an exercise in diplomacy and the politics of power. And besides," he added with a little smile, "it will be such sport."

CHAPTER NINETEEN

"But I will not," said Robbie, "do anything that hurts or offends the king." I do not believe Tom ever grasped that Rob cared for the well-meaning, troubled, and many-faceted monarch who had fallen so conspicuously in love with him.

From a position in the shadows at the back of the Banqueting Hall I watched by torchlight as the masquers danced and sang.

The Masque of Beauty – it had been a paean to the power of womanhood; and I daresay I was not alone in reflecting on its inappropriateness as a presentation to a king who gloried in male beauty and who liked to surround himself with lovely boys. It was Queen Anne that had planned the masque, and there she was as Aethiopia upon a floating island, surrounded by court ladies in diaphanous gowns. And here came the North Wind glittering with snow and icicles;and now the spirits of the ancient poets crowned with laurels! When the performance ended and the dancers merged with the watchers, the king, in silver-grey satin with a chain of diamonds round his neck, reached out for Robbie. Together they moved amongst the throng of courtiers, the

119

king with his arm about Rob's shoulder. In a blatant display of possessiveness his hands laid claim to Robbie, were all over him, in indecorous display. He stroked the velvet of Rob's breeches as he would stroke the arse beneath; he nibbled Rob's ear, played with his hair, entwined his fingers in his own. I was certain that the foreign ambassadors were busy jotting down all they observed, and hostile and gleeful no doubt, they would report that the king did slobber much about his favourite's neck.

It was understood that James and Anne had ceased to live as man and wife, with their duty done and three healthy children resulting and also a sad batch of infant deaths.

The masquers had sung: "Beauty at large breaks forth and conquers men," but the beauty which the king admired was Scottish with long golden hair. I recognised the nonchalance, the boldness of the king, so to express his love and caring not who knew it.

This was a man brought up in fear. He feared the Devil, the house of Gowrie, the power of gunpowder, the power of witchcraft, his childhood tutor, the naked blade of a drawn sword, assassination, the dark power of his own desires. His fears were eminently reasonable; and reason weighed heavily with him.

His father Lord Darnley had been strangled when the explosion planned for him blew up his house but did not touch him; strangled, they said, and his catamite with him. James had been an infant at the time. When he had been yet in his mother's womb the Italian lute player Rizzio was murdered within yards of him. Rumour and Lord Darnley accused Rizzio of being James's father. The epithet Solomon which celebrated James's wisdom was a double-edged compliment – Solomon, son of David. James's mother abdicated. That same ever-present rumour said she had tried to have James murdered with a poisoned apple. He never knew her, and they told him she was an adultress and whore and that all women had the potential to be so.

At thirteen months old James became king of Scotland. The first regent of his reign was murdered. The second, James's grandfather, was killed in a skirmish and his bleeding body was brought past the boy. The third died suddenly, perhaps of poison. Next came the Earl of Morton, a sinister red-haired figure, the murderer of Rizzio and Darnley. Meanwhile James learnt Latin and Holy Writ.

Into this darkness shone the light of Esmé Stuart, Seigneur d'Aubigny, who came riding from France into James's gloomy life, glowing with glamour. James, now thirteen, fell in love with him. The Scots lords were divided, some for and some against this new influence. One of the Scottish lords who supported Esmé's friendship with the king was Robbie's father, laird of Ferniehirst. Henceforth any man with yellow hair and fluency in French would find the way to James's heart easy. James and his lover lived in bliss, which ended suddenly and violently – at sixteen James was abducted and imprisoned by the Gowrie family and held in their fortress for ten months. He escaped, but Esmé had been sent back to France and died there soon after. It may be imagined how James took to the loss; certainly his enemies received their just deserts. A series of handsome favourites became close to the king – James, Earl of Arran – Patrick, Master of Gray – Alexander, Lord Spynie – George, Earl of Huntly. And Francis Stuart Hepburn, Earl of Bothwell.

"I canna' speak tae ye o' him," said James to Robbie.

"Then do not," Robbie said. He had no particular curiosity about what had gone before. His was the present moment, where they lay together in the royal bed. As for myself, unlike Thomas, I was one of the vulgar sort that liked to hear the details of the bedchamber and I had no compunction in asking Robbie what occurred between himself and James.

"No, but I mun, if I would tell all," said James. "His hold will be the stronger while it stays hidden. What I will say is that there never was mon like him."

Bothwell was nephew to that Bothwell who ravished the king's mother. And like that figure of notoriety he was handsome, wild, unprincipled and irresistible. He spoke French, he spoke poetry, he was a demonic swordsman – yes, demonic, for he had sold his soul to the Devil.

"He worked against my marriage," James said. "He used witchcraft – witchcraft, Robin, the Devil's tool. He met wi' witches by night and the Devil was amongst them. They passed round a wax mommet; they said it was mysel'. They said that I would be consumed by the power of Bothwell; and if I had not been protected by the Lord nae doubt but it wouldhae come tae pass. But the Lord is mighty and He prevailed. I was safe. For the moment. My advisers told me that the danger to me was of a more terrestial nature – that Bothwell was a madman, that he aspired to rule my kingdom, that he would not rest till I was slain. And so it was a mere man that I mun fear. But, God help me, there was that about Bothwell which made a man believe that he could fly through the air by night through storm and lightning!"

Bothwell was imprisoned, but he escaped. For five years he was at large, a figure of menace and terror. He led an attack on Holyrood House; men were killed; James had to hide behind the locked door of a tower. He was rescued by soldiers that had to enter secretly by torchlight; there was fighting up and down the stairs. Bothwell fled. He attacked Falkland Palace, he laid siege to it, the king within. He rode away and crossed the Border on his horse Grey Valentine – and the Devil on his shoulder, no doubt.

"Then one summer morning," James said, "he came into my very chamber. He was let in at a back door and he came tae me wi' a naked blade. He laid it at my feet. I was half-dressed and he was on his knees before me and he begged for mercy, though he was at that moment in command. All that I desire, said he, is tae be as we were before . . . And I looked at him there upon his knees and thought tae mysel': As we were before? I would sooner stick pins in my eyes! But I spoke him fair enough, and God knows but I was unsettled tae see his bonny face again sae close tae me. I temporised. I did not know if he would murder me or take me in his arms . . . I learnt afterwards that three hundred of his men were waiting outside the palace walls. I was in danger, nae doubt. I wouldnae' say this to anyone, Robin, but I trembled; I was full o' fear."

"My dear old uncle, you were brave as any lion," Rob said. "You dealt wi' him. What did you do? How did he die?"

"Die? Och, he isnae' dead," said James. "He went awa'. He went north; then I heard he went tae France. I daresay that is where he is – France or Spain or Italy. There are witches in Italy, you know. I dinnae' think he means me ill. And then if I hae pains I think otherwise and that he sits in Italy and makes a mommet of me and pierces it wi' pins. He was the handsomest creature on God's earth, and wild. Sometimes I wonder what I would do if he came back. I would sooner be a slave in the Turkish galleys than see him again. And although this be so and I do most strongly maintain it, I would give much tae see him on his knees before me once again and hear him ask for pardon and raise him up and put my lips on his . . ."

The notion set His Majesty to tremble once again. Rob calmed him and murmured soothing nothings, but they were not needed; the king was himself again, a man much practised in the art of self-control.

"D'ye ken, Robin, what it is that saves a man frae blackness and despair? It isnae' love, it isnae' drink – it's learning. While your mind is taking new ideas and grappling with useful thought there is nae entry for debilitating glooms. Aye," he reflected. "Learning and good fellow-ship. But that is not tae say that beauty doesnae' have its place! And honest lust which sees that beauty and desires it – no man need be ashamed o' that." His hand between Rob's thighs he said: "That cock of yours is more obedient than my best trained hound; I have only to touch it and it responds. I like that, Robin, it shows you care for the man and not the king, for there's no disguising natural desire which cannot be forced or counterfeited; it deserves reward." So down went

James amongst the sheets and put his mouth about this so obliging member till all was done; and now himself excited, he turned Rob to lie face down and spread his thighs. That Biblical word so abhorrent to the Lord, so glibly forbidden in the king's own law, could not be this same act of intimate affection, this homage to the perfect curves of warm and vibrant muscle – no, that word was something other, far away, set in stone tablets, writ in Greek and Hebrew; not this. The king buried his face in Rob's golden hair, he took handfuls of it and twisted it between his fingers. In the candlelight – a candle always glimmered, for His Majesty did not like the dark – the gilt of Rob's hair glinted like spun gold.

"Och, Robin," said the king. "You bring tae me the light of the sun!"

Later, recalling to mind Tom's advice Rob said: "I have a dear friend in the employ of the Earl of Salisbury who has worked across the seas for many years and done good service. Could he no' be made a knight?"

The king chuckled. "I know that I am much accused of being free wi' knighthoods, Robin, but they don't go to all comers for the asking."

"I know that, uncle. I wouldnae' ask if I did not think him worthy."

"Would it by any chance be Thomas Overbury now?"

"It would! Your Majesty is very quick."

"It is my business tae be so. Thomas Overbury has not escaped my notice. I will speak tae the Earl of Salisbury and see what he advises."

"Och," said Robbie pouting. "Would ye no' do it for me?"

His Majesty tapped Robbie on the nose. "I love ye dearly, Robin and I'll gie ye gifts enough. But even when I am most besotted – I thought ye would ken this – I never lose my judgement."

Notwithstanding, Tom became Sir Thomas Overbury in a ceremony at Greenwich, which title he affected to disdain, saying to me that knighthoods in the reign of James were two a penny. Myself I thought that Sir Thomas Overbury had a noble ring about it and I was proud on his behalf, as were his parents. My aunt and uncle hardly knew where to put themselves for their delight, and certainly there were celebrations back in Bourton-on-the-Hill, and word passed on to Moreton-in-Marsh and Stow-on-the-Wold and Compton Scorpion in Warwickshire where we had relatives. Tom was further given a post at court, that of the king's server, a position of great honour, as everyone but Thomas said. With Thomas's good looks and natural elegance he filled the post in excellent fashion and indeed was much complimented on his appearance and bearing. With something of a twinkle in his eye Rob told him that the queen herself had commented that Thomas was a pretty fellow.

"It's insupportable," Tom said to me when we were alone. "It reduces me to Robbie's level."

I knew what he meant, of course, but thought the observation inappropriate, considering how important Rob was become. But I suppose that it was a matter of some indignity to be admired for his superficial qualities for one who aspired to be Secretary of State. I wondered whether James guessed that his munificence was so disdained. I wondered even whether he knew Tom's expectations and sought to contain them.

There was a conversation that James had with Robbie once while they were out riding together.

"Oh, and by the by," said James as nonchalant as could be, "Thomas Overbury . . . have you known him long?"

"Och, aye," said Robbie vaguely.

"And where did ye meet?"

"In Edinburgh. He was my tutor. He taught me Latin."

"Not very well," said James drily.

"No," Rob laughed.

"And more than that?" said James, as an afterthought, no more.

"Than what, dear uncle?"

"Than tutoring."

"Och, nothing more," said Rob firmly.

"He's a fine-looking fellow . . . comely . . . "

"Aye, he is no' bad looking."

"But a tutor to ye, no more?"

"Aye, that's it; he was my tutor."

"I think he is ambitious."

"I cannae' tell."

"Believe me, he is so. He pours my wine, but his eyes are scornful."

"Och, no . . . "

"Tell him, Robin, that I look for natural respect in those that I employ." James's voice assumed that which in a less affable man might be taken as a warning tone. "I am easy, but I will not be rebuffed."

"I will be sure to tell him," Robbie promised dutifully. "But there's no need, no need at a'." Rob was already on the path to a nodding acquaintance with diplomacy. Since Tom's return he had to my certain knowledge shared his bed with Tom on countless numbers of occasions.

Tom was my cousin; I did not desire him. There was too much of childhood and family, shared Yuletides, childhood escapades, half-forgotten trivia in our bonding. He was handsome, yes, but I saw that in detached fashion, as I might admire a tapestry. But Rob adored him. What they had shared so long ago in Ettrick sprang to life anew now that they were together once again. Their meetings of intimacy took place in the inner room of the lodgings Rob and I shared. I know that only too well, since it was I that sat between it and the outer door in case we had an unexpected visitor, and I that made sure that there was water brought for washing (Tom was fastidiously clean) and I that suffered from the apprehension caused by fear of discovery. Perhaps fear is too strong a word; I believed that the king would not be greatly pleased if he knew about it, but I did not think him a vindictive man, and after all, why should Rob not have lovers if he chose? Jamie Hay had done so, Philip Herbert also, and his were female – all insignificant, they would have said, in comparison to their devotion to His Majesty. So wherefore my uneasiness? And yet I was uneasy.

As for personal envy I contained it; after all, I cared for both of them, both Tom and Robbie, and I wished them well; besides, I counted Rob already lost to me when he first lay with the king. So afterwards, when Thomas and Rob came from the bedroom, laughing, half-dressed, still kissing and embracing, I poured wine and helped Tom back into his clothes and sent him on his way as neat as if he had come straight from his tailor.

This latest time I heard them tease and play beyond the bedroom door, Robbie saying: "No, Tom, that's enough, I have tae talk to you; listen, Tom, it's important tae me that you listen . . . will ye no' do that, now let me be, you know I can not resist you when you do that . . . och, well, I'll talk tae ye later . . . "

With his hair much tousled Rob emerged as naked as a babe, drying himself, scattering waterdrops, and Tom with a robe about his lean frame, a sober look upon his face, following him.

"Giles," he said, "what do you think?"

"I never think; there is no profit in it." I rooted round for Rob's clothes. "Now Rob, dress yourself; what if one came looking for you?"

"His Majesty is with Salisbury and will be this long while."

"Do as I say; come here; I'll help you."

"Giles, you terrify him," Tom laughed. "Rob, do as Giles commands. Put your pretty prick away; I have finished with it for the moment."

As Rob obeyed, Tom took my arm and led me from him. "What do you think of this, Giles?" he continued. "Rob tells me the king has asked some probing questions about what I am to Robbie."

"Yes, I know."

"Why do you think His Majesty would do that?"

"He has seen you together. The world knows you are friends," I shrugged.

"You know," said Thomas stroking his moustache, "I believe the king is jealous of me."

Rob paused in his dressing, breeches halfway up his thigh. He and I both looked at Tom.

"That's it!" said Tom. "I do declare it! What a triumph! His Majesty the king is jealous of me! I am envied by the king of England!"

Robbie suddenly sniggered. I grinned – Rob looked such a fool bending there half in and half out of his breeches – not exactly a figure to inspire any kind of jealousy between two such men of respected intellect. Tom curled his lip in a slow arrogant smile.

"Jealous of me," he purred. "Jealous . . . of . . . me!"

I gave Rob a shove to take the idiot grin off his face, and he fell over a chair, and we hugged him laughing and stifling our laughter, in a tangled heap of rib-tickling amusement.

The king was jealous of Tom! We thought it monstrous droll. I swear we thought it was the funniest thing that we had ever heard . . .

CHAPTER TWENTY

As the night follows the day, so does it follow that a man who would be admired at the court of King James must excel at tennis.

Our indoor tennis court was housed in a noble and lofty building with gables and towers, fit indeed for the great and the good to display their prowess; and in warm weather out they came to perform in the Little Open Tennis Court beside the tiltyard. As well as the players came spectators, of whom many were court ladies, interested in the sport, of course, and not the sweating muscles of the participants straining in their loose-necked shirts. Robbie, now fully recovered from the accident which brought him to the king's attention, was considered chief in excellence; and I was there to mop his brow. Thomas, extraordinarily buoyed up by the assumption that he was the object of King James's jealousy, was much in evidence – taking Robbie's arm, offering him wine, congratulating him when he did well, and generally behaving as if he had produced Rob by a sleight of hand for the gratification of the vulgar.

Who could not but have admired Rob as he lunged and leapt, tossing his golden locks as he moved, laughing and panting, the sweat welding his shirt to his arms and chest? Of my own appreciation there has never been any doubt; perhaps that was why I was so swiftly perceptive of a similar warmth in another.

All the giggling girls that watched the play were much taken with Rob, this was plain to see, but one May afternoon before Tom could hand Rob his goblet of wine, someone was there before him.

Frances Howard, in a gown of honey-coloured satin, proffering a golden goblet.

"Sir Robert," she said. "Will you try mine?"

She was almost seventeen. She was slight but well-shaped, the curves of her breasts raised and visible in the fashion of the day within a round neckline trimmed with lace. Her hair was pulled back from her face and dressed with little pearls. She had a small curled fringe, the whole pretty display set off by a high wide fan-shaped collar behind the neck. Her waist was slender, her bodice laced with tiny bows that continued down to the hem of her gown. You could see her little yellow shoes.

Rob, breathing hard and receiving her offer with no more than mild gratitude and some amusement, would have taken the goblet from her hand, but Tom in an instant was beside him, and taking Rob's elbow, turned him away from her without a word, directing Rob to where I waited with our tray of wine and goblets. Neither of them gave a further thought to the spurned and disappointed lady; but I saw her face.

That personnage Mistress Turner her companion now stood beside her and they put their heads close.

"I have always found the cult of the bosom much overrated," Tom remarked in his mellifluous and carrying voice. "After all what is it but a couple of udders and any brown spotted cow hath the like."

Rob laughed, and we drank his health in fine Rhenish.

How startlingly successful he had now become! With Tom to guide him he had assumed more personal dignity than before; and now had some officers of his own – a manservant, one Copinger, who saw to the smooth running of the lodgings; a secretary, one Walter James, for Rob's hand resembled a message writ in snow by a drunken crow – indeed, not as clear; and other servants about the lodging. Walter James was sleek and dark and handsome, a little too finely sculptured perhaps, the face of too equal a proportion, lacking that fine subtlety which a slight difference gives the visage.

Thomas also was now master of his own servants – all devoted to him and who, by following in his wake, gave the observer a sense that here passed a person of some importance. Henry Payton was a young man, Laurence Davies an older; and Davies I believe was the preferred one, saying little, but, said Tom, dependable and very good at mixing potions.

This latter was a necessary attribute for a servant of Tom's. I had never seen a man so susceptible to the attractions of the chymical world – this for megrim, that to loosen the bowels, that to harden the same, and the other for a facial blemish; and all with Greek and Latin names and reeking of sulphur. A courtier Sir Robert Killigrew was his companion in this, another very fond of concocting his own medicines from chymical ingredients. Payton was forever to and from the apothecary, either for the brews I mention or, as often as not, for *aurum potabile* , which, said Tom, cures everything.

I accompanied Payton sometimes, whenever Tom thought Rob would benefit from a dose of this or that. I went mostly to please Tom, for Rob despised Tom's remedies and never took them. Rob's own receipt for long life was an afternoon of sweating at the tennis, a hearty meal and a good night's sleep; nor did he ever suffer with his bowels.

The apothecary to whom Harry and I were sent was a very reputable fellow, one Paul de Lobell; and judge how reputable he was when I say that his father was the venerable Dr. Matthias de Lobell, the Flemish naturalist, physician to His Majesty; and his wife was the sister of Sir Theodore Turquet de Mayerne, later to become His Majesty's chief physician – that same Dr. Mayerne who set Robbie's broken leg, who was a great employer of chymical remedies and in particular that curious substance mercury, which when dropped wriggles on the floor like a silver snake.

"I do remember an apothecary," so begins poor Romeo in Mantua, in his search for a dram of poison, "Such soon speeding gear/As will disperse itself through all the veins/That the life-weary taker may fall dead." And his search takes him to a needy shop, where he finds shelves of empty boxes, green earthen pots, dried bladders and musty seeds, and the stuffed skin of an alligator. This image rises unbidden to my mind whenever I enter an apothecary's shop, however reputable, and however my informed mind knows it to be fanciful; therefore I usually waited outside while Harry bought the goods. I did once go inside.

The use of alchemy for medicine sends a shiver of unease to one brought up on the mashing of elderflower and nettle. I know that alchemy is dedicated to the bringing forth of useful medicines and to the studying of elements. I know the alchemist seeks to transmute base metals into gold; more, that he searches for the Elixir of Life, panacea to all the ills of the world. I hear that our essential being is made up of salt, sulphur, and mercury – that is, our body, soul and spirit; and I know that we are composed of four elements – earth, water, fire and air – and one fifth element or quintessence, which unites the four and makes us higher than the beasts and lower than the angels. The alchemist speaks in riddles, so that other alchemists may understand, but yet his secrets may stay hidden from the general. They call the colour green a lion, grey a crow's beak, white the swan and red the blood of the Lamb, black the crow's head; and they speak of oil of Luna and Lac Virginis, chrysosperm and aqua regis. In the apothecary's shop you may buy the results of their experiments.

The apothecary shows you into his shop. Oh yes, there are the reassuring homely herbs hanging up; you will always find plenty of the sweet hedgerow plants known from childhood. And he will take his pestle and mortar and mix his potions as you watch. But what, I ask you, has he hissing and gurgling in pipes and tubes heated by flame in his back room into which you are not invited?

"Such mortal drugs I have, But Mantua's law is death to any he that utters them."

Paul de Lobell's shop was in Lyme Street, near the Tower of London and the herb market. Harry and I always made the journey there by water, taking a boat as far as the bridge, then walking up Fish Street and Gracechurch Street.

I repeat, there was nothing insalubrious about the apothecary's dwelling. It was a tall old house and the shop was on the ground floor. It had a counter and a pair of scales thereupon, and the walls were lined with shelves where neat little boxes stood, labelled; and from the beams hung any number of bunches of field herbs – some dried, some fresh, with their familiar rustic scents mingling with others that I did not recognise. To these country bunches Harry pointed, nudging me and winking, and he whispered that I well might feel at home now to see so much culled from hedge and ditch.

A skinny apprentice – not more than a boy – went off to fetch the apothecary's ingredients. William was the boy's name; we heard it spoken – "Thankyou, William" – we heard nothing that was untoward, nothing like "and now continue skinning the dead alligator and cut up the heart well . . ." Nor was there aught of the magician about the apothecary; you would swear he was no better or worse than any grocer. And yet, and yet . . . how these niggling suspicions soared and jumped like candle shadows with each movement that he made! He gave Harry all that Tom had written down on a list, he bid us good day, and he retired into his back room, closing the door.

But what had he in that back room? What in his cellar? What was the extent of his arcane knowledge? What dusty secrets – what wonders and mysteries from Arabia? What symbols had he, writ on cracked and ancient parchment? What other?

> "Put this in any liquid thing you will,
> And drink it off, and if you had the strength
> Of twenty men it would dispatch you straight . . ."

Once outside in the street Harry Payton mocked me for my pallor and I gave a sheepish grin. I was a fool, no doubt of it, but I knew that for the restoration of any dimmed vitality I would turn to tried and tested hedge cures, yes, and all the better were they gathered by the Evenlode at the right time of the moon.

"Now there is a true magician," said Harry as the boatman rowed us back to Whitehall. Plainly he was not referring to the boatman, who was straining and panting over his oars and cursing quietly and incessantly. I followed Harry's pointing finger in the direction of Lambeth.

"Simon Forman," I surmised.

"Have you ever seen him?"

"Of course not," I said with asperity. "What need have I of charms and necromancy?"

"He calls up spirits."

"So I have heard."

"Angels and demons."

"So they do say."

"They say the great ones go by night to ask for divination," Harry said, and added with a snigger: "and wives to see how much longer they must endure their husbands."

"I have heard as much."

"He uses toads and newts and the skins of snakes," said Harry warming to his theme. "And you see that pall of smoke beyond the roof tops? That'll be the wizard we speak of, making ointments from the entrails of infants and burning all the bones he digs from the churchyards."

The boatman crossed himself and I followed suit. After all, it might be so. What did we know?

Perhaps it was the matter of his personal frustration that caused Tom's growing interest in physic. He was not ill, and he kept himself in vigour – he was an excellent swordsman. But his preoccupation with those aspects of the body which left to themselves function by Nature's contrivance seemed to me mildly ridiculous. Tom certainly considered himself ill-used. He had devoted so many years of his life to His Majesty's service and where had it brought him? One more pensioner at the court when he should have ben in useful employment worthy of his fine mind and particular skills. He blamed it upon the queen's dislike of him. Whether or not Her Majesty had taken against him at that stage in his career I know not; but he so believed it.

Throughout the autumn of that year 1608 the court was given over to rehearsals of the next court masque, entitled *The Masque of Queens*. I was fascinated by the preparations, for the machinery was especially intricate, with a host of hidden wheels and pulleys, cranks and strange devices. I was happy to renew acquaintance with Ben Jonson, who had writ the words. He no more than Tom had a good word to say about Queen Anne, though of necessity he was all smiles to her face. But he and Tom together privately, how they did grouse and grumble about women! Women in power – they had no tolerance of the notion. A strong independent woman threatens the stability of the world as we know it! There were too many of the same at court, and Her Majesty should know better than to fuel their fire. Lady Bedford . . . the Countess of Suffolk . . . the little Countess of Essex . . . Lady Guildford . . . Ben's own marriage was in disarray, the which perhaps provoked his sourness; and he went away to write *The Silent Woman*, all that *The Masque of Queens* was not.

I found the rehearsals almost as intriguing as the performance; but this latter was superb. "Twelve witches fraught with spite/To overthrow the glory of this night" began the entertainment. How satisfyingly evil seemed they who had seemed droll sometimes as they rehearsed in daylight in September! Now, at the dark of the year – it was Candlemass – when torchlight and candlelight must contrive their best against the shadows, what pleasurable shivers did these witches cause, in a crowded hall where their pretence and trickery posed no real threat, and sorcery was fanciful! They issued forth from a dark cave, ugly music playing, and real smoke billowing upwards. They were the forces of ignorance and superstition which Good Fame must overthrow. And who played Good Fame's representative but Her Majesty herself, a warrior queen upon a throne, surrounded by her Amazons? There were pillars carved with triumphs – battles, sea fights, loves. I had watched them laboriously painted and now here they stood – in the half light you would swear them all of Grecian marble. The queen and her eleven ladies descended in chariots, the witches bound to the chariot wheels. Virtue had triumphed over ignorance and malice.

"All women are witches," Tom said conversationally as the performance finished.

I fidgeted in embarrassment and coughed to hide his careless words. He laughed at my discomfort.

"True," he said. "They have no function but to breed, and when they are not so employed they have no purpose, therefore they work

131

mischief. Who knows what spells they are about by midnight when they are alone and unobserved?"

"Men also," I said loudly to stop his reckless mouth, "make mischief when their talents are thwarted."

But Tom scoffed at that. "A woman's mischief is the greater, for that her mind is the more subtle and prone to morbid hysteria. Her capacity to dream up foul deeds is a hundred times greater than a man's. Leisure corrupts them. Their only salvation is to remain constantly busy in domestic charge; then they will achieve goodness, their only hope of excellence – for after all, what have they but a passive understanding? Their minds are too frail to undertake wit and learning."

"I cannot but think that the queen and her ladies would think other," I murmured. "For your sake, Tom, I hope she has no spies sitting nearby."

"The queen? Why, she more than all others bears out the truth of what I'm saying!"

I sometimes wondered whether someone overheard Tom's rash and ill-advised remarks and went and told the queen.

"Speak of me to His Majesty," Tom said to Robbie time and time again. "Tell him to find employment for me worthy of my nature."

"I have done so . . . "

"Do so again."

"Regarding my friend Thomas . . . " Robbie said to the king.

"Och, dinnae' speak o' him," said James disgruntled. "He doesnae please Her Majesty, and there's an end."

In spring Tom went beyond the seas on business of Lord Salisbury. He was away for several months. I was not sorry to lose his griping company and I believed him better suited to our country's service in the Low Countries. I thought perhaps when he returned he might be more phlegmatic, and maybe would have done so well that honours might be heaped upon him in reward. I thought that Rob would feel the same as I did and welcome the freedom that Tom's absence caused. No more hints or querulous entreaties or upbraiding for imagined slights. But no.

"I miss him," Rob said.

"He will return."

"It cannae' be soon enough for me."

"But why? Your situation is most pleasant – His Majesty adores you. Everyone remarks upon it."

"Ah; you mean Sherborne . . . "

The king had given him Sir Walter Raleigh's house and lands. I know that some were shocked at this. I would not have said so to Rob, but I myself was one. Sherborne had been given to Sir Walter by Queen Elizabeth and was intended to be his in perpetuity; and he had a wife and sons. All pleaded for the restoration of their birthright.

"No," said the king. "No, I mun hae it for Carr . . . "

How I saddened on behalf of that great man, imprisoned in the Tower, so brave and worthy, making the best of his confinement, studying, writing – ah, an inspiration to us, an echo of those golden days so long ago. King James had always hated him. It was said that the Earl of Salisbury had poisoned his mind against Sir Walter even before James arrived in England.

"It's true that His Majesty thinks well of me," said Robbie. "But I partly believe it is because he thinks that I am developing a grasp of policy. Lately he has congratulated me on something I have said. Och, Robin, he says, I didnae' ken ye knew so much – och, Robin, so ye know that? It pleases me you work tae better understand good government. I shall be able tae talk wi' ye and hear your good advice. But Giles – it was all frae Thomas that I drew the information – he told me what tae say! And now he's in the Low Countries . . . "

"But the king fell amorous of you long before Thomas came upon the scene. Nothing has changed. He loves your good looks and your affability."

"At first – but now he thinks I have a questing mind and finds it pleases him. And I am still the same dull fellow that I ever was!"

I grinned. "Ah, then you have a problem!"

Rob clouted me. I did not blame him. I did not think that he need worry overmuch about the king's regard for him, but plainly he did, and longed for Thomas's return.

At least upon the tennis court he had no anxieties.

There was a day in summer when a large group was gathered in the open air to watch the game in progress – Robbie versus Prince Harry. The king's eldest son was then fifteen years old, a tall and manly stripling, the expectancy and rose of the fair state. He was lean and muscular with eyes of startling blue and hair of darkest auburn, and a great presence. A strange lad, some thought, austere in many ways, studious and honourable, little given to foolishness and little resembling his fair-haired frivolous mother and not on the best of terms with his father. James loved to cuddle and Prince Harry kept himself aloof. There was passion in his nature, but it was for the past, for chivalry, for ships, for military glory. He despised the term Pacificus, they said, and he adored Sir Walter Raleigh. This then was the youth who was the opponent of the man who had been given Sir Walter Raleigh's house, the man who, he no doubt believed, was making a fool of his father and causing him to be mocked and despised. The only difficulty was that Rob was very much the better with a ball and racket, and Prince Harry was losing the game.

I could see how angry the young prince was becoming. Anger clouded his judgement. He made mistakes. His habitually self-control-led features showed disgust, fury, shame. And there was Robbie facing him, golden, glorious, leaping this way and that, and carelessly success-ful.

Then suddenly, it seemed, something changed. Rob seemed to lose his grip, play clumsily, make mistakes. The prince's hopes soared, he might yet retrieve the game. You might hear Robbie mutter now, with little oaths of irritation. Rapidly Prince Harry took command, now every touch of his was sure and Rob's a failure. What had hap-pened? Now the crowd began to buzz and wonder. As the game drew to its conclusion it dawned upon Prince Harry that which some of the observers had suspected and now knew for certain – Rob had let him win.

As the contenders came towards each other at the game's end, it was plain to see the prince was furious. To his way of thinking, an honest defeat was bitter but acceptable. Now he felt he had been tricked he felt a fool. It was too much – this yellow-haired catamite of his fa-ther's, this upstart, this Border reiver had deceived him, and before a group of courtiers. Eyes blazing, too enraged to speak, he hit Rob across the side of the head with his racket and strode away. His close compan-ion David Murray hurried away with him, and his servants fussed about him.

Rob stood there, his mouth agape, rubbing his head and watching the young prince go. I was the first to his side.

"Giles! Would ye no' hae thought that he would have liked tae win?" demanded Rob aggrieved. "Tom said I must make Prince Harry my friend and I thought if I beat him he would be no friend of mine. Now look at him. And he's a powerful strength in his arm wi' a racket!" And he winced and rubbed his head again. "I did it for the best," he said ruefully. "Not very wise, eh?"

"What's done is done," I said. "I think you'll never make a friend of him; circumstances are against it."

I gave him a handkerchief and he wiped his brow. And now we found ourselves surrounded by a small gathering of courtiers. I stood back dutifully.

I was surprised to see that the first amongst them was Lord Henry Howard, Earl of Northampton. The Countess of Suffolk now stepped forward. They spoke about the game, pleasantries, as if it had not been laced with overtones and concerned the discomfiture of a prince.

"And well played, Sir Robert," said Northampton heartily. "I wish that I were young again and could have challenged you myself. I never saw the like of it, your prowess today – a hero, yes, a hero, and a delight to watch. The ripple of muscle, the grace, the beauty of motion. A paragon of animals, as the poet says . . ."

With Lord Henry Howard, I found, one never knew if he were jesting or in earnest, if there were hidden merriment beneath the surface of a compliment. Rob felt the same. He grinned modestly, and mumbled.

"Here is my great-niece," purred Lord Henry. "You certainly stirred her youthful heart. And her mother's not so youthful one, eh, Catherine? Come, Frances, give the gentleman some wine."

It was a curious repetition of that moment a year ago. Frances Howard stood there with a goblet of wine. She wore a gown of honey-coloured silk, her breasts much in evidence. She offered wine to Robbie.

But this year there was no Sir Thomas Overbury to steer him away and make disparaging remarks about the female form. Rob stood there, hedged in by the little group of Howards; and when Frances raised the goblet up to him, he took it, and he drank.

CHAPTER TWENTY-ONE

Images of witches worse than those that came forth from the gaping mouth of Hell all wreathed in smoke at Candlemass – images of the black heath, the sizzling cauldron, the shadow across the moon, the spell worked at the midnight hour – these selfsame images occur to me when I write down the name of Frances Howard.

But why? It is in itself an inoffensive name. Granted, there were those for whom the Howard name conjured some unfortunate associations, but not enough, I trust, to chill the blood. And many women have been christened Frances and led more or less blameless lives. Nor, to be accurate, was the lady at this juncture even Howard, save by birth; she was a Devereux, though this meant almost nothing, one might say, since she was married in name only and had not seen her young husband since their wedding day some three years ago.

On the day that she gave Rob a drink of wine at the tennis court all that might be levelled at her in the manner of an accusation was that she seemed – in the way of women who are undeniably and more than common beautiful – to think much of herself and to encourage adulation when it was presented, and that she kept bad company. No, let us be scrupulously fair – it was not bad company in general, it was Mistress Anne Turner in particular and Mistress Turner's crone of a serving maid, who for that she had no teeth in her mouth was named Toothless Margaret, and, prejudice being as it is, her appearance, her gummy grin, her cackle gave one to think she was no stranger to the blasted heath. But on the day that Robbie received the goblet of wine there was no especial scandal or hostility towards Mistress Anne. Indeed she was very popular and her acquaintance much sought after, for she had a house in the city where she permitted any lover to meet with his mistress secretly and no questions asked; and she was a needlewoman of exceptional talent and made gowns and frills and collars; and had some skill in palmistry and astrology and the Tarot.

And so when Robbie drank he thanked the maid and thought no more about it.

"She is Prince Harry's mistress," Copinger said confidently; he would believe the worst of anyone.

"I do not think so," I said. In those days I preserved an open mind about the lady. "Not because I do not think her capable of seducing him, but knowing the character of the prince I think he would refuse her."

"Do you so?" said Copinger. "I cannot agree. Do you truly believe that a healthy youth in full vigour and prime would, Frances Devereux offering herself, say to the lady: no, let me alone?"

"I believe Prince Harry has his mind on more robust matters. He would sooner ride or run or fight, and when he takes his ease he has his male companions." I did not put it into words but I believed he cared far more for David Murray – his best-loved attendant who had slept in his bedchamber since Prince Harry was a child at Stirling – than for womankind.

"Not a whit of it!" said Copinger. "No, I see him standing, yet a virgin, looking out of a window, wondering how it would be to love a wench; and up comes Frances sneaking from behind and puts her hands over his eyes and says: guess who stands behind thee! and he feels the warmth of her questing body and he smells her lust and he finds a quickening about his person and he turns. No sooner has he done so than she clamps her lips on his and sucks the tongue from out his throat, his prick rises, and lo and behold! he is a lost man. Come to my chamber, gasps he, and away they go to where a great bed waits, and he begins to unlace her and she whispers: Take me, Harry, for my husband is across the seas and I have such an itch . . ."

"Have done," I said. "Your tale disgusts me. She may well have tried him, but if so he would move her aside and answer most severely:

go; you are a married woman; when I take a lover it shall not be you."

"His mother would have him take a lover and would settle for Frances," said Copinger sagely.

"What do you know of the workings of Her Majesty's mind?"

"Her mind? She has none; but of the workings of the hollow that she hath between the ears I know that she says: Harry, Harry – fifteen years old and still a virgin; that's no way for a young man to behave. Take some young virgin to your bed and find out how 'tis done. Whom shall I take, dear mother? answers he. Take Frances Devereux, says she, she's far the loveliest creature at the court, and all unspoilt, for Essex never had her and she's ripe now for a man. Why, now I think on it, I'll swear that old Northampton worked upon the maid and put her up to it. If you can get the prince, says he, think what it will mean for us – the Howards will be greatest of all, and you shall whisper into the royal ear what we shall have you say! Yes, dearest nuncle, simpers she, it will be no trouble at all to me to get the prince into my bed for he has been there already!"

For all I know it may have been that Copinger's lewd imaginings came near the truth. Perhaps the Lady Frances had the prince, and after him his servants and his grooms and only came to Robbie when she had worked her way through a round dozen. You see, I do believe her capable of anything lascivious and vile, each deadly sin her own especial talent.

"As for Mistress Turner," Copinger said carelessly, "they say she goes by night to Simon Forman's den. They say she buys his potions and makes castings into the future. She goes by boat without a waterman," he added cheerfully, "in the likeness of a hare."

Now that the Howard family had taken us under their wing, Rob and I dined and supped often at Northampton House, Lord Henry Howard's majestic mansion on the Strand. When Rob explained to them that Master Rawlins was a long-time friend and no mere manservant, nothing would content them but that I would take my place at the table and in the conversation, a situation more embarrassing to me than if I had been quaffing beer in the kitchens. In the beautiful chamber where we dined I was somewhat akin to that poor Scottish lord so troubled with his morbid fancies on the stage, for everywhere I looked I saw Thomas sitting there like Banquo's Ghost, not bandaged and bloody, but monstrous angry, pointing an accusing finger to see Robbie and myself so intimate with folk whom he detested. When I mentioned this to Rob he shrugged and answered:

"It's diplomacy, Giles, is it not? It seems tae me that the secret of policy is tae be on guid terms wi' everybody, whether it be frae the heart or not, and then if the occasion arise, you may call upon them as your friend. Myself I take it for a guid sign that the Howards treat us well – it means that they accept me and by implication the Scots at court; and Giles, they are the old nobility, and therefore their friendship is not tae be scorned."

"Thomas will not like it."

"Pish! He will congratulate me on my resourcefulness!"

In those spring evenings at Northampton House we all walked in the gardens that lay behind the house and sloped down to the river. Here were white violets, cowslips, cherry trees in blossom, lilac trees. There was a fountain made of marble with steps up to it and a pavement about it; and there were stately hedges with arches some ten feet high to make a closed alley to walk in. Wine was brought for us and Frances made herself the lady of the house and handed glasses round, but always making much of Robbie; indeed she brought a special goblet for him, a lovely thing made of silver, a relic from a bygone age, so perfect you would think it had come from a church; and old Northampton chuckled indulgently at his great-niece's endearing folly.

They called him Robin. I always found this irritating whomsoever did so. I never liked the name much anyway, smacking as it did of woodland elves and figures of festival and little bright-eyed birds with crimson chests; but since everything at court was to do with policy it seemed as if the Howards would lay claim to him and enthrone him in a dead tradition which included Dudley, Earl of Leicester and Devereux of Essex, all robins in their time.

These forays into the domestic situation of Northampton House were a continual source of vexation to me. Not merely the use of the name but the continual sight of Rob polite and smiling in the company of people he cared nothing for, a social whoredom every whit as repellent to me as the bedroom variety might be to others. And what, I asked myself had prompted all this interest in him, this handsome affable well-built young man with no particular aptitude for conversation whom they fêted so enthusiastically, but policy – a wish through Robbie to get closer to the king? Hypocrisy in action; and I was guilty as the rest, for I said little and conveyed no hint of my displeasure, but smiled much and admired the flowers in their garden.

Mistress Anne Turner took my arm and led me up and down beside the lilacs. "He is a fascinating man, your Robbie," she said in a low voice, disarming me by her directness and the lack of robins. "Who would have guessed that he would come this far, to see him on the journey south five years ago? I confess that I did not. Beautiful he always was, but now there is a radiance about him . . . poor Frankie wears her heart upon her sleeve."

There was the crux of it, the centre of my irritation – the sight of 'poor Frankie' making cows' eyes at Rob, following him about amongst the flowers, looking up at him with parted lips, laughing in a high silly voice, jutting her bosom; it was enough to make the flesh crawl. I gritted my teeth and smiled, hoping the resultant grimace would pass for sympathy of a detached and amicable nature.

"Tell me, Giles," said Mistress Anne. "Tell me about him – his likes and dislikes, his favourite colour, song . . ."

She was a little over thirty now and youthful still. Her yellow hair curled at her temples and her cheeks and lips were touched with her painting. Why did she want to know these things about Robbie? Women were odd, no doubt of it. I thought the questions too trivial to merit reply.

"Robbie is devoted to His Majesty," I said carefully.

Anne burst out laughing. "Whatever do you suspect me of? No one is questioning Robbie's loyalty. I would simply like to know more about him."

"Robbie is entirely honest," I replied. "What you see is what he is."

"You would protect him," she murmured. "There is no need. No one here wishes him harm. But with poor Frankie, ah, it is a different matter . . . a young girl's heart . . . Think well of her, Giles, her nature is a passionate one and easily betrayed."

This was not how it appeared to me. I thought 'poor Frankie' tiresome and I had as little to do with her as possible – an easy business, as she never sought my company but always hung about my friend. I glanced across the rose bushes. There sat Robbie on a wooden seat, and Frances kneeling on the paving on a cushion at his feet, gazing up at him like a daisy to the sun; and old Northampton leaning over him, his arm draped about Robbie's shoulders like a cloak, his crinkled pointed face close to Robbie's ear – you would be hard put to say which of those two Howards was the one that most desired him.

Fortunately the Summer Progress westward brought an end to it, and Rob out hunting with the king in the New Forest was far out of the reach of devious intriguers. But we were not done with them, for come the autumn we were once again invited to the house upon the Strand and it was as if we had never been away, for all continued as before.

The matter being thus, you may judge of my astonishment when one day an event occurred which shook the measured pattern of our intercourse into confusion.

As usual we walked about the garden, but the little chill wind and the rustle of the fallen leaves warned that the summer was now over. Frances Howard was wearing a crimson gown, embroidered all over in black. We had been accustomed to see her in amber – apricot – honey; the red became her well. Old Northampton, speaking closely with Robbie, led him back into the house. I would have followed. Frances of a sudden hesitated and let them walk on. She turned towards me. I drew level with her. Then she caught my arm and held it. I started as if I had been burnt by flame.

"Giles!" she said in a low voice vibrant with emotion. "Speak to him for me – I sense you are my friend! You always stand there oh so quiet – you say little, and I know thereby you will keep confidences. Anne says you are loyal to him; you have his best interests at heart. I think that I can trust you. Speak to him, Giles, speak of me. I love him to distraction. I fear I will go out of my mind. He is kind but he cares nothing for me. Be my friend in this. Tell him I love him and will die if he does not love me in return!"

Then she clapped her hand over her mouth as if she feared that she had said too much, and stared at me with wild anxious eyes, and I, fearing that we would be observed, said: "I will speak with him," at which she nodded and ran on towards the house.

Well, I did speak with him, but out of wonder more than out of sympathy. Secure in our apartment at Whitehall I told him of the incident.

"But it amazes me," I said, "that she should think my nature favourable to her. How may a maid be so misguided, so read all the signs awry? It must be that her passion blinds her. And you, Rob, what of you? Did you know she was in love with you? Has she said aught to you?"

"Not in words," said Rob. "I did suppose something of the sort but I hoped I was mistaken. After all, nothing can come of it. She is a married lady, and the marriage being a matter of policy and set in motion by the king, it must be treated with respect."

"What will you do then?" I said. "What action will you take, following her unlooked for declaration?"

"None," said Robbie, "and hope she will think better of it. And we will no longer dine there."

We were much heartened about this time by the return of Tom from the Low Countries. In truth we needed diversion, for there was plague in the city that year – they said that thirty poor souls died there every week. There was no mistaking Rob's elation at the prospect of Tom's being with us once again, and their old intimacy was renewed in the privacy of our apartment.

As often happens when there is sickness in the city, those yet living and believing themselves for the moment safe, tend to indulge in merriment the greater in proportion to their fear of the Grim Reaper. I have heard that in the days of the Black Death there was a madness gripped the living, and they danced and swived and played with skulls and bones and tossed them in the air. King James had always loved to trowl the jolly nut-brown bowl, and so much the better in the company of young men. In the evenings in his chambers there was vigorous horseplay, where youths ran races, one upon the back of another, in their shirts. Guffaws of raucous laughter resounded, carrying along the passageways and stairways – anyone might hear it and the bellows of noisy appreciation as the shirts of the riders were lifted and the spread haunches revealed and thwacked. Rob took part in this more than once – I blame it on the drink, which makes a man forget decorum and sobriety. Afterwards the participants would fall into undignified heaps with splayed legs and crimson panting faces, and the king would reach for Robbie and the game was at an end; and others who had been inflamed departed two by two to further joys elsewhere. Everyone knew about it.

I think it therefore no coincidence that over Christmas the entertainment of the abstemious Prince Harry's choosing was a marvellous production on the theme of chivalry. Ben Jonson wrote it, at the prince's direction, the prince in studious fashion having acquired a scholastic library and thus gaining his knowledge on the very best authority. We saw therein King Arthur and the Lady of the Lake, and Merlin the Magician arising from his tomb and making sage pronouncements. There was the House of Chivalry portrayed, all rusty and cobwebbed through lack of virtue – not, of course, that the court was not virtuous, no, the court was very fine and splendid, but the House of Chivalry needed restoration, and who was the man to do it? None other than Prince Harry – and there he stood beneath the triumphal arch, surrounded by his knights, eager to lay the first fruits of his chivalry at King James's feet and fight wherever chivalry was needed.

"King Henry V come back to life!" murmured the admiring throng. Indeed we would all have been on our way to Agincourt had it not been so cold outside.

As I came from the Banqueting House illumined redly in the glow of torches someone thrust a paper into my hand; I took it. It was addressed to Robbie. I had seen the man before; it was a Howard servant; he did not pause for answer. I took it to Rob. Later, in our rooms, he read it, Thomas and I close by.

"'Giles will have spoken to you'," Robbie read to us in wonderment. "'I am surprised that I have heard nothing in reply. Was not my meaning plain? Ask Giles to tell it how he heard it from me. Burn this and give me answer. F. D'."

We passed the note round thoughtfully.

"Foolish woman," Thomas said. "Never commit anything to paper – they should have told her that."

"She did not at first," I said. "It is because her first assay failed that she now writes."

"Puir creature," Robbie said. "I don't like tae think of her in sorrow and because of me."

Tom snorted. "Go to her then and answer her prayer. Take her to bed and have done."

"Och, no, I didnae' mean . . ." said Robbie wincing.

"Then let her stew," said Tom.

"We ought tae make some answer," Robbie said.

"What answer would you make?" said Tom.

"Och, that I'm deeply honoured by her interest but that she mun expect nothing frae me."

"Get pen and paper, Giles," said Tom.

"My hand is illegible," said Rob. "Walter James writes for me."

"Not in this instance, my dear," laughed Tom. "Giles will write it."

"Not I!" I said at once. "And besides, were it not better to ignore the matter and let it die a natural death?"

"No, she must be put in her place," said Tom. "A pleasing prospect, to put down a haughty Howard – I will write the thing myself."

He sat there at the table, toying with the quill, we watching, grouped about.

"But wait . . ." he said and gave a little smile. "What if we should tease her a little?"

"How? What do you mean?"

"Raise her hopes a little . . . moisten her with anticipation . . . then drop her later, having further to fall."

"Och, that's unkind."

"You have some affection for the lady?" Tom mocked. "A hungering for breasts?"

"No! But common courtesy . . ."

"Trust me. I'll write the letter in a very gentle pleasing manner. How – 'My lady, I was truly honoured to receive this intimation of your friendship for me. I trust that in the days to come I may show equal friendship to you. I will always be your servant and admirer. R.C.' There

– you have told no lie and you will make her happy. If she chooses to read more into it than was your intention she has only herself to blame."

"Aye, there seems no harm in it," said Robbie. "I have said that I will be her friend, no more. And 'servant and admirer' is mere formality; she cannot surely think that I mean other. Giles, be kind enough tae deliver the same tae the servant who gave you this."

And an easy enough matter that proved to be, for the man put himself in my path time and again. I gave him the letter; and we soon received another; and replied again, all in close conjunction about the writing table.

"This is one most indiscreet of ladies," Tom said marvelling. "And her manner of composition monstrous faulty."

We read: 'Robert – I have loved you from the moment that I saw you. If you could but declare the same again to me I am the happiest of women. If not I see no recourse but to die.'

"She should write for the stage," said Thomas. "There would be a place for her at any playhouse where they put on antique plays; she is mistress of the banal."

"What should I answer?" Robbie wondered.

"Oh, gratitude, as before; and let us ask her to live, shall we? 'Live and be my guiding light' – this is the language she understands. Have no fear, I'll put it most exquisitely."

We did not doubt it. Proof of Tom's effectiveness came rapidly. A Howard servant asked Rob to follow him one day, and led him down the twisting passageways that snaked between the ancient chambers, and opened a door for him. In a small room all alone waited the lady Frances in the red and black gown, velvet rich, the blackness of lace about her white shoulders, the ruff above a shimmer of wiry lace.

"Och, Lady Frances," Robbie said confused – the dimwit had not guessed that she would be here at the centre of the maze. He looked over his shoulder. The door was shut. They were alone.

"Sir Robert . . ." she began in formal fashion, but trembling like a little bird. "It is not, I know, the fashion for the lady to put herself forward thus, and I am ashamed to act in such a way that places me in such a forward part, but desperation made me bold, and trusting in your courtesy to treat me kindly . . ." Here she faltered, courage failing her.

"Och, would that I had Thomas wi' me," Robbie thought, tongue-tied, looking round for aid that did not come.

"There are some have called me proud," said Frances taking heart. "But in a matter that concerns yourself I have no pride. The plain truth is I love you. And this love makes me the most wretched of mortals."

And her eyes were full of little dewy tears. She turned away, a sob in her throat, and foolish Rob stepped forward, put his arms about her in what would have been a brotherly hug but that she fell on him ravenously, clinging to him, reaching up to him, pulling his head down to hers and kissing him, kisses so fierce and so demanding that he was obliged to open his mouth and find himself returning those same kisses.

When she desisted, she breathed close to his mouth: "I love you, Robert. Say you love me – say it – I believe you do – I love you, Robert – say it in return!"

"I love you," Robbie said, and felt the great sigh of relief and satisfaction quiver through her body.

"That is, as near as I could get tae her body for her skirt," he told us ruefully. "Whatever are they made of, farthingales? Cruck beams?"

"We will meet again," said Frances. "For the moment, enough. Our passion must be secret, stolen. But it will sustain us. It will not be easy, but now that I know you love me I am strong and you must be the same. I don't mean bodily strength – I know you possess that in abundance – but I am speaking of firmness of purpose. 'Constant as the northern star.' Leave now – and thank you, Robert, thank you for loving me."

"Och, now what shall I do?" Rob wailed to Tom and me. "I don't know why I said it. I did not want tae hurt her feelings. She was so sad and she loves me to distraction. I said it because she asked me tae – I am so easily persuaded!"

We looked at him pityingly.

"Rob, women can make tears just by blinking," Tom said, "as the crocodile does. Their mouths are shaped like crocodile's mouths too – and like a good grocer's shop, never closed."

"So tell me now what I should do," said Robbie, comic in his distress. "We are tae meet secretly and indulge our stolen passion! This was never my intent."

"*Courage, mon brave*," said Tom clapping him on the back. "If you will be so beautiful you must expect to break hearts. You must make love to the lady. You must do as she says and look upon it as a new-discovered talent."

"But how could you, Rob?" I scowled. "How could you tell that woman that you loved her? How could that declaration which should not be spoken lightly slip so easily off your tongue?" I found that I was overcome with jealousy. Stupidly I blurted out: "Why then could you not have said as much to me?"

"But I respect you far too much tae fool wi' ye," said Rob. "I have always been honest with you."

144

Thomas chortled. "Unlikely as it sounds, Giles, the buffoon is trying to pay you a compliment."

Turning from my glowering visage he now advised Rob: "Meet with the lady sometimes. Be kind to her but not intimate. Commit yourself to nothing. We are with you and will direct your course. It pleases me enormously that this scion of the house of Howard is prepared to make herself ridiculous. It shall be the cause of great amusement to us and may work much to our advantage. The lady is besotted with you, Rob, but you find her odious. It is all merriment. It is the enchanted wood near Athens – you Demetrius, she Helena." Using a feigned voice he burbled:

"The more you beat me I will fawn on you –

Use me but as your spaniel, spurn me, strike me,

Neglect me, lose me, only give me leave

Unworthy as I am, to follow you!"

We laughed in spite of ourselves, for Thomas was monstrous droll playing the lady.

"And are you Oberon, Tom, prancing here and there and rubbing magic juices on our eyes?" said Rob wrily.

"*Tarry, rash wanton, am I not thy lord?*" purred Tom. "This falls out better than I could devise . . . Forward!"

And so into the Athenian wood stepped Robbie. And at the same time into that same wood from another direction came the young Earl of Essex, hotfoot from his travels in France, panting, eager and possessive, to claim his loving bride.

CHAPTER TWENTY-TWO

I do not believe that the Earl of Essex recognised in the king's elegant and flamboyant favourite the sun-tanned sweating athlete with whom he had had an altercation at Burghley nearly seven years ago. This was apparent from the courteous manner of his salutation to Sir Robert Carr when first they met at Whitehall. Essex, however, realised his mistake soon enough; he had made himself agreeable to an upstart Scot – this must be rectified.

"My congratulations," he said to Robbie. "I would not have believed it. You wear the fashions of His Majesty's court well; yet I had heard that in your native land you all wear bedclothes pinned about your person."

Robbie either through politeness or slow wittedness could not think of a reply that would not have led to a duel, so gave none; but the seed was sown – the two would not be friends.

For myself I was greatly pleased to see that nobleman's return, because I thought that now we should be rid of the unwelcome attentions of his wife. In this, alas, I was mistaken.

The warmth of the smile upon the face of young Essex as he danced with his reclaimed lady wife was equalled only by the strength of her own lack of warmth – her rigid body held at arm's length from his closeness, her cheek turned away from his lips, her ear from his whisperings. He was not an ill-favoured man, Essex. He was eighteen, sober in demeanour, hesitant in manner, slight of build, with dark eyes and thick dark hair. But besides Robbie's glowing beauty he seemed pallid and insignificant. Frances plainly thought so. Her poignant and beseeching glance turned now and then to Robbie, who contrived always to turn away, giving all his attention to the king. On his guard now, he could not be enticed into corners by some serving man or woman to a place where Frances waited, and in order not to be obliged to frame responses to her enquiries or suggestions he chose not to see her at all, thereby causing some frustration, even desperation, to the lady. This must have been so, because she was reduced to hanging around Rob's entourage – namely myself.

"Giles!" she said accosting me quite blatantly and without preamble in the Long Gallery, surrounded as we were by hurrying folk. "Stay! I would speak with you!"

I paused and bowed. Through the windows we could see the Privy Garden, dull and rain-lashed in the wintry weather. We stood there, looking out, our backs to the gallery.

"Why does he avoid me?" murmured she.

"The king makes constant demands upon his time."

"I know that; but he seems to find time nonetheless for Sir Thomas Overbury." I think it must have slipped her mind that Thomas was my cousin. She spoke of him with a pretty lip curl, as if there was no doubt in the mind of the civilised observer that here was a matter for disgust. She continued: "I have often seen them walking together, laughing together. What do they talk of so intimately? What do they find to say?"

"They are friends of long standing."

"Everybody is aware of their particular closeness," she said. "You should warn Robert; it will tarnish his good name. Do you know what Her Majesty says when she sees them? 'There goes Carr and his governor!' There! How ugly it sounds! Robert should know what is spoken of him."

"People always resent a successful man," I shrugged. "There will

146

always be gossip about one so glamorous and in the public sight."

"He is glamorous," she agreed softening, as if it were a compliment to her. "When will he see me?"

"I cannot say."

"Giles!" she said urgently. "Be kind. Bring me something of his. Anything. Something close to him – something he has worn or handled – so that I may be near to him, as it were, by proxy. Forgive me," she then dimpled. "This must seem a strange request. Women have odd fancies. Will you do as I ask? Out of kindness to one who is unhappy?"

"Madam, you have every reason to be happy," I said greatly daring. "Your husband has returned."

"Oh, come, Giles," she said, speaking as if she considered us equals and intimates. "Have you ever seen me look upon my husband with affection? I detest him. I have forbidden him my bed, pretending nervous dread of his attentions. Make sure Sir Robert knows this. Let Sir Robert know that when at last he makes me his, I shall come to him virgin. He need fear no soiled goods; tell him so."

You may be sure I grew most uncomfortable to be spoken to in this manner upon a subject of such delicacy, and resolved to pass on no such irrelevant news to Robbie. However, and partly to escape further revelations about the Countess of Essex's private life, I agreed to procure something of Robbie's to satisfy her longings, and I hurried off to his apartments, returning with a right-handed lace-edged gauntlet whose partner's cuff had grown frayed, this one being in good condition. She had promised to wait for me, there at the window, and there she was, this great lady of the house of Howard, like some green girl, eager, expectant. I suddenly was reminded of Tom's sisters in the parlour at Bourton-on-the-Hill, throwing apple peel over their shoulders and telling Tom and me that we should both love one whose name began with S. I handed her the glove; she clasped it to her bosom.

"Thank you, Giles," she breathed. "You are a friend – dear, dear Giles, so good to me. Ah! Is it really his!" The gauntlet, bearing still the curved shape of Rob's hand, now lay curved about her breast, pressed there by her own small hand and its implication plainly causing her contentment.

I bowed and took my leave. Well, there could be no harm in the clutching of a glove, I told myself, and if so insignificant a treasure pleases her, so be it.

Did she truly loathe her husband? It was difficult to plumb the depths of women's minds, I thought. Were they born passive, with less of lust than the male, and a great desire for childbearing? What need she of desire? It were enough that she be capable of producing heirs –

this done, she could apply herself to the absorbing tasks of huswifery, the skills of still room and needle. What was she about in this misguided pursuit of Rob, particularly now that she had her husband home? Kept him from her bed? Did he permit as much and hover meekly by, not taking his rights? How did she contrive as much?

Some wayward angel must have lent its powers to Frances in this matter, for the Earl of Essex was then stricken down with an illness of a contagious nature, and for several weeks lay close confined, unable to be visited, and, if rumour were true, not like to live. And meanwhile his lady wife was seen to dance and be merry, and for all I know she took a glove to bed and liked it better than her husband.

It now seemed to be common knowledge that the Countess of Essex had no liking for her husband; that she had become enamoured of Sir Robert Carr was less widely known, possibly because Rob so plainly did not return the favour. He was that curious thing, a favourite devoted to his lord, except of course for his unfortunate predilection fot that fellow Overbury.

Thomas was not popular at court. His chilling wit and blatant self-conceit did not endear him to the well-fed precious parasites that thronged the corridors, the perfumed hothouse blooms that made parade of sigh and ogle, nor the boorish drinkers of the evening's merriment. Tom's own court was within the city, at the taverns and especially at the Mermaid in Bread Street where the university wits and lawyers met and read aloud their poetic offerings and swapped scurrilous anecdotes and murmured political dissention and grumbled at the way of the world that rewarded the unworthy and overlooked themselves. I knew some of their names – Thomas Lodge, an Oxford and a Lincoln's Inn man, a poet who had once been a pirate and had been to South America in search of gold; John Donne, also of Lincoln's Inn, who had gone to sea with Essex's father to Cadiz and the Azores. He wrote love poems known for their oddity, for while the custom was to sing of spring and hearts and tears, Donne wrote of compasses, fleas, sea discovery, mandrakes, alchemy and dissection, which be not the sweetest way to a lady's heart – or a man's – but Tom said they were poems of an excellence which would make them remembered when hearts and tears were long forgot; and Tom was always right. There was Francis Beaumont, a judge's son of the Inner Temple; and his close friend John Fletcher, two of the most successful playwrights of our day – at that time they had just completed *Philaster*. There was Thomas Coryate, an Oxford scholar, an odd looking man, but learned in Greek and a great jester and widely travelled; of which travels he was writing a book 'Coryate's Crudities, hastily gobbled up in five months' travels'. He said he meant to try next to get to

Persia and Alexandria and Greece, and everyone believed he would. And of course there was Ben Jonson, hugely successful at court now, writer of royal masques, playwright, lover of women, famous for having attended Communion and drunk the entire chalice of wine; and currently writing a play about an alchemist.

Robbie was very close to the king at that time. We heard in May the appalling news that King Henri IV of France had been assassinated by a crazed papist. A sense of his own vulnerability being ever present with His Majesty, an event of this nature reduced him to great depression of spirit, and all the heavily quilted doublets that he wore against a like occurrence and which gave him his habitual top-heavy bulky appearance were overhauled and strengthened. One remembered once again that against the sweetness of an earthly crown must be measured the sour.

The court drowned its fears and sorrows in a welter of pageantry. Prince Harry was to be made Prince of Wales and it was a summer of celebration. The prince was sixteen years old, nearly six feet tall, and giving expectation that he would rival his illustrious Tudor namesake in magnificence. Attended by a great entourage he arrived at Richmond at the end of May, and came by decorated barge to Chelsea. All around him triumphal sea creatures played – an enormous whale, a dolphin – better, we were assured, than Robert Dudley had made for Queen Elizabeth at Kenilworth. (Our age is always very eager to claim as much. The consciousness of having succeeded a legendary epoch and the need to compete with and surpass it, has always been a great burden.) Pretty John Rice from the King's Men's Company at the Globe played Corinea, Queen of Cornwall, sitting on the whale's back; and the great Richard Burbage gave a rousing speech from the back of the dolphin. At Whitehall stairs there came a volley of cannon shot from Lambeth shore in salute, and the prince was escorted to the Great Hall and thence to the Presence Chamber.

As I came from viewing the procession and made my way back towards our chambers to lay out Rob's attire for the evening I was once again accosted by the lady Frances who, seeming to be in close converse with Mistress Turner, must have been waiting for one close to Robbie.

"Ah! Giles!"

"My lady?" I asked guardedly.

"Giles, why does he not answer my letters?"

"Have you writ letters? I know nothing of this."

"I thought perhaps they had been mislaid. Does Robert understand that I take my reputation in my hands when I write to him? I take risks for him. My husband" – she winced at the name – "would be very angry if he knew that I had written to another."

"I doubt it not, my lady."

"Please beg Robert to be careful. Burn my letters, yes, but show me kindness. Giles – "

"My lady?"

"Giles, it is my birthday. I am eighteen. On this day people should be kind to me."

She looked curiously winsome. For all I did not like her I could see why folk found her attractive. Her eyes teased. She had a flawless skin. Her perfume was pleasing, sensuous, like a glade in high summer when the crushed petals underfoot gave off a rich sweetness. I suddenly noticed that close to her it was not easy to breathe. I stepped back.

"I wish you a good birthday," I said pompously.

"It has not been easy," she said, "to persuade my husband to remain at court. He would prefer to be away at his family home."

"Is that nearby?" I wondered.

"On the contrary," she shuddered with a wry laugh. "It's in the wilds of Staffordshire. Have you ever heard of it? Chartley. I've heard no good of it. It's a prison. It was a prison for Mary Queen of Scotland and I have no intention that it shall be a prison for me."

"Do you mean that the unfortunate lady was imprisoned at your lord's home? I had not heard this."

"Yes! She arrived there in winter and immediately fell ill. Horror and dread no doubt! And the bed she was shown to was stained and smelly. But the house being enclosed by deep water it was considered a secure place for a prisoner, and so there she must remain. All this being so, can you imagine what it must be like? I picture it as towers, battlements, dungeons, ghosts. *Her* ghost – prowling, its bloody head in its hands . . .Ugh! That is no place to take a bride."

"Well, it is not for me to say," I murmured, heartily agreeing with her.

She laughed. "I assure you, you will not find me at Chartley. Oh Giles, I envy you! I wish that I were you."

I blinked, a little taken aback.

"You are always near to him," she explained. "You straighten out his clothes. You handle garments still warm from him. You comb his golden hair. And you" – she passed her tongue over her lips – "handle his body. Do you . . . rub oils into his skin?"

I admitted that I did.

"Giles . . ." She touched my arm. "Bring me a gift for my birthday. Bring me something of him."

"Um . . ." I said nonplussed.

"Bring me a golden hair from his head . . ."

"Oh my lady . . ." I protested.

"Please, Giles! It's not much to ask. You are on your way to his rooms now. Surely, on a collar somewhere . . .? A single hair is all I ask."

I could give no reason why I should refuse. It was not an odd request for a lover to make. Was it not a single golden hair in the beak of a seagull that drove King Mark to distraction over the fair Isolde? I agreed to see what I could do. The besotted young woman promised not to stir from that spot until I returned. I was embarrassed by her devotion to one so careless of it.

She was right – the shoulder of a black velvet doublet showed me clear enough a forgotten golden thread (which says not much for my qualities as a manservant) and I took it to Lady Frances between finger and thumb, carefully, and all the while exasperated at myself for pandering to her whim, and thankful I would never have to expose the extent of my gullibility to my cousin and endure his scorn.

"Ah, Giles, you are a treasure!" breathed the grateful lady, and she put the hair into a little square of purple cloth edged all about with lace. "You will see me dancing in the *Masque of Tethys*, five days hence," she said. "Watch me; I dance for you."

I murmured a polite acknowledgement and withdrew.

At the beginning of June came the ceremony of Prince Harry's investiture in Westminster Hall. It was very splendid. A procession entered, composed of the earls of Sussex, Huntingdon, Cumberland, Rutland, Derby and Shrewsbury, with the twenty-five new Knights of the Bath; and the prince with the earls of Nottingham and Northampton (Howards, it will be noticed). The Earl of Salisbury read the letters patent and the prince knelt before his father, who dressed him in the Robe of Office and girded on his sword. With rod and ring and coronet the prince, accompanied by the Earl of Suffolk (another Howard) returned to Westminster stairs and the royal barge, which took the royal party to Whitehall. At the great dinner in the evening the Earl of Pembroke waited on the prince, the Earl of Southampton carved his meat, the Earl of Montgomery was his cupbearer.

Next day came the *Festival of Tethys* of which the lady Frances had spoken. It must have been one of the prettiest masques I have ever seen. They called it the Gossamer Masque, and Samuel Daniel wrote it, with most beautiful words. A dark cloud with sparkling stars was painted on the curtains. They were pulled aside to reveal a shimmering scene with caverns of gold and silver, gold pillars, pearly shells, cascading drapery. Everything sparkled; myriads of candles carefully placed caught gold-spangled lace, cobweb lace, green satin, taffeta, silver wings, glistening scales. Tethys the water nymph was played by Her Majesty in a head-dress of coral and shell, with a long diaphanous veil and a gown of blue taffeta which swirled about her like water. Beside her were half-naked Tritons, was Zephyrus with lustrous wings, were nymphs of the rivers. One of these was Lady Frances.

I was startled anew by her beauty. She wore her hair loose – how long it was! well past her waist – and her gown was blue and silver and somewhat transparent, as far as I could tell from my obscure position at the far end of the hall. There was no doubt of it – she was a graceful sinuous dancer and she danced to be seen. I suddenly recalled that day at Burghley when as a spoilt and pampered child she had discovered Rob and me in the chapel. "Look at me . . . you down there, look at me . . ."

The words washed over me, like the words of a spell.

Are they shadows that we see
And can shadows pleasure give?
Pleasures only shadows be
Cast by bodies we conceive
And are made the things we deem
In those figures which they seem;
But these pleasures vanish fast
Which by shadows are expressed.

Pleasures are not if they last –
In their parting is their best.
Glory is most bright and gay
In a flash and so away.
Feed apace then, greedy eyes,
On the wonder you behold
Take it sudden as it flies,
Though you take it not to hold.
When your eyes have done their part
Thought must length it in the heart.

The pleasure of shadows – the shadows of pleasures – I reflected much upon the same. Must pleasure then be transitory? Why was it then so fierce, a flame now bright, now gone? How can ephemeral things so please, things which maybe have no existence but in our own fanciful imaginings? There was Lady Frances, a shadowy figure believing Rob in love with her, deriving pleasure from that illusion. There were we, deriving pleasure from the beauty of the illusion she presented, which had small relation to the flesh and blood creature which she was – Howard, a trial to her husband, a recalcitrant wife. We create what we would have and we are then surprised to see it fade, something which we believed so real. We marvel something illusory can give us pain, but it seems reasonable to us that it give delight. The only answer was to grasp the pleasure though left only clutching at a shadow.

It was for the old, the regretful, the envious, to live in the shadow of pleasures; and for the lover, the man tired of the sun, the thief, the spy, the assassin, to delight in the pleasures of shadows.

And the shadows of things to come? And Frances' part in them? Fortunately these were hid from me. All I saw was a girl dancing.

CHAPTER TWENTY-THREE

"Robin, you must rid yourself of Overbury." His Majesty turned over in bed and lay upon one elbow, tapping Robbie's nose. Robbie, who hated that particular mannerism of endearment, rolled away and lay upon his front.

"Of my guid friend?" he mumbled sulkily.

"You are too much together. The queen doesnae like him."

"Or is it yourself, dear uncle, that likes him not?"

"Me, I am indifferent tae the fellow . . . I am thinking of your own guid name. It grieves me tae hear of you spoken of slightingly. *Carr and his governor* . . . it's ugly, is it not? I want the world tae see you as I do – bonny, beautiful and guid." His Majesty kissed Rob's ear. "Be less in his company, Robin. Have a care for yourself."

"I thank you for your wise counsel."

"But you will no' take it?"

"It would be ungracious of me tae spurn him who had been my friend in lean times."

"This is commendable in you, Robin, and I know you loyal. I would go so far as tae say I am the same. I can never hate the person I have once placed my affections upon – I may hate some vices of his, which may lessen my favour, but never bend my heart against him nor undo him . . . unless he undo himself."

A man more astute than Robbie might have understood a warning there for those closer to the king's person than Thomas Overbury. Robbie saw no such warning. It was a measure of his confidence in the king's dependence upon him that he argued his case at all.

"So, Robin, we may still expect tae see ye close wi' Overbury?"

"I believe him an ornament to our court."

"An ornament, aye; I do not dispute his good looks."

"And a man eager tae serve ye, uncle. He is greatly talented and underrated, and the preferment he desires comes not his way."

"I leave all that to Salisbury . . ." James hedged.

"A word frae your lips . . ."

"And is that what you want?" said James. He lifted back the sheets, uncovering Robbie's nakedness. He ran his finger slowly down the spine. "Be careful, Robin. I could give your friend the preferment you both seek – ambassador to eastern Russia, for example? How would he like that? He would be awa' for ten years. I believe he likes tae study languages – how long would it take him tae learn Russian? They say it is difficult but rewarding. There he would need tae learn tae love cabbage and tae convert his coach intae a sleigh. How does he like the cold? The carcases of beasts are piled in their thousands in heaps in the market place, frozen solid; they can be thawed and cooked wi' little loss o' flavour, they tell me. The houses, you know, are built wi' the beams o' the fir tree, and the chinks are stopped wi' moss." As James spoke his hand caressed Rob's shoulders, moving down his back. "A hearty aptitude for drinking will be required, far greater than my own – and singing in a loud voice," he said, warming to his theme. "Ah, and not to forget the bath houses. He will be required tae take his bath in steam and heat, then come leaping forth stark naked to plunge intae the river, first breaking the ice, this throughout the coldest part o' the winter; and Russian winters, I am told, can be particularly trying." The caressing hand tightened on Rob's buttock. "How d'ye think the fastidious and poetic Sir Thomas will enjoy it?"

"Your Majesty jests," said Robbie, his face muffled in the pillow. "At least, I believe that you do."

"Don't," said James pinching the arse flesh, "gie me cause tae find out."

Rob was for the moment free of the importuning of Lady Frances Devereux, because she was from court. In order to escape the attentions of her husband she had fled, like a vixen to earth, to Audley End, her parents' home in Essex. What a palace that is! I remember we had thought Burleigh splendid, but Audley End surpasses it. Big, beautiful, built about its courtyards, surrounded by its gardens, its wilderness, its bowling greens, approached by its double avenue of lime trees, it is more magnificent than Whitehall – a fact which is not lost upon King James. Frances's husband was in London, but making intermittent visits to his wife. Those interested in marital gossip passed it about that his arrow had not yet achieved the bull's eye; though, Copinger told me, the young earl had achieved the marital bed. The story was that Frances's parents had insisted that she take her husband to her bed, and she, being dutiful, had done so, and had told the wretched Essex that if he laid a hand upon her she would kill herself. Whether this were true or not we knew not, but I fear we repeated the story with a prurient relish and with many a snigger. The general opinion was Copinger's: "He is her husband. Why does he not simply take her? He has the right."

But as Thomas so succinctly pointed out: "A man with no ink in his pen may write no letter."

Was Essex that most unfortunate of creatures, an impotent lover? Or was he that strange being – a gentle courteous man who had decided to wait until his wife was ready, believing her afraid of intimacy, and hoping she would grow to love him, given time? How readily we found ourselves able to make pronouncements on matters we knew nothing of – the secret life of others!

"They say she is so fierce in lust that she has frightened young Essex away," said Copinger who knew nothing about it. "He now dare not make assay. Of course, he is a virgin," he explained.

"The luscious Frances in heat would be enough to scare the bravest," Tom sneered. "It would take a bold man with a sting of eighteen inches to attempt to plug her leak."

"Pish," said Robbie. "I could do it."

"Did I not just say as much?" Tom guffawed.

The court was now at Hampton where the Summer Progress would keep us till September. Here Rob played tennis and the king admired. And it was here that Rob received a letter from the lady. He opened it in the presence of Tom and myself and read it aloud.

"'I am now returned to London. I write to reassure you, Robert, that you need have no fear I am untrue. I constantly contrive to keep him from me. You know that I am yours and ever will be. But oh, the business weighs heavy on my heart. He takes it very ill. He says God damn him if ever he offers me a kindness till I call for it, and I say I will be damned if ever I do. But I do not think it my fault. I never asked to wed him; I was young, I knew not what I did, and I had not then seen you. It is only knowing that you love me sustains me. Be true, dear Robert, I will find a way for us to be together.'"

"Crazed," Tom decided.

"She lives a dream," said I. "Whatever can she hope for?"

"We are like carrion crows, we three, that pick over the carcase of her distress," said Rob.

We looked at him, surprised.

"You don't see the humour of it?" Tom demanded in astonishment. "That hoighty-toighty Puritan unable to come at his wife – let alone *in* his wife – and too polite to take her? The green girl holding off his advances because she believes you love her – you, Robbie, who give tongue and arse to the most regal prick in the land – and to others nearer home!"

"I wish you wouldnae' speak so," Robbie said vexed.

"*Else would a maiden blush bepaint your cheek?*" jibed Thomas. "Surely she knows you fuck with the king. And with me."

"What ails you, Tom? – you are grown coarse enough to become a Thames boatman. I wonder you don't go get yourself some oars."

"Why should I go find whores when I have thee, my sweet," said Tom stung to new heights of provocativeness. "And may I say I never had a prettier tongue than yours about my cock, nor lips that opened to it with more rapture."

"You push me, Tom," said Robbie angrily. "Have a care that you don't push me tae demand your preferment – tae Moscow."

Tom laughed uncertainly. Rob, red-faced and glowering, stood his ground, but bit his lip as if he had been goaded to say more than he intended.

"Frances Devereux has done this," I said.

"Forgive me, Tom," said Robbie warmly. "It was a foul thing I said."

"Forgive me too," said Thomas nowhere near as graciously, "for reminding you that you are good at sucking cock."

Robbie looked uncomfortable and turned back to the letter. "And what will I do wi' this?" he said.

"Keep it and turn it to your advantage," Tom said. "Or send it to Essex and cause him an apoplexy."

"No; I will not betray her trust," said Rob.

"I jested," Tom said curtly.

"I must answer it, of course, but what may I say that comforts her but gives her no encouragement?" Rob asked in all soberness.

Tom spluttered in mirth. "That one would test even a diplomat."

"If I were to assure her of my friendship and the honour that she does me tae confide in me?"

"Find me a pen," groaned Tom. "I'll write it for you. Let us not add to her pains by expecting the lady to decipher your illegible hand and clumsy sentiments. And afterwards, if you are pleased with what I write, you shall give me reward – whatever I demand of you, in bed."

"Agreed," said Robbie; and both deeds were done to mutual satisfaction.

"Giles, do you think," said Robbie later when Thomas had gone, "that Thomas could be jealous of the lady Frances's interest in me?"

"It is possible."

"But how strange! To think Tom with all his graces could be jealous of something so inconsequential!"

I smiled and said nothing. I had a word for Thomas also.

"Tom, don't forget," I said, "that Rob has been with women carnally. To my certain knowledge he has so – I once caught him in bed with some Islington strumpet. This will come as no surprise to you – you must know he is not so clear in his intent as we two are."

"What of that?"

"You seem so sure of his devotion to yourself and to His Majesty and you glory in his undoubted bedchamber talents. If you push him towards Frances, you risk throwing him into her arms."

"Oh no," said Tom dismissively. "He'll never love a woman, not as he loves me!"

We heard that Essex had set out for Chartley to prepare his ancestral home for his wife; his wife therefore had a respite.

"'Dear my lord'," she wrote to Robbie. "'For the moment, free. Free to think of you, and still untainted, though the strain of it has cost me dear. If I am lucky he will remain where he now is, and you and I will be together. I long for winter now. I long for the dark – may it hide our secret embracings!'"

Rob laughed ruefully. "Och, Giles," he said. "Myself I don't find the prospect o' the winter pleasing. I have His Majesty eyeing me for signs of too much interest in Tom; I have Thomas growling about Lady Frances. I have Lady Frances pursuing me wi' her misplaced desire. Thank goodness, Giles, for your continual dear disinterested friendship!"

He hugged me. Something about him so irritated me that my smile hurt my teeth and I was possessed of a sudden yearning to see him sent to Moscow. And obliged to take icy open-air baths.

Rob spent a deal of ingenuity in dodging Frances, who was at court for the winter without her husband, and therefore a subject of some speculation. She was living with her great-uncle in Northampton House on the Strand. Rob successfully parried all invitations to the house, but Frances was bold and would not be gainsayed. She would speak to Rob wherever she saw him.

"I would not need to do so," she complained in the Stone Gallery, "if you would see me privately."

"I am merely thinking of your reputation, my lady," Rob said cornered.

"I care nothing about it; why should you? I would risk reputation, name and all to be with you. Besides, I hate my name; it is his."

"And there we hae it," Rob said. "You belong to another."

"I belong to no one," Frances answered. "And the sooner those about me know it, the better for us all."

"But with repect, madame, you do," protested Robbie. "You are a member of a very celebrated family, and now by your marriage you are part of another such, and they both have claim on you."

"No," said Frances firmly. "I have claim on myself; that is my only bond. I am free to give myself or hold myself back. As I have done," she added meaningfully.

"I think you'll find these views are not held by our society," Rob smiled, "although I admire them for their spirit."

"Do you, Robert? Do you admire the words I say? You never tell me anything that my desire may feed upon . . . yet others seem to think me admirable."

"What would you have me say?"

"Meet me secretly," she pleaded. "You will speak louder with deeds."

"I dare not," Robbie said. "What would you? I can offer you nothing that you can properly ask for."

"You could offer me yourself, which is all that I desire!"

Rob's mouth went dry. He did not know how to handle the predicament in which he found himself. He wished Tom was beside him, whispering advice. What had happened to his preconception that the female was a passive and reluctant lover – unless of course she was a whore, a different matter altogether?

"Robert," she said into the silence. "You must know how beautiful you are. You are like no one else at court. Dazzling, golden, strong. Your image fills my dreams. In my waking hours I think about your body. I would like to be your servant and undress you and touch your skin and comb your hair; then lie beside you and . . . and glut myself upon you."

Robbie looked nervously about him. Courtiers were passing to and fro. All were staring. It was inevitable – two of the most gorgeous creatures at Whitehall in close converse, the king's beloved and the wayward wife. What had they heard? Rob wiped his brow. He felt that he was sweating. He was not; but heat seemed to drip in rivulets from him; he felt on fire, like the cold lover on the miniature with the background of burning flames.

"I felt as if she had indeed undressed me," Rob told us. "I felt that I was standing there all naked and that she was looking at me, her eyes all over me, and everyone who passed by seeing me thus, thinking the same."

"There should have been no embarrassment for you then," said Thomas cheerfully. "You have the most perfect body I have ever seen. All who passed by would have admired, envied and desired you."

"Yes, but I was . . . I found that I was roused from what she said."

"Oh, I see – you were naked and your lance at full tilt. So much the better for the spectators then! Did you hear cheering cries of Bravo! Were you showered with invitations?"

"Tom, I was awfu' muddled – it's no laughing matter! All she did was speak tae me and I was no' master o' mysel'. It would be better if I never was that close tae her again – she is an awfu' powerful woman."

"She's a whore," said Tom. "Or would be if she could. What modest woman would present herself to Robbie and speak so?"

With our undeniably limited experience of the female *modus operandi* we agreed that modest women did not so comport themselves.

"And how did you extricate yourself from her tangled coils?" Tom enquired.

"In some confusion," Rob admitted.

"Did she say aught else?"

"She said: write to me – write to me of love!"

"That is common amongst women," I suggested. "They like to hold a love letter and put it under their pillow – I have seen it in plays."

Tom flung an arm around Robbie's shoulder. "You have had an unpleasant experience, dear," he said. "I know what you need and I am the man to provide it. All this talk of women has unsettled you. Take me to your bed and I will kiss you senseless – I will lick your nipples and your armpit hair and bury my face in your balls and fling you on your belly and wrench your thighs apart and show you what it means to glut oneself upon another! Not a word now – do as you are told – it's my intent to fuck some silly notions from you and remind you where your true talents lie."

He shoved Robbie before him to the bedchamber, and Rob went unprotesting.

Some time that December Robbie encountered Mistress Anne Turner, Frances's companion, in the Stone Gallery – an encounter plainly not a chance one. Anne handed Rob a letter. He knew the writing well now and received it courteously enough. He would have walked away, but she would speak.

"Sir Robert," she began.

"Mistress Turner?"

"My lady is much grieved that it is never possible to converse privily with you."

"I am much wi' His Majesty . . ."

"Yes, but you are also free to pursue your own inclinations on the many occasions when His Majesty is occupied with affairs of state and family."

"It is not possible to be secret at court," said Rob. "Everyone knows everyone else's business."

"Quite so," said Mistress Turner smoothly. "Sir Robert, I have a house in Paternoster Row. I put it at the disposal of you and the lady Frances."

"Och, I could not so impose . . ."

Anne lowered her voice. "Have pity on my lady – she dies for love of you."

"Pish – that cannae' be; she barely knows me."

"Ah, if you but knew! You are more real to her than that illusion which goes by the name of Essex."

"Well, I am glad you raised that matter, madam," Rob said drily. "It is the name of her young husband who will have some interest in this matter."

"Essex is in Staffordshire," said Anne brusquely, "and must remain there, being unwell."

"And the nature of his illness?"

But Mistress Turner would not say.

"That makes it worse, he being unwell," said Rob. "I wouldnae' take advantage of a man sick in his bed, tae steal his wife."

"I don't think you understand," Anne murmured. "Essex cannot . . . Essex is unable to perform a husband's duties. It is pathetic to see . . . to hear. I have heard them at night, behind closed doors : *Frankie, it will not be.* Her sobs – and worse, her laughter, her ridicule . . . His pacing the floor, her bitter accusations, his sullen defensiveness, the heavy silences, the dreadful mornings – both he and she haggard, shadow-eyed . . . the growing hostility, even hatred . . . her loathing of him. Cow, she calls him . . . beast."

"So, what we heard is true? Puir fellow."

"The lady is yet virgin. But it is a state that does not please her. It is pitiable to see her. She has set her heart on you!"

"I am sensible of the honour . . ." Rob fidgeted.

"We talk now of desire and not of courtesies." Anne's voice was urgent, persuasive. "Have you never been besotted – have you never known that desperation, longing, like a fever raging inward, which can only be satisfied by the beloved? Lying in hot sheets – tossing and turning – aching with love?"

Robbie had not, and therefore hesitated. Then he said wondringly: "And Lady Frances is thus for me?"

"She is."

Mistress Turner pressed a key into Rob's hand. "This will unlock the door to my house in Paternoster Row – take it – keep it safe. Ah, Sir Robert," she breathed,"the loveliest woman at court is pining for love of you.Could you not find it in your heart to ease her longing?"

Rob opened his mouth to make the kind of answer he could relate to Tom and laugh over. Instead he said: "I could."

CHAPTER TWENTY-FOUR

"This way is perhaps better," said Thomas, as we sat there in a circle staring at the key, which lay upon a little oaken table. "How?" said Robbie.

"You meet the lady in the house in Paternoster Row. You fuck her. You then have the Howards' pride as your personal strumpet, bringing shame upon them by her prostitution. And if Essex ever gets his pen into the inkwell he discovers he has wed no virgin, and much mischief will be made. The lady will be known for the whore she is; and we shall thereby shall have much merriment."

"I cannae' do it," Rob said.

"You must – it is a Heaven-sent opportunity."

"No. I have no sentiment towards the lady. It would be unkind. I dinna' ken why I took the key at a'."

"You will offend her more by taking it and not using it," said Thomas.

"Och, tae Hell wi' her and all women," Robbie said, and left us to it, slamming the door.

I said to Thomas: "Rob's right – you must see that. Your little plan not only toys with Frances but with Robbie too. You're using him to vex your enemies."

"Well, what if I am?" said Thomas. "Consider him, Giles. So close with the king – and what has he done for me? He struts about in his pearls and velvets like a great peacock – his gait cries: behold me! And I fester here at court, my lips cracked with smiling. He basks in the sunshine of the king's good favour. It's about time he did some work for it."

And I began to understand that Tom was envious of Robbie, and I mistrusted him, for all that I was fond of him and that he was my cousin.

It was policy rather than lust which tempted Rob at that time. In Tom's close company he began to take an interest in matters of state, Tom carefully explaining to him about the manipulation of fact, the working towards a given end, of playing off one man against another, of undermining influence with a half-truth here, a seed of discord there. From what I heard when I gave ear to it, it sounded something between a game of chess and a chapter from the writings of Machiavelli, neither of which I knew over well. However, under Tom's guidance, Rob would enter the field and try his hand at the shaping of events.

"After all," said Thomas, "close as you are to the king, you have as yet no title. Philip Herbert is Earl Montgomery and you are plain Sir Robert. We must give the king a nudge. I guess he sees you at present as something to fondle and adore; we must work to make him believe you have a lively grasp of statecraft."

Robbie laughed, but knuckled down to studying Thomas's interpretation of events.

The plan was to work against the Earl of Salisbury's policies in Parliament. Salisbury had presented the Great Contract to Parliament, an attempt to secure revenues for the king, to meet his debts. The Contract met with opposition. The Commons believed that the king was in debt because of his generosity to the Scots at court, and I rather think that Thomas had a hand in suggesting it to them. There were ugly scenes and accusations. The Commons set up a committee and prepared a petition asking the king to send the Scots home. The king, disgusted, dissolved Parliament and the Contract failed, a severe blow to Salisbury. As a result the king felt obliged to reassure his Scottish friends of his affection, with rewards and favours. Robbie was created Viscount Rochester and Knight of the Garter, this latter an honour which especially delighted him. He might therefore if he chose sit in the House of Lords; no Scot had been so honoured previously, and Tom was like a cat with cream.

"Write to me of love," Frances had entreated. This was very much more to Rob's taste than to speak with the lady at close quarters. That winter at Whitehall he could not escape from Frances's baleful gaze and he had not made use of the key offered by Mistress Turner, whose gaze was no less penetrating. By dint of being out riding with the king and many an overnight stay at the hunting lodges of Royston and Ampthill he contrived to keep out of the lady's path. But he hoped to appease those hunting him by corresponsence writ by Tom.

Thomas composed for him love letters and sonnets all on the theme of Frances – her beauty, which was undeniable, her reputed love for

Rob which, she assured us, was unabated, and his for her, which was somewhat open to question. This did not inhibit liars such as we, and together we crafted verse upon verse and sent them to the lady. Shakespeare, Surrey, Sidney, celebrated sonneteers, had no need to fear the loss of their laurels – Tom was a sententious poet and I half wondered whether Frances would understand his poems, being not, as I had heard, famed for her intellect.

A servant of Anne Turner was the messenger between the two parties, and he the deliverer of the letters which he put into my hands. His name was Richard Weston – a thin and balding fellow, a man, we understood, of varied background, having been in his time a tailor's apprentice, an apothecary's assistant, and a prisoner, having been caught coining sixpences. I often found myself looking at him with distrust, simply because he had once worked for an apothecary and therefore must know a secret or two about the concoction of potions. He was, however, a ready and obliging messenger. Maybe he sensed my suspicion of him, for once he said to me, with the kind of little sly half-smile that belied his words:

"You know, Master Rawlins, you may trust me."

"I doubt it not," I assured him politely and mendaciously.

"I am utterly dependable."

"I am sure that you are." He had a habit of not quite meeting one's eye. This man, I thought, watching him, has mixed mercury brews in an apothecary's back room, measured out powders with Latin names, understands poisons. My dealings with him were done swiftly and with distaste.

"Mistress Turner depends upon me and my loyalty to her is unquenchable," he continued. This proud boast of his did nothing to reccomend him to me.

"You are both fortunate then." Try as I might I could not keep the sarcasm from my tone. I did not like him; but it mattered not – it was not my reputation that he held in his keeping. I merely handed him the sonnets and received from him the lady's grateful replies.

On New Year's night came the most memorable event of the winter – Prince Harry as Oberon in *The Masque of Oberon*. It was a fairy tale set on a moonlit rock, with creatures dressed in leaves – but enough of that: Prince Harry had grown handsome enough to die for. He wore a helmet with a fountain of plumes, a tight-fitting corselet, and the tiniest thigh-hugging breeches, showing every curve of arse and crotch, and was bare-legged, with buskins to mid-calf. The thighs were a dream, all muscle, and he walked like one who owned the world. Tom and I had only to say to one another: "Prince Harry's legs!" to melt in ecstasy.

Dream, of course, was all that one could do with Prince Harry. He was a severe young man who kept a box into which anyone who swore an oath must place a coin. He was never drunk. He was studious and thoughtful, vigorous and manly. They said he had no sense of humour, but it was not so; he had one, if a little warped. He had reduced his little brother Charles to tears with jibes about his spindly legs, and told him that he must grow up to be a bishop, so that he might wear a robe to cover them.

He had a goshawk which he had trained to be as obedient as a dog, that came at his beck and call and sat upon his wrist and did tricks to his whistles of command. They said that it had been so wild that once it tore a man's eye out in a rage, but Prince Harry had tamed it to his satisfaction – the taming a veneer, and underneath it wildness still, so that only the prince's mastery kept the bird contained. It had an unpleasant way of leaning forward watching passers by, jutting its neck and flexing itself, as if the memory of that moment of savagery was close to the surface and he yearned once again to taste eyeball.

Prince Harry liked pistols, armour, ships. It was said that he could hardly wait to go to war with Spain. In his lonely prison in the Tower Sir Walter Raleigh no doubt prayed for his accession.

The air was heavy with perfume, sweat and the mustiness of velvets. Watching the dancing that followed the masque, Mistress Turner stood beside me. The Earl of Southampton was dancing with the princess Elizabeth; Prince Harry was dancing with his mother.

"Such a waste . . ." commented Mistress Turner, then: "My lady wonders why the key has not been used?"

"It is not through disrespect of the lady," I said. "My friend is honourable and has no wish to offend the Earl of Essex."

"What offence might be caused? The earl will never know of it."

"All the world knows that the marriage has not been consummated. How would it then be if his lordship found the matter otherwise?"

"Have no anxieties there," she replied. "He will never get that close; and if he does," she added mysteriously, "tell Viscount Rochester that there are ways to counterfeit virginity, that virginity being taken."

I shuddered. I had no idea what they were, and did not wish to know.

"They are dancing together," she observed. "Viscount Rochester and Lady Frances . . . How well they look – they are the two most beautiful in the entire court." It still seemed odd to me to hear Rob called by his impressive title. Almost as if she could read my mind, Anne Turner whispered: "Tell your Robert that though my lady cannot write a sonnet as well expressed as he, yet her heart speaks most excellent verse, and longs to rhyme her lines to his."

"I will."

"There is no other lady in whom he interests himself?" she frowned.

"None." In this at least I could be honest.

"Then take this, Giles, and put it straight into his hands. It is her picture."

She slipped away. Devil take it, but I could tell I was not formed for subtlety – my lips ached from the contortions they had sufferered in my having conducted my part in the conversation out of the corner of my mouth!

If I had had sense or prescience I would have tossed the miniature aside; but no, I did as she requested and told Rob what had passed between us. He listened affably and received the miniature with interest.

By daylight we perused it. It was a pretty portrait – how could it not be? – and pictured Frances with a sort of innocence, wide-eyed and smiling, honey-coloured curls about her cheeks. Two pendant pearls showed in her hair.

"She's awfu' bonny," Rob pronounced. Then he said: "We'll no' tell Thomas that I have her picture, eh? I dinna' want his snickering over it."

I would have kept quiet about it; but once, a few weeks later, when I was tidying the bed, the picture slid from under the pillow. I found the notion disturbing and distasteful, and I thought that some of Tom's teasing would do Robbie good and show the matter for the ridiculous thing it was.

"Did you sleep well last night, my dear?" said Thomas only too happy to oblige.

"As I recall, I did," said Rob.

"You were not with the king?"

"He was unwell; I slept here in my chamber."

"I marvel that you were comfortable, with such an encumbrance under your pillow."

Rob looked startled. He got up, went into the bedchamber, came out.

"Where is it?" he demanded.

"Where is what?"

"The miniature of Lady Frances. I assume you have it, by your smirking."

"I have it, yes, and will return it when you have answered truthfully three questions."

165

"Say on, then, if you must."

"First: do you consider the lady to be beautiful?"

"That's a simple one. I do. As does everyone."

"I do not," said Thomas smoothly. "She is hid away all but her face, and that's hanged about with toys and devices, like the sign of a tavern, to draw strangers."

Rob turned to me annoyed. "Giles, that was not the act of a friend tae show her picture tae Thomas. He is well under way now, and there will be more, I know it."

"The second question," Tom said, "is why did you keep the little treasure hid from me?"

"Well, that is plain enough – to save myself frae that which I see I must now endure."

"You thought that I would laugh to see you acting like a lovesick fool? Why should you think that?"

"You have a barbed tongue, Tom."

"Not so barbed that you don't enjoy it in your mouth, your ear, your . . ."

"Have done. What question next?"

"How often do you put your lips upon the picture and your hand about your prick and think you lie upon the lady?"

Rob flushed scarlet – in anger, I would like to think; and Tom cried gleefully: "A hit, a hit, a palpable hit! You haven't answered me, Rob. Are you ashamed? Come now, tell. Do you think of her luscious breasts and her rapacious belly? What do you think of, Rob, as you lie solitary, fucking yourself?"

"Give me the picture," Rob scowled.

"I will, on one condition."

"What, more? Not more questions?"

"No, this one is more pleasurable – take me to bed."

"What, after this? I dinnae' think so."

Tom stood up. He moved towards Robbie. He reached for him. Rob stood there stiffly, unresponsive. Tom held him in his arms, began to kiss him. I watched Rob soften and permit himself to be kissed to compliance. Tom eased him toward the bedroom, and just as he reached the door, turned back and winked at me.

Resignedly I stayed where I was, reluctant to quit my post in case one knocked, and even more reluctant to remain. I knew by the rustling and the creaking of the bed that the deed took place; I knew by the progress of the grunting and the groaning when the deed was finished; and by the splashing in the tub when the participants were about to emerge.

Wearing a towel about his hips Rob came forth, moistly beautiful. He glowered at me.

"Well, Giles, and where has he hidden it? Who would suppose him a court wit to see him act so childishly?"

I shrugged. "I know nothing about it."

We turned back to Thomas who was putting the finishing touches to his dressing, beside the bed. He reached a hand beneath the pillow and withdrew the picture, holding it provocatively towards Robbie.

"Why, look, here it was all along. It has been underneath the pillow as we fucked. There were three of us in the bed!"

Rob snatched the picture and his fist closed upon it. "Out, Tom," he said jerking his head.

Tom bowed laconically and came forth most graciously. Rob waited in an angry silence, the which Tom broke by the singing of 'O Mistress Mine'as he patted perfume into his beard.

"You had best go fuck her soon in actuality," he said sweetly as he left, "or she will begin to think that you are like the Earl of Essex."

There was dancing following a feast one night in February. Robbie sought out Frances and danced much with her and was monstrous gallant. I heard one aged dame who knew no better say they made a handsome couple.

Rob and Frances now by torchlight's glow were often partners at the dance. They talked about their childhood. She remembered herself as having been a lonely child, even though her family was large. Her father, she said, was bluff and loud, her mother selfish, interested in her own concerns. Yes, she was close to her sister Elizabeth, but closest of all was she to sweet Turner, who had been her friend almost for as long as she could remember. She envied Robbie the romancy castle of his youth. There was no need, he told her, it was not his. Aye, it was considered a fine new building, he agreed, and for a dozen years now it had not been burned down, but he would never live there. At an early age he had been sent off to make what best use he might of his particular talents, and he supposed, like hers, his childhood had been lonely. It is all a question of perception. Whether it was so in either case mattered little beside the fact that both believed it so; a bond was thereby formed.

She did not speak of larger issues then – of unused keys, of absent husbands – and Rob was more comfortable so. He confided to me that he considered her a very agreeable person and nothing like as wild and forward as some would have it. I said to him that a clever woman can play any part she chooses; but he laughed and said Frances was honest – her eyes were clear as limpid pools.

"I was so very pleased for you," said Frances with becoming admiration, "when I heard you were now become Viscount Rochester and Knight of the Garter."

Rob looked modest, but there was no doubt that he enjoyed his elevation. Tom, who considered Rob's title entirely due to himself, had ceased now to call Rob by any other name than Rochester, even in their intimate moments. These, of course, continued, mutual lust a piquant glue betwixt the cracks of mutual vexation.

Meanwhile Frances gave Rob a book, *The Problems of Beauty and All Human Afflictions* by Thomas Buoni, which she said that he should read, being the most beautiful man at court. The book had been translated from the Italian and it treated of one hundred and twenty problems connected with the subject of the title.

"Why is beauty especially apprehended by the sight? Why is beauty enjoyed less desired? Why do women not born fair attempt to seem fair? Why is love so potent? Why do lovers delight in flowers? Why is the hatred of women without end or measure?"

Some of these questions of course were to prove highly pertinent to the unravelling of that which was to come, but at that stage most of the questions were considered rhetorical. Frances perhaps had paid attention to the second on the list, for now, while giving every attention to Robbie and always appearing in his company at her most exquisite, listening carefully to his every word, paying him all kinds of compliments, she never spoke of love or keys or houses in Paternoster Row; and I believe that Rob grew seriously concerned that she was no longer the throbbing lovesick mooncalf that she had been made out to be.

One day in May they were sitting in the Privy Garden, myself and Mistress Turner standing nearby, seeming nonchalant, but on our guard, positioned at the floral loopholes of the arbour walls. Rob and Frances sat facing each other upon marble seats. There was no way they could have sat side by side because the hoops of the farthingale prevented it. There were little bows down to the hem of Frances's gown, the which was blue. She wore a high wired collar, so that her neck seemed to be lying on a slim frilled pillow, her throat and breasts revealed, framed in rich lace. The sun gleamed on her honey-coloured hair; pearls hung at her ears.

Rob's eyes followed the line of bows down to her feet. The lifting of the farthingale through sitting showed her ankles, her white silk stockings. Rob's shoe brushed against hers. He did not move it, nor she hers. Looking her in the eyes he moved his feet so that they were inserted between hers, and then again, obliging her to part her legs. She did so, matching him gaze for gaze.

"Well, Frankie," Rob said, never subtle. "D'ye love me?"

She lowered her eyelids, keeping him in suspense just long enough to give him doubt of her reply. Then she raised her eyes to his with a look of such melting adoration that he caught his breath.

"And is that yes?" he asked, to make assurance doubly sure. She smiled and nodded.

"Well, that is some relief tae me," said Rob mopping his brow, "for I've been sitting here thinking that if I do not have this woman I shall burst."

She giggled. "I could not be responsible for such wanton destruction of a work of art."

He grinned sheepishly. "Och, well . . ." He cleared his throat. "And are you able to stay out overnight and come and go as ye please?"

"Are you?" retorted she.

"*Touché*," said he, inclining his head. "Well, now, then, Frances," he said carefully, " Mistress Turner has given me a key . . ."

The timing of the intrusion would have done credit to the kind of play they put on at the Red Bull.

"Mistress Turner!" I said sharply. "Have a care for your charge!"

Bearing purposefully down towards us was a noisy group of courtiers veering in our direction, laughing in loud voices. Within seconds Rob and Frances were yards apart and standing, Anne and I beside them, talking vociferously, as if we had been so doing all the time, as careless as you like, as if we had all met by chance and were about to go our ways.

"Here she is! Frankie!" called her father. "Frankie – what do you think? Your husband is returned from Chartley! Here is the good Earl of Essex!"

Frances's face froze. She gave out a kind of moan – half gasp, half sob – and then said nothing, absolutely nothing. It was scarcely noticed, for her father spoke enough for everyone, and loud enough. I saw the Earl of Southampton and the Earl of Pembroke at each side of the lady's husband – I wondered how much they had guessed.

"So, Frankie, and are you glad to see me well?" asked Essex.

"She is, she is!" her father boomed. "As are we all. And Frankie, Chartley is all prepared and waits for you, your bridal home."

Essex gave his arm to Frances and she took it. He found time to say to Robbie before he turned and led his unprotesting wife away: "I think we have no more need of your services, Viscount Rochester. You have been the escort of my wife a little more than I esteem quite necessary."

"It has been my pleasure," Rob said bowing, in a tone of warm sincerity that was not lost upon the earl.

There was no help for it – Frances must go to Chartley with her husband and make the best of it; her family would have it no other way.

I found the situation monstrous droll, though I never would have confessed as much to Robbie. I preserved a proper soberness of countenance and when Rob for the hundredth time wailed: "Och, but did ye see her face?" I nodded sympathetically, privily hoping the wretched Essex would give her her proper dues and satisfy her rampant itch and set her to breed.

We had troubles enough of our own – Thomas was banished from court.

"I mun dae it," said the king to Robbie. "It is no' for mysel'. Your friend has upset too many people. I told Northampton – I said: Harry, y'are mistaken; Overbury doesnae' work against ye, I am sure of it. He believed me. But in the case of Her Majesty – och, women, Robin, they brood over things. She feels he has offended her – well, you know that he hasnae' and I know that he hasnae'; but let's keep the puir queen happy, Robin, and if Overbury keeps out of her sight for, say, six months, the whole thing will blow over."

"It doesnae' seem fair," Rob said, "that I must lose a friend over a misunderstanding."

"Aye, I can see that it appears so to you, my dear," said James, his arm about Robbie's shoulder. "But at least we shall hae more time together, you and I, and I will hae your full attention."

There was no mistaking the warning in the avuncular tone. Rob took the point and bowed reluctantly to circumstance and set about to make the king feel wanted.

For myself it was an excellent summer. Frances was safely tucked away at Chartley, Tom was travelling, and I had Rob all to myself. The Summer Progress was to me a most agreeable diversion. Spared the need to join any of the daily hunting parties, as Robbie must, I passed gentle days in the country houses and gardens of the great, attending to Robbie's needs when required. For all that the king had intimated that he would have Rob spend more time with him, there were plenty of occasions when he was occupied or weary and Rob slept alone. This was not Rob's way.

"Giles . . ." he'd wheedle, "will ye come tae bed wi' me?"

In scented sheets, in wondrously carved beds all over southern England, we would lie, listening to the mewling cries of peacocks or the heady silences where the ticking of a distant clock seemed loud as weaponry.

Sometimes Rob would toss and turn and say: "Oh God, how is she now, alone wi' that vile brute? How may she endure it!"

Suspecting that the Earl of Essex was in no way the vile brute of Rob's imaginings, and Frances perfectly able to deal with him, I found little to lose sleep over here. I hinted as much to Robbie, but no – he would imagine scenes of pain and threat and weeping and must suffer accordingly. It seemed, moreover, that she could get no letter to us, for we were now here, now there, and no doubt she understood that any such would have been noted or mislaid or worse – opened by strangers. Rob's thoughts indeed were in distant Staffordshire, but it did not trouble me – his body was against mine, my lips in his hair, my hand about his cock. And he was not so lovelorn that he made no response when I made love to his perfection – when I kissed his skin, when I put my mouth to his prick, which in spite of Frances Devereux, was never slow to rise.

"Och, Giles," he'd murmur, snuggling against me, "how guid y'are tae me."

Was it love or stupidity, I wondered ruefully, that kept me content with the time he could spare when others dearer to him were away?

"It's my fault Tom is banished," he said guiltily. "It was because he was too close wi' me."

"It was his own fault," I corrected him. "It was because he had offended almost everybody and used his sharp wit where it was not appropriate. Listen to me – Her Majesty is the prime mover in his having been sent upon his travels. She'd like to be rid of you, but that isn't possible, so she rids herself of her secondary irritation, and if that bothers you, so much the better." I added, with a touch of deviousness that startled me and showed me worthy after all to be a Jacobean courtier, "by fretting over Tom, therefore, you play into her hands. Best put him from your mind, live in the moment, and enjoy what is to hand."

"Aye, you're right," said Rob soberly. "You always were the wise one."

I was not so lacking in subtlety as to say then: so let's to bed! – but it was soon enough that we did so, and if the strength of Rob's passion was in part to spite the queen I did not complain; I was the beneficiary. I was a very happy man that summer, with Tom abroad and Frances at her marital home and His Majesty kind enough to leave Rob sometimes to his own devices. Whether Rob's heart was with me I did not enquire, but there was honest affection between us, and the pleasure of two bodies moving in harmony, and the shared smiles of remembered satisfaction.

One unfortunate occurence that year – Philip Herbert lost his looks through smallpox. There is often talk when one has been so beautiful of whether it would have been preferable for the victim to have died. I am sure that the Earl of Montgomery was glad enough to survive; but it was sad to see him pitted and scarred. Rob was badly shaken by it, seeming to take his predecessor's misfortune personally. How ephemeral, we reflected, as many had done before us (and usually in verse), is beauty!

The pleasant summer passed, filled with the scent of roses, the playing of lutes by candlelight, the birdsong in the woods, the riding and the dancing, the banquets and the wine – and Rob, preoccupied and exquisite, asleep in our shared bed. It was with a heavy heart that I saw the return of autumn and the approach of Whitehall's chimneys.

A letter was brought to us within hours of our arrival. It read: "I write to let you know we are in London and that you need have no fear; for all is as it was before, and always will be till you make it otherwise."

"Burn me!" said Robbie whistling in admiration. "How has she held him off?"

He had no chance to enquire as much of the lady, for whenever she was seen at court she was seen with her husband. Essex never seemed to leave her side. Particularly where Robbie was concerned, there seemed to be some dark hostility amounting to suspicion, for he seethed and glowered whenever there was opportunity, and Rob's answering smiles wore thin, as he did not know what to do for the best. Not much to my surprise, Lady Frances let him know.

"It will be possible,'" she wrote, "for me to visit Mistress Turner at her house in the afternoons. She is making a winter gown for me and I must be fitted. Let me know what times you may come to us. I am in despair for lack of you and long to give you all."

Rob walked in the Privy Garden on his own, reading and re-reading this letter. There was no one about. He remembered that day in May when the object of his thoughts was taken from him so abruptly. Now the dry leaves rustled; the year was turning. The roses were yet in bloom, cut in order to come late. In the garden here were at various places stone embrasures, niches such as might have housed a statue in some other place. Rob leaned against the wall, absorbed, and read the letter once again.

What, he wondered, would he be courting by a favourable response? What would ensue? Trouble, certainly. Was the lady worth it?

"I can do wi'out her well enough," he thought. "She will grieve a while but she will mend. Though I shall be sorry not to have her for she is a bonny creature, wasted on that sour-faced Puritan . . . But it is for the best."

"'s death, an alabaster saint!"

Rob had thought himself alone, leaning there against his embrasure of stone. He now found himself gazed upon by the very man on whom he had been musing, along with that man's companion Prince Harry, majestic with his flowing auburn hair, his goshawk on his wrist.

"A coin for my poor-box, Essex!" reproved the prince. "And I think you are mistaken – we have no saint here."

"Nor no sinner either, I hope," said Robbie, conscious of having made a sound and virtuous decision and looking for the neatest way of extricating himself from this unlooked-for encounter; but the two were standing in his way.

"It is Viscount Rochester," Essex observed with heavy irony, "and he reads."

Robbie folded the letter from Essex's wife and tucked it into his glove. "Aye," he said, "it is a trick I learnt in Scotland."

"But you know other tricks, I think," Prince Harry said, "that you have learnt in England."

And now Rob began to feel uncomfortable. Essex he would have been glad to spar with, but Prince Harry was a different matter.

Whatever I may do, he thought, however I may work to please him, he despises me and will continue to do so. And there he stands, so handsome, and legs to die for . . .

Prince Harry raised his wrist. The goshawk rose and flew upward, slowly, hovering a little over Robbie's head.

"I know now how the coney feels," Rob told me. "I looked up and saw these yellow hooky talons, claws on them like Toledo blades, two inches frae my eyes. I bent my head and tried tae duck out of its way, but with a whistle of command the prince shifted the bird and sent me back against the wall. The damned bird hovered there, with its dark wings brushing my cheek. I looked intae its very eyes – they were the colour of marigolds; and its beak was bloody. Then I heard Essex say very loud and clear: 'It is a great pity about Hanley, the man who lost an eye. The eyeball hung upon a thread. It was quite cleanly done. They tried to put it back into the socket but it would not go. The false eye never looked quite right. He had it made in Cheapside but it was not well done.'

"Prince Harry chuckled, and whistled again and made the bird tae dart at me and check and pounce – it was most skilfully done. I put my hands over my eyes. I kept thinking o' puir Philip Herbert and his looks gone. I was never that much aware o' vanity but it occurred tae me then that I very much feared tae hae my face marked. I was moreover in some terror o' losing an eye. I knew that this was done for sport and if I

173

had been Essex I would hae laughed as he did. I know I looked a fool, twisting this way and that, my arms across my face . . . The bird then settled on my head; its feet were in my hair; I swear I felt the talons clench . . . At such a moment one forgets the bird is reputed tae be tamed and at the prince's beck and call and that his dad would have something tae say if I became disfigured; but by then of course it would be too late! They knew I was afraid; it was humiliating. When I felt the talons rise I put my arms down and opened my eyes. The goshawk was back upon Prince Harry's wrist and he was scratching its feet and stroking its breast feathers. He dipped his hand into a pouch and intae the bird's beak he put a mouse, cut in two and bleeding still; it gulped it down.

"'Calm yourself, my lord,' Prince Harry said, watching me in some amusement. 'Look, your lovely hair is not even ruffled.'

"They stood aside tae let me pass. I have never seen the Earl of Essex smile so; he was well content. It is of course the prerogative of the royal first-born to enjoy his sport – his was the hawk and his the skill; besides, he is so personally gorgeous and I do not overmuch begrudge him his triumph. But Essex . . . it was not his hawk; he had joined in the mirth at no cost and with no excellence, but merely because he is the prince's friend and out of spite for an imagined injury . . ."

Rob was still angry. He was laughing ruefully; but he was angry.

"I was made a fool," he said.

I let him pace and mutter. I picked up his boots from where he had kicked them. After a while he sat down and was silent. Then he looked at me. He stroked his chin reflectively.

"Where exactly is Paternoster Row?" he said.

CHAPTER TWENTY-FIVE

That Rob had made a whore of Lady Frances Devereux was considered by Thomas on his return to court in November as most excellent news. Let not Thomas be judged at fault for considering the matter thus callously – it is how the world thinks. A wife has lain with one other man; she is therefore a whore and will lie with any, and if some ruin follow for her family, so much the spicier. No, Tom's fault lay in assuming that Rob judged the matter thus.

"My dearest Rochester," he said, embracing Robbie with effusiveness. "I knew that your good looks and sexual prowess were given to you by a munificent deity with other intent than merely pleasing me!"

Rob's welcome was more guarded, but I don't believe Tom was

aware of it.

"And is it true indeed that you have bedded her?" pressed Tom. "The much-vaunted virginity whose conquest has been so feverishly and inexpertly sought by my lord of Essex is no more?"

"I have made love to Lady Frances, aye; I owe it tae ye, Tom, tae tell you as much."

"You owe it to me, aye," agreed Tom cheerfully. "Made love?" he added disparagingly. "But have you fucked her?"

"I have fucked her," said Robbie curtly.

"Several times? Once, I think, would barely count and would imply you did not leave the lady desperate for more, if she could be so easily satisfied."

"I believe that she was desperate for more," said Rob in growing irritation. "Moreover so was I, and therefore – several times."

"What, pique?" teased Thomas. "You did not use to be so coy. Come now, tell Thomas all about it. It is all so strange and new to me. You are as a sea discoverer to unknown lands and those who have not made the voyage like to hear about the havens and the storms. Did you have difficulty piercing Hymen's knot?"

"I was careful."

"And now the deed is done, is she lewd and voracious as we supposed? Did she twine about you like a spider, all legs and arms ?"

"She says," said Robbie carefully, "that she loves me tae distraction and it is true that I have had some demonstrable proof of that."

"Aye, as I said – lewd and voracious," Tom chuckled comfortably, munching a marshmallow. "But have a care; it's not the free and easy way it is with us – you'll get her with child, you know."

"I'll not; she uses a device which she – "

"Sweet Rochester, I think we'll draw a veil over a matter so unsavoury," said Thomas with an elaborate shiver of distaste. "Myself I think you should get her with child, for all the world knows Essex could not have done it and therefore her badge of whoredom will be there for all to see."

"If such occurred," said Robbie, "it would be no badge of whoredom; it would be my bairn and I would acknowledge it."

"Then by all means let her stuff herself with fifty such devices; and I'm sure that she has room," said Tom blithely. "But we should perhaps move to another subject – one that does not make Viscount Rochester to glower so. What other news while I have been away?"

I was only too willing to divert his attention to other matters. "In September Simon Forman the magician died – had you heard as much?"

"I had; but what more can you tell me?"

175

"It was Frankie who told us about it," Robbie said. "She seemed strangely cast down by the news."

"The manner of his death was very odd," I said, " for he prophesied his demise to the precise moment. 'I will die on Thursday next,' he said, and all that week he was not ill, but on the Thursday he dined well and then took a boat out on the Thames and there fell forward on his oars. He leaves a wife and, they say, papers of such incriminating nature that half London is in fear, particularly those at court who have entrusted him with their secrets."

"Aye, there was always a steady traffic from this bank of the river to his own," Tom said. "Court ladies – masked; corrupt officials, emboldened citizens, reckless players, wayward wives. They'll miss him now that he is gone. We all will, for he added a spot of colour in a drab world, if only for the rumours he engendered! And yet I fear he was most grossly misunderstood."

"They said he foretold Essex's downfall in Elizabeth's time, and he could see the movements of ships at sea and whether wives were honest, and could make folk fall in love who would not, and procure revenge from afar off, so that no one knew the cause of the disaster," I said with a shudder. "He is not someone that I would have liked to meet!"

"Giles is easily intimidated," Tom laughed. "And yet I believe he would be disappointed if someone were to tell him Forman was merely a great thinker and physician of eccentric leanings."

"No – he was a magician, everybody knows it," I protested. "He cast spells and called up spirits."

"'These metaphysics of magicians

And necromantic books are heavenly,

Lines, circles, letters and characters,

Aye, these are those that Faustus most desires,'"

quoted Tom lugubriously. "Well, well, enough of that. There was one other thing you have not told me of, which happened while I was away . . ."

"Oh? What was that?" I said.

"What did I tell you, Rochester, concerning the Earl of Northampton?"

"Tae hae nothing tae do wi' him," said Robbie like an obedient child.

"And what have you done instead?" said Tom pleasantly.

"In this matter my views differ frae yours, Tom," Robbie said. "You take no care whom you offend. Mysel' I think it does nae harm to be on guid terms wi' as many folk as possible. Northampton has made friendly overtures and I was happy tae accept them."

"Ooh, thinking for ourself, are we?" Tom said lightly. "Rochester, believe me, I know best. Northampton is a cold and calculating monster masquerading as a kind old man. You must not be taken in. It is fortunate that I am now returned and can take you in hand."

Tom's doing so consisted in a complicated series of manoeuvres to procure the position of Secretary of State. In May poor tired Cecil, Earl of Salisbury, died, largely unmourned. The office of king's secretary was originally that of dealing with the king's correspondence and holding the signet seal which authenticated the letters. As secretary a man was to some extent responsible for the security of the realm; he had access to information from at home and overseas. He went between the king and the Privy Council. It was a position of great influence. Everybody wanted to take Salisbury's place. Thomas certainly did. He felt the post was made for him; but meanwhile he supported Henry Neville and arranged for him and Southampton and Sheffield to meet in Robbie's chambers. Sir Ralph Winwood was their other choice. The other contender was the Howards' choice, Sir Thomas Lake. The Earl of Southampton supported Henry Neville his old friend, and Robbie, schooled by Tom, associated himself with them. Neville was a parliamentarian and opposed to alliance with Spain and not much favoured by the king. The Howard man, Lake, supported close ties with Spain. By the juggling involved, Rob and Thomas were become the Howards' political opponents – and yet were they so? Lord Henry, arch-intriguer, would know quite well whose influence lay behind Rob's moves. He understood Rob well enough to know he was lacking in subtlety. Tom was the enemy; and if Rob could be prised away from him, the one-time friendship of the Howards for the king's successful favourite could be renewed. But how to do it?

"Your friend the Earl of Northampton, Robin . . ." said the king.

"My friend, uncle? Is he so?"

"He would be so, and was once, so he says. He tells me that you now think poorly of him, and he fears that this is as a result of slander on the part of one often found close to you. He says his words have been powdered by malicious ingredients. Now, what d'ye suppose he means by that?"

"How should I know?"

"Could it perhaps be Overbury that he means? Does Overbury speak ill tae ye o' Northampton?"

"Och, no," Robbie assured him affably.

"And yet," the king insisted, "Northampton writes tae me of being brought by him into the compass of false dealings with Rochester."

"He writes prettily. Compasses, no less. What does he mean?"

"Dinnae' be pert wi' me, Rob. Attend me. I could say more but all I say is: in your dealings at the court give ear to others beside Overbury. There is always more than one way of assessing a given situation, and the best one is usually the middle path. Overbury is a would-be diplomatist, trying out his not inconsiderable skills. Others have been about the business longer."

Robbie looked so crestfallen at this lecture that the king began to laugh. "Och, Robbie, all I mean tae say is tae advise ye to be what y'are – a sweeting and a charmer and kind tae your auld uncle. Now tell me – hae ye ever thought o' marriage?"

"Good Lord no!" Robbie said alarmed.

"Are ye sae frightened o' the ladies?" chuckled His Majesty. "Aye, but we need 'em, Robin, for our posterity's sake, so think on't, for I will gie ye a grand marriage and be kind tae your bairns."

"Kindness, uncle, would be tae speak nae more tae me about it," Rob said firmly.

"Aye," James agreed. "For it's not all sweetness, as anyone'll tell ye. And they will paint themselves and think tae please us . . . I wonder not sae much that women paint themselves, as that when they are painted, men can love them! And I will not call those women whores that paint, I'll boldly say it is the badge of a whore! Robin, we shall choose your partner very carefully . . ."

In order to stem the rivalry between the opposing factions James took on the position of Secretary of State himself; and Robbie helped him. Strange as it sounds, Rob was thus become to some extent the Secretary of State. Walter James copied out the letters and Thomas advised Rob as to policy. In this Tom played a dangerous game. I knew that when ambassadorial letters arrived from overseas Tom opened them and took notes and then re-sealed them and sent them on to Robbie with instructions and advice. It began to occur to those about the king that if they would use Rob to press for their suit to the king they must also soften Tom, suppliants both great and mean; and I am not a wise man but I was not so stupid as not to guess that some would find this intolerable.

In typical fashion Thomas contrived to offend the Earl of Pembroke who had previously supported him and Robbie against the Howards. I would imagine that Northampton rubbed his hands in glee, for he wrote to Robbie, flattering him, calling him noble-hearted, telling him that he was well rid of Pembroke, and of Southampton – the incorruptible – who, dispirited, turned back to his own affairs.

The Privy Council asked the king to appoint a sufficient man for the place, but James would rather contain the factions and do the work himself than have an efficient administration; for James was not a man that loved paperwork. He remained, however, very close with Robbie, who was now become a privy counsellor, still intimate with Thomas and no enemy to Northampton. This was a situation which pleased neither Thomas nor Northampton. It was inevitable that one would try to oust the other from his hold on Rob's affections.

One afternoon Tom, Rob and I went to see a new play at the Red Bull playhouse in Clerkenwell. This playhouse, which was to become most meaningful to me in later days, was then merely known to me as one that had been converted from an inn. It had a poor reputation amongst courtly folk – the blood-and-thunder plays went down well there, and the beer they sold made the groundlings more vociferous. We took our places in the covered seats at the back and settled to be entertained.

It was a cynical and bitter play, its imagery sickness, deception, storm.

"Fortune's a right whore," sneered Lodovico, prowling the stage; "if she give aught, she deals it in small parcels that she may take away all at one scoop."

Courtly reward and punishment – the characters were speaking against the court, one hoping to better these bad times, and one observing that he wondered how some great men escape banishment – "there's one, the Duke of Brachiano, who by close panderism seeks to prostitute the honour of Vittoria Corombona . . ."

I grew uneasy as I watched. I seemed to hear a play concerning Rob and Frances and the court of King James. Of course, it being set in Italy I must have been mistaken; but I found the play's tone chilling in its implication for ourselves. The lines were heavy with foreboding. "O me accurst . . . Thy rash tongue hath raised a fearful and prodigious storm."

It seemed to me alive with reference to the game that Tom – and Rob to his direction – were playing:

"We are engaged to mischief and must on

The way ascends not straight, but imitates the subtle foldings of a winter's snake –

So who knows policy and her true aspect

Shall find her ways winding and indirect."

Attuned now to see coincidence within the play I found worse to come –

"She is your strumpet..

Uncivil sir, there's hemlock in thy breath

And that black slander."

This was surely redolent of the way that Tom and Robbie spoke of Lady Frances. But my companions plainly saw no similarity, but drank and munched and watched and made their observations on the lad who played Vittoria.

"Next the devil adultery
Enters the devil murder . . .
I will produce a letter
Wherein 'twas plotted he and you should meet
At an apothecary's summer house
Where after wanton bathing and the heat
Of a lascivious banquet . . ."

Yes, yes, I told myself, the mention of an apothecary and straight your mind jumps to poisons; but there was that about the words that brought to mind the house in Paternoster Row, the secret meetings under Mistress Turner's auspices . . .

Murder and lust – how many times before had I beheld them acted on a stage and yet been unaffected? I could not but suppose John Webster's verse the cause of my present discomfiture – I thought it excellently writ. I had in the past been unmoved by the guts of sheep and the livers of pigs slung to and fro to counterfeit the stabbing of a lord, nay, I had laughed uproariously at the same; but it quite chilled my blood to hear Lodovico say:

"To have poisoned his prayer book or a pair of beads
Or the handle of his racket –
That while he had been bandying at tennis
He might have sworn himself to Hell and strook
His soul into the hazard."

We watched Brachiano die of the poison in his helmet; we watched Lodovico and Gasparo gloat:

"Now there's mercury
And copperas
And quicksilver
With other devilish apothecary stuff
A-melting in your politic brains . . ."

Nor did the play leave us with any particular hope other than death's release from the pains of life:

"We cease to grieve, cease to be fortune's slave,
Nay, cease to die, by dying."

As for the court –

"Oh, happy they that never saw the court
Nor ever knew great men but by report!"

I sat back morosely, reflecting that it left one with a hankering for some tried and trusted old favourite, with clowns – but there, we will go and see new plays simply because they are new and we would be diverted.

The play drew an indifferent reception from the crowd; indeed I heard one say there never was a playwright good as old Tom Kyd, and another answered there had been no great plays since *Tambourlaine*. Robbie and Tom both said the play was fair, but it was plain their minds were upon other matters.

"And pull the brim of your hat down low, sweetheart," Tom said. "I know not if you be praised or loathed this week amongst the masses."

"No one will know me," Robbie shrugged. "The common man would not know James himself unless he wore his crown and ermine."

Nonetheless he took Tom's advice, and we made our way out of the playhouse in the crowd, with only myself, it seemed, unsettled by the disturbing power of words.

Rob and I were at the tennis court, he having finished a game, I helping him into his doublet, and both of us half idly watching the game in progress – Prince Harry and David Murray, with a group of courtiers round about them. The day was warm. All of a sudden there was consternation: the prince collapsed and fell into a faint.

The panic in the air was palpable. We hurried forward. After a while the prince opened his eyes, and Murray raised him to his feet.

"On with the game," said Prince Harry.

"Oh, Harry, no," Murray protested. "This would not be wise."

"I demand it," said Prince Harry, his eyes glittering.

"This is not the office of a friend," said Murray. "I will not be the one to tire you further."

"I am not tired," Prince Harry said. "So if not you, then who will finish the game in your place?"

Naturally no one would. Who would risk to be the one with the racket should the prince be taken ill, and blamed thereby for his indisposition? But Prince Harry was angry at his own weakness and must play to prove himself master of his physical state.

"Viscount Rochester," he said, now catching sight of Robbie. "You I know will honour me. I know already to my cost that you are an excellent player, and are not, as these, afraid."

Or the handle of his racket . . . that while he had been bandying at tennis . . .

Rob handed me his doublet and received the racket from the hand of David Murray. A very grim expression was on the face of Prince Harry's friend.

The game was played. The courtiers watched, silent and uneasy. Rob made no pretence this time of letting Prince Harry beat him. He played to win, not at his best, assuredly, since he had played already, but well enough, and won. Prince Harry shook his hand and thanked him for the game. The prince's face was white and drenched in sweat. His servants gathered round. Rob handed the racket to David Murray who received it saying: "If anything had happened to the prince, nothing would have saved you from the Tower."

"I know that," Rob said soberly. "And Prince Harry knew it too."

"Or if the favour which His Majesty bestows upon you had kept you from punishment I would have killed you myself."

"Aye, I understood as much."

"Nonetheless you did the prince a service and I thank you."

"I would do anything the prince asked of me," Robbie answered. "I am sorry that we are not friends."

Murray's lip curled; plain enough he thought there could be no chance of that. But he bowed politely and followed the prince.

It was a summer of great heat. We set off on the Summer Progress. In July we were at Theobalds, Wrest, Bletsoe and Castle Ashby, finishing at Kirby Hall, the splendid Hatton home in Northamptonshire. In August we were at Apethorpe and at Belvoir, looking over a great expanse of land from the castle perched upon the hill. Once or twice it crossed my mind to remember our journey south nine years ago, when His Majesty slept at Belvoir and Rob and I, anonymous as blades of grass, slept where we could. We travelled on to Rufford, Newstead, Nottingham and Leicester; and by September we were at Windsor.

The king startled Rob by proposing a marriage for him with Lady Anne Clifford –

"A great heiress, Robin, and an only child."

And once again I had to expend my energies assuring Robbie all would be well, and put up with his sulks and groans, the side he dare not show to James. In the king's company he was all smiles, all graciousness, the Knight of the Sun; and risked, if otherwise, His Majesty's surprised reproach: "Why now, Robin, where is your smile?"

With me Rob was edgy and terse, his thoughts with Frances. "I dare not tell the king," he said. "I fear he would be angry. I canna' tell what he would do"

We believed the Essexes to be at Chartley. "How can she keep him off for ever?" Rob despaired. "How can a man be close tae her and remain impotent? I shall kill him if he touches her," he said unreasonably.

"You know you will not."

"Aye, I will not," he agreed morosely. "After all, he has the right; he is her husband – that is the part of this affair which is ridiculous."

"It would not matter if he did – be honest," I said with the rationality of the completely disinterested.

"Aye, but it would – that is the damnable thing!" Rob groaned. "Just as it will tae him when he finds out I had her first. Neither of us will be charitable. I wish he would find out – I'd sooner have his open enmity than let him think I am afraid tae face him. I hate this secrecy. But we must preserve her reputation. How he will hate my guts if he ever discovers the truth! I wonder what he will do . . ."

We contemplated the possibilities in silence.

Rob grinned. "Who wouldhae thought that it would all come down tae this when we first met him that day at Burghley and he would hae taken his sword tae me! And I nearly felled him wi' a tree! Burn me!" he said on a sudden thought, "I hope he doesnae' want this business settled wi' a sword now! Ah, but why should he ever find out? She willnae tell him and nor will Anne; and there's only you and Thomas know besides."

As soon as we returned to London the overwhelming need of Lady Essex to be provided with a new winter gown sent her to Anne Turner's house in Paternoster Row, where Robbie, and I in attendance, waited. Rob and Frances ran to each other. Sourly I turned away; but I heard well enough the words of love, the kisses.

"No, I was not at Chartley!" I heard her say. "He was, but I would not go. I stayed in Hounslow at the Aston's."

"Why didnae ye let me know? I thought the worst."

"I dared not; my messenger could have been traced back to me, and besides I did not know where you were."

"These needless anxieties must be stopped . . ."

"There are only two ways to do that," said Lady Frances very plain and clear. "Either we never meet again, or . . . we marry."

I spun round. Marriage, no less? Here was a different matter altogether. *If that thy bent be honourable, thy purpose marriage* . . . it was always the women who remained practical, the man who dreamed and lusted.

"Marry? How can we marry?" said Rob, taken aback.

"If we could marry – if there was a way, would you take it?" She was holding his hands, looking up into his face, feverishly, with shining eyes.

"I would," said Rob, excited and frustrated by his summer weeks of desperate longing.

Then she took him upstairs, and Anne Turner and I played cards at a table, as we had done on previous occasions. Somewhat understandably my heart was not in it.

"What does she mean?" I said. "How may they marry?"

"Her intention is to have her marriage annulled," said Anne. "A marriage that has not been consummated is no marriage. The church permits annulment."

"But Essex would not, surely?"

"Yes, he would. He has agreed. He hates her now, as she him. He would like to be free as much as she would."

"Does he know about Rochester?"

"No, not yet. My lady will tell him as soon as it is established between herself and Rochester that their wishes are the same."

"She will tell him they have been lovers?" I said incredulously.

"No! No, of course not. She will tell him they have fallen in love and plan to marry – a slightly different matter!" Anne laughed brittly. She added with a grim smile: "No one must ever hear about the secret meetings now. The whole plan rests upon her being still a virgin."

I was a little out of my depth here. "But she isn't," I said.

"No," agreed Anne tranquilly.

I grew silent. I suppose that I had always known that Rob must marry. Whether Lady Frances was the one I would have wished for him was immaterial. The whole prospect depressed me beyond words – always to have a woman in our life, to have to pay attention to her wishes, to change our ways to suit her . . . Of course, others handled the same situation, did they not? Wives could be set up in a house in the country, given children to nurture, kept quiet with gifts and small excursions – this new prospect need not be so terrible. Perhaps all would continue as before?

But when I spoke of my doubts and fears to Rob he smiled, a little wanly. "I don't envisage any problems with the lady Frances. You see," he said, not without a certain modest pride, "she loves me to distraction. No, my own fears are more tae do wi' His Majesty and the Howards and wi' Thomas, and not least, wi' the church. To get Frankie to my bed within the law is going tae be a very public business."

No one had thought, during those hot summer months, that Prince Harry was sick unto death. The prince fought his illness all the way. He was never more active. He hunted, swam, worked himself into the ground at tennis. At night he walked alone beside the river while the fickle and inconstant moon lit all the fields with silver. In October he became too weak to stand. He took to his room in St James's Palace, attended by Dr Mayerne, now the king's own physician, and the faithful David Murray.

The king and queen absented themselves from the business of death as soon as all hope had been abandoned – James to Theobalds, Anne to Denmark House, where they waited for the news that soon must follow.

"How can ye – you should be wi' him," said Rob amazed. "How is it ye can go awa'?"

"I am not answerable to folk," said James. "Let's hae nae more o' this. And dinnae' presume upon my friendship tae question what I do; that is no' your place, Robin."

"I ken fu' well where you think that is," Rob scowled.

"Aye, by my side, as my guid companion," James said firmly. "And in that capacity ye'll go awa' wi' me and you'll go wi' a smile. I'll hae no gloomy faces by me."

And Rob went, and smiled; he badly needed the king's favour for the surprise which he was about to spring upon his royal benefactor.

Prince Harry's was a fearsome illness; or do I mean that the treatment was fearsome? – the glysters, the bleedings, the boiled senna and rhubarb, the stag's heart. When all these failed the prince's beautiful auburn hair was shorn and the still warm freshly killed bodies of pigeons and roosters were applied to his head. Fevered, black-lipped, dry-mouthed, tormented-eyed, delirious, the prince endured these ministrations until November, when he died in David Murray's arms.

And at the magnificent funeral of that incomparable prince, the public gaze passed along the great cortège – the banner and the riderless horse, the hearse with its black canopy, the heralds, the black velvet, the black plumes, the lone figure of Sir David Murray, the earls and bishops – to settle upon the twelve-year-old Prince Charles, of whom little was known, and whom Prince Harry had teased unmercifully for his spindly legs.

The poet George Chapman had been promised by Prince Harry that he would pay for Chapman's translation of Homer, but the promise was a spoken one and Chapman had now no claim for reimbursement. He wrote to many men of influence in search of a patron, but none would comply; but then he asked Viscount Rochester, and Rob was glad to pay this tribute to Prince Harry's memory. When the first twelve books of the *Odyssey* were published two years later, they were dedicated to Rob by the grateful poet.

Embarrassingly, almost, the court must hurry the mourning for the prince in order to prepare for the celebration of the wedding of his sister Elizabeth to the Elector Palatine in January.

"A wedding!" said the king rubbing his hands. "We need a wedding. We need good cheer. There's nothing like a wedding!"

A little heartened as to his own situation Robbie vigorously agreed.

One morning early in spring Robbie was lying in his bed in our chambers. I had cleared away his breakfast, which he had taken in bed. There came a knock at the outer door; I opened it. In came the Earl of Northampton. This visit being so unlook'd for, I hardly knew what to say. The old gentleman, however, was completely at his ease.

"Be still, Giles, all is well," he beamed. "Now, if you would remain here where you are, I will attend the viscount. He is within? You need not announce me."

Northampton went into the bedchamber, closing the door behind him. There lay Robbie, naked and tousled in the sheets, and much discomfited, not knowing whether to stand or remain supine. Northampton told him.

"Stay where you are, my dear. " Northampton strolled around the bedchamber, daintily, lightly touching this and that. "I come on business of an intimate nature," he said. "I have been talking to one dear to your heart. The lady Frances has told me everything."

Everything! That was not the plan. Rob's eyes widened, startled.

"She has told me that you and she are deep in love. Now is that so?"

"It is."

"And you would marry?"

"Aye – but – "

"But; and there lies the crux of the matter. However, though there be barriers to your bliss, they are not insurmountable. First I must tell you, Rochester, of my own delight in the proposed match. It has my complete approval and I shall do all I may to bring the business to fruition."

"My lord, I thank you – " Robbie owned to some relief; here was an ally of some stature.

"How would it be if I were to speak to the king on your behalf?" Northampton said. "I have a way with words, and no little skill in the art of persuasion."

"Oh, my lord," Rob twisted round in bed. "I scarcely can frame words tae show my gratitude. If you would do that for me I am your servant all my days."

Northampton smiled, the prospect seeming pleasant to him. He drew near to the bed. He looked at Rob's bare shoulders. Rob followed his gaze. The old earl took the bedcovers and without more ado pulled them back, to the foot of the bed, revealing Robbie where he hay. Then he sat down beside the bed. Rob lay propped on his elbows and met Northampton's gaze. This was a man famed for his debaucheries in bygone days. The Earl of Oxford's lover, a mischief maker of the first degree. Rob recognised the sight of lust in action and accepted it.

"My great-niece has been fortunate," said Northampton, idly stroking Robbie's thigh. "It is not unreasonable for a girl to want a man who knows well how to please her. Before I commit her frail bark to another venture I require a glimpse of the prospect before her. I want no repetition of past pains. I must satisfy myself that all seems as it should be."

Rob offered himself to this perusal, confident of his own excellence. With a practised hand the earl lifted Rob's prick and brought it to life. It swayed, firm and erect.

"A very maypole," purred the old man. "My congratulations!"

"You will not leave me so unsatisfied, my lord?" said Rob provocatively.

"Let me watch you," the earl said, leaning back.

Rob threw himself back and, grasping his cock in his left hand, performed the act with many a manly gasp and grunt until the juices spurted forth in liquid arcs – ("I swear I hit the wall behind me," Rob said.)

Somewhat shaken then, he lay back panting, and Northampton leaned over him and brought his wrinkled bearded visage down to Rob's face and kissed him hard upon the mouth. With Rob still breathing deeply from exertion Northampton hovered low over him like an owl and said: "My great-niece will be the dainty pot of glue that will make the bond more sure betwixt us two. A golden future is yours, Rochester, and I will guide you towards it. The two who might have limited your power are dead . . . Salisbury . . . Harry . . . You are now safe enough – the king plainly adores you. As do we all. But," and here he almost spat, "this golden future does not include Thomas Overbury. There is no place for him in our friendship. Understand this, Rochester, and drop him like a stone. Do you take my meaning?"

"Aye, my lord," said Rob; and as Northampton withdrew, all smiles now, looking like a kind old man, Rob, lying in the cold pools of his self love, shivered.

CHAPTER TWENTY-SIX

"**W**ell, my lord, if you do marry that filthy base woman you will utterly ruin your honour and yourself. You shall never do it by my advice or consent!" Tom was enraged. "What are you about, Rochester? You fuck her – isn't that enough?"

"I don't enjoy dishonesty," Rob began.

"Oh, you enjoy it well enough," Thomas said sarcastically. "And you now would have the church's approval for it."

"And yours, Tom. And yours most of all."

It was a few days after the Earl of Northampton's visit to Rob's bedchamber and the scene the same, Rob in his bed although the day was well advanced, rising late his custom. In the footsteps of the earl came Thomas and upon the same concern. The difference was in attitude thereto.

"See – Giles here doesnae' snarl and stamp; now why should you?" said Rob in a placatory tone.

I straightened my face into the fine example of a man who did not snarl and stamp, the worthy pupil, the polite child.

"Giles is a hypocrite," Tom said dismissively and truthfully. "Giles always takes the path of least resistance; you may lead him anywhere. But at heart he likes this hideous plan no more than I do. Through his misguided affection for you he has decided to say nothing, when he would like to strangle you, as I would!"

"Giles – ?" demanded Robbie.

"I think Lady Frances very beautiful," I hedged, here telling no lie.

"So is the female leopard; but she battens on the entrails of the browsing deer! Giles, she is a Howard," Thomas groaned. "A pack animal. In her train come Suffolk and his grisly wife – the senile Earl of Nottingham – the brothers and sisters – Arundel her cousin, all warts and moles and bad skin and a greed for the amassing of paintings – and the wizened old fox himself, Northampton. All her family are either buffoons or villains, and through Rochester they'll get closer to the king and all the nation's wealth and power."

This was so near the truth that I said nothing.

"Tom, say you'll gie me your blessing," Robbie pleaded. "Everything is going sae well now. Northampton has spoken tae His Majesty. Tae my relief the king is pleased. I never thought he would be. He says he only wants my happiness, and hers – an it can be done wi' honour and through the church. He promises us a splendid wedding and gifts an' a', and I am as high in his favour as ever I was. Now all I need is your goodwill. Even the Earl of Essex has put up nae resistance."

Robbie winced at the memory of Essex's speech of concession. The earl had approached him in the Stone Gallery.

"Regarding the matter which concerns us, Rochester," he said in clipped tones, "I think it fair to let you know that I shall not stand in your way in that which you propose. I loved the lady when I came from France; now I do not. If I believed her worthy of a conflict between us twain I would fight to the last to keep her; but I do not believe her so. I shall not say what I now consider her, but I will say that you are welcome to her. And there's an end."

"Nay, there is not so," Rob protested. "There is my thanks for your stepping aside sae kindly. I have nae wish tae cause you pain. I shall endeavour tae take great care o' the lady. I hope you'll no' think ill o' me for loving one whom you once loved."

Essex said dourly: "I have thought ill of you as long as it has been my misfortune to know you and I see no reason to change my opinion. Common courtesy demands some interchange between us at this juncture; I would not otherwise give you the time of day."

And Essex bowed and left, leaving Rob, as he put it, gulping like a goldfish.

"Her mother," Rob told Thomas, "is in raptures and says I am an ornament tae the family and she could fancy me hersel'. Her father exhibits less excitement and indeed told me that he preferred the Earl of Essex, he being an English nobleman. . ."

"And you a Scots upstart."

"That was implied, aye," Rob agreed drily. "But he will tolerate me, since he has no choice. Indeed I ken fu' well his true views for I was told them. "The fellow is straight-limbed, well-favoured, strong-shouldered and smooth-faced, with some sort of cunning and show of modesty; though God wot, he knows well enough when to show his impudence!" But the best thing is that His Majesty supports us and has promised to do all he can tae help us."

"So all is going very well for you," said Thomas unpleasantly.

"And I have been advised," continued Robbie boldly, "tae see less of you, Tom, for the moment. I tell you this as kindly as I may, for it is not a kind thing tae say; but I think you'll understand that the matter being delicate. . ."

"Do you realise how completely you need my goodwill?" said Thomas suddenly.

"I do need it, and I would like tae have it," said Rob, not seeing what Thomas was implying.

"One false word from me and your plot comes to nothing."

"Plot? There is no plot."

"If the marriage is unconsummated then the lady is a virgin, yes?"

Rob squirmed a little.

"We know otherwise," said Thomas meaningfully.

"Aye, but you being my friend," said Rob warily, "it wouldnae' cross your mind tae speak of what you know."

"That is something which I will consider at my leisure," Tom said. "Meanwhile I will have less talk from you of when or not I shall be seen by you. This directive has a whiff of Howardry behind it and I like it not. Climb out of bed now, Viscount Rochester."

"Why?"

"I have been teased long enough by the sight of your bare shoulders; I would see the rest."

Grumbling, Rob emerged.

"And now," purred Thomas pointing to the table, "you must keep me sweet, therefore if you would drape yourself face down you shall best please me by submitting to my pleasure."

Sulkily Rob complied. Tom smeared his bending body with the oils I used to smooth his skin, and entered him, the slippery unguent streaming down Rob's thighs.

"I think you are in danger of forgetting what you most enjoy," said Thomas rhythmically. "And you do enjoy it, don't you, Rochester?"

Rob mumbled that he did.

"Remember this," said Tom, "when next some Howard gives you some command: it is that I have made you what you are and all your undeniable success comes from my shaping of you. When I first saw you, you spoke like a pagan Pict and though you are still handicapped thus, folk more or less understand you, at least most of the time. I've led you, guided you, directed you, advised you, composed your letters, told you what to say, explained ambassadorial correspondence to you till the king believes you curiously astute. Your Howard would-be masters and your Howard strumpet would not look at you if it were not for all the work that I have done to give you a veneer of civilisation. You are very beautiful, Viscount Rochester, but you are not clever; and you need me. Whether you now rise or fall, my dear, you take me with you."

Robbie said nothing, but his gasps and grunts had punctuated Tom's recital. Thomas let him go, washed swiftly, and leaving Rob to do the same, led me through into our sitting chamber and shut the door behind us.

"Tom, don't goad him," I warned. "I think that was a mistake."

"Nonsense – he loves a good fuck."

"That one savoured of possessiveness."

"I was angry," Tom said unrepentantly. "Giles, what do you really think of this marriage notion?"

"Appalling; but it's what he wants."

"It will be a disaster," Tom said flatly. "And of course there is a way to stop it."

"Thomas, he would never forgive you if you blocked the nullity process."

Tom shrugged. "He would in time. He needs me too much." He frowned thoughtfully. "What do you suppose it will be, this annulment business – a group of divines quoting scripture and theology, with Lady Frances swearing blind she's *virgo incorrupta*? And then for fear of James they'll all agree and shuffle home? It would put the cat among the pigeons if I offered myself as a witness. I have all her letters, you know. I took copies, particularly of the ones where she wrote 'Burn this'."

The words were scarce out of his mouth when there was a knock at the door, and Copinger escorted in two visitors. Women, veiled.

"I told these ladies that they might enter," said Copinger. He used his special subservient voice, but I knew he had hoped that just for once he'd catch somebody *in flagrante delicto*. How nearly he had missed the fulfilment of his ambition gave me cause to shudder.

The ladies divested themselves of the facial veils and showed themselves to be the Lady Frances and Mistress Turner. Tom and I in our astonishment murmured pleasantries which they acknowledged hurriedly.

"Giles!" Frances turned to me as to a friend. "I know we should not be here but it was yourself and Sir Thomas that we wished to see. Is. . . Robert within?"

"Yes; he is still abed," I said composedly.

Beside me Thomas coughed as he disguised his amusement.

"We want to set in motion the plans for the annulment of my marriage," Frances said. "What I have to say is personal and private – I could not say this in some passageway, meeting you by chance. Giles! I need your word of honour that you will keep silent about what you know. . . regarding Robert and myself."

"You have it," I said readily enough.

"Oh Giles," she breathed. "You are an angel."

"No I am not," I assured her. "But I am completely loyal to Robbie."

"He knows it!" I winced at her patronising tone, her reassurance on Rob's behalf grating.

"And. . . Sir Thomas?" She looked tremulously, dubiously, beseechingly towards Tom. We all did. Conscious of what had just taken place in the bedchamber and knowing that Tom would certainly be so and no doubt relishing the present moment's piquancy, I prayed that he would act discreetly. *I have just fucked your lover; he is busy in the bedroom, washing himself* – I believed him capable of saying as much.

"My lady?" Thomas said.

"Rochester tells me that you know our secret."

"This is true."

"We are in your hands, Sir Thomas. Please be kind." She looked so soft and vulnerable that I myself was almost tempted to believe her the untouched virgin she would claim to be.

"In all sincerity I cannot give that promise, madam," Tom said, "which Giles Rawlins gave so freely."

"Why not?"

"I have Rochester's best interests at heart and I am not yet entirely decided whether marriage is the best thing for him at this time."

"Oh?" she said in a steely tone. "And what do you know of the married state?"

It was done – they had crossed swords. Inwardly I groaned.

"Sir Thomas does not mean to imply anything other than that it may be more apropriate for Rochester to marry earlier or later than the time that you intend, my lady," I waffled on unhappily.

"I believe I know what Sir Thomas means," said Frances.

"No, not so," I protested, looking daggers at Tom. "Thomas, reassure the lady."

But Tom continued, looking at Frances, unabashed:"I think your great-uncle may be unaware of the particular closeness of my bond with Viscount Rochester. Perhaps you might remind him, my lady, that I am to be consulted upon matters of importance concerning the viscount? Appropriate treatment on the one hand produces an appropriate response."

"I see," said Frances a little breathlessly. But she attempted sweetness once again. "Sir Thomas, I own I have been reckless. . . You see, I am a fool where Robert is concerned. You are his friend; therefore you understand the potency of his charms. I can refuse him nothing."

"Aye, my lady," said Tom pleasantly, " and your letters show as much."

"My – my letters?" She was pale as any ghost now. "Did he not burn them?"

"I made copies," Thomas said, "thinking he might like to read them over again."

There was a horrid little silence.

"But you would not of course disgrace a lady whose only crime has been to love excessively?" Opponents, they faced each other measuringly.

"The lady might have thought more of the consequences," Thomas said, "on those many occasions when she studied astrology through an upstairs window in Paternoster Row."

"I beg your pardon?" said Frances baffled.

"It is understood," said Thomas silkily, "that the best way to study the heavens is to lie upon your back. . ."

Frances caught her breath. She controlled herself immediately. "May I have your word," she said, "that you will do nothing, at least for the moment? I will, of course, pay any price."

Tom flashed me a look of gratification. Then "you have my word," he said. "Nothing for the moment."

"Giles, be so good as to give my kind regards to Robert," Frances murmured hurriedly. "Now we must be going. Anne?"

The door closed after them.

"How very pleasing," Thomas smiled, "to have the lady Frances eating from my hand. I think that I could grow to like it."

I opened the inner door. "Rob, you can come out now."

"Was that Frances?" Rob asked in amazement, beautiful and wholesome, naked but for a towel about his loins.

"Yes, your catopard was here," said Thomas carelessly.

"Whatever did she want?" said Rob.

"Could you hear?" I asked uncomfortably.

"No, you had shut the door. I heard your voices, and Giles at first; but you spoke like conspirators. What did you speak about?"

Thomas and I looked at one another.

"It doesnae' matter," Robbie said. "Frances will tell me everything."

"Rochester," said Thomas, "without jest I tell you that I would not trust that whore an inch. She is all varnished rottenness."

"Oh Thomas," Rob said wearily, "your jealousy has made you monstrous sour."

"She will subvert and overthrow you," Thomas declared. "She has already deserted one husband. Who would be so foolish as to cast away all upon a woman noted for immodesty. She is a strumpet and her mother a bawd."

"Have done, Tom. Will nothing stop your mouth?"

"Nothing; her unlook'd for proximity has inspired me," Tom said bright-eyed. "I see she simpers as if she had no teeth but lips; I see she reads over her face every morning and blots out pale and withered. She is the cook and the meat, dressing herself all day to be tasted with better appetite at night. She is a highway to the devil – he that looks upon her with desire begins his voyage; who enjoys her is at his journey's end."

Rob clapped ironically. Thomas grinned and bowed. I laughed uneasily – so it had been a performance merely, Tom's diatribe?

"Now let me show you what you should be looking for in a wife," said Tom producing a slim volume.

"Och, your long dull poem," Rob said, eyeing it. "I wonder you are not ashamed tae be sae full o' self-conceit you carry it about wi' ye."

"I brought it here on purpose for your instruction," said Tom smoothly. "And you shall read it."

"I would sooner get dressed; I'm awfu' cold now," Rob answered. "Giles – ?"

"Stay where you are, Giles," Thomas ordered. "I have marked the lines – now let me hear you read them, Rochester." He thrust the book at Rob who took it and cast his eyes down the page. "'O, look upon this picture and on this?'" he said sarcastically. "Is that the way of it?"

"Read it," Tom commanded.

"I'll not."

"You will, or I'll go straightways shout in the Stone Gallery that who would fuck withLady Essex shall find easy passage."

"He will not, Rob," I said distressed. "Tom, cease your provocation."

"God damn you, Thomas," Rob said; and in a sullen voice he read: "The Wife, by Thomas Overbury. You seem to have marked for me:

'Let me forget her sex. . .
Beasts' likeness lies in shape, but ours in mind,
Our souls no sexes have; their love is clean. . .
that goodly frame we see of flesh and blood
is but the lay part –
the worth of it is nothing that is seen
but only that it holds a soul within. . .
and all the carnal beauty of my wife
is but skin deep, but to two senses known. . .
her birth goes to my children, not to me –
rather had I that active gentry find,
vertue, than passive from her ancestry.
Rather in her alive one vertue see
than all the rest dead in her pedigree.'"

Rob paused, the blatant reference to Frances and her family not lost upon him; and continued somewhat through gritted teeth:

"'She must be good. . .
by good I would have holy understood. . .
next good, an understanding wife, by nature wise. . .
passive understanding. Learning and wit in womankind
what it finds malleable makes frail

and doth not add more ballast but more sail.
Domestic charge doth best that sex befit –
their leisure 'tis corrupteth womankind. . .
their carriage, not their chastity alone
must keep their name chaste from suspicion. . .'"

"That seems to be all that you have marked, Thomas," Rob said evenly. "Have I your permission tae put on my clothes?"

I marvelled at Tom's obtuseness as he stood there warm in his velvets watching Rob shiver and read out the sententious and didactic verse. I could see plain enough that Rob was angry, and that he did not dare throw down the book would further gall him.

"Do you see any relevance to Lady Frances in my image of the perfect wife?" said Tom with something of a smirk.

"I do not. You paint a creature not of this world."

"It has pleased some Puritans that have read the manuscript," agreed Tom with an affected laugh.

"Take your book again," Rob said, returning it.

"Oh, dress him, Giles," said Thomas. "Squeeze him into his wasp-waisted doublet. I daresay that affairs of state attend him and all the world knows that his majesty cannot proceed without the benefit of Viscount Rochester's advice."

The beautiful winter gown which Lady Essex had had made at Paternoster Row by Mistress Turner was black velvet, sewn all over with small pearls and gold thread, and was garnished with the latest fashion, Mistress Turner's own creation – yellow starched cuffs and an enormous yellow starched ruff. How grotesque it sounds in the writing of it – yet it was a fashion which the ladies of the court fell upon in rapture, and to some extent an exclusive one, for Mistress Turner kept the receipt for yellow starch a secret. It flattered Lady Frances – not every woman can wear yellow without looking bilious; but she could, and she flaunted her painted beauty with a brittle febrile gaiety.

She sent Thomas a silver chalice, which he took to be a kind of reward for his continued silence, and he was quite puffed up with self-conceit as one might be who believes he holds the fate of pretty people in his hand.

One day Tom said to me: "An odd thing happened last night, Giles. . . I was coming back from the Mermaid. . . I was with Ben Jonson. We had taken a short cut down an alley, when a man sprang upon us with a knife. We saw his shadow and were alerted. There was a struggle and our assailant fled. Ben picked up the knife. He is grown monstrous portly now, a great bear. He laughed and said there were a dozen men he knew who longed to put a bodkin in his guts. He assumed without question that the dagger was for him. He more or less convinced me. . . but I think I shall go walking down no more dark alleys. . ."

April now, and early evening. I was arranging Rob in all his finery, for a banquet – the doublet of striped cloth of gold and silver cut with yellow taffeta lay upon a chair. Half dressed, sipping a glass of wine he sat; I combed his hair. I liked to do this. We had taken to frizzing his hair into curls, which well became him, though it took a long time to create.

Into our chamber came Thomas frowning. Without preamble he said: "Rochester, what do you make of this?"

"Of what?"

"I have been offered an advancement. Archbishop Abbot sent for me and offered me a post, he said, that would be much to my advancement."

"That's wonderful, Tom. . ."

"No, it is not. It is not wonderful at all. The damned thing is in Russia."

"Russia?" Rob blinked. He was recalling a conversation that he once had with King James. *He would need to acquire a liking for cabbage. . . and drinking. . . and plunging naked into icy water.* "Russia? Do you think it is a joke?"

"No, I do not," said Thomas irritably. "God's teeth, it was the holiest of our churchmen broached the matter. Russia, no less! They still live in the eleventh century there."

"Then you must not go."

"You think I should refuse?"

"How can you not?"

"My dear, it is not diplomatic to refuse an offer which the king has thought fit to bestow upon one!"

"You have nothing tae fear since you are under my protection."

Thomas smiled a little at Rob's choice of phrase. "Yes, of course, you have some influence with the King." Tom mused: "I wondered if it could be something of a plot?"

"A plot by whom?"

"The Howards of course. To get me out of the country during the annulment proceedings."

Rob grinned. "Well, you would certainly be out of the country if you were in Russia."

Tom looked darkly at him; this was no time for flippancy. "You could not afford to let me go," he said.

196

"I – ?"

"Before I went I'd send copies of her letters to Archbishop Abbot."

"Then you must not go, Tom," Rob said easily. "But you don't need tae threaten me with betrayal tae the archbishop. I will not have you go tae Muscovy because you would hate it there, and moreover it would be seen tae be insulting tae me. Everyone would laugh and say: look how he thinks he has the King's affection and he couldnae' save his fancy friend frae being sent off tae the icy wastes of northern climes! And I do hae influence, Tom. Believe me, you shall not go. Tell me what you want and I'll speak tae Northampton and the King."

"What if I were to accept," suggested Tom, "thereby causing no offence; and you step in and say you will not have it so?"

"Very well, if that's what you would like. You are probably right – it sounds like a conspiracy and a clumsy one at that. And we'll not have it, eh?"

The upshot of the matter was that the Russian idea was abandoned, due, we understood, to Rob's intervention; but another possibility was presented in its stead. Lord Ellesmere and the Earl of Pembroke were sent to offer Tom the embassy of Paris or the Low Countries – he could make his own choice.

"There now," Robbie beamed. "It's what you've always wanted. Take it."

Thomas hesitated. "It is what I always wanted. But to be offered it now. . . at this time. . . Rochester, I don't like it. It seems odd to me. As if some people have got together and decided it. . . I may refuse. I'll think about it. They said that I could think about it."

"Take it, Thomas," Rob advised. Then he took Thomas by the arms and grasped him. "Take it."

Tom gently disentangled himself. "It would not matter if I refused it," he said. "You will not abandon me. You dare not. Dare you?"

"No," said Robbie. "No, you may be sure I will look after you, no matter what. There is too much between us."

Very late one night Tom came round to our chambers and settled himself down and insisted that he would see Robbie.

"Well, so you may," I temporised. "But he is not yet returned."

"Where is he?" Tom demanded.

I said nothing.

"Is he with the catopard?" Tom said angrily. "Is he so careless of his reputation and her status? Is he so sure his dainty annulment will go ahead so smoothly? The conceit of him. . . and oh, the fool! The poor misguided fool!"

I began to say some worthy words on the subject of forgiveness and believing the best of people and the like.

"Shut your mouth, Giles; you know nothing," he cut across me crudely. "Why do you think I am here? Wait until you hear me tell him what I have found out about his virgin bride!"

"Not bad news, I hope?" I said sanctimoniously but with gathering disquiet.

"You shall hear," he promised me ominously. "You shall judge for yourself."

He would say nothing to me, and I had to wait in the oppressive silence of the candlelit darkness, suffering Tom's enigmatic presence. When I could endure it no longer I opened the door and went looking for Rob in the passageway outside. Tom's manservant Harry Payton loitered there. A wall brand burned low in an aperture. Tom followed me out of the room. At that moment came Rob all unsuspecting. When he saw Tom his face fell.

"Och, are ye here?"

"Were you with that base vile woman?" Tom demanded bluntly.

"Go frae me, Thomas," Rob said wearily. "I want nae more o' this."

"Then maybe I should indeed leave you, if that's what you want," said Thomas. "Perhaps it would be better if we parted. But you'll regret it if we do."

"D'ye think tae frighten me?" Rob cried. "D'ye think I cannae' do wi'out ye?"

"Without me you're nothing," Tom said, anger growing. "Without me you'll have to stand on your own two legs."

"My legs are strong enough."

They stood there blazing at each other, equally enraged, the shadows flickering upon their faces, Payton and I awed and silent witnesses. Their voices echoed down the distant gallery – I dreaded to think who might be listening. But it was night – and all folk were abed, were they not?

"You'll not get rid of me," warned Thomas, "by thinking to shove me overseas. Is that the way our friendship is to end?"

Rob's face grew full of love and pain. "Och, Thomas. . ." he began helplessly. I think if Tom had shown willingness then he would have held out his arms and received him; but Tom turned upon his heel and stormed away. I left Robbie and ran after Tom.

"Thomas!" I said, drawing level with him in the dark and quivering silence of the Stone Gallery. "Come back! Reconsider!" A thought struck me then. "What had you to tell him? You came on purpose. Go back and tell him now."

"Oh, let him stew," snapped Tom. "He does not deserve enlightenment. Why should I let him know that Frances Howard uses witchcraft?"

Then he strode off into the shadows, Payton with him, leaving me to wonder at his dark words as I made my way back to Rob's chambers.

In the morning Thomas let Lord Ellesmere and the Earl of Pembroke know that he refused their offer of an embassy to Paris or the Low Countries. He told them that he wanted no preferment which took him out of the country and that he was unwell and troubled with the spleen – as no doubt he was.

It was from Copinger of all people that I heard the news that at six o' clock in the evening Tom had been arrested in the Council Chamber and conveyed by the Clerk of the Council and two guards unto the Tower of London. He had been taken there by boat.

"And monstrous shaken by it all," said Copinger. "His head in his hands, if you'll pardon the expression, seeing where he was bound! Consigned to the Lieutenant of the Tower as close prisoner for contempt against His Majesty. All very sudden."

Chapter Twenty-Seven

Scarcely having recovered my senses at the shock of hearing this information I hurried back to our lodgings where I found Robbie writing a letter. That he was not dictating this to Walter James gave me to suppose that it was for the lady Frances.

"Robbie!" I said, leaning back against the closed door. "Thomas has been taken to the Tower."

"I know that," said Robbie.

"You know that? Yes, of course you do – you are a privy councillor. Then why was I not told and why did I at length hear it from Copinger? You must have known it then last night when I saw you to bed; and this morning, when I dressed you for the day. And you said nothing."

"Well, I knew you would be vexed," said Rob, not meeting my eyes.

"Had you known that they proposed to send him to the Tower?"

"No, of course not. That is, I knew it when they sent for him tae the council meeting."

"Could you not have prevented it? Where were you when he was arrested? You surely did not stand by and watch?"

199

"No; I absented myself. It would have been in the poorest taste for me tae have been present."

"But upon what pretext is he arrested?" I said. "Because he would not go to France? That seems a highly spurious reason for so dire a punishment! The Tower, no less. . ."

"But you know well enough it is the conventional response – the King's displeasure – it has always been justification enough to send a person tae the Tower. It will not be for long. And listen, Giles, I have had some say in the conditions of his imprisonment."

"Indeed? Such as what? A prison is a prison."

"Sit down, Giles, and be calm." Robbie put down his pen and faced me. " At my insistence he is in a comfortable chamber where the air is good, and windows both tae the water and within the Tower. He's in the Garden Tower and I am told it is a salubrious dwelling with herbs and flowers at the door. In the upper chamber resides no less a person than Sir Walter Raleigh and he has made his place of imprisonment much like a place of study. Thomas will come tae nae harm."

"You will then persuade the king to release him? You were successful with the Muscovy appointment. It should be easy for one so high in the King's regard," I added not without irony.

"Listen, Giles," said Robbie. "Listen – I do not like Thomas's imprisonment any more than you do. But – you must see how monstrous convenient it has fallen out for me?"

I waited in a stubborn silence.

"He told me he would work against me," Rob continued. "He told me I should never have the annulment, that he would prevent it. He told me I would never wed the lady Frances if he had anything tae do wi' it. He told her he had kept her letters and would use them against her. Burn me," he said with a sudden burst of anger, "it is a great relief tae me tae hae him under lock and key!" He took a breath. "Only till the annulment, Giles. Only till then."

"Had you a hand in this – it falls so neatly into place for you?"

"Of course not," Robbie snapped. "Is this my reward for being honest wi' ye? He threatened to appear at the annulment hearing and tell them Frances is nae maid. What would ye hae me do – release him and gie him my blessing? It suits me well tae keep him in the Tower and silent. Afterwards, when I am wed, it will not matter." Then he added wrily: "And anyway he was becoming far too free wi' me. What does he think I am – his little whore, that he can fuck me when he pleases? And not always gently either. There was one day when I could barely sit down after, and the king was looking at me very oddly as we worked over some papers." He grinned at me then, looking young and boyish, inviting me to laugh. I could not. It had just occurred to me that I must be the one to write and let Tom's parents know what had happened. I dreaded to think about the weepings, lamentations and gnashing of teeth in the house at Bourton-on-the-Hill.

"Will you go visit him?" I asked.

"Good Lord no!" Robbie cried, adding more gently: "but I will keep in constant touch, wi' letters."

"Do you object if I do?"

"Giles, I dinna' think ye will be able," Rob said carefully. "He's close confined, ye see. That means he may not speak tae those who might carry his information tae the proceedings; nor write a letter."

"I shall attempt to see him nonetheless."

"Aye, if ye like, but hae a care for yoursel' – don't anger anyone within the Tower. They say Sir William Wade the lieutenant is a hard severe man."

"Oh, Rob," I said. "I hope you know what you are doing."

Rob brought his fist down on the table. "Right – since ye would hae me say it: no I do not feel easy about it; I feel a worm. There – are ye satisfied?" He looked at me almost beseechingly. "But he'll be out again before we know it – trust me, for it is the truth, I swear it!"

I did go to the Tower. All I proved by that fruitless excursion was that Rob's surmise was accurate; for I got no further than the gatehouse and was turned away upon stating my business. As I came away, I encountered Laurence Davies, Thomas's man, on the same errand as myself. This was not his first attempt.

"Oh, Master Rawlins," he complained, "this is an odd affair. What do you think of it? They would not permit my master to have any of his servants with him. I offered my services and so did Payton. We'd have gladly gone in there with him. Well – not gladly, perhaps, but we'd have gone. What kind of business is it when a man of grace and learning should endure sudden imprisonment alone with no manservant? I heard it was by the King's express wishes!"

"I hear that Sir Thomas is lodged comfortably," I said soothingly. "Viscount Rochester assured me that Sir Thomas has good airy chambers in the Garden Tower, where Sir Walter Raleigh lodges."

"The Garden Tower, is it?" scoffed Davies. "Don't you know its other name – the Bloody Tower?"

There was something that I had to speak of, though I knew that it would anger Robbie. I said, one evening as I set his hair: "Before he was arrested, Thomas told me something. He said that Lady Frances dabbled in witchcraft."

"And you believed him?" Rob said scornfully.

"Why should he say that if he had not proof?"

"Why? Because he would say anything tae annoy me and tae spoil my friendship wi' her – any low mean trick. That one is sae common an accusation made against a woman one mislikes I am surprised at Tom's lack of imagination."

"But what if it were true?"

Rob made a noise of irritation. "You've seen her, Giles; you know her. She's no' the kind tae deal wi' midnight hags in dark places. She's a creature o' light. Torchlight – sunlight. She has nae capacity for deception."

We thought about it for a moment. I knew what he meant. Frances had that about her which sparkled – her eyes, her jewels, the glints in her hair. A creature of the sunlight? In all fairness I could not but agree with Robbie. And Rob then put into words that which I thought.

"Why would she need tae dabble in the powers o' darkness? She has everything she wants. All her life she has had everything she wants. If she wants something, her family can get it for her – a new horse, a winter gown, a part in the Twelfth Night masque –"

" – you," I added without hesitation. Somehow that had seemed the logical conclusion to the list.

"Me," Rob agreed wrily, and laughed. "But I had some say in that, I think. Giles, let's hae nae more seditious talk, eh? Forget what Thomas said – his spite and rancour drove him."

With Thomas under lock and key Rob grew bolder in his dealings with Lady Frances. They were together openly now, and that meant that sometimes she visited his chambers and that sometimes they rode out into the countryside where they had the key to a house in Hammersmith, owned by some relation of Anne Turner's. I never went there. It was plain enough that the divorce and marriage were expected to go ahead, and although I did not much relish it I would have felt the same distaste about any lady else whom Rob might choose, and so I settled to put up with it.

In May the situation at the Tower was altered. Sir William Wade the stern lieutenant was dismissed, and in his place came Sir Gervaise Elwes, and this Sir Gervaise was, it seemed, a more pliant fellow, permitting letters to pass in and out of the Tower, and, more to the point, the daily visitor.

And thus I found myself, not without some apprehension, entering at last the dreaded portals of that mighty fortress.

To my astonishment I knew the man, this new lieutenant; that is, I remembered his name and having met him on the journey south when James first came to England. I remembered how he found himself in Heaven to be close to so many 'great ones', and became a knight at Burghley. He did not remember me, but after all I was not great. Here he now was, a grey-haired well built man about fifty years of age, with a quiet pleasant manner – a family man, I heard; I found his presence reassuring.

I was escorted to his lodgings by a man I thought I recognised. It was the under-keeper. After giving him barely a glance I did not study him further, only having the sensation that there was that about him which seemed familiar and somehow disturbing. But I put this from my mind, concern for Thomas and my own uneasiness in my surroundings taking precedence.

I conversed briefly with Sir Gervaise Elwes within his lodgings, and he explained the situation to me.

"I may not permit you, sir, to enter Sir Thomas Overbury's lodging; but you come from Viscount Rochester and are therefore privileged. You may speak to Sir Thomas at his window as you pass and you may call into my house to deliver letters and receive them, if they are permitted letters."

I did not at the time query what he meant by 'permitted letters'. It was enough that I might see my cousin and speak with him.

Whether one chose to call it the Garden Tower or the Bloody Tower, the place where Thomas was lodged was a small square tower above an archway. It was two storeys high, and the upper chambers housed Sir Walter Raleigh – and at times, his wife, young son and three servants. A walled garden lay between it and the lieutenant's lodging, and there was a battlemented walkway along the leads where the inmates might take the air. In the main courtyard of the Tower there was much coming and going – sellers of merchandise, servants with messages, guards eating their bread in the sunshine, little children playing, and lugubrious ravens waddling amongst it all. From the lieutenant's kitchen came the smells of cooking – of beef and beer. To my surprise it all had the air of a busy village. It was a May morning and I found nothing to alarm me. Relief made me perhaps over sanguine. I called up cheerily to Thomas.

The pleasure of speaking to Thomas at his window was, I found, a dubious one. The window was fairly high up, and therefore all converse must be shouted. Here was no opportunity for whispered intimacies; no wonder I was permitted the privilege. Thomas leaned from the window and I stood beneath.

"Thomas! Are you well?"

"What do you think?" seethed my cousin. "No, I am not well, and I am unlikely so to be while I am in this place. The room is damp and chill and I am sorely tried to find myself here at all. Tell Rochester I'll take the damned embassy, to France or Muscovy or wherever they would wish to send me – it matters not. I'm sick with mental fear and heartily baffled and confused. And you ask if I am well – no, I am scarce like to be well."

"I am permitted to talk with you and hope to cheer you a little."

"Nothing will cheer me but to be released."

"Try and be brave, Tom; this dreadful captivity may only be for a short while."

"May?" He seized on the word. " What do you know? How long must I be here?"

"Indeed I do not know! I only spoke to comfort you."

"Giles!" Thomas hissed, looking about. "That man who was with you just now – do you know who he is?"

"He's the under-keeper," I whispered back, and therefore naturally went unheard.

"He used to work for Mistress Turner!" Thomas practically hung out of the window to frame his words in a low tone. "He took the letters between him and her. This means he is a servant of the catopard."

Of course! So that was where I had seen him. I remembered now that on the occasions when Rob entrusted his letters to my hand to give to Frances's messenger, sometimes it had been Richard Weston. It was simply that I did not connect that fellow with the holding of a position of importance within the Tower. I looked back over my shoulder.

"I believe our conversation can be heard from the lieutenant's lodging," I replied unhappily. "Best keep your thoughts to yourself. I shall come whenever I can to see you, Tom; be of good cheer."

We spoke inconsequentially for a while; and dismally I understood that this would be the way of it.

I asked Anne Turner about Richard Weston; but she said there was no secret about his appointment as lieutenant's assistant.

"He was bailiff to my husband," she explained. "He's very trustworthy. An admirable man for a position of responsibility."

What did I know? It sounded a perfectly reasonable explanation. I gave the matter no more thought. Somebody had to be under-keeper – why not he?

Meanwhile Rob was well content to receive a letter from Northampton telling him that the divorce proceedings were now to begin, and Essex would put up no stumbling block. Frances added her signature to the letter, and Northampton did not doubt that God would bless her new bargain, adding a coy jest – that he hoped she would find better pen and ink in her chamber next time.

"It's awfu' kind of Essex to take it sae well," Rob told Northampton. "I dinnae' think that I could sit quietly by and let the world think that I couldnae' raise my prick."

"And if you did," purred Northampton, eyeing him lazily, "who would believe you?"

An odd thing happened about that time – some wretched female imprisoned for theft, one Mary Woods, confessed that the jewel in question was a reward for her from a great lady who had tried to procure poisons from her. Which great lady? Who but my lady Essex! This Mary was a wise woman known as Cunning Mary; and she said that my lady Essex came to her for a kind of poison which would lie in a man's body three or four days without swelling. Cunning Mary had no notion for which gentleman the poison was intended, but when ladies came to her on errands such as this the poison was usually intended for their husbands.

There were some odd looks cast at Lady Frances while this rumour circulated. She bore herself bravely, brazening it out, backed by her kindred's care and bold upon the arm of the King's favourite. But secretly and in Rob's company and even before myself she showed herself to be distressed.

"How vile some people be!" she cried. "Who can have begun this horrid tittle-tattle! If ever one is seen to be happy and successful there are always tongues to wag to try to bring a person down. Especially a woman. They hate to see a woman rise and achieve all her desires. They cannot know how hurtful. . . Why, this perfidious creature is a lowly laundress and a thief. Would they believe her word before mine?"

It was Lady Frances's word that was believed, largely, I suspect, because the Earl of Essex plainly lived and had fallen victim to no poison plot; but partly because Cunning Mary was so easily discredited. Apparently she had thieved before, and when she was found out, she always in revenge accused the woman whose jewels she had stolen of giving them to her in return for poison. Enough other similar cases were discovered to show Mary Wood a fraud.

"And no' sae cunning either," Rob laughed heartily. "You see," he said to me in private, "that must hae been what Thomas had heard about when he spoke tae you o' witchcraft. Such a paltry matter, as it turns out. . . It seems tae me there's something about Lady Frances which draws envy and malice tae her. She has everything, ye see – she comes o' noble stock, pampered frae birth, rich, beautiful, and that beauty plain for a' the world tae see. Some women hide their breasts wi' gauze because there is some defect, but Frances is perfect and she owns it. But there's nae wickedness in her. She's like the lady in the play we saw at the Red Bull – Vittoria, remember? – who said "Condemn you me for that the duke did love me? So may ye condemn a crystal river for that some melancholy fool drowned himself in it? Sum up my faults and you shall find that beauty and gay clothes and a merry heart and a good stomach to a feast are all my crimes." Remember? Frankie's like that."

"*The White Devil*?" I said drily. "Is that an apt comparison, Rob?"

"Don't push me, Giles," Rob said darkly. "I'll hear no ill spoken of the lady who will be my wife."

And so at Lambeth Palace the great divorce proceded. The commission was headed by George Abbot, Archbishop of Canterbury, assisted by three bishops and six lawyers and judges. Desirous to be made a mother, they were told, the Lady Frances offered her body to be known; but the earl could not have that copulation in any sort which the married bed allowed. He had, however, power and ability of body to know other women carnally, and it may have been due to witchcraft that he could not have copulation with the said Lady Frances. This curious accusation, it was understood, was put in to save Essex's reputation. It was well known that the devil worked upon the privities of those whom he would make impotent. A man so smitten could in no way be blamed; his manhood was not at fault.

"It is too much," fumed Frances. "This witchcraft again! It is a trial of man by men – they will not have it that one of their number could not perform. The Beast simply could not raise his prick – why look for supernatural explanation? Am I supposed to have put a curse on him? Did I go for potions back to Cunning Mary?"

"No, no, it is not you that they suspect," said old Northampton. "Why should you have bewitched his poor pudding? You wanted a good husband, but you got my lord the gelding. However, I find it offensive that he must introduce the devil to justify his failure. We shall have the unpleasant insinuation dropped henceforth; I will see to it."

Witnesses at the hearing then testified that the earl and countess had lain in bed together, and Frances swore on oath that Essex was impotent. Essex then suggested that it was not his fault but the lady's, and hinted that impediment prevented consummation.

"Is she a virgin?" he was asked.

He smiled and said: "She says so."

But what kind of answer was that? He added: "And she is so for me."

Following this ambiguity the court asked that the lady be examined.

"I am lost. Quite lost," said Frances to Robbie.

(*O me accurst*, Vittoria said.)

They sat there, in a room at Northampton House, she and Robbie, as he told me later; they were downcast and as pale as ghosts.

"What does it mean, exactly, an examination?" Robbie asked.

"Oh," she screeched like one who would have a bout of hysteria. "Oh, nothing much. All one has to do is lie upon a bed with legs spread wide while some dozen dribbling crones peer in between. I understand they are permitted to prod and probe. It has been said the evidence is more or less destroyed in the process."

"But is there nothing you can do? I mean, could not Anne – ?"

"Could not Anne what?" snapped Frances.

"This is not for me tae say," Rob fumbled, "but Anne seems tae know a deal about this sort of business. Could she not fashion a device of sorts to make it look. . . ?"

Then Frances did begin to laugh. "Oh, Robin, you are very sweet. I do believe you would refashion me a maid if it was in your power. Anne's talents are great. How endearing it is to find you have such faith in them. . ."

Plainly her laugh was mocking; Rob said no more.

"It is the Beast's doing," she then said grimly. "This is his revenge. He means to humiliate me. He will win, whatever is decided, if this foul examination goes ahead. It will show either that I lied and he has been maligned unjustly and his manhood therefore not in question – or that I took a lover and am someone's whore. And if I refuse it, my guilt will be assumed."

"I am sure that you are right. I thought it odd him standing by sae meekly. He must hope for revenge in some form."

"He does not show his anger; he controls it," she mused. "He is a cold austere man. Ugh! It makes me shudder just to think of him."

"How he must hate us," Rob said. "How he must hate me."

"Those born under Capricorn," she said, "are slow and stubborn and patient; they wait so long that in the end they are sure to have their hopes rewarded."

That evening, Rob and Frances were as gloomy as a night in November. Then Frances's mother came in. This was a woman who had always been a friend to Rob, and found him far more to her taste than Essex; a woman who had her daughter's welfare close to her heart.

"We are not come this far," she said, "to have our high hopes dashed. Leave it to me."

They looked at her, prepared to clutch at any straw.

"You are a modest girl, Frances," she said firmly. "You always have been. How could any modest girl endure the shame of an examination such as they propose? Therefore you will come to the examination veiled. Heavily veiled. They'll not deny you that. So heavily veiled," she continued, "that none shall see your face. I shall escort you there and I shall never leave your side. Trust me. Trust mother."

And so a heavily veiled female was brought to the examination by Lady Suffolk. This modest maiden was examined by five matrons and two midwives. She was found to be *virgo intacta*.

Rob's personal relief must have made him deaf to what was said at court. The general conclusion seemed to be a simple one – that either Frances Howard was a maid or that the veiled lady was not Frances Howard. It may be well imagined which conclusion was the one most readily believed.

And now the proceedings of the divorce commission reached a halt, for Archbishop Abbot brought matters to a standstill by declaring that such a divorce did not exist within canon law. It would be an immense disgrace to the Howards if this should not go forward, he was told. "They should have thought of that before they did begin it," he retorted. "Must I to save them from disgrace send my soul to Hell to give a sentence whereof I see no ground? I will never do it."

Strong words; and here the proceedings stuck.

"What kind of justice is it," Frances said, "that intimate details of the marriage bed be mauled and picked over by elderly divines? Archbishop Abbot is a grim-faced bachelor, and a Calvinist. The Bishop of London is a pious preacher. The Bishop of Ely and the Bishop of Lichfield are Devereux men. All the rest are lawyers – doctors of divinity. How dare they presume to judge the truth or otherwise of my miserable nights with an ugly pocky bedfellow?"

"These old black crows find it somewhat difficult to see a woman claiming her right to happiness in marriage," said her mother. "If you chose to suffer and endure, our age would call you virtuous."

"We should proceed with great wariness in this cause," the Bishop of Lichfield said. "The world looks upon what we do; and there were not more eyes upon Essex's father losing his head than there be upon the earl now losing his wife."

"Why do they take so long?" cried Frances. "What is so difficult to prove, now that they have evidence of virginity?"

"Be patient, dear," said Robbie. "You know the king is on our side."

"I cannot wait," said Frances imperiously. "I will brook no hitch to the achieving of my heart's desire!"

Rob put his arm about her, plainly pleased to be the object of such passion.

Her mother smiled indulgently. "She was always wilful. Even as a little girl she would move heaven and earth to get her way."

Chapter Twenty-Eight

As the two halves of the wheel of fortune, Robbie's fortunes soared and Tom's plummeted. Although I saw him almost every day I could learn nothing of Thomas's true state of mind or situation, for all our converse must be shouted in the air, I on the ground, he at his window; Richard Weston strolling past, smiling affably, chewing on a chicken leg or quaffing beer, waving to me in a most amicable manner, and indicating as plainly as if he had said it, that he could hear our every word.

I was moreover much hampered by a strong wish not to cause annoyance to Sir Walter Raleigh, whom, as I have indicated, I revered with an intense ardour, and who lodged in the rooms above. What if I disturbed whichever great work he was embarked upon, with my inane shouts to Thomas about trivialities? I am ashamed to say I sometimes grew irritable with Tom for keeping me talking there, when our conversation was of nothings.

Every day Tom told me he was ill and every day I spoke of it to Sir Gervaise when I went in to deliver Thomas's letters from Robbie and receive his, in the nearby lieutenant's lodging, whose door, by the way, was always ajar, as if to catch the residue of conversation scattered dust-like on the breeze.

"No, no, he is not ill," Sir Gervaise reassured me constantly. "I know he says he is. He says as much to me. All new ones go thus. It is a morbid depression of the spirit and it clouds their judgement. They believe themselves ill. Believe me, all this would instantly disperse if they were to be set free. And your Sir Thomas is one of these gentlemen that fixes his thoughts upon his own body, always probing it for symptoms of disease. This kind always makes the matter worse."

I could not deny this. Thomas had ever been a man that interested himself in potions for a matter which another man would leave to nature's course.

"Besides which," said Sir Gervaise, "look – he is surrounded with the love of those who care for him. Every day comes food and wine from a rich lord's kitchen."

On the table at that moment stood indeed two bottles of wine, a pigeon pie in a great dish, and several bowls covered and tied with cloths, smelling, I thought, of strawberries that were somewhat over-ripe.

"These have all come from Viscount Rochester," said Sir Gervaise. "Better than our poor kitchen fare, eh? You see, the great ones look after their own."

"Sir Thomas has asked me for medicine; may I bring it?"

"You may, because you come from Viscount Rochester. And Master Rawlins, pay no heed to wild tales. If Sir Thomas should fall sick I will inform you at once, believe me. Trust me."

Laurence Davies waited for me as I came away.

"How is my master?" he demanded.

"Well enough, I think. Why do you not go in and speak to him?"

"I am not permitted to, as yet; though I have hopes. Meanwhile, Master Rawlins, have you not noticed that the only folk that may go in or carry correspondence are those that come from my lords of Rochester, Northampton and Suffolk? And tell me – do the letters go directly to Sir Thomas or do you take them and receive them by courtesy of the lieutenant? I thought as much. It seems to me they have him very well sewn up."

I had to visit the apothecary's in Lime Street to have the medicines made up – Paul de Lobell's place, within easy distance of the Tower, where Thomas used to send for his emetics. De Lobell knew Thomas's constitution and made up the powders he had made before. Here I encountered Sir Robert Killigrew, another frequent dabbler in apothecary's potions, and, moreover, a loyal friend of Tom's who had just spent a few days in the Fleet prison for having a conversation with Tom at his window in the Tower.

While we talked, the apprentice went to and fro between us, weighing powders, grinding the same with pestle and mortar. William his name was – that same William whom I had seen before when I had come with Tom's man Payton some time ago to take a powder for Thomas. He had grown into a mean-eyed shifty-looking youth, sullen in his manner, with nothing to inspire confidence in the work he was about. I had to give myself a hearty mental shake for seeing bugbears where there was none. The poor lad could not help it if he had squinting eyes; no doubt his mother loved him. It was no use – I would always feel a nervous dread when I stood in an apothecary's shop. I had to confess as much to Killigrew in order to explain my jittery comportment.

"I am a fool, I own it," I admitted.

"You are," said Killigrew. "Lobell is an excellent man and knows his business. I come here every week. I would not be without my glysters – they clean the back passage and take away the impurities. I'm sending some in to Thomas; he's asked for them. And *aurum potabile* , the cure-all. I've sent him a vomit also. But the glysters are the thing; you should try them."

I shook my head vigorously. "I will let my impurities make their own way out, I thank you." But I knew Thomas agreed with Killigrew, therefore I took all I was given, and kept my judgements to myself.

Payton came round to our lodgings a few days later with a letter from Thomas for Robbie. I received him; Rob was in the bedchamber.

"When you hand him the letter," Payton said, "tell his lordship that Master Weston bids me say that powder which my lord sent made Sir Thomas very sick."

Rob must have heard this through the open door. He came through, greeting Harry Payton. "Ah, you have a letter for me. How does Sir Thomas fare?"

"He is sick," said Payton bluntly.

"How sick?" Rob said.

"Very sick."

"Oh? Very sick indeed?"

"Yes, my lord, in great danger of death. In one day he has endured threescore purges and vomits."

Payton eyed Rob with what would have been hostility if he had dared. He waited Rob's reply, and Rob made the immortal rejoinder which in later days he was bitterly to regret. Having thus been informed that Thomas was sick unto death he answered: "Pish!" And Harry Payton never did forget that that was what he said.

With Payton gone Rob said in mild exasperation: "His illness is pretence, Giles. Burn me, he told me so himsel'. He's taking potions to make himself seem ill – so ill that he will have tae be released. D'ye know what? – he's asked me tae do the same – take vomits and glysters to make myself ill, so that the king believes I'm missing Thomas tae the point of physical illness. I'm supposed tae ask for Thomas's release so that I may have converse wi' him once before I breathe my last. Lord, Lord, he never stops the intrigue, the windings of policy – even now he thinks tae manipulate me tae his direction. . ." He added broodingly: "But if Tom was truly taken ill it wasnae' frae the powder I sent in, for it was his old emetic which he has been taking for as long as I can remember. If he asks for it again, Giles, maybe you should put a note in it and tell him not tae be sae anxious. If he was sick it will be something frae the Tower kitchens – I hear it's no' the best o' fare."

"He supplements his diet with the pies and jellies which you send," I said.

"I? I have sent no pies," said Robbie in surprise.

"Pies have been sent. They must be from the Earl of Suffolk then. I thought Sir Gervaise said that you sent them."

"No. But if Suffolk sends in pies and jellies I will do the same, or they will say I have withdrawn my friendship. Apricot is his favourite; I will send that." Rob added then vexed: "It grieves me that Tom thinks the medicine I sent in made him ill. If indeed he does think so. You never can believe Tom's servants. They all have an axe tae grind. They glower at me as if I was Auld Hornie."

And then he settled down to read the letter in the bedchamber and did not show it to me. There were a good many letters now. Robbie kept them all in a small chest which he kept locked. He replied to them himself and made no use of Walter James. I never saw them. In this, Rob, a habitually honest man, was secretive.

When I met Lawrence Davies at the corner of Tower Street he said without preamble and accusingly as if I was myself to blame: "That powder which your master sent has made Sir Thomas very ill."

I shook my head. "No, no, it was his usual powder. If Sir Thomas felt ill it must be for some other reason."

"I saw the vomit!"

"Good Lord! How came you to do that?"

"Richard Weston kept it by to show me that it was loathsome."

"I understand that vomit often is," I said with heavy sarcasm, all lost upon the much aggrieved manservant.

"I wanted to bring it directly to Viscount Rochester and show him the nature of the sickness," Davies persisted. "But Master Weston would not permit it. He said that it was not a fit sight to show him."

"And by God he was right," I cried. "If you ever think to bring a heap of vomit to his lordship again I will undertake to press your face in it."

"Forgive me," Davies mumbled. "I am over zealous."

"My cousin doses himself," I said. "He always has done. He has brought the sickness upon himself. He takes foul waters – I have known him sick with them before. Sometimes this is done on purpose to take impurities from the body, as with the glysters which he also takes."

Even Davies had glumly to admit that this was true.

When I looked up at Thomas at his window I peered anxiously for signs of deterioration. He was in shadow. Indeed, he seemed all shadow.

"Speak louder," I encouraged; but he said he was too tired.

Sir Gervaise Elwes said: "Your friend is not well. What did I tell you? I said that if he was not well I would let you know. We have sent for a doctor."

Dr Craig, a Scot, a member of the College of Physicians, pronounced that Thomas had a lingering consumption. He was thirsty and he could not eat; he was let blood. Dr Craig said that the highly flavoured tarts left standing in the sun had worked upon his stomach; this was why he vomited. Dr Craig attended him all summer.

I wrote to my aunt and uncle with the details of the situation, and Bourton-on-the-Hill decided it would come to London. When I told Rob what I had done he was heartily vexed.

"Whatever did ye that for? It makes the matter seem much worse than it is. Dr Craig will see tae Thomas. Everyone considers him a good physician. You will only make Tom's parents anxious. We need have said nothing, and Thomas would have been released and they none the wiser."

"You say this because it now puts you in a poor light. They will expect you to have enough influence with the king to secure Thomas's release, and you dare not tell them Tom is being close confined until your marriage, so that he may not blab."

We scowled at one another. "I don't deny your assessment of the situation," Rob said curtly. "You put me in the position of having tae keep them happy while pretending helplessness in the face of a hardhearted monarch. If I had wanted tae become a juggler I would hae set up at Bartholomew Fair."

Robbie was kindness itself to Mr and Mrs Overbury. He took them around Whitehall and showed them the Privy Garden and the tennis courts; he escorted them along the galleries and pointed out the famous Holbein Gate. But in the gentlest possible way he had to inform them with regret that they would not be able to enter the Tower. A message could be got to Thomas saying that his parents were in London; more than that he could not do.

"Thomas must have the very best medicine that can be provided," my uncle said, and, as a result of Robbie's speaking to the King, His Majesty's own physician Dr Mayerne was sent in to see what he could do. What could he do? He could work in conjunction with the apothecary Paul de Lobell, who was his brother-in-law; and into the Tower went de Lobell and made up potions. Thomas began to recover.

The date of the Summer Progress now drew near and Robbie must accompany the king out of London.

"I think I shall not go with you," I said.

"Och, Giles!" said Robbie in dismay. "But I need you."

"I'm pleased to hear it," I said drily. "But you can do without me for a couple of months. Copinger – Myton-Fargus – they can attend you." I have not spoken much of Robbie's other helpers – they existed and they were useful; they are not important to my story, but they were competent and Rob would certainly do well with them in attendance.

"I cannot quit London while Tom is in his cell," I explained. "He likes to see me even though we talk of trite things and in hoarse voices."

"Well, I understand, of course," said Robbie. "But I shall miss you sorely."

I must admit I found Tom's parents something of a trial. They were not comfortable in London; they were sweet folk but they were rural Gloucestershire. They were staying at the house of their son-in-law Sir John Lidcote, that same Lidcote whom Tom considered reliable, kindly and dull. There was nothing they could do to help Tom. After all, he was now in the hands of the King's own physician. I was reduced to taking them around the sights, the most popular one at the moment being the wreck of the Globe playhouse which had just burnt down and smouldered still.

"Why not go home?" I said as kindly as I might. "Tom's on the mend. And surely we'll have good news soon."

They saw the sense in it. They set off back into the country. My aunt left me some cowslip wine.

Once they had gone back, Lidcote said to me: "Now, Giles, what's all this about?"

"Eh?"

"I would not have said a word before the old folks; but I am not happy about this and I assume you share my opinion."

"Which is – ?"

"I cannot make up my mind about your Viscount Rochester."

"Whatever do you mean?"

"I mean he could have brought Tom from the Tower by now if he had a mind to do it. Has he said anything to you? You are close to him. Do you know his mind?"

"No. I fold his clothes and frizz his hair."

Lidcote looked at me with something of pity, as if he thought our time on earth was given us to spend in more worthy pursuits.

"I may be wrong," he shrugged. "I hope I am. Mrs Overbury says he's very charming."

"And Mr Overbury?"

"Mr Overbury said that he could barely understand his heathen speech," said Lidcote drily. "But I daresay your Rochester thought the same about him. Did you know I have a warrant to visit him?"

"What? No! To visit Thomas?"

"Yes. Your Rochester procured it for me. I think he had forgotten that Tom had a family. I am permitted to accompany Sir Robert Killigrew, and in the presence of the lieutenant I may speak to Tom and reassure myself."

"Giles, he looks dreadful," Lidcote told me. We were sitting in the corner of an upper room in a tavern on Fish Street Hill – the Star. The high backs of the settles framed us in. We spoke in low voices. There was no one in the room. A smudge of amber from the setting sun showed in the sky beyond the leaded panes.

"But we were told he had recovered," I whispered.

"No. . . we were not told the truth. Or if he had recovered he has now relapsed. He was in his bed, Giles; he looked an old man. His hands were like parchment. He was talking about making his will. . . What troubles me is that I cannot believe that Rochester knows he is thus, or he would not have permitted us to see him."

I frowned. "You mean that Rob himself – that is, Viscount Rochester – has himself been misinformed of Tom's physical condition? After all, he does not visit. But I don't understand – Rochester believes Tom's illness to be self-induced. What did Tom say? He was surely able to speak?" I said alarmed.

"Yes. But there was a moment which gave me some disquiet. Elwes was showing us out and speaking to Killigrew in the doorway. I remained at the bedside for a moment. Tom raised himself up a little and said: 'Is Rochester juggling with me?' 'I believe not,' I answered. Then he whispered: 'I suspect Mayerne. I suspect his physic. Tell Rochester I would have thought by now to have heard more of him. . .' I had a sudden understanding that somehow he was counting on Rochester to save him. I believed it then appropriate to make him see that this was a false security. I was in a dilemma – I did not want to lower his hopes, but I thought it right he should know what I feared. I whispered: 'Study by all means your getting out speedily, for by God, never any man was so cozened as you are – as for Rochester I think there is no honest quarter to be held with him.' I am sorry to have had to say that, Giles, of a man you admire; but it seemed important to me to let Thomas know what I believed true, so that he might put his hopes elsewhere."

"And what did Thomas say?"

"He had no time to reply. Sir Gervaise pounced upon me then and said, much flustered: 'No whispering! What are you about?' He ordered me away. I think I shall be given no further warrant." Lidcote looked at me, large-eyed. "What do you think it means? I am a rational sober man. I try not to think the worst. I know that there are tales about the Bloody Tower. I have told myself not to be fanciful. But I ask myself now – *if they meant ill by Thomas, who would know?*"

"This is fanciful, John," I whispered. "Fanciful and dreadful."

"Yes, I know," he replied. "The answer came immediately to me: Rochester could mean no ill to him because he procured the warrant for me and permitted me inside the Tower. I felt suitably ashamed of my vile suspicion."

"And so you should," I seethed. "Reason, as you say, came to your rescue; but reason alone is a poor advocate beside the fact that Rochester is an honourable man and Thomas is his friend."

"You do well to remind me and I am doubly chastened."

As if further to allay Lidcote's misgivings, throughout the month of August Tom seemed very well. Lidcote's grim recountment seemed no more than a fevered dream. I stayed in close touch with Lidcote. The shared glimpse of the horrors that had opened up to us in that upper room at the Star had bound us in a curious intimacy, perhaps like men that have been scared by the same phantom and now wish to deny they ever saw it; but know all the while they did.

I saw Tom at his window; he called to me that he grew bored for want of occupation. He told me which books he planned to read when he was released. I guessed he must have had some good news in a letter, for he spoke of his release as something likely, nay, probable. One day he said more upon the subject.

"The Earl of Suffolk himself has promised me my release – I am to be out by Michaelmas. I've been a fool, Giles – I believed there was some kind of conspiracy to keep me in here, and I believed now one, now another of them, to be the source behind it. I see now it was my own bitter despondency that warped my mind, and the dark imaginings which this place induces. . . I see now all our differences were due to misunderstandings. Suffolk and Northampton are in constant touch with me and have given me promises of friendship. I've written at some length to put myself right with the Lady Frances; I've explained that although I may have spoken with less respect than was fit I never meant anything against her honour. . . Suffolk wrote in reply, most graciously. He signed the letter 'your loving good friend'. The Earl of Suffolk has been to me generosity itself. My only grief is that unhappily I have been a stranger this long to his lordship. . . It was Lidcote advised this course of reconciliation to me and I see that he is right. I was a fool to speak so rashly; I much repent it. But now we will all be friends, and I look daily for my release." His voice was strained and cracked with emotion and the effort of speaking to me from afar. He forced a smile. "All will be well," he said. "I have Northampton's word on it."

I listened to this speech with gathering bewilderment. It embarrassed me to hear my cynical and arrogant cousin sounding so penitent. Knowing that Richard Weston was never very far away I wondered if it was all done for his benefit, so that he might reassure Sir Gervaise of Tom's quiescence.

I had never been one to question Tom's judgement, but it seemed curious to me that he placed his trust in the Earl of Northampton, a man whom he had always told me was a master of the devious. But Tom was always right – always had been, and must know even now exactly what he was about. I chided myself for looking for trouble – too much closeness with Lidcote, no doubt.

I had a treat then – a long glimpse of Sir Walter Raleigh who came out and walked along the leads. In gazing at my hero I barely noticed that Thomas had gone in and closed his window, and my thoughts were as much of Raleigh as of Thomas as I came away.

CHAPTER TWENTY-NINE

When the court returned to Whitehall Rob and I embraced with heartfelt pleasure. "How good to see you!" I declared, holding him tightly. "So bonny and so –"

"So?" he teased.

What did I mean? So substantial, so human, so plainly of this world and not of the shadows of a man's imagination.

"So well," I answered lamely.

My previous misgivings, I found, had been much alleviated by seeing Thomas to continue in good spirits; and having a great respect for Thomas's perception of a given situation I had no doubt that he was right and would be out by Michaelmas, in some three weeks' time. I was greatly relieved that he had chosen the course of diplomacy and discretion towards the Howards and I assumed that they for their part would find Thomas no danger once the divorce commissioners had reached a verdict favourable to Frances. At present the commissioners were meeting regularly at Lambeth Palace, studying legal precedents and ancient authorities; but I understood that they were in a state of deadlock, for fear that if they granted the divorce, the floodgates would open for any that were unharmoniously married. "Whatsoever couple therefore have no children and live discontented come presently to take part of this general jubilee. . ." They were to gather for their final verdict later this month.

I spoke of this to Robbie as I happily resumed my duties as his manservant. He lay face down on my bed all naked while I rubbed the scented oils into his skin. How beautiful he was! How very pleasant to feel again under my palms the firm and supple curves of his buttocks, the hollow of his spine, the muscles of his shoulders. I parted the wealth of golden hair and my fingers played about his neck.

"Och, Giles. . . no one does this as you do. How I missed you! Did ye miss me?"

"Surely you get compliments enough from your fair lady, without my poor praise?" I said good humouredly enough.

"Aye, the Lady Frances does seem tae dote upon me," Rob agreed mischievously.

I tweaked his ear.

"But your continued good regard is also necessary tae me," he continued.

"Rest assured you have it."

"And so how did you spend your time awa' frae me in London?"

"Mostly I visited Thomas."

Rob fidgeted under my ministrations. "How is he?"

"Don't you know?" I said sharply. "Are you not kept informed?"

"Aye, but you've seen him, which is something other."

"When I say visited," I explained,"I mean that I stood under his window and shouted my good wishes and received his called out in reply. We have no private conversation and his keeper, that man Weston, is always nearby to pick up our scraps. However, Thomas was well and cheerful when I saw him last, and confident of his release by Michaelmas."

"I think it most unlikely he will be let out before we hae the divorce under our belts," said Rob cautiously.

"Yes, but if the commissioners meet on the 18th that would mean his hopes were justified. Michaelmas is on the 29th."

"I ken fine when it will be Michaelmas," said Robbie tetchily.

"Northampton and Suffolk have both written to him in a friendly manner and both have told him he will be released," I persisted. "I think it is generally understood now that the imprisonment is only in part a punishment for the refusal of an embassy, and that he is to be confined until you have your annulment, for the trouble it was once thought he might cause."

"Aye – he threatened to reveal all that he knew and damn our cause."

"I believe that he is heartily sorry for those threats. He has settled upon a policy of reconciliation. You will find him a good friend to Lady Frances now, as well as to yourself. He even understands that he must tolerate the Howards. You will find him changed by his incarceration – less domineering," I added pointedly. "It is a pity that he must wait for the annulment before putting his new-found amiability into practice. Is there nothing you could do?"

"You speak as if the result of the annulment was a foregone conclusion," Rob said grimly. "I fear it isnae' so. I hear that Archbishop Abbot is bringing in the evidence of Pope Alexander III who wouldnae' grant annulment tae King Henry VIII. He is suggesting that there ought tae be a reconciliation between Frances and that man she so despises. He is an awfu' powerfu' man, the archbishop. I personally wouldae' risk Thomas at large, for the damage he could do. Have ye no' thought his sweet words might be spoken in order tae achieve his release? He hated Frances – you know he did! – and I cannae' believe he's changed his mind. I feel sure that Frances's relations think as much. Let him be patient a wee while longer, eh? Did ye see any new plays while I was awa'?"

September was a few days advanced when I next made my way to the Tower for my visit to Thomas. The Thames had been choppy, whipped by a sharp little wind with a snatch of autumn in it, and I was feeling queasy as I plodded up towards the Tower. I was a familiar sight by now, and since I came under the auspices of Viscount Rochester I made my way unhindered towards the window at which Tom was accustomed to sit. He was not there. I called but I could not make him hear me.

Richard Weston sidled up beside me. "No use, Master Rawlins; he is not there."

"What – has he been released?" I said, delight and disbelief straining together to rise uppermost.

"No, no," said Weston almost with a laugh, I thought, at my naivety. "The chamber is empty now and your cousin has been moved to another place."

"Oh? Where?" I looked about me stupidly, as if I would be able at some window of the thirteen towers that made up the great fortress to see Thomas waving down at me. Just for a moment, in the silence that followed when Weston did not instantly reply, I felt a rising wave of nausea. My careless glance had brought home to me with shocking clarity that this was indeed a prison – the Wakefield Tower where King Henry VI had been sticked full of deadly holes with his foes' daggers –

the aweful White Tower with walls fifteen feet thick behind which they had racked the Powder Plot conspirators and from whose battlements a Prince of Wales plunged to his death, his head and neck crushed between his shoulder blades – and all those other towers whose unwinking eyes looked down upon the courtyard, repositories of their own dark secrets, ancient mischiefs which would never come to light. The walls whirled.

Richard Weston caught me, all solicitude. "Master Rawlins, you are not well?"

"I found the river journey unsettling. No, I am very well."

"Come with me to the lieutenant's lodging; take a glass of wine."

I sat in Sir Gervaise's kitchen; he was not present. Master Weston explained, all kindliness.

"I will be honest with you, Master Rawlins. The matter stands as follows. The great ones, as Sir Gervaise must call their lordships, believed it to be politic for Sir Thomas to be moved out of the public gaze. It is as simple as that. You know the matter, Master Rawlins, the matter of their concern – your master's hopes and fears that hang upon the outcome of the great annulment. A word from Sir Thomas in the wrong ear – well, you understand me, and seated as he was at that window, who knows what careless whispering might have ensued? And those letters, which he smuggled out in empty wine bottles, yes? And so, just for the moment he must be out of sight and hearing, all this business being of so delicate a nature – if you take my meaning, sir?"

I sipped the restorative wine. "And so where is Sir Thomas now?"

Weston looked undeniably shifty, as a man will do that may not deal honestly in his answer, howsoever much he might like to. "I may not tell you, sir."

"Why not?"

"Those are my orders. Sir, it's only common prudence. If none knows where he is, there is no danger of an indiscretion."

"Is it a place with windows and good air?"

"Sir, I must say nothing. Although I will say it is not as spacious as the Garden Tower."

"It is not – God forbid – a dungeon?" I began in gathering alarm.

"Oh, Good Lord, no – what do you take us for? And his physicians come and go and bring his physic."

"His physic? Is he sick?"

"Now Master Rawlins, you know as well as I do that Sir Thomas is a man always over-anxious for his health. Ever since he has been with us he has been taking physic. And the physic is prescribed by Dr Mayerne himself, so you see your cousin is in good hands."

"Who brings his physic?"

"The apothecary Master Lobell, a very reputable man; and his assistant comes in with him – a youth, carrying the basket. They have a shop not far from here."

"I know it." How to prevent the nervous dread that clutched about my heart? It was my own morbid imagining that plucked at me, my foolish fear of an apothecary because he dealt in powders and sublimate of mercury and *aurum potabile* and I was a country bumpkin whose physic had to have an old English name to be acceptable. Whatever excellence had lungwort and five-fingers over potions prepared by skilful fellows who understood their trade? I took another gulp of the wine.

"When I last saw Sir Thomas he seemed fairly well and cheerful. Can you assure me that he is still so?"

"Master Rawlins," said Weston severely, "you presume upon your privileged position. We have permitted you familiarities denied to Sir Thomas's family. On whose behalf do you ask these questions? Not on the part of the Viscount Rochester, who is satisfied with what we do. Therefore is it the Earl of Northampton whom you find fault with, or the Earl of Suffolk? Who are you, to ask the lieutenant's under-keeper if he does his duty by the prisoner?"

It was true – I had overstepped the mark. I felt confused and not a little fearful. My hand shook as I put the glass down on the table.

Perhaps Weston relented at the sight of my befuddlement.

"Your Sir Thomas is, I think, not a well man," he said. "Some of the physicians who have seen him have pronounced him consumptive. He was always lean, ever since he came in here, and, as I understand it, he believed himself sickly from the first. He brought with him the seeds of whatever sickness has tormented him under our care. A rheumy cough he has of nights. Consumptive, that is what they say, and with the turning of the year the walls take on a chill." He shrugged. "There's nothing we can do about it. But as I tell you, he has physic every day. There's no cause to alarm yourself. He will be as well cared for here as if he was in the King's own palace. Indeed, we are sending for the prisoner's own furniture and hangings to make his chamber more agreeable."

I stood up to go.

"Oh, and Master Rawlins," Weston said.

I paused.

"I wouldn't trouble to come here again; there'd be no point. Sir Thomas is permitted no visitors."

I came away from the Tower sunk deep in thought. Thomas, I thought, was not a lovely man. He made enemies easily. He was self-opinionated and arrogant. He did not inspire the affection of the common man and the great found him insufferable. But no man deserved this curious incarceration brought about because through circumstance he was possessed of information which he had threatened to divulge and thereby ruin Lady Frances Devereux's marriage hopes. This man was being punished for neither crime nor sin. And now he was hidden from sight in some dark chamber where no man might come to him save whom Sir Gervaise Elwes permitted on orders from his masters. Too well could I imagine my fastidious cousin now in his dire plight and he who for his biting wit was well received by the poets and playwrights at the Mermaid alone with only Richard Weston for diversion. Whatever did they talk about? And how would Tom retain his reason in these circumstances – what philosophy might sustain a man of fine intelligence so unjustly treated?

In happier times Thomas had written a character study of a gaoler. "Of that red earth of which man is fashioned, this piece was the basest; of the rubbish which was left and thrown by came a gaoler. He wears the vizor of a man, yet retains the fierceness, currishness and ravening of a tiger. A gaoler's soul stands not upon those two pillars that support Heaven – justice and mercy. It rather sits upon those two footstools of Hell – wrong and cruelty. His conscience and his shackles hang up together and are made very near of the same mettle, saving that the one is harder than the other and has property above iron for that it never melts. He must look for no mercy for he shows none and I think he cares the less, because he knows Heaven has no need of such tenants – the doors there want no porters, for they stand ever open."

I doubt that Thomas ever thought he would ever put his theories on the subject to the test when he wrote that.

In welcoming Robbie back from the Summer Progress I was obliged perforce also to welcome Lady Frances. This personage was now and henceforth to be part of our lives and I must habituate myself to it. She, however, with surprising sensibility, I thought, now put herself out to be agreeable to me, as if she considered me a figure of some worth. She made me a present of a pair of excellent gauntlet gloves perfumed with musk, and said it was for my care of Robert. I bit my tongue on the ungracious reply that this care was not given for her sake and thanked her heartily, wondering if it were some kind of bribe for my goodwill or even a gesture of sympathy, since she must have known that I was troubled about Thomas's incarceration, of which she was to some extent the unwitting cause.

I could not help but notice that Lady Frances was almost constantly in a condition of febrile excitement, taut as stretched lute strings.

Before the end of the month she would either have her heart's ultimate desire or her hopes dashed to pieces; there would be no middle way. The divorce commissioners would either give her Robbie and a wedding and a glittering future or condemn her to a life of misery and gloom with the man she loathed. No wonder she was nervous, brittle, tense. Myself I wished the outcome might be swift; for until then my wretched cousin must endure a life of solitude and darkness in diminishing health.

"Weston hinted to me that Thomas was become consumptive," I told Robbie. "He suggested that he was so when he first came to the Tower."

"Was he? I dinnae' think so," Robbie answered. "He was well enough. I wouldnae' hae agreed tae his going there if he had been ailing."

"Surely if he is consumptive this is a condition which will worsen within those damp stone walls. . ."

"Giles, listen tae me," said Robbie, and I saw that he was roused to anger. "I dinnae' want tae hear of Thomas. Ye ken the matter as well as I do. There he mun stay until we hae the divorce. When I am wed tae Frankie he may come forth and he may say she is nae maid and it will no' matter for she will be my wedded wife and indeed nae maid. He shouldhae learnt tae curb his poisonous tongue when he was free and then he wouldnae' be in such a pickle. And if you pester Weston wi' your questioning it's certain that he'll pass it on tae Elwes who will tell Northampton and you may well find yoursel' along wi' Thomas – d'ye hear me, Giles? The situation is sae tricky nae man kens which way the wind shall blow and you mun keep your head down till it blow itsel' out." I must have looked somewhat shaken and alarmed – I was – because he added winsomely: "It's only till we hae the divorce, Giles. Be patient. Only till then."

Robbie came back late to our rooms from a banquet, and I thought as I made him ready for bed that I did not know him at all. His gradual slipping into the orbit of the Howards and his close involvement with that woman was making him a stranger to me. He spoke little of the times he spent with Frances, knowing I resented her growing influence upon him. That night of all nights we were what the world assumed us to be – Viscount Rochester and his manservant. Not a word of intimacy passed between us. You would never have thought that we had ever made love. We kept our thoughts to ourselves and his were as unguessable to me as the nature of the composition of the moon.

In the morning while Rob was still abed a servant of the Earl of Northampton brought a letter for him, which I handed to Robbie and which he opened sitting up in bed. He pushed the hair out of his eyes. I heard him catch his breath. I heard his whispered oath.

"I think that you had better hear this," he said, plainly stunned. "It seems that in the night Thomas has died. Of natural causes, my lord writes." Rob looked at me bewildered, still bleary with sleep, his look a query: "So he was consumptive after all?"

"But dead?" I gasped. "So sudden?"

"But all the world knows he was ailing," Rob blurted out. "It's scarcely sudden. But it is unexpected," he murmured, shaking his head. "It is unexpected tae me. I wish most fervently that it had not happened."

We stared at one another. Rob groaned. "Och, Giles, it's all my fault!" he cried. " I never was easy about his arrest. He was put in prison for his silence. I never was easy about that business of offering him an embassy. Northampton said it was the only way. I let mysel' be persuaded by him. He talks sae well; he makes you believe whatever he wishes. And at the time I thought how neatly it had fallen out. . . But this annulment has gone on sae long. . . I thought it would be a matter of a few weeks. Who would hae guessed that it would be postponed and that the summer would pass by and nothing settled? I did not think that he was truly ill. He wrote tae me – you shall see the letters – he wrote tae me that he would feign sickness. He sent for physic that would render him unwell. He told me so. . . Do you think perhaps he took his own life? Och, no, that wasnae' Thomas. . . He had great plans for his own future. Och, Thomas! It has all gone wrong and I am much tae blame. I shouldhae demanded his release. Och, why did no one tell me that he was sae ill? I did not know. . . I am the indirect and unhappy cause of his death, a man I loved and admired since my youth. However will I bear this guilt? Giles? Answer me!"

What could I say? I myself could barely take in the enormity of the dreadful news. I listened to Rob's impassioned outpourings as someone in a daze.

"Giles," insisted Robbie urgently. "It's not my fault – believe me, won't you? You'll no' turn against me? I would gie all I own tae hae him back alive. But d'you believe me? Tell me you dinnae' think I am tae blame?"

I struggled to be fair. "I do believe some blame to be yours for that he was imprisoned to procure your marriage. But no more than that. Of course I will not turn against you – how could you think it? You could not have guessed that he would die. None of us could. You are no more guilty than the rest of us. Be still."

He was distressed; I took him in my arms and soothed him, sitting with him on the bed against the pillows, holding him close. I did not know what to say. Looking beyond his bent head all I could see was the haze of my own confusion.

CHAPTER THIRTY

I rode that very day to Gloucestershire, the reluctant bearer of the news to Thomas's parents. In the quiet parlour, with the ticking of the clock and the shifting of the hearth logs, we spoke about the funeral requirements, of bringing the coffin back to Bourton-on-the-Hill. I promised that Lidcote and I would make all arrangements.

I was back in London within three days. To my astonishment I learnt on my return that Thomas was already buried, and the whole matter considered more or less complete. Rather than the business being a subject upon everybody's lips it was news already cold, and all the talk was of the progress of the annulment.

Now in my foolishness I had assumed – and so had Tom's parents – that there would be an inquest and a gathering of 'great ones'. I thought Sir Gervaise might be called to account, that Weston would be obliged to explain the events of that last grim night and his own personal negligence. I would have liked to have heard the exact cause of Tom's death. 'Natural causes' did not in my mind suffice as a description of a young man's passing – if one is still young at thirty-two. If death had been expected, Lidcote should have been sent for, and word got to Tom's parents.

Robbie, it is true, wrote a gracious letter to the grieving father. "Your son's love to me got him the malice of many and they cast those knots on his fortune that have cost him his life, so in a kind there is none guilty of his death but I, and you can have no more cause to commiserate the death of a son than I as a friend. But though he be dead you shall find me as ready as ever I was to do all the courtesies that possibly I can to you, your wife and children. In the meantime I desire pardon from you and your wife for your lost son, though I esteem my loss the greater."

He sent for Weston to enquire further of the details of Tom's last hours – indeed, I found the man waiting at the door of our chambers and was obliged to escort him in. I heard them talking within but not what they said. When Weston left, Rob stayed in his bedchamber alone. When he came out he told me Weston had done all he could for Tom and, not thinking he was in extremity, had left him for a quarter of an hour; when he returned he found him dead. He told me he rewarded

Weston for his care of Tom. I said that was unnecessary since it had been to no avail. Rob said he did not wish to dwell upon it; and indeed his eyes were red with weeping.

But even Robbie, in his gathering excitement, seemed prepared to put his grief aside to concentrate upon what was to come. That great hive, Whitehall, buzzed, but it was over the ups and downs of the annulment and the exciting possibility of a wedding; not over a misfortune in the Tower.

"It seems to me," said Lidcote, "that this is what occurred."

Lidcote wrote to me suggesting that I meet him at the Star. He did not like the palace of Whitehall; he found it intimidating – too many people, too many passageways, too many unexpected corners. He was as countrified as I – more so, since I through my service with Robbie had acquired the kind of polish any oaken cupboard would be proud to own. At the Star, obscure, unknown, we sat privily ensconced in our high-backed settles and drank indifferent ale. Two weeks had passed since we had heard the news of Thomas's death. It occurs to me now, with something of a shudder, that it must have been Michaelmas, the day by which Tom thought he would be free.

"On the night of the fourteenth," said Lidcote, speaking low, like a conspirator, "the apothecary's apprentice brought Thomas a physic. Weston received him. They were all three together for a while. The boy went home. Weston remained with Thomas who said that he felt unwell. When I first heard of this, I considered it a kindly act to stay with Thomas – Weston could have left him to his pains; but he remained. At an early hour Thomas sent Weston to fetch beer from the buttery. When Weston returned he found Thomas dead. We cannot know the awful details of those last moments; but then Weston told Sir Gervaise of his grim discovery. Sir Gervaise sent for de Lobell, and the apothecary came at once to view the body. He pronounces that a speedy burial would be most appropriate and so Sir Gervaise arranges an inquest. Because of the urgency of the matter the inquest is made up of six Tower Warders and six fellow prisoners. They agree upon a verdict: death from natural causes. The body is laid out for burial." Lidcote paused. "Then was I sent for." He took a sip of ale. "I arrived at the Tower expecting to arrange to take the corpse away for burial. I was told that was not possible. The body must be interred immediately. A lecture was delivered me upon the state of corpses. Some, I was told, and in particular the corpses of the blessed saints, give off the odour of sanctity. A perfume not unlike the scent of violets rises from the sanctified remains. But in ordinary mortals there is natural decay. In some corpses this may take a time to set in. In others it occurs at once and in cases like these the body must be buried swiftly, as in Thomas's case. Though I did not peruse the body closely it is true I was aware of an unpleasant odour. Sir Gervaise told me that Lobell had viewed it, that twelve men had further seen the same, that there was nothing hugger-mugger in the business. I assured him that I had not thought there was. Let me say, I had not thought so; but this urgent protestation was beginning to cause the very doubts these good folks would dispel. And I was angry not to be permitted to return the body to the family. Sir Gervaise thought to placate me. 'He will lie amongst the great!' he said. 'In the chapel of the Tower his close companions will be Queen Anne Boleyn – Queen Catherine Howard – the Duke of Northumberland – the Duke of Somerset; also Lady Jane Grey and the Earl of Essex!'" Lidcote smiled wrily. "No doubt this at least would have well pleased Thomas."

"Yes," said I with cynicism. "Who would have thought as much when he first set out from Bourton-on-the-Hill?"

"Unpersuaded by Sir Gervaise's gracious offer of so noble a resting place," said Lidcote, "I protested; but to no avail. Mistress Dunne, the beldame who laid out the body, was brought in, and when requested, nodded her head to verify that for the dignity of the deceased and for the health of those yet above ground, my kinsman's corpse must be interred as a matter of some urgency. What could I do? I left them to it. And it is true that Thomas lies now with the great ones in St Peter ad Vincula." He added in clipped tones: "His parents were not asked their thoughts upon the matter."

"I agree; it is not as we would have wished it," I said.

"I made my way out of the Tower," continued Lidcote. "My intention was to take a boat upstream. As chance would have it, as I thought at the time, Mistress Dunne fell into step beside me as I went along Tower Street. . . I see now that chance played no part in her meeting me; she had been waiting for me. I greeted her and thanked her once again for her care of Thomas's body. I said the family would be very grateful; it is no pleasant task, the laying out of a corpse. 'It is no pleasant task,' Mistress Dunne agreed, 'but it is one that I have done so often that it causes me no particular grief. Some folk make a pretty corpse – the ladies who have died young, the little childer, and the old whose faces often recover something of their youthful comeliness when cares have fled their earthly form.' She fixed a claw-like grip upon my arm. 'Sir Thomas was not like that.'

"I began to feel uncomfortable. I am not a squeamish man but I had had my fill of corpses for one day and the combined presences of Elwes and Weston had worked upon my equilibrium and I was not at ease. You know the feeling, Giles? A kind of sharp desire to be walking in the meadows of the Evenlode and hearing all the larks of Oxfordshire?"

"I know the feeling well."

"However, the old dame would speak, and I must hear her. 'I have never seen a body like it,' she continued. 'It was all skin and bone and covered all with sores and blisters. Between the shoulder blades was a great black ulcer. All over the belly, amber-coloured blisters big as peas seeping with noisome pus, at least a dozen, all cracked and foul. The stench of him so strong that nobody wanted to lay hold of him. I did not think I should have been asked to do as much and I demanded a greater fee, the which I got and gratefully. But even worse, thought I, than the foulness I have spoken of, was that his face was not a man's face that had died in peace. What you caught a glimpse of today was done by me, in that I rearranged his features for him. They were not like that at first. How shall I say? – the teeth all bared into a ghastly grin as men who meet their end in battle often have; the kind of face you do not see upon one that has died in his sleep or with his family about him and his hand upon the Holy Writ.'

"You may imagine, Giles, my state of mind on hearing this alarming recountment," Lidcote murmured, "and by your looks I see you are perturbed as I. I asked the woman what she might infer from such a condition then. She gave a cackle. 'What do you think I am – a halfwit? I think nothing. I infer nothing. I have more sense. I shall work again for Sir Gervaise and thereby make my living, and inferring, as you call it, has no place in the laying out of limbs. But I pass on to you what I have seen. You are a kinsman. You must do as you think fit. Good day to you.'"

"She darted down a backstreet, leaving me to stand and ponder over what she told me. I made my way down to the river, very slow and thoughtful. And now I say to you, Giles, what do you surmise from this strange tale?"

"What do I surmise? That this was not a man that perished from a slow consumption."

"Now unlike yourself," said Lidcote, "I have no close dealings with the great ones. You catch me talking as Sir Gervaise does. . . Therefore I may view the matter with detachment. I had believed that Weston was a kindly fellow, keeping Thomas company when the apprentice brought the physic, staying with him in the lonely night. But villain that I am, I now begin to ask myself *was Thomas unwell before he took the physic or after?*"

"You cannot suspect a poor apprentice boy of – of what, John?

What do you suspect him of?"

"Of bringing physic, which he did; after taking which, some hours later, Thomas perished in some bodily agony."

"Poison. . ." I whispered. My mouth was dry as gravel. "De Lobell? I cannot credit it."

"Lobell is the apothecary, no more. Who tells him what powders to grind?"

"Dr Mayerne? The King's physician?" My voice shook. "No, no, we are in too deep waters here. For God's sake listen to yourself. You seem to be accusing – I dare not say it. Who is it you suspect? And whisper it in your softest tone; I am all of a tremble."

It seemed to me that he accused the King. Now I knew even better than Lidcote that James hated Thomas and always had done. It was a mean and petty hatred dating back to the early days of his friendship with Robbie, for that Robbie was so close with Thomas and that all the world knew it. And it was certainly contributory to the King's arrest and imprisoning of Thomas on a slender charge. But the leap was too great from the king as a jealous lover to the King as poisoner. I could not accept it.

"Who is it you suspect?" I said again.

The answer came and not what I expected. "Who but your Rochester?"

At this I gave a laugh of derision.

"Ask yourself – if there had been foul play, who had the most to gain?" said Lidcote undeterred.

"We should not assume foul play upon the evidence which you have presented," I said. "Wretched as is the picture you have conjured, what you describe is the position of any prisoner close confined, as Thomas was in his last days. The diet is poor, the walls damp, the cell foul. We have no cause to suspect poison. But even if that were the case, Rochester could have no part in it. His is an honest generous nature, and besides he has been in love with Thomas for years, and although there came irritation between them because of the marriage, it would have all blown over, given time."

"In love?" said Lidcote with an unbecoming leer. "I knew of course that Thomas had no inclination towards women. But if it was indeed love between they two, remember hate and love are horns on the same ram."

"No, no, no," I said firmly. I shook my head. "Robbie was shaken to the core by Thomas's death; he thought it was all his fault. He meant that it was out of love for Robbie that Tom made enemies and therefore entered his imprisonment. He is heartily distressed. Believe me, he has wept upon my shoulder."

"Oh, tears," shrugged Lidcote. "But who is now riding high? Whose star is brightest in the firmament?"

The Court of Delegates was now gathered. The delegates hesitated; they talked of recalling Essex to the bar. King James intervened. He said the principles had the right to a verdict without further delay. In order to achieve it he added the Bishops of Rochester and Winchester to the commissioners, knowing they were in favour of the divorce. It was decided to put the matter to the vote. Archbishop Abbot told the king he could not in conscience grant the annulment. They voted. By seven votes to five the great cause was decided in favour of the Countess. Frances was free. Free to marry again. Because the marriage was declared null and void the Earl of Essex would be obliged to return the dowry of £5000. Of course, he had already spent it. He had to sell some of his woods and manor and to borrow money.

But Robbie. . .

Robbie is busy arranging his wedding, kissing Frances in full view of any passer-by, preparing for his golden future. He sends to Italy for fine paintings by Italian artists – Titian, Tintoretto, Veronese – whom he has been told are very good.

And two months after Thomas's death Rob is created Earl of Somerset, which begins with S; and I must of necessity believe in the divinatory power of apple peel.

CHAPTER THIRTY-ONE

Amongst the birch trees of the Forest of Ettrick the young Tam Lin was a shape shifter, hero of the romancy ballad which first drew Tom to Robbie when he pursued the dazzling figure on the milk-white steed and followed him into their doomed adventure. Now here at Whitehall Robbie was a shape shifter. Raw reiver lad, page, favourite of a king, knight, viscount, husband, earl.

It was the 26th December. In the Chapel Royal, Robert, Earl of Somerset, wed the lady of his choice. Or should I say the lady who had chosen him? He was almost twenty-seven years of age.

What would Tom have made of this, I thought, looking on Robbie and his bride?

Shame betide her ill far'd face
And an ill death may she die

For she's ta'en awa' the bonniest knight
In a' my companie.

But had I kend, Tam Lin, she says
What now this night I see
I wad hae ta'en out thy taw grey een
And put in twa een o' tree.

They were a glittering pair, Rob and Frances. Everything about them shone. The torchlight caught the jewellery in a myriad dazzling arcs. Frances wore a gown of silver, and her honey-coloured hair combed in waves down to her waist to proclaim to all the world she was a virgin. She was conducted in by old Northampton, who had the look of a cat with cream. Robbie shone with equal splendour in gold satin, and the torchlight glinted on his golden hair. The sun and the moon. . .

It was all celebration. There was a special masque. Campion wrote the words, who wrote so well of pleasures and shadows. The musicians wore taffeta robes and caps of tinsel. A curtain was drawn to reveal a sky of clouds. There were pillars of gold, a sea with rocks and ships. Error and Rumour were dispelled by Eternity and Harmony. Queen Anne with a somewhat fixed smile took a branch from the Tree of Grace and Bounty, setting free the masquers from enforced enchantment and showing that the marriage was accepted by the court. The couple were then put to bed noisily and bawdily. Both the king and queen assisted; myself I had no wish to see it. In the celebrations that followed over the next few days two Cupids vied with one another for supremacy in verses of lewd language. There was an Irish masque. There was a tournament. There were torchlight processions through the night-time streets. There was a banquet given by the Lord Mayor and citizens in the Merchant Taylors' Hall. On Twelfth Night there took place *The Masque of Flowers* – the young gentlemen of Gray's Inn dressed up as hyacinths and daffodils and danced corantoes and galliards, and there were fountains, blossoms, myriads of lights. This masque was paid for by Sir Francis Bacon who was grateful to Robbie for helping him achieve promotion to Attorney-General. If ever a man crashed his own bark on the rocks Robbie did then with that act of generosity; but alas, the future was, as is its wont, an uncharted sea, veiled in clouds.

All the poets wrote in praise of Rob and Frances. Poor Ben Jonson who despised the great ones grit his teeth and wrote an epigram expressing his hope for the couple that: 'When your years rise more than would be told/Yet neither of you seem to the other old.'

One William Alabaster wrote an epithalamium in Latin, which

neither Rob nor Frances could properly understand. Wretched Chapman wrote an allegory in which he likened Frances to Andromeda chained to a barren rock, prey to a monstrous whale and saved by Perseus – Robbie – and thereby got himself into trouble with the supporters of Essex and obliged him to deny that Essex was either the monster or the barren rock, but it was all intended merely symbolically; the monster was the base ignoble barbarous giddy multitude who criticised poetry.

Poor Essex. Of course, he kept away from the festivities, nursing his wounds far away at Chartley; but he had to return – his world was of necessity at Whitehall where the power source lay. He made a splendid debut in the House of Lords, but personally he was very much the loser.

There was one occasion on which Frances engineered it so that by dint of hurrying Robbie along a circuitous route they were able to descend a staircase together just as Essex was coming up it; and whereas Frances's face wore a triumphant radiance and Rob's a becoming modest pride, it must have been all Essex could do to preserve a polite indifference. How could he not be aware of them? – banquets, dancing, walking in the galleries and the Privy Garden, anywhere where the king was – there they were, the cynosure of all eyes, and for Essex a constant throbbing reminder of his humiliation.

Even John Donne who had writ such excellent love poems previously came up with verses in celebration of the wedding.

I think it all rather went to Robbie's head, then and in the days to come. How could it not? Thomas had often told him he was none too clever; and now look at him. He was the most powerful subject in the land. He was Earl of Somerset. He was handsome, rich and healthy. He was married to the most beautiful woman at court, who plainly adored him. The king would do almost anything for him.

"No man should marvel that I bestowed a place so near myself upon my friend whom I love above all men living," he said. Frankie and Robin, as he called them, were the King's new passion, his family, his stepchildren. It was Robbie's time of triumph.

What was less apparent to him – as it would have been to Thomas – was that it was the Howards' time of triumph too. The Earl of Suffolk, Frances's father, was Lord Treasurer, and had completed for himself the fabulous mansion of Audley End, a palace fit for a King, except that it housed a Lord Treasurer. A Howard son-in-law Lord Knollys was Treasurer of the Household, another son-in-law was Lord Salisbury; Suffolk's eldest son Lord Walden was married to the heiress of the Earl of Dunbar; and all the younger sons had livings of £1000 or more. And old Northampton the cackling patriarch surveyed it all with the satisfaction of a grandame basking in the sun.

Now by his marriage Robbie was become firmly joined to the fortunes of the Howard faction, where before he had been free. And there were plenty at court who made no secret of their resentment of the Howards' success. Some of these were powerful, some politically astute, all discontented. We might mention Sir Ralph Winwood the Puritan, ambassador to the United Provinces, later Secretary of State; George Abbot, Archbishop of Canterbury, still smarting over the divorce; the Earl of Southampton, Essex's friend; the Earl of Pembroke; Lord Chancellor Ellesmere; Sir Thomas Lake; Her Majesty the Queen.

However, politically inept as Robbie, I could in no way take any credit for observing this or passing on a timely warning. I speak from hindsight. I thought Robbie was secure as any man might be. My reservations were personal ones, and they were two.

The first was that it gave me no joy to watch him dallying with a woman. I had been pleased and honoured for him when he had been chosen by the King, and jealous but tolerant of his devotion to Thomas. But to have our lives disrupted by this female was not easy for me.

We had to leave our rooms overlooking the river, to move into a more suitable dwelling, the Cockpit Lodgings, the other side of the Privy Garden at the north end of the Palace of Whitehall. It was beautifully positioned, overlooking St James' Park, and it was a very fine dwelling. Our move was mainly to accommodate all Frances's possessions, clothes and ladies-in-waiting. I had a small chamber to myself within call of Robbie and therefore of necessity within the sound of the murmured voices of the marital bedchamber, a situation not much to my liking.

But you should have seen that bedchamber! I had often believed before that we lived in splendour here at Whitehall. But this place surpassed all others. The bedstead had gilt pillars. The bedcover was purple velvet lined with yellow damask, trimmed with lace and fringes of gold. There was another bedcover of white velvet lined with carnation velvet, and another of crimson damask trimmed with gold.

The wedding presents arrived there – enamelled silver dishes, gold basins, silver knives and spoons, ewers set with gems, six candlesticks whose worth was reckoned to be more than 1000 marks; and from the Earl of Northampton £1,500 worth of gold plate and for Robbie a sword with a gold enamelled hilt worth £600.

I can still see Frances kneeling in the middle of it all and laughing over two presents that were exactly the same – a set of fire irons, tongs and shovel all in silver from Sir Robert Carey and the same from Sir

Robert Mansfield.

"When we sit and poke the fire," she giggled to Robbie, "you shall hold one shovel, I the other."

It became a house of women; you could always hear high-pitched laughter and the awful grinding of indifferent lute playing; and the whispering of gossip. Anne Turner had a room here, which she shared with Toothless Margaret. Anne was as high in Frances's favour as she had ever been. A superb nedlewoman, she made all Frances's dresses. She must have been nearly forty then, and still much celebrated about the court for her saffron-starched ruffs and collars. She was very close with Frances, always casting her horoscope. As for Toothless Margaret she was no ornament to the place, and her odd way of speaking made her seem simple; but I knew she was not – the eyes were bird-bright and missed nothing.

I very much regretted the loss of my private friendship with Rob and I spoke to him of my misgivings. I was curling his hair. Rob followed the progress in a jewelled hand mirror which he raised from time to time to contemplate the effect.

"I am not certain that my future lies with you," I said, "now that you are a married man. You do not need me – anyone may fold your clothes. You have Copinger and Fargas. I have been thinking I might try my luck elsewhere."

"Och, pish!" said Rob heartily. "Stuff and nonsense! Of course I need you. You know I do. And where else could you go?"

He had a point of course. I glowered at him for having made it. "Back to the playhouse for a start, or join with travelling minstrels. I daresay I have wind enough yet to blow a cornet."

"I don't doubt it, and you're wasting it on this daft notion," Robbie said. "But I want you with me. Och, Giles – you've seen me through the lean times – how can you think of leaving me when everything is going sae well? What would you like? Name it – it's yours."

You to lose that woman, I thought; but did not say it.

"I don't need bribery," I began in irritation. "Although I see you could line the walls of my hovel with gold and silver just at present I don't stay with you for the comforts of Whitehall, enjoyable as they are. I simply wonder whether it is time for me to leave."

"You're not in earnest, Giles?" Rob said winsomely and put his arm around me. I disentangled myself. "What has brought this about? Are ye no' well content?"

"We are not close," I said, "as once we were."

"How are we not, when you still curl my hair and rub my skin with perfumes?"

"You do not confide in me as you once used to do." Lord save me, but I sounded like a querulous wife, like a fretful playhouse quean. Where had I heard a scene upon the stage where some poor wife spoke lines like mine? Yes, I might be Brutus' Portia for my female reproaches. I winced.

"Well," Rob answered reasonably, "that is because I ken ye dinnae' think sae much o' Frances and I guess ye dinnae' want tae hear what she has said or done in bed."

I shuddered. "Spare me," I agreed.

"I used tae talk tae ye about the King; I had nae secrets frae ye then, but this is different." He laughed. "I dinnae' understand the lady mysel', so I cannae' talk o' her tae ye."

"Whatever does she think about you and the King?"

"We never talk about it. She kens fine that the Gentlemen of the Bedchamber take turns tae sleep in the King's chamber tae guard and protect him and keep him company and see tae his needs. She doesnae' need tae know more than that."

"Do you think perhaps she doesn't even know. . . ?"

"She has never asked and if she did I wouldnae' tell her. It is between me and His Majesty."

"And I suppose the same goes for me," I said.

"In what way?" Rob's eyes in the hand mirror met mine.

"If you thought I did not need to know something then you would keep it secret."

"Secret? What have I kept secret?"

"Well, how would I know?" I said testily. "That is, I believe, the essence of secrets; they are hidden." I sighed. "Have you somewhere along the way, Rob, learnt to be devious?"

"What d'you believe I havenae' told you?" Rob said, putting down the mirror and turning to face me with a frank and honest gaze.

And this was my other reservation (I said there were two). I could not tell him. How could I say: *Do you remember John Lidcote? He thinks you poisoned Thomas. I see him sometimes. We take a meal together. We talk about the news from Gloucestershire and Oxfordshire. And every time we meet he asks me to look into Thomas's death. You are his cousin, he says. You should send a petition to His Majesty asking that the circumstances of Tom's death be fully investigated. And I hedge and stall, for fear that they will be so, for fear of what I will find out. . .*

"Nothing," I said lamely, coward to the last. "I am sure that you are honest with me, Rob, and as long as I believe that, I will stay with you, if that is what you want."

"It is! I do!" There was no doubt about the warmth of Rob's reply.

"The key to the matter is that apprentice," Lidcote persisted.

"The apothecary's apprentice? The sour-faced boy who works for Paul de Lobell and took the physic in?"

"He was the last person to see Thomas alive," said Lidcote. "That is, apart from Weston."

"And what do you suppose that we should do?" I said scathingly. "Ask him if he took in poison? He would be likely to reply in the affirmative, no doubt, and make the matter easy for us."

"Talk to him, at least," said Lidcote. "Sound him out. Discover what manner of man he is."

"I did not like the look of him," I temporised. "But of course he cannot help his face."

"Speak with him," Lidcote insisted. "It had better be you, Giles. I have already met Lobell and so am known."

Although I had ventured within the portals of the apothecary's shop I did not think that I would be remembered except as a messenger collecting for another; and as it happened it would not have mattered, for Lobell was not there on the day I screwed my courage to the sticking post and entered on the pretext of buying *aurum potabile* , one of the few preparations whose name I recollected.

A young man I did not recognise prepared the mixture for me. I leaned against the counter, watching him.

"You are not the apothecary's apprentice, I think? Or perhaps he has acquired a new one?" I asked.

"You're thinking of William Reeve," the youth answered readily enough. "No, he's been sent to Paris."

"Dismissed?" I ventured boldly. "Was he unsatisfactory?"

"I don't believe so. He had money and he had a letter to take with him to see him all right. No, he's done very well for himself," he laughed. "That is, if you don't mind the French! Me, I wouldn't be able to speak the language." He laughed again. "Nor can William."

I laughed with him, a sickly grimace on my face and feeling anything but amused. The new apprentice began to chatter about other things and I joined in frenetically in order not to seem only interested in William. I took the potion away with me and later dropped it in the gutter – foolish, maybe, as it was not cheap – but I would as soon have eaten rotten apples as a Latin potion.

"So. . ." mused Lidcote. "He has been hustled away, our apprentice. Suspicious, very suspicious. . . By whom, I wonder?"

"Robbie, I suppose that you will have it," I said sourly.

"Do you believe in the Earl of Somerset's innocence?"

"I do!"

"Then set in motion the petition I request, or I shall believe that secretly you agree with me."

I shrugged. We sent the petition. We heard nothing more about it. It seemed as useful as having dropped a pebble down a well. Perhaps it was because we were not important, Lidcote and I.

"Or maybe," Lidcote suggested darkly, "those in high places made sure it came to nothing."

"Have done with this," I answered vexed. "I tell you plainly that the Earl of Somerset is an honourable man and loved his friend. It would never have crossed his mind to wish him ill."

I spoke vehemently, believing what I said. I was shortly to have cause to think differently.

CHAPTER THIRTY-TWO

The orderliness of our previous way of life was very much disrupted by the move to the Cockpit lodgings and the invasion of our space by females. Small details were overlooked, daily rituals postponed; a certain carelessness crept in. One result of this was to cause me some disquiet and dismay.

I was standing in the marital bedroom sometime in late spring; I had come to sort out what Rob would wear that evening. I had my hand upon the lid of the little coffer where Robbie kept his private letters; it moved beneath my hand. Absent-mindedly I fiddled with it and it shifted. I looked. It was unlocked. I could see the key now, lying a little apart. Rob had forgotten to lock the box.

I was alone. I would be undisturbed for some time. I am ashamed to say I lifted the lid.

There was a pile of Frances's love letters. I had read some of them; they belonged to the days when Thomas composed sonnets on Rob's behalf and love letters in exquisite prose which no lady and certainly not the besotted Frances might resist. I put them down on the table. I found one from Northampton in florid style: "My heart is full of the love of you. Reading your poor writing is like the cracking of a nut for the sweet kernel." You'd swear he was in love with Rob. Maybe he was. He had certainly overseen his rise, his courtship of Frances, and his reputation linked his name with celebrated males of past times. It would be understandable if he lusted after Robbie. Perhaps Frances confided in him, shared the secrets of the marriage bed with him, told him how

237

completely Robbie satisfied her, after her unfortunate experiences with Essex. Perhaps he lay by proxy in the arms of Robbie, savouring Frances's confidences. *And then he. . . and then he. . .*

Here was another one from Northampton – short, compact.

Sweet lord, Overbury being viewed, there was found in his arm an issue and on his belly twelve kernels likely to break to issue, each as big as three pennies; one issue on his back with a tawny plaster on it; this was strange and ugly. He stank intolerably in so much as he was cast into the coffin with a loose sheet over him. God is good in cutting off ill instruments from off the factious crew. If he had come forth, they would have made use of him. Thus, sweet lord, wishing you all increase of happiness and honour, I end, Your Lordship's more than any man, Henry Northampton.

I sat down suddenly. The nauseous facts, the callous tone of the writer, which plainly was not assumed by Northampton likely to give offence to its recipient, hit me sharply in the gut. The assumption that the neat outcome was the work of the Almighty – that Thomas was an ill instrument. . . The factious crew – Lidcote? Archbishop Abbot?

But Northampton? I knew of course that he had written to Thomas in the Tower; Thomas had told me so. But I had assumed that this was in connection with procuring Thomas's release. Tom had been writing in placatory tones; Northampton had been replying. He and Suffolk had promised to work for Tom's release. Tom had said so. I knew so little. I did not know what to believe. But Northampton then had viewed the body or had been in close touch with those who did? I had not been aware of this. Who would pass the details on to him? Elwes. Why would Elwes do that? What was Northampton's part in the business? Had Lidcote set out on the wrong track when he told me that his suspicion lay with Robbie? Northampton. . . He was a very old man now, seventy-four and ailing. He was laid up at his country house at Greenwich, with a festering sore upon the thigh. But. . . a murderer? The man who gave the order for the poisoning of Thomas? For Frances's sake? Did he love Frances then so much that he would order murder done to grant her her heart's desire? But it was to Rob he wrote. His fellow conspirator?

I had no sooner attempted to digest the implications of this letter than I caught sight of another. My heart jumped. It was in Tom's handwriting. It was different from the other letters, folded so many times that it was creased and stained; and greasy it was, as if it had been smeared with lard. . . hidden in pastry. . .

This paper comes under seal and therefore I shall be bold and speak to you as I used to do myself. I understand you told my brother Lidcote that my unreverent style should make an alienation betwixt you and me and that hereafter we should never be as we had been. With what face could you tell him you would be less true to me, to whom you owe more than to any soul living, both for your fortune, understanding and reputation? Five months' miserable imprisonment, all down to you! And now to say you'll alter towards me for the style of my letters! Alas! This shift will not serve to cover your vow, your sacrificing me to your woman, your holding a firm friendship with those that brought me hither and keep me here, and not to set me free. And you bid my brother keep your intent secret so you might not steal away with your wickedness. But that shall not be. You and I shall come to a public trial before all the friends I have. They shall know what words have passed between us heretofore of another nature, I upon the rack, you at your ease, negligent of me. When I heard how notwithstanding my misery you visited your woman, frizzled your hair and daily were solicitous about your clothes, held daily traffic of letters with my enemies without turning it to my good, sent me nineteen projects and promises for my liberty, then at the beginning of next week sent me some frivolous account of the miscarriage of them and so slip out of town. . .

By God, since I came in here I have not found the advantage of a straw, by not so much as a servant in my extreme sickness, nor my friends free to speak my last words to. . . That this wickedness can never die I have writ the story betwixt you and me from the first hour to this day. . . what secrets have passed between you and me before I was caught in this trap. All the particulars I have set down and sent by a friend of mine whom I dare trust. So if you deal wickedly with me I have provided that whether I live or die, your shame shall never die but remain to the world, to make you the most odious man alive. . .

My hands trembled as I read the letter. I could feel Tom's rage and sense of betrayal rising up like steam, hot as the day he wrote it. Five months. . . just shortly before his death. I heard his voice speaking the words. I saw him, as Northampton's note described him, covered in sores, weak, ill and neglected.

But even as I shared his outrage, I sensed the emptiness of his threat. If he told the world of his mistreatment, I thought dismally, who would care? The bickerings of rejected lovers, they would say, and smile and sneer and pass on to some other matter. Yes, Rob had treated Thomas shabbily, but as to whether the cynical world would consider him the most odious man alive, I doubted it.

Moreover I did not believe that even if Thomas had written such a letter as he threatened he could have sent it out. I knew how difficult it had been to send and receive letters; everything was searched by Weston. It must be bluff. One whom he dare trust? They never let such near him.

But the most damning part of the letter was Tom's plain fear that one way or another he might die in the Tower. I do not believe that he would have considered Robbie capable of ordering his murder; but there was that phrase 'if you deal wickedly with me' which could be much open to misinterpretation. It could mean anything at all; but Lidcote, for instance. . . Lidcote would assume it meant that Thomas feared Rob meant to murder him.

Lidcote – he must not see this; it would fuel his worst suspicions. I would say nothing of it.

I cast a hurried glance through some of the remaining letters. There were several more from Tom, all creased and greasy. I read snatches here and there:

> – for you know the king is jealous of me for that you love me better than him. . . let me know whether that in the scurvy greasy bottle was legible. . . others are not kept in the Tower so long; it must be on account of our passionate love. . . when I come out they may be afraid I shall divert you but you must assure them I will not. . . I pray God you may not be sorry for this. . .

But I now began to grow nervous on my own account. I would do myself no favour to be caught here reading Robbie's letters. I replaced them, as best I could in the order in which I found them, and I shut the lid.

My own apprehension alarmed me. It could not be that I had now cause to fear Robbie! It was ridiculous, impossible. What a damnable thing suspicion was, causing one friend to doubt another, seeing demons where there were none!

There was, I understood now, much more to this matter than whereof I knew or Lidcote knew. The involvement of Northampton, whom Tom hated and had warned us both against so long ago, put a more sinister complexion upon the matter. *Into whose hands Rob must not fall.* . . Well, Rob had fallen very neatly into those hands. Under Northampton's influence he had been led to interest himself in the Spanish policies favoured by the Howards; he had been seen to speak at some length with the Spanish ambassador. He was considered a Howard man now, and all Protestant and Puritan parties would consider him their foe. Had Tom lived he would certainly have had something to say about the folly of this kind of policy, particularly since Northampton was rumoured to be using his position as Lord Warden of the Cinque Ports to smuggle out priests and spies; and the word treason had been mentioned.

But how deeply was Rob allied to him? And did that alliance go as far as murder? *If you deal wickedly with me.* . . If this letter were to fall into the wrong hands a man distrustful of Robbie could see in it a motive for murder. He might interpret it as meaning that Thomas feared for his safety, that to prevent him revealing to the world how badly Rob had treated him, Rob might order one to stop his mouth. That I knew this was nonsense was irrelevant; but an enemy could make much of it.

That Rob should leave the letter in an unlocked box – that Rob should have kept the letter at all – exasperated me; this action – or lack of action – smacked of folly beyond belief. However, I dared not take it upon myself to destroy it and nor did I wish to confess that I had seen it. But I did pick up the key and lock the box; and then I came away.

With the movements of someone in a trance I sorted Robbie's satin suits, his shoes, his collars. And all the while I rebelled against the notion which presented itself to me with such a vibrant clarity – that Rob had had reason to wish Thomas dead and that Northampton was a creature devious and powerful enough to fix it. No, I thought, not Robbie. Northampton maybe. But not Robbie. Whatever the evidence against him – and it was only Lidcote's suspicious nature and Tom's distorted fears – if anyone had poisoned Thomas it could not be Robbie.

Why not? I could hear Lidcote asking it as clear as if he were at my very elbow. Why not? What is your evidence to the contrary?

And all that I could offer were those most illogical, those most unanswerable of reasons: because I know him. . . because I love him.

One morning very early Lady Frances came into my room. I was still half asleep and the sun was warm on my pillow. The first I knew of her presence was when her hair brushed against my face, like the soft-draped wing of a mythical bird. I opened my surprised eyes on to a honey-coloured thickness and like honey there was an over-sweetness about it from the unguents she combed into it.

"Giles," she murmured, her lips close to my eyes.

She was wearing some light chamber robe and I could smell her skin and the almond flavour of her breath.

"I want you to know, Giles," she said in her low soft voice, "how very grateful I am for your service to my lord. I want you to know from my own lips how much I value you."

I muttered something stupid about thanks and kindness.

"I know there was a time," she said, "when you wondered whether your place was with my lord or elsewhere. I never desired to come between you. I know your friendship goes back into the past. I am so glad that you decided you would stay."

I mumbled idiocies about loyalty to Robbie.

"Yes," she said. "I know that you are loyal. I know my lord values your loyalty. And so do I. So you will stay with us, Giles? Let me hear you say it. Look at me, Giles, and say it to my face."

I knew what she was doing. She was so stunningly beautiful that she believed herself irresistible to all men. Not that I mean anything immoral or unworthy, no, I never have denied that she was absolutely devoted to Rob. No, she was working her own particular enchantment upon me. She was Titania, I a mortal who had strayed into the forest. She had done the same with Walter James, Rob's good-looking secretary. He thought her wonderful and would do anything for her. She was using her presence, her glowing sensuality, to win us over, to bind us to her. Copinger, Fargas, James, everybody. . .

I was obliged to raise my eyes to look at her, from somewhere beneath her bosom since she was leaning over me. I was startled to see the complacency showing in her brilliant topaz eyes, the sense of power. She reminded me of a hawk – predatory, strong, able to escape by flight. The words caught in my throat as I replied to her direction:

"I will stay with you, my lady."

She gave a little smile from perfectly shaped lips, like someone who has breakfasted on her husband's mistress. She leaned down till I had all but suffocated in her hair, and very lightly touched my lips with hers. Then the great wing of hair was lifted and she moved away. In the doorway she paused and turned.

"There is a gift for you, Giles," she said, and was gone.

I turned to the wall and all but choked. I said that her enchantment had worked with Walter James; it nauseated me. I sat up in bed and shook myself, like a hedgehog of its fleas. I felt patronised, if one may use the term of a female, and I felt used. I heartily resented her assumption of my devotion, and as always it enraged me when she spoke to me on Rob's behalf. I never could endure the scent of almonds after that.

The damnable thing was that the gift she left me, propped against the door jamb, was an Italian lute of perfect proportion, already strung and with an excellent tone. It would have looked odd to have refused it, even if I had wanted to; in truth I could hardly wait to get my hands upon it. I set about to tune it there and then, all naked as I was. I played 'Bonny sweet Robin' carefully and with a good deal of passion; and then 'Love's god is a boy' very merrily. It was a joy to handle. I leaned back, my fingers resting on the throbbing strings. At the back of my mind the gift seemed to savour of a bribe, but I had not the least idea why Frances should be bribing me to do what I had already chosen to do – remain in Robbie's service. And so I rarely felt entirely comfortable strumming that lovely lute, though everyone complimented me upon the music.

When Lord Northampton came back from the country it was apparent that he was not well. He did not appear at court, but went straight to Northampton House and took to his bed. Robbie and Frances visited him there. Rob told me about it in the evening.

"He cannae' walk at all – there is something spreading in the flesh of his leg. And Giles, it stinks. We sat there making pretence we couldnae' smell it. Frankie felt quite ill afterwards. His face looked awfu' grey. Puir auld man."

"What do you truly think of him, now that you know him so well?" I asked.

"He has always been awfu' guid tae me," shrugged Robbie. "This last time I had the impression he had something on his mind. Mortality, as I guess. It would gie a man cause tae think, with the flesh o' the thigh mouldering awa'. I guess he's troubled that they'll tell him that the leg must be cut off. And at his age. . ."

"Do you believe him devious as they say?"

"I do, aye. But in his dealings wi' me I'm sure he has been honest. With his foes I guess it tae be a different matter. But he's devoted tae Frankie and tae me. He says his best wish is tae live tae see a bairn or two."

"Perhaps it is something else that he has on his mind," I said, ignoring such an uninviting prospect, and thinking back to what Robbie had said before.

"Then why did he say nothing about it?"

"I don't know. Perhaps you are right and he was thinking about his condition, physical and spiritual."

But next day a messenger from Northampton House brought Rob a letter, which he opened upon the scene of domesticity before him. I was sitting to one side, playing the lute, and Frances and Anne were sitting together sewing.

"The auld man wants me tae go and see him," Robbie said. "He says he has a thing tae tell me and would see me alone. He says tae come tae supper."

It was all I could not not to break the rhythm of my playing. This savoured to me of something of importance. To me it seemed as clear as day that Northampton feared his time might be at hand and there was something that he wished to impart to Robbie. Ah, but my mind ran only in one direction these days. Why should it be anything to do with Thomas? My fancy pictured them – Northampton propped upon his pillows, a cage about his leg beneath the blanket, his face drawn with pain; Robbie leaning to him the better to catch his drift, forcing his face to hide the revulsion that he felt as the stench of the decaying flesh assailed his nostrils. What would it be? – advice on whom to trust with Northampton gone? Warnings to burn all letters concerned with Thomas? A confession? An admittance of guilt? Oh, how I longed to be a fly on the wall at such a meeting! Then sourly I reflected that Rob would never tell me of the substance of it, if it did indeed concern Thomas. My fingers slipped on the strings and the chord jarred, which vexed me, as I rarely made such an elementary mistake when playing for others. Curiously no one seemed to notice. You would swear that everybody there was deep in thought, oblivious to me.

I helped Robbie later that evening to prepare himself for supper at Northampton House.

"You'll come wi' me, Giles, of course?" said Robbie.

"Gladly!" I said, with a leap of the heart. So – perhaps I would learn something after all. . .

As I was brushing down Rob's doublet, Frances entered, her hair loose, her gown excessively low cut, lacking the lace that sometimes covered part of her bosom.

"Robin. . ." she said meltingly.

Robbie gazed at her cow-eyed.

"Rob. . ." I murmured warningly.

"Leave us, Giles," said Frances. Then she glided over to him, into his arms.

When I combed his hair next morning I was not gentle, letting the comb tug at his curls.

"You did not go!" I accused. "You did not see Northampton."

"Frankie wanted me," Rob said sheepishly. Then he said a monstrous stupid thing. "Och, Giles! Is she not the loveliest creature you set eyes upon? I cannot resist her when she comes tae me. . . last night she was sae guid tae me I could think of nothing but herself."

"The puir auld man?" I mocked. The comb tore at his curls with vigour.

"I'll go tonight," he promised, wincing under my ministrations.

He did not so, for a message came that the old man had sunk into unconsciousness. Northampton House then filled with Howards. Within the week the old man died, the tumour in his thigh his death warrant. Frances wept and Robbie comforted her; and I thought about Thomas and I wondered grimly what secrets the old man had taken with him to the grave.

"We must all comfort each other," said the king to Robbie. "He was a guid friend tae us all. It will do us all guid tae leave the dirty town behind us and take the clean air o' the country."

The Summer Progress! How splendid we all were as we set out that July! To show his love for Robbie King James created him Lord Chamberlain. Robbie seemed like the northern star, the most constant star in all the firmament. For years now he had been the darling of the warmhearted loving monarch. He was twenty-eight years old, beautiful, adored by his besotted wife, fawned upon by all who would rise in this wicked world. It seemed that nothing could mar his radiant glory.

And yet there was something, though as yet we did not know it.

He was twenty-two, tall and slender, with the face of an angel and gorgeous legs. He was of good family but more or less penniless. Someone had just advised him to try his luck at court.

CHAPTER THIRTY-THREE

A Magdalen flood
Never did good. . .

The old rhyme was very much in our minds when it rained upon the July day which honours that particular saint; but worse was to come next day in the way of unseasonable weather, presaging doom for someone, no doubt – but for whom?

The royal party had reached Bedfordshire where the king purposed to remain for several nights, but when he received word that the Queen's brother was arrived in London His Majesty decided to make a swift trip to the capital. He travelled south by coach, Robbie with him. The sky darkened.

Within a few moments there came heavy rain, so that nothing could be seen from the windows of the coach. Louder and louder sounded the rain upon the glass, till it became apparent that this was no rain but hail – hailstones that battered on the panes in the month of July, hailstones so fierce that the coach was obliged to stop and the horses' heads were turned away from the onslaught. The dripping coachman explained that there would be a halt.

"Where are we?" James enquired, trying to peer beyond the elements.

"We are not anywhere, sire," replied the hapless coachman glumly. "That is our difficulty. If we could see through the rain, which we cannot, we would see woods and fields and trees. Otherwise we might have sought shelter. I am certain that the rain will cease; then we may go forward."

"Then it seems that we must make the best of it," said James.

The coachman returned to the horses – it is not an easy life, a coachman's – and the king and Robbie were alone, surrounded by the noisy whirling world of water.

"It is no hardship at all tae me tae be here with Your Majesty," said Robbie.

"And there are many that would envy me," said James, "alone with the comeliest creature of my kingdom. Rob, give me a kiss."

They embraced. Enclosed in that curious placelessnesss they shared a long deep kiss. The hailstones rattled at the window. The King's fingers touched Robbie's face, his eyes, his hair, his little golden beard.

"And then he tweaked my chin," gasped Robbie still quivering with outrage at the memory, "and said tae me that I was fleshly! He said plump as a chicken, and he chuckled. I was speechless. I opened my mouth to protest at such an insult. I glowered at him; but he only laughed.

"'What, are you sulking, Robin?' then said he. 'Come, come, I meant nae harm. We all grow heavier as we grow older; it is only nature.'

"How do you think I then felt? In no way comforted, as you may suppose. He then said worse. He said, all thoughtful-like: 'But Rob, you are not the fresh-faced boy that once you were. What are ye – nearly thirty?' And I went cauld about the hairt."

The smile upon my face that had settled when I heard the king describe Rob's chin as fleshly vanished as rapidly I understood his meaning.

"Aye," he nodded. "D'you remember when Southampton came tae Burghley and they wondered if the king would take him as a lover and they reckoned that it didnae' come tae be because Southampton was too auld – at thirty? It seems that thirty is the knell o' doom at King James's court; and ye would do well to remember, Giles, that all our fortunes hang upon whether I am fleshly in the jaw."

"I think perhaps you see trouble where none is," I said soothingly. "The King's affection for you is such that he will never let you go. All the world knows that he cares for you."

"Aye, but he need not think that he shall put me out tae grass, as he has done wi' Philip Herbert and James Hay. I am of another stamp and I am here tae stay. And if he doesnae' ken that I shall tell him."

"Have you remarked any particular change in his bearing towards you since he discovered what he terms fleshliness?" I said – no, in perfect soberness; this was a matter of the greatest importance! There was not a trace of amusement in my tone.

"No, none," Rob answered with equal gravity. "He seemed tae think the matter mildly humorous and it has proved no bar tae his kissing me again and more than once there in the coach, and pressing his hand intae my crotch the while. And shortly afterwards the coach gave a great jolt and flung us apart and we were on our way again. But I was awfu' sour. I thought: then let him win me if he wants me; and I made him pay me compliments then for an hour or so. 'I'll never come tae your bed more,' I told him, 'if ye dinnae' ken how ye mun treat me.'"

"Whatever did he say to that?" I asked uneasily.

"He laughed and smiled and said that I was fair as ever and he couldnae' do wi'out me and he begged me to be kind. I said I would be kind if I were treated wi' consideration. And he was guid tae me then, as he should be, and has been since, and never a word said about fleshly. Well, Giles – do you think I am fleshly in the jaw?" he said very fierce.

But at the end of seven years
we pay a tiend to Hell
I am sae fair and fu' o' flesh
I'm feared it be mysel.

"Of course not," I said; but he was, a little, and I own to some misgivings on the subject. I know nothing of these matters, as is obvious, but it did occur to me that threats and petulance were not the most diplomatic of weapons against a monarch who had one's entire wellbeing in his hands and who had just discovered one was nearing thirty and putting on weight.

The royal progress had now picked up its original course and having reached Northamptonshire was approaching Apethorpe, where Sir Anthony Mildmay would be our host.

It was early August and the corn harvest was beginning in the fields about us. No presage of disaster was in my mind as we drew near to Apethorpe. Dismounted, standing some way behind the royal party, however, I saw the whole scenario, impeccably arranged as on a stage. I saw the main doorway; I saw James and Robbie enter, and King James was leaning heavily upon Rob, his arm about Rob's shoulder. Beyond them was a staircase, and light from an upper window, with some curious effect of sunlight that gave an amber cast to the scene. Sir Anthony came forward to greet the King, and behind him, on the stairs, was positioned a young man, caught in the light. Somehow, his immobility and the amber light contrived to call to mind a stained-glass window. The young man wore a suit of tawny-red, not unlike flame in colour, and it would not be an exaggeration to declare that, like a flame, he glowed. Perhaps he had gold earrings – something dazzled about his face. You would swear he had been planted there to catch the eye.

The royal party moved past the staircase then; but the king looked back over his shoulder.

A room near to the King's had been placed at the disposal of Rob and Frances; but Rob went to the king that night.

"I was sickeningly sweet," said Rob. "Whatever my true thoughts were I presented a front of deep devotion. The king was a very lucky man that night. I was at my best – all the tricks – he might do anything he liked wi' me; and did. He will be a tired man for a week. He did not sleep; I worked my balls off tae gie that man his pleasure. Praise I got, and thanks and promises; and this ring I have upon my finger. Then as I was getting ready tae depart and go back tae my loving wife he said tae me frae the bed: 'Och, and Robbie, did ye see the lovely boy upon the stairs?'"

The King's careless glance over his shoulder had been remarked by everyone – no meteor in flight leaving a trail across the night sky could have had greater effect. We all discovered soon enough that the young man with the stained-glass-window face was one George Villiers. He came from Leicestershire. His father was dead and his mother was ambitious. He was good at dancing and poor at French. He had dark brown hair, a fresh-faced countenance and gorgeous legs. He was stunningly good looking and only twenty-two.

Planted, I had thought, when I saw him on the stairs. What we did not know then was that I spoke truer than I knew. Planted was he indeed, as carefully as a sapling on a lawn, by the anti-Howard faction, who had practically dragged him out of Newmarket where he had been trying his luck at the races in a threadbare suit with the elbows out. Prepared as finely as the main course of a banquet, pricked out in satins, washed and perfumed, this dish was then presented at the table of the king. The court hung poised to see if James was ready to eat.

"I dinnae' want that Villiers on the progress," Robbie told the King. "And if you care for me you'll send him awa'."

"I do care for you and you know it well; but it doesnae' please me when you make demands."

"I wouldnae' hae tae make demands if you were kind."

"What further proofs of kindness do you need than the many which you already have?"

"This one: send that man awa' and let us get on wi' our lives. Do it. I warn you," Robbie said, "I am no' someone you may push aside – I will be heard."

"Ah? You threaten me? With what?" Curiosity perhaps was uppermost in the King's tone; but underneath there must have dawned a gathering wariness.

"I dinnae' ken," said Rob and grinned disarmingly. "But I'll think o' something, and ye willnae' like it."

"Very well," said James placidly. "I will consider not inviting Villiers tae follow the court. In return I shall expect tae see you at your most generous and docile, Robin, and very obedient tae my wishes."

Surprised and delighted at what appeared to be so easy a victory Rob promised that he would be everything that James desired. It must have been a happy moment for His Majesty – Rob at his most endearing was an answer to prayer. And he kept his side of the bargain. It was small wonder that Frances showed no sign of conceiving a child – Rob was more often with the king than with her.

I watched them, Rob and the king, in their public moments – setting off to hunt, banqueting, admiring the gardens of the country houses where we stayed. No, there was no threat to Robbie. King James was as devoted to him as ever he was, leaning on him, his arm about his shoulder, his face close to Robbie's, his hand stroking the satin of Rob's breeches, resting on the curve of his bum, possessively, in easy ownership, as it must have done last night upon the naked skin. And Rob – how could the king not love him, lovely as he was, with his curly hair and his merry eyes that hardly ever left the king, conveying all he might of willing servitude and mutual lust. And was he not Earl of Somerset? Had he not ridden with the king to the opening of the Parliament, for all the world to see how much the king depended on him? Yes, I thought, these two will be close for many years to come – we have nothing to fear from the leggy youth hovering in the background, procured for James by Pembroke and his Protestants. He was no more than a little blot upon an otherwise creamy parchment.

"What I thought," said James to Robbie, "was that we all three might be friends together."

"I'd sooner see us all in Hell," said Rob.

It was autumn and young Villiers was at court. Moreover, he was plainly here to stay.

"Robin, I need not ask your permission tae make him my cupbearer."

"I dinnae' wish him tae be made your cupbearer."

"I wish it. It is a very small honour, one that need not vex you. It in no way threatens your position if I see him sometimes handing me a cup."

"Was I guid tae ye in the summer? Was I guid tae ye in the big bed at Apethorpe?"

"You were."

"Do you remember all I did for ye, and time and time again?"

"How could I not?"

"I will never do those things more, never, if you make Villiers your cupbearer."

"Och, Robin, why do ye dislike him so?"

"Why? Ha! I dinnae' like his face."

"His face? I thought it like an angel's face. You cannae' take against his face. It is a church face, haloed as a saint's. He called tae mind Saint Stephen."

"Saint Stephen, d'ye say? Bring him here and I will show ye what can be done wi' a heap o' stones!"

And cupbearer young Villiers became – but nothing more.

"You see," said James in a placatory tone, "I could advance him now by leaps and bounds but I do not, tae please you, Robin. Now come tae bed now that we talk o' pleasure."

"You do not please me and you know it," Robbie scowled. "There is no pleasure for me while that person is at court and there will be no pleasure for you either, until I am pleased."

"Get in tae bed; you will catch cauld."

"D'you like the look o' me?" Rob said flaunting himself. "Would you like me in your bed?"

"Have I not said so?" said the much tried monarch.

"Take a guid look; you will find me worth the viewing."

"I admit it, Robin. Tease me no more; bring all that excellence here tae me."

Rob clambered into bed. The king reached for him and Rob let himself be embraced. His Majesty slowly excited himself upon Rob's perfumed skin. He murmured sweetnesses. He called Rob darling. . . sweetheart. . . He sighed. Rob wriggled free. Rob scrambled out of bed. He hustled on his clothes.

"If Villiers was sent awa' you couldhae known great pleasure here tonight," he panted. "I came tae your bed tae show you what you're missing!"

"Robbie, come back," the king begged. "Come back tae my bed."

"Can ye no' see what he is doing?" Robbie told the king as they rode side by side beneath the trees. "It is well known that Pembroke brought him here tae draw your love awa' frae me. They dangle him before ye like a bauble tae a bairn and you reach out just as they intended. It makes you no more than a puppet, jiggling about tae their direction. Are ye sae weak and simple, tae fall in wi' their scheming? Are ye?"

"I have something that I want you tae consider, Robin," said King James politely, "and it is this: bearing in mind who I am and who it was that raised you to the heights that you now straddle, is it appropriate for ye tae talk tae me like this?"

"I say no more tae ye than you should know," said Robbie sulkily, "and that you choose tae remind me o' your station – which seems tae me an underhand trick – shows tae me that the truth of what I'm saying hits the mark."

"It is monstrous, Giles, the way the king must take his part," seethed Rob after one particular banquet. "There he was prancing about in his rose-coloured satin suit – I daresay Essex sold one of his manors tae buy it for him! – and his legs in shiny rose-coloured stockings like some kind o' silly ostrich. I gave the word tae Myton who was handing round the meat that if he could contrive in passing tae spill a plate down the rose-coloured satin I would see him well rewarded; and he did so and an awfu' guid mess he made. There is a manservant to be proud of! The suit was ruined unless Villiers has an excellent laundress. Villiers was beside himsel' wi' rage. He turned round and clouted Myton round the head. Now tell me what, Giles, tell me what is supposed tae happen tae a man that strikes another in the presence o' the king."

"It is a very grave offence."

"It is! It is! And d'ye know the penalty? The right hand is cut off with a hatchet and the stump is seared wi' searing irons and a mighty sizzle. And d'ye know whose task it is tae carry out the punishment? –

the Lord Chamberlain's! That is, mysel'. Aye, if justice had been allowed tae take its course I should have chopped his hand off at the wrist. It is not fair," Rob persisted, "how laws are changed and changed about tae suit the felons who commit the crimes."

"I take it you were thwarted in your intent."

"The king intervened. He has the power tae grant mercy. It is his prerogative," Robbie said in disgust. Then he sniggered. "But for a moment Villiers went very pale!"

In the December of that year Rob and I were amongst the throng that pressed into the Blackfriars playhouse. A great staircase led to the chamber where the play was performed and here the watchers sat on benches for which seat they paid one shilling. We were sitting in one of the boxes – half a crown. On the whole a better class of person used the Blackfriars playhouse. It had a roof, and seats for all; and, being small, it lent itself to the less rowdy plays and had no room for stage fighting. The play was *The Duchess of Malfi*.

I noticed that once again much criticism of the court was implied. In an ideal court, it was suggested, the king rids his royal palace of flattering sycophants, of dissolute and infamous persons. I hoped that Rob would not be recognised! There might be some that would consider him such. *And let my son fly the courts of princes.* I was glad my uncle Overbury was not there to hear. Disrespect to the great continued: "Search the heads of the greatest rivers in the world; you shall find them but bubbles of water."

I found the play a gloomy thing, full of imagery of disease – "Apply desperate physic – we must not now use balsamum but fire – though we are eaten up of lice and worms and though continually we bear about us a rotten and dead body we delight to hide it in rich tissue. . ." and as if it were contagious, it was difficult not to be infected with the play's same sense of foreboding – "yet fear presents me somewhat that looks like danger."

I felt that Antonio looked straight at us when he declared: "Make scrutiny throughout the passes of your own life – you'll find it impossible to fly your fate."

The relentless tribute to the sickness of the world rolled on – "Pleasure of life, what is it? Only the good hours of an ague." And they spoke of poison, murder, death – "It must be done i' the dark – it is a secret, that, like a lingering poison, may chance lie spread in thy veins, and kill thee seven year hence."

Rob was as preoccupied as I. He said: "He plays the lady well. I wish she did not have to die."

"We have seen much of death this day," I agreed, having had my fill of stabbings and stranglings. "Has it made you melancholy? It serves us right, Rob, to go see a play by Webster on a dull day in December!"

We laughed ourselves uneasily out of our doldrums. As we made our way out we were jostled amongst the crowd. I heard a voice close by say: "It is the Earl of Somerset!"

And then the same voice, before it was hustled away by a prudent companion, called:

"Somerset! Who murdered your friend Thomas Overbury? Look close to home!"

CHAPTER THIRTY-FOUR

"Did you hear that?" I said in a clumsy attempt to portray innocent surprise, as we made our way to the river. "No, I didnae', and nor did you," said Rob aggressively, "so let's speak nae more about it."

We did not in the company of the waterman that rowed us back to Whitehall. But late in the evening in the little room where I prepared him for bed Rob shut the door and brought the subject up himself.

"It's no' the first time I have been aware of this rumour," Rob said in a low voice. "I know that people talk. . . there are little flurries and then you hear nothing. I have even received letters. Nothing signed. Just a few scrawled lines; I tore them up."

"A few scrawled lines? Saying what?"

"Och, nothing o' any consequence. Questions. *Why was Thomas Overbury silenced?* – that sort o' thing. And once: *Who poisoned Thomas Overbury?* Folk will always look for trouble. All the world knows that he died of a consumption. But what we heard at the playhouse. . . I have not heard any accusation made before. *Look closer tae home.* Have you ever heard anything, Giles? What do you think he meant?"

I hesitated, as any prudent man would do.

"You have heard something then?" said Robbie urgently.

"Only that some of Thomas's friends had their suspicions about the way that he was buried so hurriedly. It looked as if there might have been something to hide."

"But there was! The putrifying corpse. It was only right and dignified tae attend tae it at once. Northampton said so."

Our eyes met.

"Northampton?" Robbie frowned.

I shrugged.

"Northampton. . ." Rob mused. "They disliked each other, of course."

"I did wonder," I said cautiously, "whether he meant to tell you anything on that evening when he asked to speak to you alone? But you did not go."

"No, that's right, I remember – Frankie came tae me and we made love instead."

"An unfortunate coincidence."

"Well," Rob grinned, "a coincidence, but not unfortunate for me; she was wonderful that night."

"Her wondrousness prevented you from learning something of importance," I said severely.

"Och, but how do we know?" said Robbie irritably. "We are only guessing. These rumours always follow the death of one that goes suddenly, or young. Look at what happened when Prince Harry died. I heard so many rumours of poison. It's the same in this instance. How could anyone have got past Weston and Sir Gervaise Elwes and sneaked in and murdered Thomas?"

"No one could have," I agreed. "No one was allowed in or out, nor letters either, only those that came from Suffolk or yourself or. . ."

"Or Northampton," Rob finished. He was silent for a moment. Then he shrugged. "Well, let the dead sleep. Thomas is gone, and Northampton also. Whatever was done is done. I cannae' bring Tom back however hard I try."

"Would you want to?" I said curiously.

"Well, I don't deny that it would make life difficult for me and Frankie if Tom were here," Rob said. "They would fight like cat and dog. But for mysel'. . . I do miss him. He always knew what tae do. He gave me guid advice. He'd tell me how tae handle this Villiers problem. I get sae angry I cannae think straight. Tom knew the tricks to get one jump ahead and make folk do what you want them tae." He grinned. "And he was awfu' guid in bed."

We had never spoken much of Thomas. I was unwilling to let this oppoprtunity slip by. "So you prefer not to pursue any enquiries over the matter of Thomas's untimely death?"

"Och, what would ye hae me do?" groaned Robbie. "Believe me, Giles, I have enough tae fret about in the present moment. I seriously believe my place in the King's favour is in jeopardy. I am, you might say, fighting for my life, my life at court, the only life we both have known. I cannae' be doing wi' an ancient mystery. I have troubles of my own."

Indeed I knew that Rob was right. The masque that January contained

George Villiers in all his excellence and the king ordered it repeated a few nights later. Some grotesque creatures made by alchemists danced about, and then in company with Mother Nature came twelve courtiers dancing perfectly to show the perfection of the years to come under James's benign rule. One of the dancers was George Villiers, and there was no doubt about it – he danced very well. Rob attended both performances, aggressively gorgeous in peacock-blue satin. He knew well enough that people were shaking their heads and nudging each other and saying that his day was over. He brazened it out. I thought that he was admirable. It looked very much as if George Villiers was here to stay, although as yet he was for the king the cherry on the plate that is saved for last, a pleasure to come, but for the moment something to be savoured in fancy only.

"How could you be so insensible of my feelings?" Rob demanded of the king – yes, you could hear him; he spoke in what he thought to be a subdued whisper; but rage is not subdued and its whisper carries. "One masque was bad enough, with that person in it, but two – and he there jumping about and showing himsel' off, a silly spectacle, and yoursel' like a green girl slavering at the mouth. . ."

His Majesty contrived to sidestep Rob's tirade, and later he wrote him a letter. In his privacy he no doubt could unburden himself of measured thought, a thing he might not do in Robbie's presence, for Rob close to His Majesty was gentle as a fire that spat forth coals and sparks.

It was a very fair if wordy letter:

As trusty friend and servant none comes towards your merit. But as a piece of ground cannot be so fertile unless it's fertile also to weeds, even so these merits since the strange frenzy took you, so powdered and mixed with strange streams of unquietness, passion, fury, insolent pride and settled obstinacy as it chokes and obscures all those excellent parts God has bestowed on you. Greatness and trust and privacy betwixt us allows you an infinitely great liberty and freedom of speech unto me, to rebuke me more sharply and bitterly than ever my old schoolmaster did. I bore – God almighty knows – with those passions of yours, dissembling my grief thereat in hope that time and experience would abate that heat which I thought to wear you out of by a long suffering patience and many gentle admonitions. I told you twice or thrice that you might lead me by the heart, not by the nose. My love has been infinite

towards you. Let me be met then with your entire heart but
softened by humility. You may build upon my favour as
upon a rock that shall never fail you, that shall never weary
to give new demonstrations of my affection towards you.
But if ever I find that you think to retain me by one sparkle
of fear, all the violence of my love will be changed to as
violent hate. It lies in your hands to make of me what you
please – the best master and truest friend or something
other.

"And ye ken what he means by it," said Rob, beside himself with
fury and disbelief. "We live in harmony with Villiers! What? One night
Villiers, one night mysel'? All three in bed together? And d'ye ken the
worst of all – he says he will not mind if I should take a lover. We all
know what that means – he doesnae' gie a damn. So – will I take a
lover? Who shall it be? I think I'll take young Villiers. He's pretty, damn
him. I could teach him how tae gie best pleasure tae His Majesty. I
would be doing them both a favour if I fucked the fellow's arse and
made the way plain for the royal prick. Or maybe that has already been
done for him. They say that he was penniless when Pembroke found
him – they say he would do anything for a roof over his head. No
wonder he has that beatific smile upon his face – he's thinking o' his
memories."

What could I say? Myself I would not have cared if James had cast
Rob into poverty and he and I had been obliged to beg for a crust on
street corners. I was that odd creature at the court of Whitehall, an
unmercenary man. I would have been delighted to take to the road with
Rob as players, if we could but share a bed at night. However, this was
not a viewpoint shared by Robbie; and so I murmured soothing nothings. Frances neither shared my phlegmatic attitude and her support
being more genuine at this time, Rob relied heavily upon her to bear
out the injustice of his position.

"It's monstrous, Robin," she said. "Monstrous. After all you've been
to him – devoted your life to him – and he rewards you thus – for what?
This nothing creature. Did you know his brother is a halfwit or a madman or both? Villiers will bear the same strain, mark my words. He will
prove a trial to the king and the king will know it soon enough. Saint
Stephen! I wish he were indeed Saint Stephen – I would cast the first
stone!"

"There's my fierce darling," Rob said gratefully. "I am glad you are
not my foe, dear Frankie, for I swear that you would terrify me!"

"I would do anything, Robin, to keep you where you are."

"And where is that?"

"High in the king's affection – for so you are in spite of everything – secure in your place at court and close in my arms at night," said Frances; and I turned away from the inevitable embrace that followed.

"There are no factions at my court," James told Rob. "You are quite mistaken. Your own stubbornness sees menaces that have all the substantiality of a bubble."

These imaginary factions now hit on a merry plan. April brought Saint George's Day. Why not mark the occasion with a celebration for anyone whose name was George! This George might be knighted and made a Gentleman of the Bedchamber, with £1000 a year for life. That was a good notion and would give pleasure to so many, the George in question being a sweet good-natured young man who only lived to please.

Rob lay quietly for once with the king and spoke into the darkness. "I feel like one that hangs from a tree and one by one my limbs are hacked away."

"That is the language of excess," the king said. "You speak as if the raising of Villiers were done on purpose to offend you; it is not so."

"Each fresh honour to him being one more stab at my own self-esteem," continued Robbie, martyr-like.

"Your position is secure. Has anyone threatened you with loss of any honour bestowed upon you?"

"I believe that in our closeness there is room only for two; and when I see one creeping nearer and nearer to all that we share it occurs tae me that one must go in order tae make room, and since it willnae' be Your Majesty it will be someone else."

"Robin, now what of your lovely wife?"

"What of her?" Rob said guardedly.

"Become in truth the married man! Love her – it's plain she dotes upon you. Give us children. settle down, in a house with a garden! How I long tae see you happy!"

Rob threw himself out of bed with a shriek of outrage. "How dare ye speak tae me like this, you who say you cannae' do wi'out me? You would send me tae the west country, nae doubt, a good journey awa' frae London, leaving you free tae play wi' Villiers in the same warm place that I have just vacated!"

"All I said was. . ."

"I ken fine what you said. I heard ye but too well. Eight years I hae been wi' ye and now they count for nothing. Thank you, Robbie, now be off tae the country and fuck your wife. But you'll no' take your own advice, will ye? No – for you'll be fucking Villiers!"

Yes, Rob had probably overstepped the mark here, and tried even James's patience.

"Aye, I'll go tae Frankie," Rob growled, prowling round the bed. "Shall I send him in on my way out?"

And so Villiers was knighted, in a very foolish ceremony that had all the elements of that boisterous interlude they write into a sober play to keep the groundlings happy. Why, I half expected morris men and a man dressed as a horse to come prancing in and we all to sing a chorus of *summer is icumen in*.

The imaginary faction had worked upon the queen to initiate the event and it took place in her bedchamber. The king accompanied by Prince Charles, now a thin lad of fourteen, went in, and there was Queen Anne, all dressed and ready to receive visitors. And how do we know as much? Because everybody who was somebody was waiting in the passageways, blocking the doors, pushing and shoving for a better view, and Rob and I at the front, thrust inside the very room.

"There is someone waiting nearby whom I would bring to your attention, sire," says the queen, and out pops Villiers from some alcove and down on his knees goes he. What a surprise to find him within call! The queen then also kneels in a beseeching pose and begs the king to knight this noble gentleman whose name is George, upon this, Saint George's Day.

"I have no sword," the king says as if taken by surprise.

"Charles, give His Majesty your rapier."

Out comes a naked sword; the king leaps back, his fear apparent even amongst his joy.

"Joyfully I dub thee knight," says James.

"The scab," Robbie breathes into my ear.

"Arise, Sir George," His Majesty continues unregardless. You can hear a pin drop, then a buzz of murmur from the throng. Now some to-ing and fro-ing and milling about, as the queen rises and makes clear her next request.

"I thought perhaps," says the queen, "that Sir George should serve you in a practical way as Gentleman of the Bedchamber."

Robbie went stiff as a post. "No – only Groom of the Bedchamber. Giles – tell them so," and he shoved me forward. I had no need to say a word; he had been heard. Villiers's imaginary faction, which looked uncommonly like Archbishop Abbot, sent in one of their party to whisper in the queen's ear. "Gentleman of the Bedchamber," she repeated.

And Gentleman of the Bedchamber it was. Persuaded so eloquently by the queen, what could His Majesty do?

The new knight, the ceremony over, came bounding from the room, to where Archbishop Abbot stood, and flung himself at his feet.

"My lord archbishop!" he cried in a voice that cracked with emotion. "I swear to love you my whole life long as my very father!"

"Take me frae this place," said Robbie loudly. "I may puke."

It was not an easy matter to be with Rob in the weeks that followed. He was constantly irritable, restless, fretful, impatient, subject to moods. This was not Rob as I was accustomed to him. He had been easy-going and affable ever since I had known him, but the present situation was more than he could bear. Villiers was of necessity now always at court, always smiling, grateful for his good fortune, presenting an agreeable contrast to Rob, who prowled about like a leopard only waiting for a chance to show his fangs.

Truly I think the king did not dare take Villiers to his bed. I believe he thought that Rob was angry enough to do him a mischief. Maybe he was right. There was one time in the royal bedchamber when after one of their many arguments Rob took hold of the king and shook him, and Rob had always been physically strong. The very muscles which the king had so often admired were now used against him. I daresay he was somewhat alarmed.

"Aye," said Rob still shivering with rage, "and there'll be more o' that for those that think they may cast me aside."

Poor James – this monster was his lover, while wearing his halo and with sunbeams emanating from his head, pretty Villiers behaved himself and gave every indication of a promised land with green pastures and still waters to the weary traveller.

So gently did the day of reckoning begin. It was a day in June.

Frances, all smiles, put her hands up to Robbie's shoulders. "Dearest," she said, "what if you and Giles should take yourselves away out of it all this afternoon? Go and find some open land and ride. It will do you good. You have been so tense and crabbed. . ."

Rob thought it a good idea, and as for myself I could hardly believe my luck. Alone with Rob, away from the court on a summer day! So I encouraged him to take up the suggestion and we set off. We rode through St James' Park into the fields that lay to the north. By common consent we rode at speed, as if to shake the dust of Whitehall from our feet, and then slowed to a gentle pace with time enough to relish the abundance round about us – the starry elderflowers, the creamy cow parsley, the hedge roses, the daisies.

I looked cautiously at Robbie. What was his mood now? What might this day achieve? He was preoccupied, his eyes downcast. I sighed.

"Are we to bring Villiers with us, even here?" I said.

He jumped, and stared at me, startled. He gave a wry laugh. "For once I wasnae' thinking of that churl. I was thinking about Frankie."

My heart sank. A private fancy I had had of our dismounting under an elder bush and lying in the long grass and kissing and toying and forgetting those that vexed us dispersed like wind-blown petals.

"Frankie?" I said. "Why?"

"Did ye no' think it odd that she asked us tae go out?"

"No; I thought it very kind of her. She's anxious on your behalf."

"Ah, but is she? She has been a little strange of late."

"Has she? I have not remarked it."

"Distant, you know – quiet; and pale about the face."

"As I said, she is troubled for you. And for us all. Please, Rob, put her from your thoughts and let us go on."

His next remark astonished me."I wondered if she has a lover, maybe?"

"Oh no!" I said scathingly. "That's a ridiculous idea!"

"But is it? I have not been with her much of late and when I am I fear I am unkind. I havenae' been mysel' – you may have noticed."

"Just a little."

"What if she is seeing someone?"

"No, Rob, this is folly. The one constant thing about your wife is her devotion to you."

"Why did she want me tae go out and take you with me? I keep thinking about it. It feels tae me as if she wanted tae do something neither of us must know about. And what could that be but a secret assignation?"

"It isn't that – I know it isn't that. And so do you. Your troubles with the king and Villiers have made you think of that subject alone, and you have grown overly suspicious."

"Giles, would you think it very odd if we turned back now and went quietly to see what she is doing, with us gone from home?"

"I would."

"But will you come back wi' me now, and quietly sneak in unannounced?"

I groaned. "I will, the more fool I."

And leaving the elderflower and the long lush grass we rode back towards the smoke of London.

Like felons, in we crept, through a side door of the Cockpit lodgings. The house was very quiet. It looked as if some of the servants also must have been sent away. Some of Rob's disquiet settled on me. Then we heard voices. We went softly towards the parlour, and we listened.

260

The voice was indeed a man's – a deep rough voice with an accent which I could not place, a country burr but not from the Midlands or the west. His tone was menacing and his voice was raised in anger – or was it fear?

"I tell you this, my lady, you are in some danger now and you must know it. And as for me I don't propose to go under because of it. If you would keep me quiet it will take a deal more than your wedding ring. Think on't."

Without more ado Rob burst into the room; I followed. The room was very dark and musty, wall hangings drawn against the sunlight. Frances was seated on the settle, Anne in the corner on a low chair. In the middle of the room stood a great hulking brute of a man, crook-shouldered, hanging over Frances with his fist raised. When she saw Rob she gave a little scream and fell back with her hand lifted as if to ward off a blow. Rob took a stride and punched the stranger on the jaw; the man staggered back and knocked over a stool in his fall. He sprang up. He looked as if he would have returned the blow – and he certainly had the strength and build to do it – but recollected where he was and who it was that had knocked him down. He wiped his mouth and glowered.

Rob drew back the hangings, letting in a burst of sunlight. It showed them, Anne and Frances, looking dazed and guilty, blinking, like the creatures found beneath a stone. Robbie stood there breathing heavily, nursing his knuckles.

"Frances," he said. "Will you introduce me to your visitor?"

But Frances had been struck dumb. She gaped at us like a halfwit. Anne also seemed bereft of speech. She had risen to her feet and her mouth opened and shut like a fish's.

"Franklin," replied the man brusquely. "My name's Franklin. And maybe it is no bad thing your lordship knows it, for you have been a long while in my debt, unknowing. If your lady does not make her confession to you I will tell you myself, for she is deep in trouble, and it may be only you can save her."

"What is your business with my wife?" said Rob. Under his show of anger it was obvious that sheer bafflement was uppermost in his mind. The man so plainly bespoke villainy, both by manner and appearance. It was almost laughable – you would have thought him made up for the stage. His hair and beard were reddish, and he wore his hair long in a pigtail down his back. His face was pock-marked, his expression threatening. And there he stood in Frances's parlour, an invited guest, a man to be seen while Robbie was away.

"I'll leave your wife to tell you about that, my lord," said Franklin, "as I think she must now, not simply because you have surprised us, but because she will need all the protection that your high position and friendship with the king can offer her. And you should know the worst of it, my lord, which plainly you do not."

"Frances – ?" Rob said.

"I cannot. . . not now. . ." was all she stammered.

"But what was that about a wedding ring?"

"Oh – not yours," she gasped holding up her hand, on which the ring showed. "No – I sold the one that Essex gave me, for –" she hesitated.

"For services rendered," said Franklin. "To me. She'll not get that back. And now she owes me more, so when she gives it I will take my departure. My lady?"

"She gives you nothing," Rob said. "And you'll mend your manners or you'll no' be leaving unless it be tae Newgate."

"Oh, Robin, you don't understand," wailed Frances. "Please treat him fair. He has it in his power to ruin me. Here, take this." She took a coin from her purse and offered it to Franklin. He did not take it.

"It's not enough," he said. "Do you think I am a beggar that you throw coins to me? Come now, my lady, you can do better."

With immense dignity and a face like thunder Rob took a ring from his own hand and gave it to the man. Franklin gave a grunt of satisfaction.

"Is that enough, Frances, for whatever it is you have been guilty of?" said Rob with heavy sarcasm.

Frances turned her face away and buried her head in her arms.

Rob sat down beside Frances and tried to put his arms around her. She shook him off and collapsed into a dreadful bout of weeping and would not be comforted. Rob looked at Anne for explanation.

"She fears to lose your love," said Anne.

"Whatever has she done?" Rob blanched.

"You have no idea, have you?" said Anne pityingly.

"I have not. But I will hae and I will hae it now."

"We hoped that you would never need to find it out," said Anne very soberly. "But Archbishop Abbot is in possession of some letters, which will bring it all to light, and Franklin came to tell us that the news is about to break. Folk that should not have spoken have done so, and the word is about. If word gets to your enemies, my lord, we are all lost, I fear, unless something can be done. We thought the truth was dead and buried with the corpse. It had all gone so well."

"Be silent, Anne," snapped Frances. "You make it worse – my lord has no idea what you mean. I'll tell it in my own way." She threw a glance at Robbie. "Send Franklin away. Giles may stay. Yes, Giles had better stay – he is in as deep as anyone, though he does not know it. Oh, give me strength," she moaned. "I am about to lose all I most value in the world."

Rob looked at Anne. "May I ask if it is safe for us tae permit this villain tae depart?"

Franklin answered it. "Aye, I'll not blab. We're all in this together. One goes down, all go. Like ninepins." Then he bowed. "I wish you fortitude, my lord. You have a droll tale to hear."

And he was gone.

Chapter Thirty-Five

"Remember, Robert, all was done for love of you." Dry-eyed now, Frances was prepared to speak. She remained seated, Rob beside her. Anne returned to her corner seat, and I sat upon a stool, far back, but a position from where I could see each face. Frances was wearing a honey-coloured gown exactly the same colour as her hair. It was sewn with threads of gold. Whenever the sunbeams caught them, they gave a sudden leap of brilliance bright enough to dazzle the eye.

Rob radiated sympathy, goodwill, an eagerness to be convinced of her innocence.

"I loved you from the first moment that I saw you," Frances said, looking at him. She saw in his gaze all the old familiar affection. Far from reassuring her this seemed to give her pain. She turned away and looked at her hands, and not at Rob at all throughout her terrible recital.

"I was a little girl then, remember," she said. "Pampered, headstrong, accustomed to getting my way. Your lovely yellow hair. . . everyone remarked upon it. The one with the lovely yellow hair. I wanted you. Not, of course, that I had any conception of what that meant. I simply wanted you, as I would want a necklace, or a dish of strawberries. And then we all came to court and it was a new reign, an antheap upon which all the ants must jostle, and my family climbed eagerly into the heap. Not you. No one knew where you had gone. France, they thought. But I never forgot you.

"And then I was married. I thought it very glamorous. I had a new silk gown – Anne made it for me; it was lovely. And I had jewels and was much petted. My mother told me that it was a good marriage for me. My father spoke about political harmony. My great-uncle made me laugh. He said it did not matter – if I did not like my husband I could take a lover; everybody did. Suddenly I found myself to be a wife. Nothing much was said about the husband. I looked at him as he gave me the ring. He was very shy and hardly met my gaze. He had cold hands. Everyone was very kind to us; there was much kissing of hands and compliments. we had a banquet; afterwards I was a little sick. Rich food, my mother said. Then I went home with my mother and with Anne. We put my wedding ring in a little box and no one then said much about it and the husband went overseas. He was absent for three years.

"Three years is a long time when you are young as I was. I completely forgot what the husband looked like. No one strove to keep his memory alive; there was too much to do. Pleasant things. Masques, poesy, dancing, riding, reading, new clothes. After he had been away for one year, Robert, you came back to England. The first I knew of it was when you rode up to the king bearing Sir James Hay's shield. By then I had read something about Lancelot. I was in the crowd at that tilt. I saw you fall and carried from the field. I saw your golden hair spread on the ground. Everybody wanted to send you gifts as you recovered. All the ladies were in love with you. You should have heard the gossip – you would have laughed. They all thought they could be your lover. They made wagers. They cast horoscopes. But I knew all along it would be me. . .

"You remember that I used to watch you play tennis. You scarcely looked at me. I had Anne make me a golden gown. As she fitted it we talked about you, about how you would admire me. I was sixteen. Most people did admire me. I had my hair curled; it took a long time. We thought I looked as fair as any. You always drank after you played. I waited with a goblet. You would have taken it. I thought at last that you had noticed me and afterwards would speak to me. But Thomas Overbury pulled you away. He looked me in the eyes as he did so, and smiled. It was a horrid smile – possessive, masterful, as if to say: this man belongs to me. It was as if we understood each other, he and I. Then he insulted me with a vile remark, calculated for me to hear. You, you saw nothing of it. You are too easy going, it meant nothing to you. You would not remember it. But I understood it. His look, his insult, said: 'If you want Robert Carr then you must deal with me.' No matter. By then I had an inkling of the ways of court. I spoke to my great-uncle. Do you know, that dear old gentleman would have done anything for me! We had a special bond, he and I, a particular closeness. He always gave me good advice. I told him that I thought Thomas Overbury hungered for a place beyond the seas, and this was true. My uncle spoke to the Earl of Salisbury and shortly afterwards your unwelcome bodyguard was sent to France. I confided all my feelings to my uncle. My desperation: 'Robert Carr never looks at me. . . I am too young.' 'No, no, it is not that,' my uncle chuckled, 'you are too womanly!' But I paid no heed. I knew that you would love me if you knew me. . .

"'Frankie, Frankie,' said my uncle, 'you are someone who should have all that she desires. But here I fear you may be backing a lost cause.' And then he laughed and said: 'you had better give him a love potion!'"

"Yes! Like Tristan and Isolde. Why had I not thought of that before? I pictured the strand of golden hair in the beak of the bird that flew across the sea. A strand of golden hair was the shackle that bound King Mark, just as it was binding me. I thought about the sea voyage, the boat with the jewelled hangings, and the knight and the lady drinking from the same goblet, the wine that contained the magic draught. 'Anne,' I said, 'you know of such things. Can you find me a love potion?' 'Nothing easier,' said Anne.

"'Where will you find it?' I asked.

"'I will go to Simon Forman,'" she replied."

At the introduction of this name Robbie for the first time began to look uncomfortable.

"You gave me a love potion? Concocted by Simon Forman?"

"It was perfectly harmless; they always are; everybody went to him," shrugged Frances dismissively. "Anne had been Simon Forman's friend for years. He had given her countless love potions for other people at court. People just don't understand his work. He used plants, just as the old hedge witches do – wormwood, thyme, angelica, fumitory – wholesome herbs. Anne went to see him and she brought a love potion. I put it in the wine I handed you after your game of tennis. And you drank."

"Well, as I recall, it did not work," said Robbie brusquely, and not a little proud of his resistance to the powers of Dr Forman.

"There was more than one," said Frances.

"There was?"

"You came to dine with us at my great-uncle's house, and Giles also. Several times. I gave you love potions. I thought that you became kinder to me. But not as kind as I would have liked. So Anne began to talk to Giles. She asked Giles more about you. If we had more information we could cast a spell. Just a little one. Nothing troublesome, you understand. But Giles was not very forthcoming. He would reveal no more about you than we already knew."

Rob turned to me and gave me a small ironic bow.

"And so," continued Frances, "I confessed my love. And one day at Whitehall we met and kissed and there you told me that you loved me.

Either the potions had worked or your heart had softened. I did not care which. You loved me. You wrote me beautiful letters, sonnets that any woman would be proud to receive. . ."

Rob's eyes met mine for a moment and my lips twitched. He looked away.

"We were to meet in secret," Frances said. "We would know each other better. My life would be a lovely thing. My years of patient waiting would be rewarded at last. Then the husband came home.

"Oh God," she shuddered. "If you could imagine my confusion. And my rage. A man I did not know – a stranger – suddenly appearing and believing he had rights upon my body, that same body which I longed to give to Robert undefiled and pure. At first I felt darkest despair. Then I felt anger. It was not just. I felt used. I had been handed over to this man when I was hardly more than a child, never consulted, nothing explained to me. Now I was a woman, grown, my mind formed and my choice made. I was angry. I decided there and then that I would refuse to be a part of it."

She looked across at me, dark-eyed. "You have no conception, have you, you and Robbie, either of you, what it is to be a woman in this world where men are judges, masters of households, physicians, lawyers, soldiers – all the parts of consequence. We are like ornaments, collected, shared, given away – little pots of glue that men use to cement alliances. I had not thought about it very much when it suited me to be such an ornament. But now I did. Now I thought: well, this is not for me.

"But I needed to be sure, Robert, of your love. You began so lukewarm; and I suspected Overbury's influence upon you. Everybody said he ruled you. I persuaded Giles to get me some of your possessions. He gave me a lace-edged gauntlet. Anne went to Dr Forman for a spell. You take the gauntlet of the beloved. You light four candles, and the moon must be new and waxing. By earth, water, fire and air, you say, I conjure you to love me, Robert Carr. . . and that is how the spell begins, and there is more – I have forgotten it. Besides, it did not work. And then I got from Giles a single golden hair."

Rob stared at me amazed. I gulped. I saw again her beseeching expression; I heard her wheedling voice. Yes, I had gone off to do her bidding, thinking no more of it. I met Rob's gaze. I nodded; it was true.

"And this I carried in a purse of silk close to my heart," said Frances. "I tell you this to show you how I did all I did for love of you, how my desire became so great that I acted so, that love for you so overruled me that I did more than what in modesty I should have done. This single golden hair I placed upon a saucer and poured in the potion Anne got for me. I lit four candles and I cut an apple in half. I folded that hair in with a leaf of caraway to bind your life to mine, and I put it between the two halves, and I knelt in the garden at Northampton House by moonlight and I buried the apple in the earth. *As it becomes one with the earth so shall Robert Carr become one with me* – I said this three times. The apple is one with the earth, and you grew kind. . ."

Rob fidgeted. "An enemy would say then that you got me by witchcraft," he said.

"I don't think it can be witchcraft," Frances said, "since I am not a witch. It is no different from the country girls that throw hayseed over their shoulder and say

'hayseed I sow, hayseed I throw,

who would my lover be, come after and mow.'"

"Or those that cast the apple peel over their shoulders and find the letter S spread out upon the floor and thus foretell whom they will love," I said with feeling. "It is only country ways."

Frances looked at me, surprised and grateful, I thought, for my unexpected support.

"Then if this is the extent of your wickedness," said Robbie, "why were you sitting there in darkness and talking of danger and plots about to break?"

"It is not the extent of my wickedness," said Frances.

There was an uneasy little pause.

"You forget," she said, "that all this time there was my husband."

Robbie looked blank. His mind was still on love potions.

"The first thing that the beastly Essex did on his return to England," Frances said with sudden venom, "was to catch smallpox."

Rob gave a grunt of laughter. "I do not believe he did that on purpose tae offend ye, Frankie."

"Nonetheless," said she coldly, "it did offend me when he put his pocky cheek so close to mine that I could feel the pustules, pits and hollows. It quite turned my stomach. There were some that bore a little scaly rim. And for a time some of them oozed, then dried, then oozed again; and some all pale and pasty, crusty, like. . . like biscuits!"

She shook herself, as if casting herself free of the unpleasant memory. "The truth is that he had grown ill-favoured, and I was fair and in love with the handsomest man at court, whom I believed my destiny and whom I was close to achieving. A lady who loved Essex with a deep affection might have loved him in spite of his pockmarks, which after all in time may fade. But to a lady who loathed him already it was an added cause of revulsion. I could not bear him near me. As for the thought of a more intimate proximity I knew that I would rather die a thousand times over. About that time Anne said to me that Dr Forman had potions to make a man impotent but that she was unwilling to speak to him on my behalf, for my personal presence was necessary, but that she would go with me if I would go there. And so I did, my situation being desperate."

She looked up. Robbie's face bore no expression. My own must have shown astonishment and indeed admiration. I would never have gone across the river to Simon Forman's house, however dire my circumstance. He had conjured devils, had he not? He had called up spirits. He had been a Dr Faustus, and Dr Faustus had been dragged away to Hell by devils. Yet Frances had dared visit him!

"I was afraid," she agreed, "at first. We used to go in secret, no one knowing that we went. I was trembling with fright when Anne first introduced me to the doctor in the room where he received me. There were charts upon the walls – a figure showing the astrological aspects that work upon the body; and one all composed of letters of the alphabet in a great square, and one composed of numbers and another with symbols which I believe referred to angels. And there were pots of herbs on shelves, and waters in jars, and one that hissed and made steam; and many many books. Amongst it all, Simon Forman." She paused, seeing once again that figure of dark repute. "He was a man short in stature, wearing a purple gown and a velvet cap. He must have been quite old – sixty or so. His brow was broad and furrowed, and also furrowed was the bridge of his nose. He had a thin face with high cheekbones and flared nostrils. His mouth was bitter and sensuous. He had a thick beard and moustache. He had the most piercing eyes that I have ever seen. I could not look at them for long; they made me feel quite ill. But this strange and powerful man put me at my ease and soon became like a father to me. He said that he could help me." She paused again, hesitating before treading deeper waters. Then she went on. "He cast my horoscope. And the Beast's. And when I went back he had ready all that I required. It was. . . something to go in my husband's clothes and in the sheets and. . . on his prick."

Robbie now looked most uncomfortable and loosened his collar as if it had grown warm.

"I had to get close to him, of course, to use it," Frances continued. "And when I could not I paid his manservant to do it. You rub an ointment on the privy member and be sure that some goes inwards," she explained to us, quite naturally, as if it were most reasonable; but I swear my own prick twinged in an awful sympathy for Essex.

"It worked very well," Frances continued. "And there was other to go in his food. And when we went to Chartley I took it all with me."

"The puir devil," Rob said wincing.

Frances suddenly stood up. "What do you know of my own suffering?" she cried. "I would have done anything to keep him from me. It was a nightmare to me, Chartley. Far away from London, far away from you. So many fields and woods and roads between. You feel as if you are going towards the end of the world. And the house. . . it is near nowhere. Only woods and trees, encroaching trees, like sentinels to keep me in. Thousands of acres – herds of wild oxen – silence, silence, silence. I was like a mad thing. I refused to leave my room. I locked the door. I had a wax mommet of him – Anne helped me make it – the size of a doll. Every night I stuck a fresh thorn between its legs and pressed it in hard and left it embedded there all day. And then at night I came forth, cloaked, and wandered out, and tore the roses for the thorns they bore, and watched the moon in the black clouds and cursed him. And all that time," she gloated, "he could never raise his prick." Her voice throbbed with triumph and with pleasure at the notion. She continued: "But the measures would be only temporary. I could not continue with this intermittent dosing all my life. I determined to ask Dr Forman if he had some stronger brew. . . more lasting. . . to make the Beast unwell, sick in his bed, leaving me free. But when I got back to London I learnt that the good doctor had died. He died that September in a boat on the river and he forecast his own death to the very moment."

She sat down on a chair beside the window. "I was devastated. Where would I go now for help?"

I remembered Robbie saying that Frances had told him of Forman's death and had seemed troubled by the news. We had attached no importance to the matter.

"Without the good doctor's aid, the Beast was like to recover. I could not permit that. Then Anne told me about Mary Woods, whom they called Cunning Mary."

"Och, I remember," Robbie cried. "That hag who accused you of buying poison frae her – tae murder your husband!"

"Yes. And how you laughed and said old crones would threaten anything for money, and how eager some folk were to stain my good name. She came to Anne's house. She wasn't an old crone at all. She knew of a hundred poisons, all with different properties, all potent to a greater or lesser degree. A poison for every occasion!" Frances laughed, a little wildly. "Who would have believed it! Here in London! Poison, she said, was so easy to procure. She knew stories. . . we would be surprised, she said, to learn how many deaths of natural causes were helped to their conclusion! 'Ah – not to kill him,' I said, 'merely to render him incapacitated.' And then it seemed that we might get the marriage annulled. And so I ceased my dealings with that woman. But if there had been no legal means I sometimes wonder whether I would have been tempted to go further. She had the means. . . Then someone started the gossip about me. I knew Mary Woods was not to be trusted. Rumour of my dealings with her floated about for a short while. Well; we lived it down. But Mary Woods had given me a potion. More than one. And then the Beast grew sick."

I had a vague recollection of Essex's withdrawal to Chartley at various times, illness being mentioned.

"His hair fell out," said Frances, "and he lost some of his fingernails. But nothing could be proved concerning me. And who would believe Cunning Mary, who rants and raves and accuses anyone to save her own skin? But she had roused my interest. . . I had some of her potions left to me. More than once I found myself tempted to use it on that man I loathed, in a greater amount, to see what would befall. . ."

"But you did not," said Robbie, plainly shocked and plainly wishing to bring to an end Frances's rambling contemplation of further villainies. "Essex is alive, thank God, and you are spared the knowledge that you committed murder. As you say, no one believed Mary Woods. At least, no one of any consequence. My God, Frankie! Tae go tae these lengths – tae consider taking Essex's life – tae flirt wi' necromancy and the filthy ways o' ditch crones! And all for my sake!" He gave a rough laugh. "I hope you found me worth it."

"I did," she answered levelly. "I have been happier beyond my wildest dreams. I have accounted myself the luckiest woman in the kingdom. I know that I am now to lose it all, and in the days to come I shall look back upon our time together with a passion all the fiercer for the happiness being of so short duration."

"Is it over?" Robbie said in some confusion. "I dinnae' see it. You have been ill-advised; and Anne is much tae blame, but dreadful as your confession has been, it has not destroyed my goodwill towards you. What do you mean? Lose your happiness? Wherefore should ye do that?"

Frances began to laugh in a silly helpless sort of way. She shrugged her shoulders.

"Frankie?" Rob said, with the look of a man at sea who understands that he may be about to drown. "Is there something that ye havenae' told me?"

CHAPTER THIRTY-SIX

"Even now," said Frances, "I believe I could have kept the matter quiet were it not that those I trusted have been weak." "Who?" demanded Rob. "Who has been weak?"

"Sir Gervaise Elwes, obviously. He has blabbed to his 'great ones', to exonerate himself of blame. He has shown my letters to Archbishop Abbot. He was a fool – I did suppose it all along; but my uncle frightened him into acquiescence. It is since my uncle died that all has fallen into disarray. He was an excellent plotter. He had been practicing for years. It was all down to him, that clever scheme to get Overbury into the Tower and out of the way. And show me no innocence here, Robert, you know this as well as I."

"So help me, I was party to it," answered Robbie. "I very much regret my action, seeing what followed; but at the time I was glad tae be free of Thomas's attentions and his accusations regarding yourself."

"Robert, there was more than accusation," Frances said darkly. "My family honour was impugned by him – an upstart from nowhere. We have served the monarchy for generations. He stirred up hatred against us, rashly, for no one slanders my great-uncle and gets away unscathed. And for myself. . . what did he not call me? – whore, witch, base, vile, filthy, stupid, unworthy of your love. He exuded hatred towards me. He tried to turn you against me. He sneered at me, insulted me, ridiculed me. And once, Robert, at the tennis court, he saw me looking at you – adoringly, no doubt – and he, standing close beside you, nibbled your ear, and looked me in the eye as he did so. He was laying claim to you – physically – gloating, boasting. He was issuing a challenge. He despised me and he underrated me, because I was a woman. He felt contempt for women, did he not? He felt contempt for me. He underrated me. Well, that was his mistake."

There was no doubt about the quiet triumph of her tone. She was almost purring.

She continued: "What could I do? He was banished for his arrogance, but he came back again. Like the winter. It goes; but it comes back again. Accusations and abuse, yes, but then came the threats. The annulment hung upon a thread. The grey churchmen picked over the private trials of my marriage bed, spoke words unfamiliar to them – penetration, ejaculation. . . I never knew until the very last moment whether I would be a free woman. I never knew till the last whether I would live shackled to the Beast. and all the while the scurrilous verses were sung about me in the streets, with always someone kind enough to repeat them in my hearing."

We knew what she meant; we had heard them too.

There was at court a lady of late
That none could enter she was so straight
But now with use she's grown so wide
There is a passage for a carr to ride. . .

From Catherine's dock there launched a pink
Which sore did leak but did not sink
A while she lay on Essex' shore
Expecting rigging, yard and store

She was weak-sided and did reel
But Some are set to mend her keel
To stop her leak and mend her port
And make her fit for any sport.

"Only marriage to Robert would clear my good name," said Frances, "and raise me from the slime of gossip and rumour. And Overbury swore he would prevent it. If it was proved I were no maid I would not get my freedom; and Overbury said that he would tell the world I was not so and that I had used witchcraft for my ends. I tried to stop his mouth – I paid a man a vast amount to stab him in an alley, but nothing came of it. And so my uncle got him in the Tower; but even there his voice was heard. He spoke to people daily at a window. He wrote letters hid in pies. My uncle got rid of Sir William Wade who was too high principled for our purposes and made Sir Gervaise Elwes lieutenant of the Tower because he would do all my uncle said. But uncle only wanted Overbury closed in till we had the annulment. It was not enough. When he came out he would be once again a troublemaker. So Anne said to me: *well, he must not get out.*"

An image came to me of Thomas telling of an attack upon him when he was walking in an alley with Ben Jonson. Ben Jonson thought the dagger had been meant for him. But it had been in the hand of an an assassin, sent by Frances! Slowly I began to digest the implications of her last remark.

"Elwes needed to be provided with an under keeper," Frances said. "Anne knew a man – Richard Weston. He was in her service, her husband's bailiff. We told him what we would require of him. He understood. I paid him well, with promises of more when the deed was done. So into the Tower he went, our creature."

"We thought it was Northampton!" I blurted out.

"No," said Frances without expression, knowing what I meant. "No; it was me." She laughed bitterly. "I never knew there were so many poisons to choose from – did you? Realgar – *aqua fortis* – white arsenic – mercury – powder of diamonds – *lapis causticus* – great spiders – cantharides. Who told me? Master Franklin, whom you have just met. He is an apothecary. Anne found him for me. We needed a poison which would lie in the body a little while, and he languish little by little. Franklin gave us *aqua fortis*, which we tried upon a cat. We could not use that for it was too violent. As was white arsenic. It was decided to use rosalgar. I put it in a little phial, wrapped in paper, and gave it to Weston's son to take within the Tower and hand it to his father. But nothing happened. Weston behaved stupidly. He thought Elwes knew what was going on and asked him: *Shall I give him it now*? And Elwes became righteous and made him throw it away. 'What shall I do?' Weston asked us. 'We must think of something else,'" I said.

Cautiously I stole a glance at Robbie's face. It was completely without expression, immobile as if carved from stone. *She had tried to poison Thomas.* She had procured the services of an apothecary – and just such an apothecary as my over-heated fancy had so many times envisaged! She was sitting here in a golden gown and talking of rosalgar and the killing of a cat. She had suborned the man in whose hands Thomas lay, who had chatted to me politely, affably, who had a mandate to give my cousin poison. The sunlight danced upon a gold pin in her hair. A creature of light, we called her, a woman to whom deeds of darkness were unknown. She said:

"So we put the poison in the tarts and jellies."

"Oh, not all of them," she added, as if to ease our minds. "Some jellies were wholesome. Some contained letters; some contained poison. Then there was the physic – you sent that in, Robert, and you, Giles, you delivered it. White powders, remember, asked for by Overbury, acquired by Killigrew from Lobell's apothecary shop. All going to and fro. Elwes knew all about it by now. What could he do? He was a poor tool of my uncle, a weak man. He told Weston: *Let it be done so I know not of it*. It could well have been he thought the poison came from Robert and of course he would not have dared offend him. Anne cooked the brews. There were luscious partridges seasoned with pepper and *lapis costitus*; fruit and jelly flavoured with mercury sublimate. We were lucky not to be found out, for there were several mishaps! Someone licked the syrup which had oozed from a tart – some of his hair fell out and several of his fingernails; it must have been the same as Cunning Mary used on the Beast. And then a warder's wife ate some of the broth and was up all night with vomiting. But what we could not understand was why the Scab did not die! We called him the Scab. Everyone had names in cipher. Anne wondered if Weston played us false and gave no poison, taking our reward for nothing; but he swears he gave it. And then we heard the Scab was regaining his health, which gave us a fright. And then you told me, Robert, that you planned to bring him forth. My heart turned over. 'Anne,' I said, 'my lord means to release him – whatever can be done?' And Anne said: 'let us send for Franklin.'

"It was then very difficult to get pies and jellies to the Scab for he was close confined in a small dark room and only visited by the apothecary who gave him his glyster. And Franklin said: *Then with the glyster must it be done.* I did not understand his meaning. But I gave him money to be spent as best he knew how, and he gave £20 to William Reeve the youth who served Lobell, and promise of a safe passage to France; and so by night comes Reeve into the Tower and he with Weston administers the glyster and therein was poison and it was of that he died."

Rob put a hand to his forehead. He stood up and began to pace about the room. Myself I was as silent as a mouse. Rob stood, his back to us.

"And then my uncle dealt with everything," said Frances. "He always got me out of scrapes. He thought at first it was my father who had procured the poison. He laughed when he discovered it was me. 'I did not know you had it in you, girl; Lucrezia Borgia would be proud of you. A poisoned glyster – it ranks with the best of Italy and as apt a death as as old King Edward's. But you are not safe while the corpse is above ground. Leave it all to me, Frankie,' he said, 'leave it all to me. You have done well and we shall live to find ourselves grateful. But till the corpse is buried we shall know some tricky moments and it must be done in seemly fashion. But quickly. No prodding and poking, just a brief glimpse to satisfy that damned Lidcote and his country cronies. . .'"

I guessed she had forgotten by now whom she might offend or what horror she might provoke in her listeners as she told her story. Having made her decision to tell the truth she was telling it, and it was our own fault if we did not like what we were hearing. I thought about myself and Lidcote in our alcove at the Star, making our guesses, mulling over our suspicions, fearful, ineffectual, confused. Would Lidcote ever get to hear what I was hearing now? Whatever would be the outcome?

Frances cast a glance at Rob's back. Then she continued. "My great-uncle told Elwes to bury the body quickly and he'd stand between him and harm. He said best let Lidcote see it and be satisfied – but briefly – and then to get it below ground. Elwes did as he was told – he dare not do otherwise; we Howards are too powerful. And therefore we could marry, Robert, all unhindered," she finished breathlessly. She looked at Rob's broad back. "Well, you say nothing, Robert," she cried out accusingly, "but if you are honest you are glad of what I did. I know you wished him dead. You told me so. You said how much easier it would be if he should die of natural causes in the Tower. *How marvellous convenient that would be*, you said. I did you a favour. I did what you dared not do and what the king himself wished done. If truth be known you all have cause to thank me! If you are honest you will see that I am right."

Rob turned slowly round. Then he reached out to Frances and he shook her till her teeth chattered.

"You stupid stupid woman," he said shaking her as if she were a doll. "Do you not see what you have done?"

She did not. She gawped at him wide-eyed and probably with her head swimming.

"My grieving for my friend," said Robbie stonily, "and the foul death that he died – that must wait. But I congratulate you, Frances – you have done what Villiers couldnae' do nor all the Puritan gang that wish me gone. You have handed to them on a plate the gift that they will use tae bring me down. And all of you along wi' me." Then with a movement of disgust he flung her from him, his own strength being such that she fell to the floor and landed in a heap, there being no way that a person in a farthingale may fall and graceful, for the skirt and hoops go one way and the petticoats another, and the general impression much like a capsized boat.

Anne, who had said nothing during the ghastly narrative now darted to Frances and caught her in her arms and looked towards Robbie, who had turned away.

"My lord," she said. "Take care – she bears your child."

A statement always calculated to have some effect; and so did it now. Rob spun about and lifted Frances up and placed her on the settle and himself beside her and his arm about her and contrition overlaying all his features.

I put my head in my hands and closed my eyes against the nauseous whisperings. I had preferred Rob angry. If he had stamped on her where she lay I would still not have been satisfied.

So Lidcote and I had been right in our suspicions. Poison, we had thought, poison from the apothecary's boy, the last visitor shown in to Tom in his dark and lonely cell and now unaccountably absent from his shop, sent over to France, a reward beneath his belt. Lidcote had believed Rob the instigator, I Northampton. I recalled how he had asked to speak to Rob alone in the week before he died, and how Frances had waylaid Rob with her body and distracted him from accepting the old man's invitation. He must have meant to warn Rob of the dangers that might lie ahead if the truth came out, so that Rob could be forearmed. Frances must have guessed as much and prevented it.

Why had I never suspected her? Was it because she was a woman and we are accustomed to consider them passive and without access to the darker side of the age in which we live, unable to go freely through the doorways to the seamy underbelly of the city? And Anne, who had sat there so quietly with her sewing, seeming a frivolous and shallow creature, with her love of fashion, her delight in yellow starched ruffs and her penchant for astrological games. . . It was true she lent her house in Paternoster Row to courtiers that lusted in secret, but of greater sin than bawdiness I had never suspected her. Yet she had known Simon Forman, she knew Franklin, and her use of Weston had made Tom's murder possible.

I had sat with Weston in the kitchen of the Lieutenant's lodgings in the Tower, the pies and jellies steaming at my elbow in the summer heat. I could have tasted one – I could have absentmindedly licked the oozing syrup and lost my finger nails next day, and had my hair fall out. So casually, so carelessly had these jellies been placed. Flies settled on them. *There had been dead flies on the table.*

But what should I do now? I longed to run into the presence of His Majesty and shout out all I knew. *You should have paid attention to my petition – you should have ordered an investigation into my cousin's death – the beautiful darling of the Howards ordered his murder, in as vile and sickening a way as any that we see upon the stage! What punishment? What punishment for so villainous a crime but death?* Her rank, I supposed, entitled her to the scaffold. She was Countess of Somerset. Countess of Somerset and she had killed my cousin. . . And Rob was fussing over her now, stroking her hair; I could hear his voice, all low and gentle, and his mind no doubt distracted from the threat that Villiers presented, while it filled with images of a bonny son or daughter.

Despising myself, I knew that I would say nothing. I would put Rob's reputation first. It was unforgiveable of me, I knew, but what else could I do? No one would believe he did not know what Frances was about. He would be tainted by association. Much as it sickened me I would keep the damned secret.

I stood up and went out of the room. I don't think Rob or Frances knew that I had gone. I went upstairs into my own room and I picked up that lute that she had given me. I took it by the neck and smashed it hard against the door jamb. I smashed the beautiful thing with all my might and then sat down amongst the wreckage, drained.

Anne was standing in the doorway. "What was the point of that?" she asked. "Everyone knows that you accepted it at first. They will assume it was a bribe."

"I know that."

"And you took potions into the Tower. Everybody saw you. Weston knows that you took powders in, sent by the Earl of Somerset. The earl sent in food, just as my lady did. Who knows which were dosed and which were good? The fine lines of goodwill and malevolence are very much blurred in this instance. We are all in this together, Giles. Fine scruples are out of place. I am sent to bring you back into the room. We have to decide upon what story we are going to tell when we are challenged. The Earl of Somerset's enemies will not be slow to move against us."

Chapter Thirty-Seven

But nothing happened. It was a dreadful summer. I believed that everybody knew the truth but had decided to say nothing, biding their time, like cats watching the mice at play. Maybe they thought that Rob and Frances would incriminate themselves further and entangle themselves more deeply in the net that was beginning to be cast about them. What was it they were waiting for? And meanwhile we must live in the public gaze and act as if we had not a care in the world.

Rob decided it would be best if Frances spent the summer with her sister Elizabeth in the country; and he saw her settled in at Greys in Oxfordshire. The infant was expected towards the end of the year. The king was overjoyed to hear the good news and said the country air would do Frances good. I was very glad of the decision for I could not bear to be in the same room as the lady. Rob returned to London.

"Letters. . ." Rob mused. "They may entrap us through letters. Burn me – I writ so many! Where are they all? We have tae get them back."

What is it about this age of ours that everyone keeps the letters they are sent, and very often in a pretty coffer which even the dullest servant knows is stacked full of suspicious correspondence? Lord Northampton had kept the ones that Robbie wrote to him, and when Rob sent round to Northampton House for them a veritable trunkload was delivered. We sat one night before an unseasonable fire in the hearth, rooting through them. Some were burnt outright, unread by me, others, after having asked the advice of an antiquary, Rob altered, saying it would look odd if there had been no letters at all between men who were such good friends as Northampton and himself. And so dates were changed and parts cut out and put into other sections. And then I was sent to Tom's one-time servants to buy back letters Rob had writ to Tom.

Of course I knew Laurence Davies well and he knew me. We had also encountered each other at the Tower. He had taken service with Sir Humphrey May since Thomas's death, and because of that he was frequently at Whitehall. Our meeting took place in an alcove by a window that looked down upon the river.

"How many letters have you?" I enquired.

"I have brought thirty with me."

"That's very good of you."

"Not at all; I have made copies."

My heart sank. But then I thought optimistically: of what value are copies? Folk will say he made them up, if they are in his own hand.

"You have them here?"

He handed me a package, bound about with a black ribbon. I gave him in return the sum we had agreed upon.

"Do you miss your cousin, Master Rawlins?" he said then.

"I do."

"You were boys together, as I understand?"

"Yes, in the Midland shires."

"Fished together in the river?"

"The Evenlode runs just nearby."

"I daresay there is still much grief in the old house on the hill."

Why was he speaking so, stirring at my memories, probing at my pains? I looked at him curiously. I thought that he had changed a little from the anxious doting manservant I had spoken to on Tower Hill. He seemed more worldly, and his casual remarks seemed heavy with meaning.

"It was a dreadful death he died," said Davies.

What had he heard?

"It was a slow consumption, as I understand," I said.

"Not so slow, I think," said Davies, "for the end came in one night."

He knows. . . Who has he spoken to? Where did he hear it?

"I never knew the details," I said.

"You should ask your master," Laurence Davies said. "I think you'll find he knows a little more."

"I know the earl was very saddened to hear of Tom's death," I stalled. "He was his dearest friend."

"I thought so," Davies agreed. "And Sir Thomas thought so too. When Sir Thomas died I asked to enter the service of the earl – did you know that?"

"I don't recall. . ."

"But he would not take me," Davies said. "I wonder why that was? Do you suppose my presence would have been a constant reminder of something he would sooner forget?"

All Davies's remarks seemed double-edged.

"I am not privy to my lord's thoughts," I replied, taking refuge in the manservant's proper docility.

"If the time should come when you should wish to leave his service," Davies said, "Sir Humphrey is a good master. Don't forget. I hope the earl enjoys reading over his old letters. He will see again how completely my old master trusted him, and how he felt himself betrayed. And he will read about the many times he promised to achieve Sir Thomas's release and raised his hopes. It does not make for easy reading. Fare you well, Master Rawlins."

"Mommets," said Toothless Margaret, unravelling a bundle on to the table.

"What is their purpose?" Rob murmured, handling them.

It was a heap of dolls of varying sizes, some naked, some clothed, all about eight inches high. Some were made of wax, others were of cloth, sewn together; and there were two made out of brass, entwined in a representation of copulation.

"Mistress Turner said that I should go again to Dr Forman's house and get these from his wife."

"His wife?" said Rob. "I never heard that he was married."

"Oh yes." I write the words not as Toothless Margaret spoke them but as we perceived her meaning, habituated as we were to her gummy deformity. "Oh yes," she said. "A very shrewish female. . . pretty, but sour. I think that she was jealous. Mistress Turner used to be enclosed with Dr Forman in his study and Mistress Forman had to wait outside, with me, and that did not go down well. Mistress Turner said there might be mommets left which belonged to us, and got me to go again and find them. And Mistress Forman found me these and said I could take them."

"Why should you want them?"

"I don't want them, Lord bless you, sir. Mistress Turner said that you would want them, my lord, as being representations of yourself and your good lady."

"What?" said Rob aghast.

"Yes sir. This is Lady Frances, with the long yellow hair, and naked, and this is yourself. . ."

I caught Rob's eye and could not prevent an unbecoming snigger. The golden-haired wax figure was as naked as the other, with an Order of the Garter round its neck, and a privy member as long as its own height. Even Toothless Margaret smirked.

"It's common, my lord, in love workings, to put the couple to the deed in play. Lady Frances ordered these made, when she was unsure of your love."

"Aye," said Robbie grimly. "Well, she had better make another."

I would have liked to pursue the meaning behind that remark of Rob's; but Toothless Margaret pressed: "what shall I do with them, my lord?"

"Leave them. . . I will destroy them."

Toothless Margaret left us. Rob and I handled the mommets thoughtfully. Rob held up the naked female with its legs splayed and a painted smile upon its face. "What do you say, Giles? Has it something of my wife?"

"It's vile," I said. "And therefore, maybe. . ."

"You're right – it is vile. Intae the fire wi' it. Let it melt. This one now. . ." Rob picked up the representation of himself and surveyed it carefully upon his hand. It could not stand upright for the weight of its extended prick but tumbled forward till the prick supported the body weight. "This one. . ." Rob said with a sudden mischievous grin. "Pretty like, would you not say?"

Anne did not go with Frances into the country. She returned to her house in Paternoster Row where she could be in touch with what was going on within the city.

"I don't like it," she confided to me. "The atmosphere is very bad. It's almost as if the whole business is already known, and yet an invisible blanket stifles it all. I know that old woman who prepared the body for the coffin has been talking. And then Franklin told me that he had seen mommets with yellow hair passed around in tavern backrooms. I don't know if someone has made more to incriminate us, or if they are from Mistress Forman, who dislikes us. When the doctor died I went over to his house across the river to get back all the papers relevant to Lady Frances. I swear that malevolent woman kept some back. I could not remember all our interchanges with the doctor. For all I know the wretched woman has kept papers and means to use them against us. And when Franklin went into de Lobell's shop upon an ordinary matter, Lobell shook with fright to see him, and ordered him from the shop. I tell myself all will be well as long as Weston holds. Nothing can be traced to us if Weston keeps his head. And why should anyone suspect him of anything? I'll speak to him again. . . I'll tell him what to say."

Anne was rambling, talking to herself. She was a woman very much afraid. She had been in the matter for so long I do believe she simply could not remember who knew what and who was trustworthy. It seemed to me that there had been no master plan. My cousin had been murdered by a muddle, by guesswork, by trial and error, and finally by sudden panic. There were too many loose ends, too many mouths to blab indiscreetly, and fear was loose amongst them. What if Rob's enemies found the fellow whose hair dropped out through licking of the syrup? His evidence alone would tell the world of a poison plot. And where had the pies come from? Frances's kitchen! The lack of cunning and cohesion, the curious ineptitude of the whole business would have been laughable if it had not been also terrible.

With His Majesty yet in ignorance of rumour Rob had this notion to get for himself a written royal pardon for any fault he might have inadvertantly committed, this to include treason and murder. He had it professionally drawn up. Amazingly James would have granted it, no questions asked; but Lord Ellesmere the Lord Chancellor would not put the great seal to so bold a proposition.

"He always hated me," Rob muttered to me. "He would do anything tae foil me. Has he been talking wi' Archbishop Abbot? Does he guess my intention?"

The Summer Progress was upon us. On the night before we quit London Rob spoke to me of his fears.

"How may I trail round the south of England wi' a set smile on my face and leaving all this sizzling brew in London? I should be here, tae stem the rumours. You never know what you will hear next. It's like a leak of foul water – you block one hole and it seeps out of another. And then – so nebulous it all is, you begin tae think you have imagined it, that there is no plot, that Anne is merely hysterical, that Abbot is in possession of no letter, that my opponents dinnae' sit like crows upon a branch waiting tae feast upon my carcass. And if there is no plot, then maybe we have all grown crazed and run about like headless chickens for no reason, making ourselves ridiculous. . . But I could do wi'out the Summer Progress. Villiers will be with us. God, how I do detest him. . . Younger than me, taller than me, and, if I am honest, more handsome; unburdened by a guilty wife, unhindered by a Scottish accent. Why don't I make a mommet of him – that seems tae be the way of it, eh, Giles? A funny little wax figure, with GV carved upon the chest, and pins stuck in it – one in the face tae spoil his guid looks, one in the backside. . . Giles," he said then. "Sleep wi' me tonight."

We lay together in the great ornate bed he had shared with Frances. Perhaps the infant had been conceived there. Here had been the imprint of her body. He could not hate George Villiers as much as I hated her who killed my cousin; and it tore me apart to keep my loyalty intact, like a lid of bronze over the cauldron of smouldering rage beneath. What he felt for Villiers was jealousy and natural resentment and a reasonable anger at the ways of kings and favourites.

> All kings and all their favourites
> All glory of honours, beauties, wits,
> The sun itself which makes times as they pass
> Is elder by a year now than it was
> When thou and I first one another saw.
> All things to their destruction draw,
> *Only our love hath no decay. . .*

Love. . . I must not stain this moment with the smear of hate. I put my arms around him and he clung to me. He was shaking with fear, Rob who was so strong and so light-hearted. He held on to me like a shipwrecked mariner upon a mast.

"I shall lose him, Giles, I know it," he said. "It's all over. I shall lose everything."

"No," I said, "no. . ."

I held him close all night, his breath upon my cheek, my lips upon his perfumed hair.

Next day he rode beside the king, wearing amber satin, and a dazzling smile. You would have sworn he was the happiest man alive.

The progress was a generally ghastly affair. Like the balances on the scales of Libra the fortunes of Rob and Villiers seemed poised in equilibrium. The courtiers did not know whom to appease. They dared not be over-subservient to either in case it was the other who retained the royal favour. It made for some silly scenes. James either could not or would not see what was going on. Robbie was sour and ill at ease, taut as a pulled thread, smiling hollowly and veering frequently towards a cynical sneer. Villiers smiled at everybody, like a child allowed at last into the company of its elders. Either prompted by his backers or through an incredible optimism Villiers made several gracious attempts to be agreeable to Rob; Rob told him to get out of his way.

"Robin! You must find it in your heart to feel affection towards our George," reproved the king.

"Would you have me dishonest?"

"I would have you as you used tae be and no' this wild and sullen thing you have become. I never withdraw my love once it is given, but you try me sorely. I say again – it would please me tae the heart if you could bring yourself tae care for George."

"I never can and that's the truth."

"I will send George to you; face tae face you may resolve your difficulties."

"I wish ye wouldnae'. I cannot answer for what I may do."

Jacobus Pacificus. . . Undaunted James proceeded. We were then at Lulworth, in the heat, in the new castle built of white stone. Rob had received a letter from Frances and he paced about in some irritation reading it.

"She writes tae me as if nothing had happened – sae bland and untroubled. And here I am in a fine sweat. . ."

"In all fairness she could scarcely do other," I said drily. "What would you have? 'And by the way, you remember who I had murdered in the Tower. . .?'"

"Be silent, Giles – are you mad? There are those who watch and listen. . ."

As if upon a signal, there came a knock upon the door, and we both jumped, proving the abysmal state of our susceptibilities. Sir Humphrey May entered self-importantly. "My lord," he said. "I have been sent by His Majesty to prepare you for a visitor."

"Very well; do so."

"My lord, it is Sir George Villiers."

"Tell him tae go tae Hell. He knows I wish him there."

"My lord, Sir George is waiting outside your door and he has been sent by His Majesty. His Majesty hopes that you will be kind enough to show him friendship."

"The king knows my thoughts upon the matter."

"I beg your lordship. . . please permit Sir George to enter."

He was here. He came in. He was gorgeous. He must have been about as physically perfect as a man could be. He was all dressed in blue, the which picked out the colour of his eyes. Those few months in the sunshine of the king's favour had caused him to bloom. He was like a flower whose petals had opened. He looked sure of himself, yet with a studied modesty, as if to say: they love me – everybody seems to love me, but I know not why! He stood there for a moment, just long enough for Rob, who looked a little stocky by comparison, to notice how tall and slender was his frame; and then he bounded in and knelt at Robbie's feet.

"My lord of Somerset," he said. "I desire to be your servant and your creature and shall desire to take my court preferment under your favour. And your lordship shall find me as faithful a servant unto you as ever did serve you!"

"I will none of your service," Rob replied. "And you shall have none of my favour. I will, if I can, break your neck, and of that be confident."

Young Villiers's glowing upturned face fell. Plainly he had not anticipated this response. He looked uncertain. He had probably supposed that Rob would raise him to his feet and clasp him warmly. Rob whirled about and turned his back upon him; and Sir Humphrey helped the young man to his feet and eased him somewhat ignominiously from the room.

I knew it for a moment of some magnitude. I suddenly remembered the scene in the hospice at Charing Cross – Rob young and tousled, dewy-eyed and in some discomfort from his broken leg; and Philip Herbert strolling in with his greyhounds and eyeing Rob with frank appraisal.

"It seems I have no choice but to wish you luck. Be glad I do, Kerr, for your rise would be more difficult with my enmity. That I feel none count yourself fortunate. I wonder if you'll remember this moment when you stand where I do now."

Rob turned, his face expressionless. "Has he gone?"

"He has."

"What a buffoon, to throw himself at my feet and think to gain my favour!"

"A complete buffoon, no doubt of it."

"Damned handsome. I had not remarked how beautiful his lips."

"As lips go, I suppose, they are fair enough."

"And eyes like cornflowers. One could not miss 'em."

"They are fairly blue."

"And a penchant for flinging himself upon his knees. It is perhaps his speciality. He did so before Archbishop Abbot when he promised tae look up tae him as a father." Rob curled his lip. "It is a habit that will come in useful tae him when he is called upon tae suck the royal cock."

When the royal progress reached Beaulieu, the home of the Earl of Southampton, the guests settled into their pattern of hunting and feasting, the wonderful forest providing excellent sport. But all was not to run smoothly.

A party from London came with an urgent and secret matter which they must lay before the king. Amongst them was Secretary Winwood who had just received some disturbing news from Brussels.

James spoke openly of the matter to Robbie. Plainly he thought that Rob would share his own concern for the pursuit of justice. He told him all about it, as they rode together in the leafy glades of William the Conqueror's New Forest.

"An apothecary's apprentice, falling dangerously ill and thinking himself like tae die, has made a strange confession. He says that he was given £20 by an apothecary tae administer a poisoned glyster tae a gentleman in the Tower. The gentleman died. . . Robin – it was your old friend Thomas Overbury! Winwood advises me tae look into the business with some urgency. My own good name is threatened if those that live at my pleasure in my prison are subject tae foul play. It is important that we find out who that apothecary was and his motive for bribing the wretched youth tae do a deed sae foul! I remember at the time your man Rawlins raised the matter, but Northampton reassured me, saying Overbury died of a consumption. . ."

The sick look on Rob's face was no doubt put down to the shock he must have undergone to hear so vile a story. He asked leave to ride to Oxfordshire and spend some time with his poor sick wife who missed him sorely. But there was more to Rob's request than the need to talk to Frances about this hideous new development. I guess that he did not want to be on view when the inevitable happened.

At Farnham castle late that summer King James at last took Villiers to his bed.

CHAPTER THIRTY-EIGHT

I have a confession of my own to make now: I was a traitor in the camp; and the reason is that I was glad the news had been broken to the king, glad that he saw fit to have the matter investigated, and most of all, glad that the dirty trail was leading back to Frances. I hoped that it would all come out, the whole vile filthy business, and I hoped that she would get her just deserts – namely death upon the scaffold.

Lord Chief Justice Sir Edward Coke was the man in charge of the investigation. A big loud good-looking Norfolk man, he had risen rapidly through many high offices to become Chief Justice of the King's Bench and privy councillor. He was well known for the vigour and aggression with which he pursued his prosecutions. Queen Elizabeth's

Earl of Essex, Sir Walter Raleigh, the Powder Plot conspirators had all felt his rancorous venom. He feared no nobleman in his pursuit of a conviction. No one would be safe in his hands, I thought gleefully, and I longed for the day when Frances would fall victim to his questioning.

But I sat there, quiet, as usual, my loyalty assumed, and I listened to the sounds of fear.

It was late September. In the parlour of the Cockpit lodgings were gathered Rob, Frances, Anne and I; and James Franklin. Rob stood, his habit being much to pace on occasions such as this. Frances, unwieldy, being about seven months into her time, sat on the settle. There was a space beside her. That Rob was not in it, with his arm about her, was, I thought, indicative of something. Anne sat in a low chair, I upon a stool. Franklin also paced.

"What will we do?" cried Frances. "We shall all be hanged, for Weston has been sent for by a pursuivant and will confess all!"

"He may confess nothing," Franklin said.

With all the instruments of torture which the White Tower had at its disposal? I thought cynically. He will confess. You may count upon it.

"But he knows about you, Franklin," Frances whispered.

"I will deny whatever he accuses me of," said Franklin with a shrug of bravado. "I'll tell any lie you like."

"Listen," Frances urged him. "You must swear to me you'll never confess that you let me or Anne have poison!"

"You may count upon my utmost devotion," Franklin answered readily.

"Oh! If only I could believe as much!" wailed Frances. "The Council are bound to offer you a pardon if you confess. But you see – you must not believe them, for when they have got out of you what they would, we shall all be hanged!"

"Not you, Frances," Rob said drily. "I can promise you the king will never hang the Countess of Somerset."

What did he mean? – that James would spare her life or that she would be taken to the scaffold? I fidgeted.

"But what of we others?" shivered Anne. "Whatever will befall us now?"

It was Sir Gervaise Elwes who had implicated Weston and caused his arrest. He had unburdened himself to Sir Ralph Winwood and the Earl of Pembroke, Rob's known opponent, thinking to clear his own name, falling over himself to explain that although he had known Weston had orders to poison the prisoner and that the poison came in with the tarts and the jellies, he, Elwes, had been shocked and appalled. He had tried to prevent the murder, telling Weston to throw away the contents of the phial, himself throwing away many of the jellies – the ones that stank and oozed, the ones that changed colour in the heat, the ones that killed the flies that settled on them. He had seriously believed thus to exonerate himself from blame.

"Dinnae' fear, Anne; I will do all I can tae protect you," said Robbie curtly. "I still have some influence upon the king."

Rob and I rode back to rejoin the court at Theobalds. Here Rob spoke at some length with the king.

"The matter is now grown very grave," the king said. "This Weston has made some terrible accusations. After an initial silence he has given names – de Lobell, Sir Robert Killigrew, one James Franklin – but these are small fry. He speaks of Mistress Turner, whom we know at court. And then, Robin, he speaks of Frances. Of your wife. What do you know of this? Let me be open with you – he says your wife employed him tae give poison tae your friend."

"Well, that is nonsense," Rob said. "Arrant nonsense – criminal nonsense – and should be suppressed."

"And now your own name has been spoken," James continued quietly.

"Mine?" said Rob in genuine amazement.

"You sent in a white powder, it would seem, by your man Giles Rawlins, he who is ever with you." The king was looking at him oddly now, his gaze of a steely penetrating quality.

"Good God, who is sae vile as tae suppose that I wouldhae poisoned Thomas?" Rob said. "How can you repeat this tae me? You know only too well what Thomas was tae me – you upbraided me bitterly for it. Cannot you see that this whole disgusting business is a plot hatched by my enemies to discredit me and bring me down? And will ye go along wi' it and play into their hands? I wouldhae thought better o' ye!"

"Aye, that was my first thought," said James. "And that was why I knew that I mun hae it all investigated. Tae disprove it, Robin. Tae establish your innocence."

"My – ?" blanched Rob. "But I am innocent! I need no one tae prove it."

"Then you have nothing tae fear frae an investigation," James said eyeing him guardedly.

"I cannot believe that you are saying this! Do you mean that you suspect me?"

"I know you wanted the annulment, you and Frankie both, and that your friend stood in your way."

"Oh God!" Rob swore with strong emotion. "If you of all folk are against me what chance do I stand? Let us call in my enemies and have done."

"I am not against you. I am for you. I want nothing better than tae prove you innocent. And therefore Coke will see if there is a case tae answer and he will then dig out the truth. This business has a stink about it and we mun clear the air."

Rob was shaken by this conversation. "Giles, I believe the bugger thinks I was the one that worked it all. Whatever position does that put me intae? *No, sire, it wasnae' me – it was my wife.* I am a fool, I know, but never did it cross my mind that I would be accused! I thought that I would be the one tae save Frances and Anne through my long-standing bond wi' James. I thought I would be pitied for that my wife turned out tae be a murdress. And now I begin tae see that I may not be able even tae save mysel'. It could well be that I – och, no, it is unthinkable! They dare not! And James would not permit it – he'll never throw me tae the dogs. At least. . . I didnae' think he would do so. . . Giles, you'll sleep wi' me tonight, will you not? You willnae' leave me?"

I was monstrous uneasy myself. I felt it was an apt punishment for me over my uncharitable wishes concerning Frances. Every pain I had wished on her could be Robbie's, if this business was ill-handled. I felt afraid. A husband could well be damned with his own wife. Who would believe that Rob had no idea what Frances had done? What if he were deemed guilty as she?

And me? Now I knew fear upon my own acount. If a case could be made against Robbie, innocent, then would not I his servant and his messenger be damned by association? I do not know which of us two was the more fearful that night as we clung together in that bed at Theobalds while the future gaped, a black unknown through which we were about to flounder, for all we knew, in peril of our lives. It was as if the court which had nourished, fêted and supported us had ripped off its gaudy mask of inconsequential frivolity to show a death's head beneath, its laughing eyes mere sockets in the bone.

One by one all of us that had been in any way connected with the to-ings and fro-ings in the Tower that summer two years ago were sent for by Sir Edward Coke and the Commission of Enquiry, and obliged to present ourselves at York House to be questioned.

I was apprehensive because of the hideous extent of my private knowledge; but of course the Commission did not know that, I told myself, and I therefore would not be asked about it. All that was required of me was to establish who I was and that I carried messages.

And thus I found myself face to face with Sir Edward Coke, a table between us whereon lay papers, very neat, in piles, with quill and ink. I looked at him, the man whose purpose was to ferret out the truth, the man who had called my boyhood hero 'a spider of hell, the vilest viper on the face of the earth'. He was somewhat over sixty, but very sharp-eyed, and even sitting down, an energetic vibrant man, big limbed and powerful. He had a long broad brow, an aquiline nose, and a grey-white pointed beard and curled moustache.

"Giles Rawlins. . . Thomas Overbury's cousin. . . Robert, Earl of Somerset's man. . . H'm!" There seemed a wealth of meaning in so small a grunt. He had a loud clear voice which in the small room boomed like a bell.

"You delivered into the Tower a white powder sent by the Earl of Somerset?"

"Yes. It was *aurum potabile.*"

"How do you know? did you taste it?"

"No. But I know it was wholesome."

"I do not ask for your opinion about what kind of powder you delivered; merely that you acknowledge that a powder was delivered, and by you, and from the Earl of Somerset."

"Yes; this is so."

I was not long in his company; I was asked nothing which I might not with honesty reply. Why was it that an interview of so short duration and so simple in essentials should prove so unnerving? Lord save me, but my legs were shaking as I came away.

Rob and I rode up to Royston to be with the king – Royston, the red brick hunting lodge in Hertfordshire. It was Rob's intention to protest most strongly about the Commission. "The commission you are setting up is composed entirely of my enemies. Lord Ellesmere has always hated me and you put him at its head. . . if you were my friend as you have often professed to be you would quash this commission entirely. . ." Our brief stay there was not particularly pleasant.

It was October, a sullen dripping month of sodden leaves and heavy skies. Through the windows the trees in the garden soughed and shifted in the rain. Holly berries showed bright, and shrivelled elderberries hung down low. The rumour and gossip were unbearable. Everyone could speak of nothing else, but when they caught sight of Rob they grew suddenly silent or whispered behind their hands. To cap it all, came Villiers at once to Robbie and said all unasked: "My lord, there is no love lost between us, I know. But I have never wished such trouble upon you, my lord, and my heart is heavy for you. I would have you know my warmest thoughts are with you at this time."

"God give me strength," said Rob.

"Amen!" said Villiers piously and with feeling.

"– tae bear such hypocritical sentiments as you now show me," Rob said. "You cannae' wait tae see me quit the field and leave you room tae put down roots."

Stung no doubt, Villiers added: "And we were all distressed to hear of the arrest of your wife's close companion Mistress Turner. . ."

Rob had not heard as much. He pretended that he had, while feeling chill and sick at heart. "It was a shock," he agreed grimly calm. "But we are sure that she will soon be released. A misunderstanding. . ."

He hurried off to find the king. "I think it would be better if I was permitted tae return tae London, if Your Majesty agrees," said Rob. "I should be with my wife and I am helpless here against rumour and slander."

"Aye, go," said James. "Do all you may tae ease your mind."

A flock of starlings settled on the elderberries and the tree shook, black with wings.

James came right to the door of the coach that was to bear Rob and myself and our baggage back to London. For a moment it was as if George Villiers had never been. The king put his arms around Robbie and sobbed into his neck.

"Och, Robin, I never wanted this. . . I would give half my kingdom tae hae all as it used tae be. . ." And there he fell to kissing Robbie before all folk. "For God's sake, when shall I see you again?"

"Well, soon enough, I hope," said Robbie.

"I shall neither eat nor sleep till you are here again," wept James.

"You do me too much honour," Rob said.

"Honour, no; between us twain it was ever love, true love. . ."

As we sat back in the coach Rob said: "Well, that was promising. He loves me still. He'll never let me go."

"How much has Anne confessed?" said Rob when he and Frances were alone.

"I don't know! I am going out of my mind. The messages I send no longer reach her. But Robin – there are more letters! Anne wrote some to me and I to her from Chartley in which I spoke too freely."

"What do you mean? You spoke freely about what?"

"About my pain and sorrow."

"You are entitled tae pain and sorrow."

"But in my pain and sorrow I spoke about the Beast and my hopes and fears about yourself. A person might construe from what I wrote that my intention was to cause Essex harm in order to gain your love."

"God's heart, but you have been an awfu' fool, Frances," Rob said despairingly.

"I may have been; but so have you," she retorted. "The letters between you and my great-uncle in which you said you often wished him dead, the Scab. . ."

"I'll thank you not tae use that word when talking of my friend."

"It's how I think of him," she said sulkily, "and how we always spoke of him – my uncle, Weston and Sir Gervaise. 'The Scab is like the fox, madam,' Sir Gervaise wrote, 'the more he is cursed the more he thrives.'"

"Sir Gervaise wrote that?" Rob gasped. "Tae you?"

"Yes."

"And where is that letter? I don't recall seeing it."

"Anne had it."

"You gave it tae Anne?"

"Yes, she put them all in a trunk."

"With the letters frae Chartley?"

"Yes, I suppose so. These are the letters I was speaking of. We have to get them back."

"Oh Christ – and where are they?"

"I believe they are in Anne's sister's house. I know the address at least; it is near Temple Bar."

"Leave it tae me," said Rob.

"And Robin. . ."

"What more?"

"You have heard that Franklin has been arrested?"

The house that Frances described was locked and barred. Under Rob's direction a pursuivant and a locksmith broke the house open and found a trunk of letters in the cellar and brought them to the Cockpit lodgings. Rob took them privily away. I know the trunk did not contain the letters that he sought; but what therein was damning he destroyed.

King James's written reply to Rob's protestations was hardly encouraging. "That I should suffer a murder (if it be so) to be suppressed and plastered over, to the destruction both of my soul and reputation, I am no Christian. . . will you still rail and scribble against me? In a business of this nature I look into my conscience before God and my reputation in the eyes of the world and I do not change my course at the instance of the party without any other reason but they will have it so."

"He speaks so awfu' pious out of guilt," Rob muttered savagely. "He put Thomas in the Tower and kept him there and wished him dead. He was ever jealous of him because Thomas was more handsome than himsel' and looked down his nose at him for all he was the king, and because he feared that Tom and I had fucked."

Rob and Frances's attempts to bribe servants to get messages to and from Anne in custody met with no success. When it was discovered that they had tried to reach Anne, orders were given that they must be kept apart and speak only to their servants. Rob was forbidden to leave the Cockpit lodgings. *It is for your own good, my lord, for fear that you will incriminate yourself by the suborning of witnesses.* Frances was asked to place herself at a house in Blackfriars and to keep herself henceforth out of trouble.

Richard Weston was now brought to trial at the Guildhall. It was generally held that he looked nothing like a poisoner – more like a schoolmaster, they said who saw his trial. Sir Edward Coke spoke with great bombast and panache about the vileness of murder by poison – "A crime detestable and foreign to Englishmen" – and finished with a splendid ring: "Jury, do your duty, notwithstanding the greatness of any!"

Neither Rob nor I said anything to each other about what this might mean. A hunt? A long drawn-out pursuit, with Weston the poor bait and Rob the quarry? I knew so little. Was it all to grow into a plot to bring down the Earl of Somerset so that James might have his way cleared for the favouring of Villiers? This was certainly rumoured. I did not ask Rob if he knew of it; I hoped that I was wrong. I kept my own counsel, sharing none of my fears with Copinger and Fargas, merely waiting on events; but I was monstrous fearful in my heart.

Weston was charged with mixing realgar in the prisoner's broth, arsenic in his food, mercury in tarts and jellies; and finally with helping the apothecary's boy to make and administer a poisoned glyster. But Weston would not reply. He called out: Lord have mercy upon me! and would not plead, though threatened with torture. Unlawfully Coke barged ahead, freely naming Frances, calling her a dead and rotten branch which being lopped off, the noble tree would prosper the better. Other branches of this noble tree had already departed to Audley End – her father and mother had decided to stay clear of this, their own futures now uncertain. Weston's trial was adjourned through his impassivity; but later inexplicably he changed his mind and pleaded guilty, and at his second trial the jury found likewise. Only two days later Weston was taken to Tyburn and hanged. Sir Gervaise Elwes was now taken prisoner. The Dean of Westminster then came to inform Rob that men were now gone to question Frances at her house in Blackfriars. It is an old and well-worn adage that speaks of the sensation of a net closing in but such are well-used because they express a truth.

On the first day of November in the morning when I had finished helping Rob to dress, he said without preamble: "Giles, you would do me a favour if you quit my service and went home."

This was something I had not expected and amazement took my breath away.

"Giles?"

"But you need me," I protested.

"I have Copinger and Fargas and Myton. Anyone of those can do the duties of a manservant."

"But for frizzing your hair. . ."

Rob gave a grunt of exasperation and something akin to amusement. "The frizzing of my hair is the least of my troubles at the moment. I grant that there is no one who makes curls for me as you do but just at present that is of no consequence; I wish you to go home."

"Home?" I said uncertainly. "Oxfordshire?"

"You have always maintained it is the queen of countries."

"And so I do – but now? At this time?"

"Exactly," Rob said grimly.

"Have you grown tired of me?" I demanded hotly.

Rob grabbed me, held me, pressed me in his arms. "You fool," he said. "The converse, don't you see?" Breathless from the rough embrace and the sudden unaccustomed wamth of his demonstrativeness I said nothing, but savoured the lovely moment as a hungry man takes bread.

"Aye," said Rob with understanding. "I've been a stranger tae ye a' this while, a brute. . ." He let me go and he stood back, but holding my arms. "Ever since I heard of Frances' guilt I havenae' been mysel'. Or rather I've thought only of mysel'. Running about in circles – meeting wi' folk I thought could save my cause – railing at the king – writing pages of gibberish tae him, threatening, cajoling – indulging in self-pity and righteous rage – I've been a bear – bad-tempered, thoughtless. . ."

"You had reason," I pointed out.

"Aye – my world as I knew it – the only world I know – falling apart about me. . . and many's the time I've wished that I had Thomas wi' me, tae tell me what tae do." He winced. His hands tightened on my arms. "Make it easy for me, Giles. Don't add more guilt tae my account." It was the same voice he had used, the same intent look that he had offered Thomas when he had advised him to take the chance of an embassy. *Take it, Thomas!* It made me shiver. He had known then what would happen to Tom if he stayed in London – at least, he had known that he would be arrested.

I felt confused. "What do you fear?" I said, a stupid question, tactlessly phrased. I wished that I could take it back. But Rob laughed brightly.

"Fear? Nothing? They dare not hurt me; the king will see tae that. I merely want you out of this. You never were one made for intrigue, any more than I was. I know how frightened you were when you were sent for by Coke on my account. I should never have permitted you tae be put through that. It troubles me that you had to endure it, all through knowing me. I would feel better if you were somewhere else. Just for a while, eh? Believe me, it's for the best."

I must admit to a sudden cowardly impulse to agree without demur. The idea of leaving London seemed monstrous appealing. The heaving city, rife with rumour, the blood lust and clamour, the fear and uncertainty, the confines of house custody. . . Even in November it would be no poor thing to ride beneath the open skies to kinsfolk, countryfolk. . .

"You need me," I said woodenly. Or had I mixed the pronouns?

"I need you, aye, but I mun do wi'out you. Burn me," he grinned, "I never thought you were sae puffed up wi' self-conceit as tae think you were the only one who could look after me! And d'ye think I'll go tae pieces when you leave?"

He made me smile in spite of myself. After all, it would only be for a short time. And there were Copinger and Fargas.

"Then if you think it's best. . ." I began.

"I do – indeed I order it! Burn me, what is the point of being Earl of Somerset if I cannae' make my manservant obey me!"

The jest rang hollowly. "When would you like me to go?" I asked.

"At once, Giles," he said calmly.

"What – now?" I frowned.

"This very day no less. And don't add tae my pains by disputing wi' me. If you are my friend, do me this kindness."

I was his friend; I did so. I was not happy about it.

Within the week my setting could scarcely have been more of a contrast. I dismounted at the Lamb Inn, Stow-on-the-Wold, my boots in good country mud, my ears assailed by the bleating of the sheep that were close penned behind a nearby drystone wall. Of course, this Gloucestershire town was not considered the back of beyond by its inhabitants, as I admit it seemed so to me, fresh from the source of power. At the confluence of five cross-country roads, and famous for its market, it was a thriving place of trade and commerce, and at its Court House no doubt business of great moment was discussed. Rob had been right – it had done me good to breathe some clear air. I will not say that I was light of spirit – far from it – but I had shed the burden of nervous dread that I carried about me in London. I had been too long among Sir Gervaise's great ones, the rich and powerful, the men who made events and lived in fear of betrayal and calamity; and I had shared all the strain and misgivings of folk carrying a guilty secret that must one day break. It was bliss to me to listen in on conversations about matters of true importance: whether winter would be cold or warm, discovered by the cutting of a chip into a beech tree – whether to begin the threshing of corn – how to concoct a mixture of wheatbran and water to lay upon chilblains.

I had arranged to meet my uncle, Tom's father, in the Lamb, to dine, when he had finished his business at the Court House, and though I was not entirely looking forward to it, I saw no reason why it should not be agreeable enough. We need not talk of Thomas. And here was my uncle, sitting in a corner by the opened window, muttering about the smoke that gusted fitfully down the chimney and from the tobacco pipes about us. Our entire conversation took place to the background noise of bleating sheep, penned beneath the window.

He was in his sixties now, my uncle, good-looking, vigorous; his face lined and severe. He waved me over to him cheerfully enough and disarmed me quite with pleasant conversation about our mutual relatives while we ate our way through mutton steaks in ale and butter, with sliced onions and bread, and plenty more ale beside. I was a little disconcerted when he told me Lidcote would be joining us.

"Yes," he said. "He has just returned from London – as I have myself – and I told him to bring all news he might."

"I have not seen him lately. And I had no idea that you were in London."

"No," said my uncle in a voice heavy with censure. "You have been too much closeted with that Scot, I daresay." He looked across at me sharply. "When are you going to quit his service?"

" I – but why should I do that?"

"If the fact that he had your cousin Thomas murdered is not reason enough, I do not know what to suggest," said my uncle in clipped tones.

"But he did not!" I gasped. "I assure you he did not."

"Your opinion is not the one held by most people."

"I think I know the Earl of Somerset a little better than most people."

"The Earl of Somerset!" said my uncle disparagingly. "What is he? Plain Robert Kerr till his good looks got him advancement! His father was a Border reiver – they pass all their time in burning, pillaging and cattle stealing. *Blood will out.*"

"Tell me," I said. "Is His Majesty considered to be knowledgeable and shrewd and something of a scholar?"

"Eh?" said my uncle.

"And who has His Majesty judged worthy of honour and friendship these past eight years?"

My uncle grunted. "With all respect to His Majesty's undoubted learning, I venture to suggest that Robert Carr would not have been so fêted if he had not had a pretty face."

I paused in my reply. The wretched sheep bleated outside the window.

"Uncle, I understand your hostility to my lord of Somerset. . ." I began.

"As I do not understand your devotion to him, Giles. What kind of a creature are you that can stand by him through thick and thin? Lord save us, Thomas was your cousin – does not that count for anything?"

"It has caused me no little grief," I said, straining to retain the politeness due to an elder. "But you are wrong in your suspicions. The Earl of Somerset had no part in Thomas's death."

"Murder," corrected my uncle. "Do you deny that he acted in a shifty and deceiving manner when your aunt and I met him, Thomas being in the Tower?"

"No; I know he was not open with you," I admitted. "But that was because he was obliged to keep Tom confined and could not tell you why; it was nothing to do with any plot to injure him. . ."

"Do you deny that he refused your aunt permission to visit her sick son?" my uncle glowered.

"No," I admitted unhappily.

"That he said that he would plead our cause to the king? He lied to us!"

"He could do no other at the time. The circumstances were so. It grieved him that he could not be more honest with you."

"Him it grieved?" my uncle thundered. "And Thomas?"

Everyone who sat about us at the Lamb was listening unashamedly. The silly sheep bleat on. I glowered back.

"I see I am in the service of a monster," I agreed with heavy sarcasm. "Fortunate that you have opened my eyes to his defects in time for me to escape his clutches."

My uncle grunted. He too was vexed at our having become so lively a diversion.

"I did not take to him at the time, your smooth-faced charmer,"my uncle said, ignoring my remark. "I am a judge of faces – I found your

Somerset superficial, bland, all smiles, no depth; a deceiver."

"These are faults, no more, and pertinent to many."

"Did you know that I have been approached by Sir Edward Coke?" then said my uncle.

"No. As I said, I did not even know you were in London." I hoped that I might be able to conceal my growing uneasiness; I doubted it – my uncle's eyes were like gimlets.

"There is a man to get things done!" said my uncle warmly. "He made mincemeat of Sir Walter Raleigh; he will wipe the floor with your fancy earl."

"In what way?" I said cautiously.

"Why, when the bugger comes to trial," expostulated my uncle. "When he comes to trial for Thomas's murder. There's no way he will not be found guilty, in Coke's capable hands. And then nothing will save him from the scaffold. "

"It seems you know very much more about this than I do, uncle," I said, keeping my temper and my alarm under control.

"I do. I was there to see Weston hanged. I saw him in his cell. He sent for me – did you know that? – and he asked for my forgiveness. He was a poor tool – weak and wicked – but not so much to blame as those that paid him."

"Those unknown. . ." I reminded him.

"Aye, there is much that is unknown now that will be known later," said my uncle enigmatically. "There were no straight answers got from him. Lidcote tried and failed. Lidcote followed him to the gallows – he thought the verdict inconclusive. He troubled himself much over which was the pie that had the poison that took effect – whose was the poison that went in the glyster – where was the apothecary's boy? *Did you poison Sir Thomas Overbury, yea or nay?* he shouted to the wretched man in the gallows cart. But he got no answer that would satisfy him. Ah, but this is mere quibbling. Weston told me that he put a pillow over Thomas's head to silence him in his sufferings and that was how he met his end. By then the foul deed had been done. I shall not rest till I see proper justice done. And nor should you, boy, if you had a streak of honour in your nature!"

"I do very much hope the wrongdoers are punished," I said. "But if they mean to hound the Earl of Somerset – whom I know to be innocent – I can only regret it with all my heart, and pray it does not come to that."

"Come to that? I do assure you that it will. And I shall be a part of it, for Coke has asked me to bear witness when he comes to trial. And if I were you, Giles, I would get myself clear of the villain for you risk to go down with him. "

"It is inconceivable that the Earl of Somerset will come to trial," I maintained with a firmness that I did not entirely feel. "The king will not permit it. The king will protect him from his enemies for the old affection they had for each other."

"I think you will live to be proved wrong," my uncle said in quiet chilling tones. Then with much lightening of expression:"Ah – and here is Lidcote, hotfoot from London."

Lidcote hurried into the place beside us, mudstained and wind-swept. He barely had time to murmur his civilities before he blurted out his news – news of such import that it must be heard before all else.

"The Earl of Somerset is arrested and imprisoned in the Tower of London! He is to be brought to trial and no one gives a halfpenny for his chances of acquittal!"

CHAPTER THIRTY-NINE

"You should never have come back," said Rob embracing me yet once again. "But I am awfu' glad you did." With ironic amusement I imagined the reaction of my uncle when he learnt that I was in the Tower of London with my fancy earl, my smooth-faced charmer, the villain whose downfall my uncle so confidently proph-esied. A month or so had passed since that meeting at the inn. Overjoyed at Lidcote's news my uncle had called for wine to celebrate the occa-sion. Three glasses were brought. My uncle proposed a toast.

"To the swift and speedy trial of the Earl of Somerset – to his conviction – to his death upon the block."

They looked at me, he and Lidcote, waiting for me to declare my allegiance, daring me to go against family and upbringing, to throw away righteousness and morality for the upstart son of a Border reiver who had surely brought my cousin to his doom. I did so without hesi-tation.

"I cannot drink to that," I said; and stood and hurried from the room. The sounds of the bleating sheep pursued me as I rode away into the windy gloom.

When, my affairs in order, my farewells said, I made the journey back to London I thought often about my uncle's accusations, trying to make sense in my own mind of what I had done. It was perfectly true that Rob had behaved shabbily to my aunt and uncle, had lied to them, had kept Thomas from them. This was dastardly behaviour, yes, but every action of Robbie's, every charge levelled against him was also such as might be levelled against the king. It was the king who had imprisoned Thomas, had forbidden him a manservant, had ordered the terms of his confinement. Who accused him? He was now become the arbiter, the judge, the embodiment of integrity, who was as much to blame as Rob. I had no particular idea what I would do in London but in my heart I knew that I must be with Rob.

London was every whit as ghastly as when I left it. During my absence Mistress Anne Turner had been tried; indeed I arrived there on the day of her execution. I heard that she came to trial in the yellow starched ruffs that had made her famous and her best gown and hat. She had pleaded not guilty. But Sir Laurence Hide in prosecuting told the court of Simon Forman and love potions and spells. He read the letters Frances wrote to her from Chartley: "I cannot be happy as long as Essex lives. . . if I can get this done you shall have as much money as you can demand – be careful you name me not to anybody, for we have so many spies that you must use all your wits, and all little enough, for the world is against me." As evidence the jury were shown mommets of a naked couple copulating – the dolls with yellow hair – and spells cast using strange letters and a piece of human skin. As the watchers crowded forward in their eagerness to see these wicked things the floorboards cracked and everyone panicked, fearing the devil was amongst them. Mistress Forman gave her own malicious evidence and Anne was doomed. Sir Edward Coke said she had all the seven deadly sins – she was a whore, bawd, sorcerer, witch, papist, felon and murderer; and chillingly for us he said that Thomas had been a prisoner to all his friends but open to his enemies or such as Somerset sent to him. The trail was set to lead to Rob. A week after her trial Anne was hanged at Tyburn and in a horrid jest of Coke's the hangman wore a yellow ruff and cuffs. They said Anne made a pious end.

Next came Sir Gervaise Elwes's trial at the Guildhall before Coke. Elwes made an excellent defence. He pointed out that Coke had aggravated every evidence and applied it to himself and therefore he stood condemned before he was found guilty. But largely as a result of Franklin's evidence the jury found him guilty. At no time did he hint that Rob was to blame, to the despair of the prosecution. To the last he revered the great ones whom he had served. He was executed on Tower Hill.

Sweet Franklin was an altogether different matter; he accused everybody. He was brought to trial at Westminster towards the end of November. Yes, he had procured poisons for the Countess of Somerset and Mistress Turner but he did not know what they were for. It was all part of a great poison plot, he believed. The Countess of Somerset's mother was the instigator, and if more details about witchcraft were wanted he could give them; he could name several witches. And, he said, there are great persons in this matter more than are yet known. Oh yes, one of them was certainly the Earl of Somerset and he intends to poison Princess Elizabeth and he poisoned Prince Harry and if more names were wanted, Franklin could tell any number of knights and gentlemen who deal in poison. . . He was hanged; and his ending was undignified.

For myself, learning all through hearsay, sleeping on a trundle in the back room of the lodgings of an old acquaintance from my Fortune days, trudging the streets in the newly-fallen grimy snow, it was a dispiriting time, and I was nowhere nearer seeing Rob. Some time in December most reluctantly I made my way to the house in Blackfriars where I knew Frances to be confined, because it seemed to me that here I would find news of how he fared. I was let into the house by Walter James, whose devotion to Frances was undimmed, as witnessed by his presence here. News indeed I found – the babe was born; it was a girl; its name was Anne.

"Named after Her Majesty," said Walter James, looking me in the eye, daring me to query this.

"Of course," I said.

"They believe my lady chose the name to curry favour." Wat and I exchanged wry smiles. We knew well enough which lady Frances had in mind when naming of her daughter.

But much more pertinent to me than the birth of the babe was the other news I had from Wat – that Copinger and Fargas, Rob's servants in the Tower, were arrested for smuggling out a letter, and that the Earl of Somerset required manservants to replace them.

"So you are come in happy time," said Wat, "if you dare take the office; for I swear there will be no rush, arrests and imprisonments being the way of it. Will you go into the Tower? You were always his favourite."

"I will; it seems to me that chance has played me very fair in this."

"Will you see my lady?" he asked, his thought more upon Frances than Rob. "She is in low spirits since the birth."

"I doubt the sight of me will raise them." I observed drily.

"Would you like to see the babe?" he offered, plainly considering such an invitation a great privilege to me. I had no interest in the infant; and the notion of conversation with Frances gloomy after the event of the birth filled me with revulsion.

"Has the infant's father seen her?"

"No. . ." Wat looked uncomfortable. "How could he?"

"Then it's not for me to take pride of place; but if I may assure his lordship she is well?"

"You should never have come back," Rob groaned. "Whatever possessed you? I believed that I had got you well clear of my disgrace."

"I was always something of a fool," I said, and set about to tidy up the room.

It was cold although a fire was lit, and with wall hangings and a little furniture it had been made into something like his rank demanded. I found it curiously disturbing to see some of his familiar clothes hanging up in such a place. There was a good-sized bed. I prodded it. I thought the pillows clammy and set about at once to air them, the mundane action masking my distress at seeing Rob in this predicament. I told the Tower servant who lurked nearby to go and fetch me as many warming pans as could be got, to be filled with hot coals from the fire. He hesitated, as well he might, at orders from this bumptious nobody, but he went quickly enough when I reminded him fiercely: "This is the Earl of Somerset you have here under the king's protection!"

Rob and I were now alone. He knelt down beside me before the fire, taking the other pillow, holding it to the blaze. I looked at him with love and exasperation.

"You knew that you would be arrested," I supposed.

"Aye, and that you would go wi' me if I didnae' prevent it. As if I hadnae' enough on my conscience bringing Thomas intae the Tower, wi'out bringing in yoursel'! And besides," he added with an odd and shamefaced glance, "I didnae' want you tae see me here – it is. . .somewhat humiliating."

"Nonsense – it's home to the greatest in the land," I said cheerfully.

"Och, aye, it's quite a fellowship, I suppose," he said bitterly. "Sir Walter Raleigh has been here for years and he has made his lodgings very comfortable. Lord Cobham in the Beauchamp Tower has brought in all his books – I'm told he has over one thousand. Then there's the Wizard Earl Northumberland in the Martin Tower – he dines off gold and silver plate. A man of taste can make his lodgings all that he has been accustomed tae at home." He fell silent. Rob's home had been the palace of the king.

"I shall never forgive him for this, never," Rob said.

"No; you are not charged with any crime; your situation is laden with ambivalence; you are right, it is unforgiveable. Who is the lieutenant here?" I wondered with understandable uneasiness. "Is he fair minded?"

"Sir George More – oh, properly polite. Elderly. He's the father of

John Donne's wife. His first unpleasant task was tae inform me that I would receive no visitors nor was I tae write letters tae the king. He sends in a couple of his men tae keep an eye on me. But not at night," he added significantly. Our eyes met, flickered, dropped. Then he made a movement of impatience. "How long d'you think I will be here? A month already. Two months? Over Christmas? Those puir buggers in the other towers have been here for years. Somehow I don't see mysel' reading a thousand tomes and writing a history of our time!"

I said nothing. I waited for Rob to broach the subject which had been in both our minds.

"I keep thinking o' Thomas."

"It is hard not to do so."

"All the time in the barge when they brought me here I thought: this way came Thomas, as bewildered as I. He must hae sat there in the boat and seen the offer of the embassy as a trap and realised too late that he had been caught. He must hae thought of me and doubtless believed that I would get him out. He must hae thought: och, I shall be frae here in a week. And then the days came and went and he still here and I out there in satins with any pleasure I might wish tae take laid out for me. How he mun be laughing now! In polished tones he would now speak tae me of a certain justice in the falling out of events."

"I don't think he would laugh, Rob," I said soberly.

"Well then, he would curl his lip," shrugged Rob. "What would he say tae me, I wonder? What would he gie me by way of advice?"

"I think I know," I said with half a smile, "but I will not offend you by repeating it."

Rob grinned. "You don't need tae – I ken fu' well your meaning. He would say: if Frances sends in any jellies, send them back."

We sniggered mirthlessly.

"The first night that I came intae the Tower," said Rob in low tones as if the walls indeed had ears, "I wasnae' in this room but in another. It was the cell where Thomas died."

I caught my breath, appalled.

Rob laughed roughly. "Save your gasps, Giles – I have seen enough upon the stage tae comprehend the intention behind the gesture. I half expected tae be plagued by a dismembered hand as the Duchess of Malfi was and to hear a hollow voice of accusation, some buffoon speaking through a crack in the stone. *This is the room where Sir Thomas Overbury died*, they told me, *that is his very bed*. The devil it is!" I said and drew back – it was a vile hole of a place – no windows and no light. They all want whipping for incarcerating Thomas there! *Just for this night, my lord, this room will be your lodging while your chamber is pre-*

pared. I said nothing but went inside. There was a trundle bed in there – not Thomas's, I know, because Northampton had it burnt, but that it was Tom's chamber I hae no doubt and I was put in there because they think that I am guilty and Tom's ghost will haunt my conscience." I took the pillow from his hands; it was about to catch fire.

"However," Rob said grimly, "I did not order him put in that dark place and that is not upon my conscience, nor am I afraid of the dark. That is not tae say," he added, "that I didnae' think o' Tom as I was put in there tae do. I am not a man that indulges much in fancy. When Tom was in his prison I didnae' gie much thought tae his solitude. I didnae' think the terms of his imprisonment harsh and I knew it tae be temporary. That night, of course, I understood what it means tae be immured within walls of many feet's thickness wi' a single flickering candle, and it being November I was cold and shivered; and that made me angry. And so I lay in a fine rage for that I was made tae be so cold and tae shiver."

I knew horrors of my own that night, with far less justification. As Rob and I lay in the well-warmed bed he slept; but I did not. His grim little story convinced me that they meant to do away with him – after all, there was something of a tradition of it in this place – and my mind wavered between the various ways the nefarious deed might be done. The well-aired pillows seemed no comfort – merely the wherewithal by which we might be smothered, much as the hapless princes were rumoured to have been – and after all, when Lord Darnley was strangled after the explosion failed to kill him, his wretched manservant lover was murdered with him. And so I surely would not be spared to tell the tale! Failing murder, of course, there were in the White Tower the implements of torture used upon the Powder plotters, any one of which might well oblige either of us – particularly myself – to confess to prior knowledge of the poisoned glyster and secure Rob's conviction for his part in Thomas's demise. I dared not go to sleep. I lay in a cold sweat, gripping the sheet, listening to the awful silence, sucking my thumb like an abandoned babe, starting at each imagined sound. Oh Thomas, I thought more than once, now am I well paid for my inadequacy, for my cheerful ignoring of your anxieties, my assumption that all would be well, my eagerness to squint for a sight of Sir Walter Raleigh instead of your signs of debilitation! What cunning twists and turns Dame Fortune offers us – what just rewards for our folly!

Our situation in itself was not that uncomfortable. Servants came and went, under the eye of the Tower guards; Myton – that obliging man who had spilled food over Villiers's suit – saw to the changes of clothes and bed linen; Rob's own cook and bottleman oversaw our food; but even from the Tower kitchens came not one pie nor jelly. It was possible Sir George More was nervous also. Lord Cobham sent in some of his books, and – more welcome – the Earl of Northumberland sent in his home-brewed beer. It was the fact that we were there at all that grated, and we feared the closing in of circumstance, for we knew that evidence was being gathered with the aim of bringing Rob to trial.

As Christmas drew near Rob had been cooped up in that place some seven weeks. In a curious way it grew to be a happy time for me, for I had Robbie to myself more now than I ever had before. I was essential to him, hearer of his thoughts, comforter of his despair, soother of his impatience; and I slept with him at night, free from the rival claims of James and Frances. But of course it was not that simple. Sometimes a Tower servant slept in the trundle bed nearby. But even when we were alone although we comforted one another with our hands one does not make love with a light heart, imprisoned, angry and afraid, and Rob was all of these. He demanded constantly of Sir George to be permitted to write letters to the king. But plainly James believed that if Rob were an accessory to murder, the king could not afford to be in any way connected with him; as it was, he would not come out of this with an untarnished reputation. Rob was moreover furious that his baby daughter was kept from him and understandably bitter about King James's part in this decision.

"When I remember the intimate care he took tae oversee our wedding ceremonies. . ." he said.

Rob was not the sort who could find solace in philosophy. Lord Cobham's books went unread. How to fill the days? We tried to think how he had filled them in his days of freedom – hunting with the king, meeting foreign dignitaries, handling state papers, working with the king, making himself beautiful for the king, playgoing, feasting, masquing, dancing, riding. . . an empty kind of life, a farm worker in Bourton-on-the-Hill would say, but full enough compared to these interminable days of inactivity.

The curling of his hair which had been pleasurable to us both and absorbed hours of leisured time Rob had no interest in now and we let the curls grow out and the golden hair retain its naturalness. I made him keep himself as beautiful as was possible and refused to allow him to go to seed as he was tempted to do now no one cared, he said, what became of him.

"Think," I said, "if you are suddenly sent for. . ."

I bathed him in a tub before the fire. The water in the Tower always smelt odd, but we perfumed it heavily, and Myton brought in additions to our requirements. I read to Rob sometimes and he sat listlessly, his mind on his wrongs. I had a lute brought in and twanged away, but most of the songs we knew recalled happier times.

"He will ask for me back," Rob said. "He must ask for me back."

As one day succeeded another with no word from the king Rob became more and more dispirited. He began to grow obsessed with Thomas. He noted down the date of Tom's arrest – April 21st – and counted the number of days Tom had spent in the Tower before he died.

"One hundred and forty-five days," he said marvelling. "How long have I had? Fifty. And he was alone and ailing. And I wrote such gibberish tae him and did not believe his complaints. Led him along wi' false promises. He was right – I am the most odious creature alive. It serves me right that I am here; it is my penance for neglect of him. It's right that I should suffer and be neglected when I think of all that he endured. All for that woman who came between us. Giles!" he said turning to me all hollow-eyed. "She got me by witchcraft!"

"Have you thought, Giles,"Rob said one night as we lay in bed alone, "that Thomas is here with us? That he lies not a stone's throw from where we are? That I am closer to him now than I have ever been since we lay in one another's arms?"

I did not like the sound of this. I had a vision of him waking crazed one night and running to St Peter's chapel and tearing up the flagstones and flinging open the coffin, an act more nauseous for the reports of what we had heard about the condition of the body. That night he awoke in a cold sweat and though for one penned in by walls of stone in the darkest part of December a shivering fit was not the most unlooked-for of occurences yet this was feverish and strange. He tossed and turned, his hair plastered to his forehead, his teeth chattering; I had to hold him still.

"That trick tae get him intae the Tower. . . the false promise of an embassy – I was party to it, with Northampton and the king. I thought myself sae canny – diplomacy it was called, and I was fooling Thomas, whose trade it was. The number o' times he called me stupid, and I thought: well, I hae fooled you well enough who was sae clever! I was awfu' proud o' mysel'. Can he forgive me? Of course he cannae'. I shall burn in hell for what I have done."

"Rob!" I shook him. "You have not done anything. This is madness. Calm yourself."

"And then I left him tae his fate. I did not get him out."

"You would have done. You were going to. But he died first."

"She murdered him first."

"Yes she did," I agreed, being human and pleased to see him latching on to that at last. "She murdered him. She has said so. She had her reasons, and no doubt she will suffer also, in her way."

"Her sufferings are as nothing compared wi' his," he said savagely.

"Yes. His death was vile."

"I wish the same for her. Oh God – if I had never seen that woman I would have my friend today – I wish tae God that she were dead instead of him." His voice, intense in the complete darkness within the bed hangings, made me shudder. No, if I am honest, it was not his voice that did so – it was the great surge of elation that I felt in my own heart to hear him talk of Frances with such venom. And as I held him he began to weep and sob so full and freely that his tears streamed down my neck and his whole body heaved and shook in an ecstasy of remorse and self-loathing, spattered with incoherent oaths and prayers, the which I heard in an ecstasy of my own; for this wreck in my arms was the Earl of Somerset, late favourite of the king, the jewel of the court, and he had understood at last the damage he had done, the terrible mistake that he had made, and was now making to Tom's cousin a gift of his repentance and his burgeoning hatred for the woman. *Ah, Tom,* I thought exultant, *now it is you are revenged!*

And then I checked myself and gave myself a hearty mental shake for acting like one in a Webster play. I would be cackling like a crone and drinking out of a hollowed skull next if I was not careful!

And so the year turned, passing over Rob and I, leaving us to grapple with our conflicting emotions. And all unknown to us the careless court was celebrating with a new masque for a new era. Justice was summoned. Jove announced that he intended to create a new Golden Age, spiritual and fresh. A curtain was pulled aside to reveal George Villiers sitting in a scallop shell in an Elysian bower lit by the glow of many candelabra. Sweet voices rammed the message home.

Then earth unploughed shall yield her crop
Pure honey from the oak shall drop
The fountains shall run milk
The thistle shall the lily bear
And every bramble roses bear
And every worm make silk.

CHAPTER FORTY

"I would strongly advise you to plead guilty, my lord Somerset," said Sir Edward Coke, rustling his papers with a flourish. "That way you throw yourself upon the mercy of the king and make the path clear for the graciousness of a royal pardon. And believe me, my lord, a royal pardon is the only chance that you have to escape condemnation and the punishment that must follow."

"It is very kind of His Majesty," said Rob, "tae offer me pardon for something which I havenae' done. But then, His Majesty was ever kind."

They faced each other across the table, the lieutenant seated near the door. It was January and bitter cold.

"It is kinder than you deserve," said Coke. "I think you are not properly aware of your own danger. You will come to trial, my lord of Somerset, and you must take heed of what you say, both at this present moment and in the days to come."

"I will never come tae trial," said Rob. "His Majesty will not allow it, for though it may seem otherwise tae you at this time I have been held in high affection by His Majesty. And though you have been very busy, my Lord Chief Justice, ferreting in dark corners, you have no' found anything which may be proved against me, for there is nothing tae be found."

"Oh, as to that," said Coke, "pray do not deceive yourself, my lord, that you will be spared a trial on the grounds of insufficient evidence; for I have gathered already enough evidence to ruin you twice over."

"Och, so I am already tried then, and condemned? What – on hearsay and rumour? – for you hae nothing else. And you suppose I will present mysel' before you voluntarily tae endure that?"

"My lord, I would remind you that four have already been executed, none of whom had any malice toward Sir Thomas Overbury but were instruments of the bloody malice of others. God forbid that the authors of so heinous a crime should pass away with impunity!"

"Threaten me all you please, Sir Edward – I am an innocent man, and no' the person you sae darkly hint at," Rob replied. "But I warn you, it will be very much tae His Majesty's discredit if he dares bring me tae trial, for not only will his own guid name be stained by association, but if I chose tae speak out loud concerning him it would be very much against his interests."

Coke frowned. "And would you like to explain to me here privily just what you mean by that insinuation?"

"I would not. I would sooner save it till I stand in a crowded hall and all tae hear me. But I will say this. No one wanted Thomas Overbury dead more than His Majesty himsel'; the whole world knew how bitterly he hated Thomas, for His Majesty was consumed with a vindictive jealousy over my requited love for Thomas – aye, love, Sir Edward Coke, and the bodily lust that goes wi' it – now let the king think on that and ask himsel' whether he would like tae hear that I hae spoken of such things before a crowd tae whom it will come as something of a surprise." Rob paused, defiant. Swiftly he continued: "And it was the king whose warrant put Tom in the Tower, and it was the king's own physicians that saw Tom in his cell and did not guess that he was being poisoned; and it was Dr Mayerne that placed de Lobell in attendance upon Tom and the glyster was administered by de Lobell's assistant. And Dr Mayerne took his directions from His Majesty. . . Now tell that tae His Majesty and see if he would like tae have me go into a public place and speak!"

Coke was plainly disturbed by this outburst and shuffled his papers about with studious care. But he had a trump of his own.

"Your wife, my lord," he said, "has already made a full confession of the offence. Do you understand me, my lord of Somerset? Your wife has admitted she gave orders for the murder of Sir Thomas Overbury." And he watched Rob's face closely, with eyes like a hovering hawk's.

"I am sorry tae hear that my wife be guilty of sae foul a fact," said Rob without a change of countenance.

"And the king has heard of it," pursued Sir Edward.

"She has been promised a pardon also, then," Rob surmised.

"It is not for me to say."

"She has made a full confession. . ." Rob said thoughtfully. "And am I implicated in it?" he demanded.

"That is also not for me to say."

"Ah – then I am not. I am not, am I?" Rob said jubilantly. "At least she has shown honour there. You hae no case against me, if Frances has been honest."

"My lord," said Coke severely. "You are indicted for procuring and consenting to the murder of Sir Thomas Overbury as an accessory before the fact, and you will come to trial, I promise you. You must make a declaration in writing to the king, which the lieutenant here will take down. And when you come to trial," he added with a sudden jovial smirk, "may I offer you some advice?"

"I see that you intend tae do so and that I mun hear it."

"Then here it is. Take some practice in the days to come to speak in English which the civilised ear may comprehend, for as you speak at present nobody will understand you."

Leaving Rob smarting under this jibe the Lord Chief Justice indicated to the lieutenant that the interview was at an end.

"Phew," said Rob. "He came at me like a battering ram. If I am tae stand trial before him I will stand no chance at all."

"Do you really believe that the king had anything to do with it?" I murmured.

"Put it this way," Rob said loudly, for the flapping ears of the lieutenant's servant. "If I stand trial His Majesty should be there beside me."

Rob's declaration to the king was dignified and honest.

"Being told by my Lord Chief Justice that I was indicted and was shortly to expect my arraignment I did not then believe him for I did not look that way. Your Majesty has three kingdoms wherein to exercise the prerogative of your power and but few that taste of the first of your favours, in which number I did think myself, if not the first, then inferior to very few. And having committed no offence against your person nor the state, I hope Your Majesty will not for this bring me to a public trial which for my reputation's cause I humbly desire to avoid. But if I must come to my trial, knowing the presumptions may be strong against me in respect I consented to and endeavoured the imprisonment of Sir Thomas Overbury (though I desired it for his reformation not his ruin) I therefore desire Your Majesty's mercy and that you will be pleased to give me leave to dispose of my lands and goods to my wife and child and graciously to pardon her, having confessed the fact. . ."

" I did not like the word 'mercy' in that it smacks of my guilt, but the lieutenant said it did not – it was his word. I thought 'favour', which is less loaded wi' implication. But I abided by his advice – I never was an excellent writer of letters. But I think that this one may a little touch His Majesty. . . Have I lost him, Giles?" said Rob wistfully of a sudden. "Will a' that mean nothing tae him?"

"How may we know?" I said helplessly, believing the king much at fault and Rob's surmise a true one.

"At heart he loves me," Rob insisted. "All that time we were together. . . nights of love and days of pleasure. . . does that count for nothing? It is this business which has come between us, that is all. When I am proved an innocent man I know that he will ask for me again."

I would never have said so to Rob, but it occurred to me that even so must Tom have likewise in vain believed, thus with false hopes sustained as day succeeded day.

Some excitement within the Tower now, for Sir Walter Raleigh was to be given leave to depart and go in search of gold across the seas. The new Golden Age, you see. If Sir Walter was successful he would be a hero and the gold he brought back a symbol of the brave new era.

I went into the courtyard to watch him leave. A crowd from within the Tower had gathered to see the great man leave his prison. I was much moved at the sight. He was handsome yet, but ah he looked so old! His once black hair was grizzled and his shoulders were bent; he walked with the aid of a stick. My boyhood hero! I was able to stand close enough to wish him luck. To me he would always be magnificent.

As if that were not excitement enough, now into the Tower was come the witch, the self-confessed poisoner, the wicked wife herself – Frances! Her arrival I did not see, but she was allowed to make her home in Sir Walter's vacated chambers until her trial.

Robbie was given leave to speak with his wife, the Lieutenant being present. He came away very thoughtful.

"I was touched tae the heart tae see her," he told me. "She is awfu' cast down. She can barely raise a smile. Very beautiful; but ashen pale and thin about the cheek. She misses the bairn. She says our daughter has fair hair and blue eyes. She's three months old now; Frances's sister is looking after her. A good quiet babe, she says. And it is true – in her confession she did not name me. I looked at her in her distress and I couldnae' believe that she did what she did. And I thought: will I ever know if it was love or magic that brought us together? Whichever it was, because of it we are in awfu' trouble. I cannae' see a guid future for us now. As I came away I thought of that play we saw, you and I, at the Red Bull playhouse, and how the puir man says tae the lady: 'I was bewitched, for all the world speaks ill o' thee,' and how he loves and hates her both and says: 'Thou hast led me like an heathen sacrifice, with music and the fatal yokes o' flowers, tae my eternal ruin.'"

I curled my lip and made no comment.

Myton said the London streets were full of nothing but talk of Rob and Frances. You could buy pictures of them – horrid little likenesses, he said, with yellow hair and lewd eyes. And there were verses made and sung and sold – of a somewhat different nature from the panegyrics that accompanied the marriage festivities.

A page, a knight, a viscount and an earl
All those did love a lustful English girl

A match well made, for she was likewise four -
A wife, a witch, a poisoner and a whore.

And there was:

When Carr in court at first a page began
He swelled and swelled into a gentleman
And from a gentleman and bravely dight
He swelled and swelled till he became a knight
At last forgetting what he was at first
He swelled into an earl and then he burst.

"Let not his lordship see them," I said. "For myself I think it good
to learn the generosity and tender heartedness of the town we live in."

When he was told that the date of the trials had been fixed – Frances's
for 24th May, Rob's for the 25th – Rob told the Lieutenant flatly that
he would not go.

"You see what their intention is," he cried. "Frances has confessed
and is already guilty. All the vile trappings will be dredged up and smeared
about, much talk of arsenic and glysters and jellies turning black in the
sun, and then, this fresh in the minds of folk, I will be brought in and
be damned by what is hers."

"I will pass on your protestation to the commissioners," said Sir
George.

"Do it or not as it pleases you, but I will not stand trial."

They sent in Walter James to try and persuade Rob to agree to
stand trial, speaking to him as one who cared about him.

"I am bid to say His Majesty wishes you no ill. He wants to pardon
you, my lord. He wants you to emerge unscathed. He says he knows
that you are innocent. He says if Lady Frances be the villain you are well
rid of her. Oh, my lord, consider – there is no other way. They have
decided upon it and will do it."

"They cannae' do it if I am no' there," said Rob, "and there's an
end."

His good humour on having decided never to stand trial made for a
merry evening after Wat had gone, and, left to ourselves, a night of
strenuous love-making that for once was not prompted by the need to
comfort or console or stifle fear. Suddenly it seemed as if we had not a
care in the world. That the weather was now warmer helped our mood,
for we could lie without blankets and see each other naked in the half-

light. We laughed as we kissed. We wrestled in our nakedness and scrapped and tousled, tickled and bit each other – we were like puppies in a meadow. I could see the whiteness of Rob's teeth; and it occurred to me how rarely I had seen him smile at all over the past few months. I clamped my mouth on his, angry that so open-hearted and affable a man had been so twisted out of character, had known so much of sterile darkness in the power of others. Passionate we clung, and in our mutual delight we forgot where we were and gave ourselves up to pleasure. Panting, groaning, we lay back in the turmoil of our sheets, our bodies slippery and sweet with lust, and our hearts light.

"Myton has brought in some poems," I remarked. "I wondered whether to show them to you, Rob, but you are strong enough to bear it, and the ironic humour of it may sustain you."

"Give them to me."

"Do you guess the subject?"

Rob read:

Tis dangerous to be good, well may we praise
Honesty and innocence, but who can raise
A power that shall secure't gainst wrongs to come
When such a *saint* hath suffered martyrdom. . .

Thomas?

And as the blood of that first slaughtered saint
For vengeance to Jehovah made complaint
So did the blood of Overbury cry
For justice to the throne of majesty. . .
True life alone
In vertue lives and true religion
In both which thou art deathless. . .

Rob looked at me wondringly.

"Yes," I agreed. "These, and also Tom's poems, are selling on the streets; and 'The Wife' proves particularly popular."

"That dreary tract?"

"Even that."

Rob laughed mirthlessly. "I daresay Coke has paid the booksellers tae flood the market wi' them. The scene is set. And they expect me tae go forth into it and receive my judgement. I had sooner go naked in a blizzard."

"Should you ever do so, let me know. I would be there in a warm coat to watch."

He kissed me. "You'd share your coat wi' me, Giles. You've been good tae me so long and I have taken it as my due. I'll be a better friend tae ye henceforth, I swear it."

Having made his decision not to stand trial Rob became cheerful to the point of frivolousness; and if the week that followed had not had a flavour of the unreality of a dream it would have been our happiest time together. We made love every night – vigorous rapturous love, so intense and prolonged in drawing out its finer ecstasies that we slept little and sat about in the daytime drinking Northumberland's heady beer with aching heads and backache.

Once Rob gazed bleary-eyed at me from his chair. "It is as if I only now discovered how necessary you are tae me. . . how handsome you are. . . how good your body. I've been so stupid. Tom was right – I've nothing between the ears, everything between the legs! And dearest Giles, you've been wi' me all along, there when I needed you, there when I ignored you. It'll all be different now, Giles, I'll put you first. If we have tae stay here as long as Raleigh did we'll make best use of our time and know each other better, and it will be as if Tom was here wi' us, because he knew us both and loved us both, as we loved him. . . Is it no' tomorrow Frances goes tae her trial?"

That evening the Lieutenant came most soberly to speak to Rob about the arrangements for his trial. He had sent word that he would visit us and so Rob was ready – he lay on the bed and groaned much and told Sir George that he was sick.

"It is a fever," I agreed. I could not resist adding wickedly: "I recollect he ate a jelly yesterday, one that came from your kitchen."

To my delight Sir George looked for a moment deeply uneasy, but his composure swiftly returned.

"My lord of Somerset, prepare yourself. You are not sick, I know it – this is a counterfeit sickness."

"I fear not," Rob sighed. "No – you must carry me there in my bed if you would hae me go."

Sir George grunted. "I will send a physician to you."

"He will find nothing," Rob said. "It is an inward malady."

"These games are beyond my capabilities," said Sir George. "I will write for my instructions to His Majesty."

On the afternoon of the 24th May Sir George came in to tell us about Frances's trial. At least, delivered somewhat in the form of a sermon, his account smacked of the pulpit, and had not the racy humour that Myton's would have shown had he got to us first.

"I have just escorted your wife back from Westminster Hall, my lord," said Sir George. "And may I say she bore herself most bravely. Her gown was modest and becoming, being black, with cuffs of cobweb lawn. Her sad and penitent demeanour was remarked by all. Her eyes were shadowed and downcast. What a most beautiful woman she is indeed! And beauty repentant strikes a chord of sympathy in the beholder. I led her in. The hall was a press of folk. Some had paid fifty pound for the edge of a bench. The lords and the Lord High Steward and his procession then took their seats. The Clerk of the Crown read the indictment. Your wife wept gentle tears and hid her face in her fan.

"'Frances, Countess of Somerset, what sayest thou? Art thou guilty of this felony and murder or not guilty?' 'Guilty,' she replied in fear and dread.

"And now the Attorney General praised the nobility of her confession. We recalled her noble parentage and the weakness of womankind. The countess was asked if she had anything to say for herself why judgement of death should not be pronounced. She humbly asked for mercy, admitting herself at fault. Her voice being so low with shame and remorse the Attorney General was obliged to repeat what she had said. Lord Ellesemere then passed judgement and sentence, which was indeed that of hanging; but in a kind voice he explained that the countess's humility and grief would weigh much in her favour. Not one there but did not pity the poor woman in her grief. My lord of Essex was most visibly moved! The whole sad business was but of two hours' duration. I led her weeping from the hall." Sir George looked assessingly at Rob. "I see that you are recovered from your fever, my lord, and your inward malady has not prevented you from putting on your clothes and receiving me in your accustomed manner. My lord, it is permitted that you come to your wife and briefly comfort her."

"Oh?" said Rob surprised. "Och, very well, if you think that is what she wants. Come wi' me, Giles."

I followed them across the court to the Garden Tower, the small two-storeyed building on the river side. This being the place where Tom had been first housed I entered with some misgiving; but we did not go into the lower chamber where Tom had lodged; entering a dark passageway we mounted a twisting stone stairway to an upper chamber where I caught a glimpse of Frances all in black, seated, her maids about her. Not Toothless Margaret. Toothless Margaret was in Bridewell, for her part in this business.

To my surprise the Lieutenant waited outside Frances's door, and I with him, when Rob went into her room. It occurred to me – and no doubt was beginning to occur to Robbie also – that for all that they seemed to be private, whatever he and Frances said would be heard by the Lieutenant, and that this unlooked-for meeting was perhaps contrived to furnish further evidence.

"Did ye say out loud I wasnae' guilty?" Rob said urgently. "Did ye say it before folk?"

"No. . . I don't know what I said. I was so frightened. I said what they told me to say. I was so ill all week. . ."

"Well," Rob answered bitterly. "You have lost an opportunity to speak out on my behalf and help my case. And though I do not flatter mysel' that you would have thought of me at such a time, if you had said as much it might have made the world of difference between whether I am spared or no."

"I did not think. . ."

"Or did ye think that if ye mun go down, better I go wi' ye?" Rob said grimly.

I heard Frances weeping noisily. I heard Rob mutter platitudes of consolation. This done he called for the Lieutenant, and the two set out down the stairs and back across the courtyard. I was the last to leave, hesitating dumbly in that place where Sir Walter Raleigh writ his books – that wronged and noble man. Here was his bedroom, there his walk along the leads, the horrible confines of a man who had known the limitless freedom of the seas.

Thus I was able to hear Frances's voice from within the room.

"Have they gone? God! The strain of being pious! I fear I shall burst. Cream this black mess off my eyelids, Mary, and wipe my cheeks. Well, was I penitent enough to please the mob? I hope the wretches will be satisfied now they have had their pennyworth of gawping. . ."

I rejoined Rob and the Lieutenant as they regained our lodgings and we entered.

"Now it was with your own case in mind, my lord, that I told you of your wife's impeccable deportment at her trial," Sir George said firmly. "Your own trial, as you know, is to take place tomorrow. Once again I ask you to be wise – plead guilty, throw yourself upon the mercy of the king, as your remorseful wife has done."

"I thought that I had made myself clear upon the matter," Rob said stiffly. "I will not go. I am an innocent man and I will no' be so degraded. If you want me there at Westminster you'll have tae drag me there by force."

I winced. I did not believe this suggestion as unlikely a possibility as Rob seemed to do.

"My lord, you have nothing to fear from the king's justice," Sir George declared.

"Don't you understand?" cried Rob. "I cannae' – what, put mysel' before those who have worked for my downfall? Ask them tae judge me? Stand before the mob who have been led tae believe Thomas Overbury a saint and would pay fifty pound tae watch me squirm when they could watch bear-baiting for a penny? And now you say my lord of Essex is amongst them?" Rob began to pace about. "It has all been a carefully laid trail leading up tae mysel', like a cabinet of wonders, each one more glittering than the last. And because you may be sure I shall not snivel and hide my face behind my fan I am likely tae prove more excellent sport than Frances. Why should I collude in this? They willnae' dare tae find me innocent for it would make the king look like a fool – moreover a vindictive and malicious fool, that brought me down only tae clear the air and raise up Villiers. I cannae' understand why he permits this proposed humiliation of me." He turned and stared at the Lieutenant. "Are you sure that he has said nothing privily upon the subject?"

"My lord, he has, and it is this. That unless my lord of Somerset be sick or witless he must come to Westminster tomorrow. And that if he refuses I must do my office. That means," added Sir George as if for the slow-witted – and not without some satisfaction; Rob had not been the easiest of prisoners – "that I must get you to Westminster, my lord, by whatever means it takes."

Rob gasped involuntarily, his face white and his eyes scared. He looked at me, trapped, helpless.

"Giles – what can I do?"

"Nothing," I replied. "But I have your black satin suit ready; and I suggest we curl your hair."

CHAPTER FORTY-ONE

"Robert, Earl of Somerset," said Lord Ellesmere, "you have been arraigned and pleaded not guilty. Now I must tell you, whatsoever you have to say in your own defence, say it boldly without fear. But remember that God is the God of truth. Hide not the verity nor affirm an untruth. Take heed lest your wilfulness cause the gates of mercy to be shut upon you."

The courtroom was stiflingly hot. Who would have believed the air in so vast a hall as Westminster, with its high walls and windows and its great majestic beams, could grow so oppressive and close? The sunlight streamed in upon the steaming throng who had paid ten shillings for a seat and ten pounds for a family box; upon the Lord High Steward, Lord Ellesmere, the officials and sergeants-at-arms, the peers in their raised galleries, the judges in scarlet; upon Sir Edward Coke, upon the Earl of Essex sitting in the front row, upon Sir Francis Bacon the Attorney-General; upon the lawyers and the scriveners, and the bar at which the prisoners made their defence.

I had a seat on the end of a bench against the wall near the door; Sir George More got it for me.

"It is a condition of my going quietly," Rob said. "I daresay Giles's will be the only friendly face that I am like tae see."

"Why, my lord, they may not even bring you to trial," he was assured. "To satisfy justice you must appear; but it may well be that you are permitted to return instantly again without any further proceding."

Rob favoured him with a contemptuous smile.

He had slept little. We had been awake since early morning while I worked to make him beautiful. In order that he should make his appearance looking much as folk remembered him we curled his hair and he sat patiently in his shirt while I fiddled with the golden tendrils. As my fingers moved about his face my heart lurched – he looked so pale and haggard. How had I not noticed this before, in all our rompings and close dealings together? Had I grown so habituated to this gradual change in him that I was not aware of it? Beneath his eyes were great black shadows and his eyes seemed sunk into his head. He was twenty-nine; this morning he looked older.

"What is it?" he asked, seeing me stare.

"Nothing. I was thinking once again how beautiful you are."

Everyone turned to stare as he came into the hall, and the great chamber buzzed with mutterings and murmurs. Sir George More brought him in, framed by two men-at-arms. These had orders to hustle him from the court if he began to speak a word against the king.

"And how will it appear," Rob had said scathingly, "when I am hustled out in an undignified scuffle after having berated His Majesty? Who will then believe that he has nothing tae hide?"

It was all that I could do to look at him, my heart so ached with love and pity. He looked so alone. The black satin of his suit became him well, relieved by the sash of his Saint George medal, but the harsh sunlight showed his gaunt cheeks and his trapped and sunken eyes, as I had feared it would. But he bore himself well. Later, I thought, when he grew more accustomed to the awesome and hostile surroundings, his natural anger would carry him through. The implication that this was a trial at all was plainly specious. If he had chosen Frances's course, pleaded guilty and thrown himself upon the king's mercy, this trial would be a formality and he would be out of this place in an hour or so. That he had come stubbornly to maintain his innocence obliged the law to bring him down. I only hoped it could be done without leaving him too much bloodied.

Turning to the peers Lord Ellesmere told them to free their discourse from all partiality.

"I was placed in some confusion as to where tae put my gaze," Rob told me bitterly. "If I looked down at my hands they wouldhae thought I couldnae' look them in the eye; and if I looked straight ahead I found that I was looking at the Earl of Essex."

He was permitted pen and ink to note down his defence; he would get no other helper than his memory that day. And so when Essex's smooth and predatory stare grew too much for him he took to his pen and wrote whatever he might assemble there and then against the clear analytical mind of the most astute lawyer of our day, the Attorney-General Sir Francis Bacon. But first Sir Henry Montague for the prosecution rose and said that as Weston was already found guilty of the murder, what the prosecution had to prove was that my lord of Somerset had instigated the crime, which he confidently affirmed to be the case.

In melodious prose then spoke Sir Francis Bacon, whom Rob had always deemed his friend, and who indeed in part owed his present position to Rob's goodwill. He spoke of carrying the lanthorn of justice upright and promised not to use wit or art to carry the day otherwise than upon sure grounds – a promise which he did not keep. His was a devious task. He must condemn the Earl of Somerset but not besmirch him overmuch for as it was supposed the king was loath to order his execution there must be room left for the king to show clemency.

Forget the street ballads which say that Thomas Overbury was a saint, Sir Francis advised his hearers; Overbury was insolent and corrupt; and this was the man that Somerset took as his oracle. But when he incurred the hatred of Somerset and Northampton, Thomas Overbury became the victim of a plot, a poison plot. Sir Francis now reminded us of all the famous murderers, beginning with Cain – a chilling list! And how much worse in this case that the victim was a prisoner in the king's protection, for whom the king and state were responsible! Sir Francis summarised the evidence, and speaking to Robbie he told him he would have three cogitations to answer, but in explaining them he spoke at length; he spoke in lawyers' language.

"Words," Rob told me gloomily. "I couldnae' get his meaning

through his words. I am a plain honest man, I thought, and when my turn comes I cannae' speak so and I will seem a fool."

And now Bacon set himself to prove that there was a mortal hatred between Rob and Thomas. Harry Payton was then called to speak. It was read out that he had been there when Rob and Tom had quarrelled outside Rob's room and he had given Giles Rawlins a letter to carry in to Robbie. I remembered the occasion he described. He told the court:

"The Earl of Somerset asked if the physic had worked. I said Sir Thomas was now very sick. How sick? his lordship asked me. Very sick, sick unto death, said I."

"And how did my lord of Somerset reply?"

I winced, remembering.

"My lord of Somerset said pish and turned away."

The court buzzed.

"If I die, my blood lie upon you." Yes, Payton had seen a letter from Overbury to Somerset and this phrase was in it; but no, he had not the letter now. And he had seen plenty more letters; but no, he did not have them.

Laurence Davies's evidence was read, containing more hearsay and more accounts of letters from Overbury to Somerset – but he did not think the Earl of Somerset had seen them.

"I pray you, my lords, note this," Rob said. "He says I never saw them."

There was then much talk of the white powders, the white powders which had been delivered to Thomas in the Tower on separate occasions, ostensibly physic for his ailments. I felt that there was a startling omission here – I was not called to speak, and I had delivered a white powder. I had got it from Sir Robert Killigrew and it was harmless. And therefore it was not mentioned in this court so heavily weighed against the accused. My evidence being not hostile to Rob it was considered irrelevant.

Letters from Tom were now read out – those written from the Tower when he thought Rob had turned against him. They caused some murmurs; but Lord Wentworth questioned their veracity. More hearsay evidence followed, from one Simcocks, a disreputable friend of Weston's whom we had never seen before. It seemed that as they could not now produce the villainous Franklin, to damn Rob by association they produced this Simcocks. He said Somerset had obscurely threatened Weston with death if he permitted Overbury to live.

"I had never seen Weston until after Overbury's death," Rob said. "He had no access tae me." Rob asked whether this threat had been contained in Weston's evidence; but no one answered him. It was of far more interest to them to listen to the pack of lies that Simcocks told about Robbie – that he was hand in glove with Weston and rewarded him with gold.

Sir Francis said that Robbie had rewarded Weston for keeping Tom close and hinted that Tom knew dangerous state secrets, and it was for this he had been murdered. He suggested that both Frances and Rob had plotted to have Tom assassinated.

"I intend to prove that Somerset had a hand in all the events that led to Overbury's imprisonment, which event seems to tend to no other end but empoisonment!"

"No!" said Rob but it was barely audible.

On went Sir Francis. "And now to the Puddle of Blood – the first link of which is that the means to entrap Overbury for the Tower was by the means of my lord of Somerset."

They then produced Rob's declaration in writing to the king, in which he admitted as much. Prefaced by a puddle of blood it had a somewhat sinister ring which on its own it did not have. Coke jumped up and said it was the brink of a confession; and then some of the scaffolding within the court fell down and there was a great disturbance till all was righted again.

Robbie mopped his brow and rubbed his hand across his eyes. He wrote down something that occurred to him – lefthandedly as was his wont. There would no doubt be some to take this as a sign of deviancy.

In the calm that followed the interruption my uncle Overbury was called as witness. True to his promise in the Lamb at Stow-on-the-Wold he was here to speak against the man whom he considered responsible for Tom's death. He related how he had tried to procure Tom's release and how Rob had pretended to help him in this and told him he was doing all he could on Tom's behalf. He thought that Rob intended mischief when he heard Tom was allowed no servant with him by orders from outside and he believed Rob had prevented his and Lidcote's attempts to have Tom freed. My uncle looked a dignified old man. He gained the sympathy of his hearers. Then he caught sight of me and stared and gave me such a withering look that I all but shrivelled down to nothing. Something told me I would not now be welcome in the house at Bourton-on-the-Hill.

Next came Lidcote, saying he also had been much hindered from close communication with Thomas and this all done by orders of the Earl of Somerset. There was that in his tone which smacked of one who has had his darkest suspicions confirmed, of one who had always suspected Rob's guilt and was now proved right – for there was Rob accused and like to be condemned.

Letters were read out from Lord Northampton to Rob saying that Tom's death would be the most sure and happy change for all. Northampton! Slippery to the last, he had avoided standing there beside Rob and answering his judges, which he must surely have done had he lived.

Shortly after this Sir Francis sat down. The Lord High Steward turned to Rob with a most severe countenance and said: "My lord, you have heard what hath been urged against you and may imagine that there rests much behind, and therefore you had best confess the truth."

Now all eyes turned to Robbie once again. I thought of Frances weeping judiciously, hiding her face behind her fan, gaining the sympathy of the court for her becoming penitence.

"My lord," said Rob in a firm voice, "I came here wi' a resolution tae defend mysel'."

The procedings coming to a pause I went outside with many others in search of fresher air. I had a piss against a wall and bought a pie from a pastry seller with a tray, and some over-warm ale from a stall. You would have sworn it was a holiday. Innumerable pedlars waited for us outside the door. Not only food could we buy, but verses, and pictures of Rob and Frances looking evil, and of Thomas looking saintly. All Tom's books were on sale, and in the murmurings of the little groups outside you could hear every shade of opinion voiced:

"What do you think? Guilty?"

"Guilty beyond a doubt. I never saw one look so guilty."

"His wife drove him to it."

"Poor man – with all the ladies at court to choose from and he settles upon that one! Many a good man has been brought low by the wiles of a scheming woman."

"They say it is a plot contrived to rid the king of one he has grown tired of. His Majesty has a new fancy now, they say."

"This man had everything and now will have nothing. It makes you think about the wheel of Fortune."

"He's good looking. . . prettier than his picture; at least, he would be if he was not so troubled – poor soul, he looks exhausted. I wish that I could take him home."

"Save your longings – he has been the king's beloved bed boy this many a year."

"I won't believe it! Two men together and one His Majesty? Don't talk to me so filthy!"

And from two sober gentlemen as we went back in: "Yet he has come to plead his cause and face his accusers. I would not fancy crossing swords with Sir Francis Bacon. Young Carr shows some personal courage. . ."

"Courageous?" said his cynical friend. "Or stupid?"

When we had all regained our seats I found to my vexation that one of the doggerel verses sung by a pedlar was fixed in my mind – a merry thing composed of letters of the alphabet and beginning:

I C U R good Monsieur Carr About to fall. . .
and ending: S X Y F whose wanton life will break your back.

The balladeer at least concurred with the general opinion then. The wretched thing had a jolly tune and I had picked it up on one hearing, and the damned thing buzzed in my head like a trapped fly at a window.

Even this, however, was somewhat more edifying than Sir Henry Montague's prosecution. Accusation followed accusation – that my lord of Somerset did direct the poison, did deliver the poison, that he waited eagerly to hear that the poison had taken effect.

"No," said Rob. "I deny it," and then gave up, looking pained and irritable.

Sir Henry muddled us all with his accounts of white powders. He told the court that the white powder he had been referring to – the one that must have come from Rob – gave Sir Thomas fifty or sixty stools and vomits for four or five days; and I swear that everyone there shuddered in sympathy.

Letters from Frances were produced and read, and inferences drawn, and hearsay from Franklin's confession – everything mounting up to make a vile and sorry heap. Judge the effect which Northampton's letter to Sir Gervaise Elwes produced:

"If the knave's body be foul, bury it at once. I'll stand between you and harm; but if it will abide the view, send for Lidcote and let him see it, to satisfy the damned crew. When you come to me, bring this letter again or else burn it."

The day was eaten away with what seemed more of the same. I saw Rob's gathering impatience.

Sir Randolph Crew, Serjeant-at-Law, prowled about as if he were upon the stage. "Now I behold you, my lord of Somerset. Methinks I hear the ghost of Thomas Overbury crying unto you in this manner: *Et tu quoque Brute!* Did not you and I vow a friendship of souls? Did you not sacrifice me to your woman – did you not oppose me cruelly and treacherously, by whose vigilance, counsel and labour you have attained your honourable place? Have I not waked that you might sleep, cared that you might enjoy?"

Rob sighed laboriously, his eyes skyward.

Crew continued, accusing Rob of acting guiltily after Tom's demise. "All he did," he told us, "detected a guilty conscience." He had some of the details of the night that Franklin came to the Cockpit lodgings. He knew about Rob's attempts to get back his letters. He was going to refer to every letter, date by date.

Rob interrupted, leaning forward. "Concerning the dates you need not trouble yourself, for it now grows late and I shall have very little time tae answer. I confess that my letters tae Lord Northampton were delivered tae me and that I burnt them and cut off some parts that were not relevant."

Crew told us about Rob's attempt to get a pardon for any ill he might have done, and once again they read Rob's letter to the king. Sir Francis Bacon seized upon it. "You see, my lords, he urges that because he has been formerly so great in the king's favour and has never committed any treason that he should never have been called to an account for this fault, though he had been guilty!"

"That isnae' what I said!" Rob gasped.

The Lord High Steward now spoke to Rob concerning his plea.

"My lord of Somerset has behaved himself modestly in the hearing." There was relief in his tone. Once again he suggested Rob should throw himself upon the mercy of the king. "There never was a more gracious and merciful king than our master," he reminded him.

"I am confident in my own cause," said Rob, "and am come hither tae defend it."

Lord Ellesmere answered kindly enough: "Be not troubled that your answers shall be abridged by time. It is indeed very late, but we will borrow some hours of the night. Whatever you can say to clear yourself of this murder, in God's name speak freely and fully and you shall be heard with all patience."

A long pause ensued, with shuffling and moving about, comings and goings. Evening had come on. The dusky twilight hung about the hall. Servants brought in candles and lit torches. I saw Rob riffling through his papers and run his finger round his collar. Myself I was drenched with sweat, and all about me bodies steamed and stank. Some during the course of the day had been carried fainting from the chamber, and at least one had vomited and been the butt of irreverent jests about white powders and arsenic. I heard one piss where he sat, for an unwillingness to leave his seat.

Rob at the bar looked drained and tired. Somehow he must put together a coherent defence; his life depended on it. I could not bear to watch. I clasped my hands between my knees and closed my eyes.

"It is true," Rob said, "that I helped Overbury tae the Tower, but not for evil purposes, but tae prevent him threatening my marriage, the which he had proposed tae do. But I had a care of his lodgings, that they should be where he might have the best air and windows both tae the water and within the Tower so that he might have liberty to speak wi' whom he would. The letters of Elwes and Northampton show there was a conspiracy, aye, but only tae keep Thomas prisoner.

"There was no deep-seated malice against Overbury on my part. Whereas the breach of friendship betwixt Overbury and me is used for an aggravation against me, it is no great wonder for friends sometimes to fall out, and least of all wi' him; for I think he had never a friend in his life that he would not sometimes fall out with and give offence to. As tae the cutting about of the letters I was ill-advised; but if I had ever thought those letters of my lord Northampton would be dangerous tae me, is it likely that I wouldhae kept them?"

Point by point he dealt with every accusation, not as it were in order of importance but as they had occurred, and not in lawyers' language, but speaking as any ordinary honest man accused would do. I began to feel a little eased. I opened my eyes. I believed that he could make a convincing case for innocence.

"For the declaration which I lately sent tae the king and particularly the word mercy which is now so much urged against me, it was the Lieutenant's. I would have used another; but he said it would be nothing prejudicial tae me. When I writ it, I did not think thus to be sifted in this declaration."

He spoke slowly and carefully. I could tell that he had taken Coke's half jesting advice to heart, and I was vexed on his behalf that as well as having to answer all the evidence against him he was obliged to listen to his own voice and to regulate it constantly for the benefit of those that found his accent offensive.

His opponents turned to the attack. He had sent in poisoned tarts! Rob replied: "Frances in her confession said there were none sent in but either by me or her and some were wholesome and some not. Then it must needs follow that the good ones were those which I sent and the bad hers."

"My lady says in her letters to the Lieutenant of the Tower 'I was bid to bid you do this'. Who should bid her if not you?"

Rob did not know; and Montague suggested this must be inferred. Simcocks's allegations of meetings with Weston?

"I never did see Weston till after Overbury's death."

Franklin's allegations?

"I do not believe Franklin should be taken for a good witness."

The hearsay evidence was now juggled with. I heard Rob grow confused in battling with each detail against so powerful an onslaught, lapsing into partly incomprehensible Scots, repeating himself, stumbling over a word. And as to the letter about a sea of blood, which Franklin swore that he had seen?

Rob declared passionately: "But I call heaven now to witness I never wrote any such letter, neither can any such be produced. Let not you, my noble peers, rely upon the remembered words of such a villain as Franklin, neither think it a hard request when I humbly desire you to weigh my protestations, my oath upon my honour and conscience against the lewd information of so bad a miscreant."

He looked towards the nobles who had so lately buzzed about him for his favours. His skin glistened in the light of the torches and his hair gleamed golden. Suddenly, unaccountably, into my mind came half-remembered words and images conjured up by Thomas so long ago.

"*Not an ounce of brain between his ears. His only chance of rising is to trade on his good looks and marry well. How will you find him? Oh, I shall pluck a rose. . .*

Giles, it was very strange – you see, he rode a milk white steed like young Tam Lin. . . then in a grove of silver birch trees he dropped down from a bough, straight into my arms. . . the honey of that first embrace, the sweetness of his lips. If I should live a thousand years I never shall forget it."

I forced my mind back to the present, to the dark-clad figure half in shadow standing trial for Frances's murder of his friend.

Rob spoke on, fumblingly, gripping the bar, but upright in carriage in despite of his exhaustion. At last he gave up. "More I cannot call to mind," he said, "but desire favour."

I believe that his listeners were not unmoved. I am sure that they admired his dogged and courageous stance in a losing battle. And he had put up a reasonable defence for one fighting with straws and his back to the wall. But of course he had not been brought here to be found innocent.

"My lords," Rob said with great dignity, "before you go together I beseech you to give me leave to recommend my self and cause to you. As the king has raised me to your degree so he has now disposed me to your censures. This may be any of your own cases, and therefore I assure myself that you will not take circumstances for evidence; for if you should, the condition of a man's life were nothing." He continued: "In the meantime you may see the excellence of the king's justice, which makes no distinction, putting me in your hands for a just and equal censure." Splendidly he declared: "For my part I protest before God I was neither guilty of nor privy to any wrong that Overbury suffered in this kind," adding ruefully: "a man sensible of his own preservation had need to express himself."

And so the peers went to deliberate and Rob was taken out while they came to their decision. It was a long half hour. The hall grew restive. There was more coming and going. Somehow I thought such sympathy as there had been began a little to evaporate. It had been merely the instantaneous reaction to Rob's stubborn useless fight. Now reason reasserted itself. No smoke without fire. . . The lords thought so too. They returned, and Rob was brought back to the bar for the sentencing. Every peer said "guilty". Rob had expected no less. Had my lord of Somerset anything to say?

He did not doubt, Rob said, that the peers had acted according to their consciences, but his own was clear.

"It is a pity that pure weakness of memory on my part has been the reason for you to condemn an innocent man," he said. "I only desire a death according to my degree."

Not hanging, not the Tyburn mob, the degrading deaths that Franklin, Weston, Elwes and Anne had suffered.

"But about what Simcocks said. . ." he suddenly remembered.

"My lord, you are not to speak any more in your defence but why judgement of death should not be pronounced."

Rob inclined his head. "Then I have nothing more tae say, but humbly beseech you, my Lord High Steward and the rest of the lords to be intercessors tae the king for his mercy towards me. . ." Then he added with a touch of his former defiance, "if it be necessary."

Sentence of death was now pronounced.

"Robert, Earl of Somerset, whereas thou hast been indicted, arraigned and found guilty as accessory before the fact of the wilful poisoning and murder of Sir Thomas Overbury, it is now my part to pronounce judgement which is that you are to be taken from hence to the Tower and from thence to a place of execution where you are to be hanged till you are dead. And the Lord have mercy upon you."

Rob bowed with a most elaborate flourish. I gasped in admiration. Elegance – contempt – indifference – ironic thanks – the gesture said it all. And now, the court being dissolved, he was led out of the hall.

It is a chilling sensation to hear sentence of death pronounced upon him dearest to one's heart; and when I stood up I found my legs so weak I scarce could use them. I stumbled to the door and through it and looked about in great agitation for Rob's procession.

The night was dark but glimmering with the lights of torches. I caught up with them – Sir George, the guards and Rob, and room was found for me in the barge that would take us all back to the Tower. No one spoke of anything of any consequence. Rob said not a word.

Within the Tower we were escorted back towards our lodgings. As we passed the Garden Tower we could see a light burning at the window. When we drew level with the door a figure ran out – Frances in white, her hair loose. The torches that accompanied us lit the scene with a lurid red and amber glow. Our faces showed roseate and shadowy in the flickering flame.

"Robert!" Frances squealed. "Robert! What happened? What happened at Westminster? I have been out of my mind with anxiety. Tell me what was said!"

She would have touched him, but she stood there rooted to the spot, frightened at what she saw. It was the look he gave her. If it might be said that a look might slay a person she by rights had been dead there where she stood. And then Rob turned about and accompanied by his keeper strode quickly across the courtyard.

"Giles!" she jibbered now to me. "Giles! Speak to me! Did they condemn him? I must know – I need to know."

She clutched me in a feverish grip. I looked down at her fingers and removed them from my arm as if they had been slugs. Then with a creditable attempt to emulate Rob's exquisite gesture, I turned and followed him.

CHAPTER FORTY-TWO

"But my lord, you never were in any danger," said Sir George More. "The king has never wished your death. But with so many vile rumours buzzing it was necessary that you came to trial, and if His Majesty had not decided so he would have been deemed a poor purveyor of justice. He had to show that great ones must stand trial as well as lesser folk – that fame and name are no protection against wrongdoing. And though you may not be guilty of murder – as you continually protest that you are not – yet are you guilty of much along the path to murder. You are moreover close to the lady who confessed her guilt – so much so that none may honestly believe you were not privy to the offence. It is a pity that you did not confess and receive a pardon thereby; but the king has always wished to show you mercy, and though you are now a convicted felon," he added reassuringly, "it is not supposed that you will hang."

It may be imagined with what serenity Rob received this piece of news. "I am pleased tae hear it," he said bitterly. "It is good tae know the king's justice so unprejudiced. And what, by the by, will happen tae me instead?"

"You will remain a close prisoner here in the Tower for as long as this remains His Majesty's pleasure," replied Sir George.

"Aye," said Rob with a curl of the lip. "His Majesty has ever been known tae find his pleasures in a manner which another might deem perverse."

Sir George pretended that he had not heard. "And in the fullness of time," he continued, "it may well be that the king will pardon you."

"How very gracious of him," Rob observed. "A pardon for no crime committed."

"Of course," added Sir George, "it may take several years."

"And in the meantime?"

"My lord, I think you should resign yourself to an imprisonment of some duration. However, if you were to sue to one who has the ear of the king and might speak to His Majesty on your behalf. . ."

"Have you someone perhaps in mind?"

"Sir George Villiers is the man now closest to the king. If your lordship were to write to him and humbly beg him to intercede on your behalf. . ."

"No," said Rob levelly. "No, I shall no' be doing that."

It was not an easy matter to be with Rob in close confinement in the days and nights that followed the trial. That first night, after we had peeled the satin suit from him, it was his sense of anger and humiliation that obsessed him – "on show, paraded like a trophy before Essex" – and then the paralysing fear of one condemned to hang. All night he truly thought that he was doomed to die a shameful public death; and neither of us slept, in contemplation of the same.

Then as it slowly dawned on him that James had never intended he should die, that the trial was a show trial to appease the lords, the lawyers and the multitude, to clear the king of conniving at the murder, he understood how shabbily he had been dealt with. I was obliged to put from my mind the lover who had promised me a better life – one where I would take precedence; instead I found that my companion was the Earl of Somerset and he was monstrous angry. I bore the brunt of it.

"Playing wi' me – using me – making me do tricks – obliging me tae answer all those vile accusations from the mouths of men not fit tae clean my shoes – and Essex looking on. And putting me in fear – burn me, when I went from that hall I believed I was going tae my death. I never will forgive him – never. If he should ever send a pardon tae me

I'll throw the damned thing back in his face. And tae think I honoured him and kept his name back – what an opportunity I lost there! They have made such a fool of me and I permitted it. . ."

And then he would go over what he said and what was said to him. "I could have done it better," he said time and again. "I fell rather for want of well defending than by the force of any proofs. If I had been permitted one like Francis Bacon to help me state my case and put my words in order I shouldhae made a better show. As it is. . ."

Why should I waste time telling him he had seemed noble, that under the circumstances he had nothing to reproach himself with? It was necessary to him now to rant and rave. Let him – he had cause. It was as if he thought: I am imprisoned for being the Earl of Somerset and all that he represented; very well, him will I be. His pride had been so dented; now he buckled it about about him like a suit of armour.

He insisted on being dressed to perfection every day, though there was none to see him, and I created him anew each day as fair as if he was about to meet a gathering of the entire court, ambassadors and dignitaries, upon the arm of the king, though alas! we had not access to his better clothes. He was brusque with me, morose, authoritative and withdrawn. There was no love-making, for there was no love in Robbie; he was consumed with bitterness and he felt utterly betrayed.

I understood it; but it must have been about this time that it occurred to me that I did not have to put up with it.

It must have been about a month or so later that the Lieutenant of the Tower announced to us that we were to quit our present quarters and move into the Garden Tower. With Frances!

"It's lovely there," Myton told us. "Lady Frances has made it like a palace. She has the upper chamber that faces towards the green, and there is aroom adjoining for my lord. You would never suspect it was a prison."

Indeed I had a fair idea of what Frances had been about. As I crossed the courtyard on my various errands, I had remarked upon the arrival of furniture and hangings, all heading towards the Garden Tower. One day I saw two satin chairs standing self-consciously on the cobbles, and a tapestry that had half unfolded and lay incongruously spread upon some travelling chests, crimson and green showing bright amongst the weave. A couple of ravens picked their ungainly way amongst this rich debris. A maidservant flapped a cloth at them and they regarded her with baleful dignity and remained. When they lifted their wings and made a move towards her she fled screaming.

Frances had three maids at that time. The Garden Tower was become a women's house. The air that had once stank of Sir Walter's tobacco was now heavy with perfume. The big chamber that overlooked the courtyard was taken over by the women. Rob's room was smaller. He would be able to go from it and walk along the leads as Sir Walter had been accustomed to do. Frances had furnished it with taste. All signs of ancient stone were quite disguised, and tapestries hung from ceiling to floor – hunting scenes, as is usual, and perhaps not the most tactful of choices for a man who once hunted every day with the king and was himself a fair horseman.

It would be noisy in this new abode, I thought, as I unpacked Rob's clothes. The maids chattered and laughed – indeed, the air of jollity that hung about the place was palpable; one might almost think it smacked of defiance. They all had lutes; there would be plenty of indifferent music. Through the opened windows of the room where Sir Walter Raleigh had written *The History of the World* the female faces leaned and waved and called out to the people in the courtyard; yes, this was not a close confinement – people came and went. It did not matter now – the secrets were all told, the Golden Age was unravelling at Whitehall, the Somersets irrelevant.

Lady Knollys, Frances's sister, brought in Rob's child for him to see at last, a pretty infant six months old. I watched him standing there with Frances and the babe, holding the infant in his arms as clumsily as most men do, with Lady Knollys teasing him and showing him how it should be done. The maids fluttered and squealed and cooed, as if they never had seen a babe before, and when Frances asked us all whether we had ever seen such a perfect child before in all our lives, I do not think there was anyone who answered that they had seen one fairer. Lord Hay also visited – the favourite who had known how to behave, how to retire gracefully and therefore to continue to live well.

Servants shifted Rob's furniture and belongings. I sorted out his clothes and hung them. As the days went by the rows began. I caught snatches of conversations between Rob and Frances. Her voice came strident, accusing, reckless, up the narrow spiral stairs.

"I know you wished him dead. You told me that you wished him dead."

And Rob's reply: "I may have said as much. I may have wished it. But madam, in the course of these last weeks, believe me, I have many times wished the same of you."

Cynically I observed her attempts to get him to her bed – her sweetnesses and cajolings, her self-display, her enticements and her tears. I watched his studied unresponsiveness with satisfaction. Later I heard her screamed reproaches. "Robert! Why? I am still beautiful. Robert – I am your wife! You used to love me – what must I do to regain your love?"

Rob answered sourly: "You might try making a mommet."

Her attempts now took a new direction, a ploy to make him jealous. "I have been talking to the Earl of Northumberland – the wizard earl."

"You should have much in common."

"More than you think – I believe that he is not immune to what some people consider my charms."

"I wish you joy of each other."

And then more tears and accusations and – which I found worse – pleading and hysteria of a curiously penetrating quality. Certainly in the upper rooms there was no difficulty hearing where she was.

Myton and I once stood in Rob's room listening to these sounds from the adjoining chamber.

"Would you have her if you were him?" said Myton.

"I would not. I would be frightened every time she handed me a drink."

"But of her beauty there's no question. She's a very fine made woman. And only twenty-four or so. It's pitiable to think of her immured so young."

"She did do murder," I said with sarcasm.

"Aye, and it being your cousin, you naturally would find it hard to forgive her. I think, I being the earl, I would forgive her," Myton decided. "It's such a waste, her being just nearby and desperate." He grinned saucily. "Do you think she might consider me?"

Then once he said sagely: "She'll wear him down, you know. No red-blooded man may resist a woman that pursues him. And in this confined space and no other to hand, his natural urges will get the better of him sooner or later."

"You're talking gibberish," I said savagely.

Rob came into the chamber. I was alone and lighting candles. He sat down heavily and sighed.

"These are not easy days," he said.

"No, my lord," said I. "You will need to show much fortitude. You have a trying time ahead."

He may have caught something of my drift from the manner in which I spoke, for he looked at me oddly and waited as if he expected me to say more.

"I shall not be with you," I said.

Complete disbelief showed in his face. "Why not? Where will you be?"

"I have been pleased to be with you throughout the years that we have been together. . . your friend and servant," I said carefully. "I was glad to share your imprisonment and cheer you when I could. There has been no alteration in my love. I have loved you from the first moment that I saw you – do you remember? At the Lion at Stamford, when you burst into my little dark room and hung over me with a lanthorn and said: 'You want me; I am Robbie Kerr.'"

"Did I so? I don't remember."

"But Rob, I cannot live with Frances."

"Ha! D'ye think I can?"

"You, my dear, have no choice. You should have thought about that when you married her. You will not get a second nullity."

"How hard I worked tae win this woman!" he agreed.

"I never liked her," I continued. "I was jealous, of course. I was jealous of you and Thomas, but that did not seem to matter. I did not feel so excluded then. But I was ever much in the background of your thoughts and certainly when she decided to achieve you, and you succumbed."

"But it was witchcraft," he protested.

"Not entirely," I said drily.

"But Giles," Rob said winsomely, "you have no reason tae be jealous now – you see how it is between she and me; we are cat and dog. Whereas you are ever first in my affections!"

"Somehow that has ceased to matter," I said with a sudden weariness.

Rob stood up, troubled. "I don't understand," he said.

"It's simple; I have had enough."

"Of me?" His face fell, like a little boy's.

"Of what it means to be close to you. I have lived with you and known with you the sweet days and the sour. And now I find I want no more of it. I would have stayed, if we could be together on our own. It's not this place that drives me away. You, however, are obliged to remain here. But I am not."

"This is very cruel of you so tae desert me."

"Myton will fold your clothes. There are dozens of Howard servants to take care of you. You will be always well dressed and pleasing to the eye."

Rob stared at me. "I cannae' believe that you are saying this. As if I wanted you here for those reasons"

"You will get used to my absence."

"I will not! I will be like a man that has lost a limb."

"I hate her, Rob," I said. "I cannot be with her. If you saw the way

Tom's father looked at me, for having chosen to stay with you. . . if you knew the pain his family endures."

"Of course I know it. I am not insensible. I feel some pain upon that score mysel'," said Rob aggrieved.

"I look at her as she eats or sews and think: this very woman murdered my cousin, and she lives and breathes and laughs and talks."

"I know," said Rob. "The others died, but she lives, because she said that she was sorry, and because she is a Howard." Then he cried: "but this is to no purpose. The true matter is: how can you leave me? I thought you said something about love?"

"I did," I said unhappily. "I love you; but I can't stay here."

"Have I tae pursue you up and down the stairs as she does wi' me, with wailing and gnashing of teeth?"

"Even that, Rob, gratifying and diverting as the prospect might be," I said with a wan smile, "would have no effect upon my determination."

"Where will you go?" said Robbie gloomily.

"To one of the playhouses if they'll have me. I can still blow a horn, I daresay, or carry a spear."

"You cannae' know how much I envy you," said Rob.

I was afraid that I would be diverted from my purpose by the longing in his voice. To be deprived of liberty – not to be able to go where one would go – not to see fields and trees and highways – others to order your life – what worse could there be?

Rob opened his arms to me and we hugged each other close.

"Well," he said with an attempt at humour, "if you change your mind, you will always know where tae find me."

CHAPTER FORTY-THREE

No sooner had I quit the portals of the Tower than I was made aware of how much hated Rob and Frances had become. A small crowd was assembled, lurking malcontents as I supposed; but as I drew nearer I saw that they were ordinary citizens.

"Do you come from the Tower?" they demanded of me. "What news of the Lord and Lady Somerset?"

"None; none at all."

"They are not to be beheaded today?"

"Good Lord, no."

A great groan. "We had heard that they were to be beheaded. We had it on good authority. We came to see their end."

"You have been misinformed."

"Shame!" they clamoured. "Are they still to be spared, guilty though they be? Where is justice? All the small ones hanged and the true murderers to go free? She because of her high family and he because he too much pleased the king? Let them be brought to the citizens of London who will treat them according to their deserts! Fortunate they have the walls of the Tower to protect their wicked hides. Hand them to us, we say, if the law cannot touch them!"

"Go home," I said. "There will be no execution today."

"When the execution is announced, we will be here, believe it. We are always on watch. We shall not miss the day. We shall be here to cheer them on their way to hell."

I left these pleasant folk behind and wandered into the London streets. The air seemed curiously bright, the distances over long. For six months I had been immured. For a foolish moment I regretted my decision. I longed to rush back to the safety of the walls thirteen feet thick. The timbered houses swayed about me and I put out a hand to support myself against a wooden buttress. This would not do. Afraid of freedom? Whoever had heard of something so ridiculous? I plodded slowly on into the town. I must begin anew, and on my own; I must not look back.

The Red Bull playhouse in St John's Street used to be an inn. It had been a playhouse for some ten years now. Its nearest rivals were the Fortune where I once had worked, and the Curtain just nearby. It sold bread and beer to be munched and slurped during the performances. It was known mostly for clownery and clamour. It put on old plays, loud plays, plays that showed battles and blood. Its stage jutted into an unroofed yard.

A glance through its chests, coffers and store rooms gave an indication of the substance of its repertoire. A damned cave – severed heads and limbs – a rack for the Virgin Martyr – the Mouth of Hell – three coffins – two dozen bottles of blood – a red hot spit – a bleeding heart upon a knife point – a pot of lily flowers with a skull in it – a gobbet of flesh – a severed tongue – a dozen eyeballs, dangling.

I worked at anything that came my way, and for a meagre payment. After all, I had some skills. Where the stage directions called for a sad funeral march – a great noise saying: Arm! arm! – a noise of tumult within – a strange confused fray – a noise of knocking down the bridge – hellish music – bells – there was I. I was also rain (a rattling shower of dried peas from the tiring house garret) and I played trumpets, cornet, lute and recorder when occasion required. I sewed costumes

– I was skilled with a needle – and kept the players' apparel in good repair. I should have known my years of waiting upon Rob would come in useful.

I was surprised at the lightheartedness I now felt to leave Rob behind – and his disagreeable ménage. I had thought there would be pain. No, I was glad. It appalled me to consider how I had lived my life at second hand for so many years, recounting someone else's story, always at someone's beck and call, going without bed pleasures if it did not suit Rob to indulge. As may be imagined, one of the first things I did was fall in love.

I lie, of course – it was not love. I had lost the faculty to love, as if it had been drawn out of my body by pincers, like a tooth. Amongst the players there were always pretty boys, either playing or attracting followers. I was twenty-nine, not young, but neither old, and I was handsome. I have not made much of this, being obsessed with Rob's golden good looks; but now away from him I no longer felt obscured by his radiance, and able to shine somewhat for myself.

After a performance of *If it be not good the devil is in it*, I went home with the man who played Lucifer. It must have been the way he declaimed:

"This yew tree blast with your hot scorching breath!"

All the while that we made gyration about his bed I thought: 'How odd it is to be this intimate with someone other than Rob! How different! In time I daresay black hair will come to seem natural and right and not a freak of nature as now it does. I may grow to admire it. I may think black hair a great improvement and consider all that have not black hair something to be pitied'. I came with a gasp over his bending buttocks. A wealth of release was in that rush of lust. He laughed, pleased, and later asked me to move in with him. I thought to myself: 'If it be so easy to get myself a handsome bedfellow, why ever did I stay so long within the Tower?'

Fool, I replied, knowing the answer.

But I found that a lifetime's habit of living through another is not easily broken. What is it about you, Giles Rawlins, I wondered, that you seem to have no existence in your own right, being nothing but a mirror reflecting another's face?

I was at the Red Bull playhouse for six years; but what can I say of it? My life was very much as other folk's lives, and one play following another, one season following another, work and more work, the more exhausting the better.

The Virgin Martyr – Philenzo and Hypollyta – The Fair Foul One –

The Younger Brother – A Fair Quarrel – Herod and Antipater – Richard III – Edward II – and then again *The Virgin Martyr.* Some of these were performed in summer heat, some in sleet and hail. Autumn leaves blew into our faces – blossom speckled our hair – snow kept the crowds away.

News of the great ones reached us of course. Players, watchers, the shopkeeper in the street – everyone cared about the doings of the great. I even one day witnessed the moment when a five-foot high picture of Rob was taken down out of a tailor's shop and an equally large likeness of George Villiers was hoisted into its place. There was some confusion over what to do with Robbie. What if Villiers fell and Somerset was returned to favour? They had better have the previous favourite to hand. Ah, but he was under sentence of death? Yes, but the king was soft-hearted and wept easily; he would not let him die, you may be sure of that. Better safe than sorry, however, so the picture of Robbie was turned face to the wall and stacked towards the back of the shop, along with rolls of worsted and muslin.

When the Countess of Somerset received her pardon in that first July the fury of the common man knew no bounds. She was pardoned, we heard, because she came of noble stock, had confessed, and had been led astray by bad company.

"And who believes that?" said the baker who sold me bread. "She knew what she was doing, the minx. One law for the rich, eh, one for the poor."

I heartily concurred; I was bitter about Frances's pardon on my own account.

A fresh spate of street verse gushed forth:

Our summer sun is set
And winter is come on
The robin redbreast leaves to chirp
Because his voice is gone. . .

Now coaches creep and cars do fly
To four fierce ladies this Carr did trust
Called Pride, Oppression, Murder, Lust. . .

– and clever folk made anagrams, cheating to work a meaning. Francis Howarde became 'Car finds a whore'; and Thomas Overburie became 'O! O! a busie murther!'

"Let her stay in the Tower," I heard. "If she venture on the street her life will not be worth a pin."

"And him?" I asked.

"Oh, him," they shrugged. "He was the dupe of a wicked woman. A witch, a murderess, a whore – what chance had he? Thus is many a good man cozened."

Making fair copies of the plays that we possessed, warming my hands at a candle in the room I shared with the man who had played Lucifer, I grumbled to myself as I tried to make sense of the playwright's stage directions.

"'Climb to the main top' – with five lines to ascend there. 'Enter in bed.' 'Enter Godfrey as newly landed.' And the expressive: 'Dorothea's head struck off.'

I worked hard and found it diverting and engrossing, and I swear that I was well content.

And in the task I often found the writing gave me pause, for as I copied I was often made to think of those that I had left within the Tower, as when Frankford in *A Woman Killed with Kindness* cries:

> O God! O God! that it were possible
> To undo things done, to call back yesterday,
> That Time could turn up his swift sandy glass
> To untell the days and to redeem these hours
> Or that the sun
> Could, rising from the west, draw his coach backward
> Take from the account of time so many minutes
> Till he had all these seasons called again
> Those minutes, and those actions done in them,
> Even from her first offence, that I might take her
> As spotless as an angel in my arms!
> But O! I talk of things impossible
> And cast beyond the moon.

Villiers was made a viscount shortly after Rob's trial. Now he was Earl of Buckingham. Now he was Privy Councillor. Now he was marquis. All his relatives had titles. Now he was Lord Admiral of England. Now he had married an heiress.

Sir Walter Raleigh's expedition failed. When he returned to England he was arrested, tried and executed, and died with the immortal lines: "What matter how the head lie, so the heart be right?"

King James was hated for the deed.

Richard Burbage our great player died. The Banqueting House

337

burned down and was rebuilt much better than before. Queen Anne died. All the Howards fell into disrepute. The Earl of Nottingham resigned as Lord Admiral; the Earl of Suffolk and his wife, Frances's parents, were found guilty of embezzlement and taking bribes and they were placed within the Tower, where their reunion with Rob and Frances must have been interesting.

Prince Charles became Prince of Wales. The king visited Scotland. Southampton was arrested, then released, now in open opposition to the king and much out of favour. Parliament was dissolved. The king was rumoured to be forever drunk and often ill. Sir Francis Bacon was accused of taking bribes and found guilty by the House of Lords. I wished I had been at his trial for bribery and corruption. He was fined £40,000 and imprisoned in the Tower; but not, alas, for long. And strange the wheel of Fortune, for Sir Edward Coke was also sent to the Tower, having become something of a man of the people in his beliefs and an opponent of Spain and James's policies.

Surpassing all these happenings was one of great moment to the Red Bull – our great rival the Fortune in Golding Lane burned down one day in December. It burned down completely within two hours. All their apparel and play books were lost. We could see the blaze above the rooftops and the wind blew charred fragments our way. A candle had blown over, as it was thought, and the philosophers amongst us noted that of such small accidents come events of great magnitude.

And then all went quiet regarding my lord and lady Somerset. They were in the Tower and that was that; they seemed to have been quite forgotten. Perhaps I now might begin my own forgetting.

One day the handsome man whose bed I shared said, seeing me sewing: "How is it that you do that work so neat and fine? Were you a tailor?"

"No. . . I was manservant to a lord."

"You never speak of other times. I know you come from Oxfordshire. I know you worked once at the Fortune and you used to know Ben Jonson."

"That is a life quite full enough for anybody," I laughed.

"Yes, but you have spoken of it. It's always the unspoken about which a man is curious."

"What do I know of you?" I countered. "Only that you come from Aylesbury and you play the hero and the villain with equal relish; and that you are an ardent lover."

"I have no secrets; you may ask me what you will. And yet you never do."

"It is my delight to dwell in the suburbs of a man's affection; I have had my fill of the heart of the city."

"When a man makes such a secret of his past life," said Lucifer, "a man that's close to him is tempted to become inquisitive."

"Why? Best live in the moment is the sum of what I've learnt. All is uncertainty. The past and the future are so different one from another; and Fortune is a wayward hussy."

"So you would throw me off the scent with those old adages? Do you think so little of me? It is ungenerous of you not to share your heart when you are bounteous enough of your body, to my great advantage."

"No, to my own!" I assured him. "You are the loveliest man this company has to offer and I the beneficiary. It's not that I do not value you, as well you know. I have such poverty within. I have nothing to offer."

"I would like to meet the man who caused it," Lucifer said darkly, "and take a cudgel to him."

"Yes," I said wrily. "There was a time when many others felt the same."

"He lives? Is he in London?"

"I have no more to say."

"You have not?" said Lucifer quizzically. "Then watch your dreams – you have more than once spoke *Robbie* as you slept."

"That is someone I knew at home in Oxfordshire. Someone. . . who has died."

"Ah – so I must be jealous of a ghost!"

"There is one asking for you at the playhouse."

A January morning. Heavy fog; the houses blurred shapes in the murk. When the lad brought the message to me I had no prescience as to who the stranger might be. He was standing in the playhouse yard, drinking beer, cloaked against the cold. Myton, Rob's manservant. I recognised him at once – his craggy face, his grizzled beard, his lazy eyes with their sudden spark of levity.

"Ah, Giles, is it you at last? I've been to every playhouse in London, I swear, not knowing where you were, and all the while half supposing I was on a wild goose chase after all."

"Speak softly, friend. No one here knows about. . . where I once was. Whatever can you want with me? He is all right? Not ill?"

"Not ill, no, and he will be in better health soon enough. They are both to be released."

The havoc that my body played with me then should have given me clear indication that I was not free of him, that he had power to move me, six years having passed. I was thirty-four and I was shaking

339

like a green and lovesick youth. I could not speak. If I had spoken I would have gibbered like an idiot.

"Giles? Now I must ask the same of you – you are not well?"

"Speak on, Myton. You come at me like a phantom through the fog and you speak to me of. . . and you suppose that I will be unmoved?"

"Ah, yes, I see," he grinned. "The suddenness. . ."

"I had not heard that he had received a pardon."

"He has not. I say that they will be released, but only to confinement elsewhere. They are to go to Greys in Oxfordshire – Lord and Lady Knollys's house – you know, my lady's sister who has been looking after the little girl. It is another kind of imprisonment, but a gentler one."

I knew the house. I had visited it in Rob's company in balmier days. It lay near Henley, near the river. It was surrounded by fields.

"Well, I am glad of that." I could hardly breathe; my heart had come up into my throat. "It is kind of you to let me know."

"Oh, no, that was not the purpose of my errand. At least, it was in part. No, I am come with a particular message."

"What – ? A message?"

"His lordship bids me tell you that for the first night of their liberty they go to Northampton House in the Strand. He says you will remember it. You are to come to him there. His lordship bids me tell you to be there and waiting."

CHAPTER FORTY-FOUR

The Earl and Countess of Somerset were to be released! And she a self-confessed murderess and he a condemned felon under sentence of death! You would think the streets of London had been slumbering these six years, only waiting for this moment to burst into life.

Portraits of the monstrous pair were back on view. Portraits, but horrid things – two people bearing superficial traits of Rob and Frances dressed in rich clothes, leering in sinister fashion at a supine figure representing Thomas, with the towers of his grim prison round about him. Some displays on walls and windows showed pictures of the victims of the gallows – Mistress Turner in her fancy ruffs, Franklin pockmarked and contorted, Elwes and Weston with their hands folded in prayer.

And now a rash of plays infected the stage. Middleton's *The Witch* was performed again at Blackfriars, a pretty story about a scheming female named Francisca. The astute will notice a similarity here between her name and that of Frances Carr. Within the play a husband is bewitched, a man and wife separate so that the wife may remarry as a virgin; a duchess means to murder her husband and attempts to murder one who might prevent her marriage. Love charms are used and witchcraft. A test for virginity is recommended.

"Tis so uncouth," says Francisca, "living in the country now I'm used to the city, that I shall ne'er endure it." The watchers guffawed, showing that they had understood its aptness. A gentleman from the northern parts with a terrible Scots accent enters; he was received with whistles and hisses. One of the characters observes that the great ones get away with anything. The duchess admits: "Blood I am guilty of, but not adultery." The duchess is pardoned.

In May there came *The Changeling* at the Phoenix in Drury Lane, an excellent play, and the more effective for its excellence. A lady engages the services of a poxy villain (it was commonly believed that Frances had been Franklin's lover). This ominous ill-faced fellow is to murder her unwelcome betrothed so that she may marry one with whom she has fallen desperately in love. This villainous accomplice tells her scathingly:

Fly not to your birth, but settle you
In what the act has made you. You are no more now –
y'are the deed's creature.

She tells her husband in self justification that the murder proves the depths of her devotion to himself. . . *remember, Robert, all was done for love of you*. . . There is much talk of poison, and a virginity test; and the murdered Alonzo's body lies hid within the castle, waiting for vengeance. Looking at the towers of the city one remarks:

Our citadels
Are placed conspicuous to outward view
On promonts' tops; but within are secrets. . .

Within are secrets! How pertinent seemed that phrase to certain places known to me!

I shuddered as I came away from the Phoenix though the day was warm. Lucifer was with me. No devil he; he was Lucifer, Light Bearer, bringer of enlightenment. But just at present he was very taken with the boy who had played Beatrice Joanna. I would not have minded overmuch if he had decided to pursue the matter further. We were lovers, friends, we worked together; but we held each other as gossamer upon an open palm – a breath might shift it.

And what was I about, playgoing in May in Drury Lane when I had received that imperious summons back in January to present myself at Northampton House and be waiting when his lordship came forth from the Tower? Simply I had ignored it. What did he think he was about, the Earl of Somerset, commanding my presence, as if I were a servant at his beck and call? I was no such thing. What was I, I wondered then? A hired hand at the Red Bull, I answered ruefully. But nonetheless a valued one, I replied, and if his lordship thought that he could stride back carelessly and claim me like a glove, he was mistaken.

This is not to say that I was comfortable on the night that he expected to find me there; I was not. I thought about him constantly. I was eating and drinking at The Three Pigeons hard by the playhouse, with a group of players in the dark inn parlour by a spitting hissing fire, and someone said I was poor company.

I saw in my mind's eye the rooms at Northampton House. I pictured the Earl and Countess of Suffolk – would they be there to welcome their errant daughter and their son-in-law? Servants would have warmed the house, and, dazed and chill, after six years within the Tower, and a trundle through the London streets in a covered coach, Rob and Frances would – what? eat and warm themselves and – what? did they sleep together now? I did not know. I might have added: nor did I care; but it would have been a little less than truth. I did not think that my absence would weigh heavily with his lordship as he settled into scented sheets. Next day he would have gone into the country; and I had work to do.

It was as well the wicked pair had quit the city, was the general opinion. If they had ventured forth into the streets of London no one could have answered for the consequence. Like the noble lady of Alexandria, Hypatia, who was resented for her beauty and her learning, they would certainly have been torn limb from limb. There were beery arguments as to who was most to blame, he or she. At the Red Bull Frances was deemed the greater villain because she was a woman and had quit her first husband and slated his manhood which of course no wife should do, and was shown by this to be voracious in her appetite for lust and pleasure. As for Robert it was generally held he was the poor fly in the spider's web, as so many hapless men before him, victim of female enticements. Nonetheless he must have known about the poisoning, and after all it was he that put the gentleman in the Tower. And he was the king's minion and a Scot at that, and came not even of the old English nobility. Let them go into the country where no one would hear of them. They deserved each other. Let them fade into obscurity.

Early in February Myton had sought me out again. He was drenched with rain and very muddy and I took him into the parlour of The Three Pigeons and gave him a meal and beer. We sat together at a pocky table near the fire.

"You come from Oxfordshire!" I marvelled.

"Aye, and all on your account," he grumbled. "I have a letter for you." He produced from deep within his shirt a moist and smelly missive which he placed upon the board. I stared at it, recognising the abysmal hand.

"Come now, take it; it will not bite," Myton encouraged.

I opened it, half turning away, while Myton, squinting, tried to read over my shoulder.

I read: "Why were you not where I requested you to be? I thought that you might send some answer but a month has gone by. Send answer by Myton and join me here. You remember this place. Ask directions of Myton if you have forgot."

I drew in my breath. "There is no answer," I said.

"Now, Giles!" reproached Myton. "This will not do. I have ridden seventy miles and I will not go back with such a leaden reply. He's asked for you, hasn't he? Oh, go to him – he's monstrous despondent. Oh, I was not to tell you that. But have a heart – he wants you and you would do us all a service if you cheered his dumps."

"Let him send for a jester," I shrugged.

"No, that's not what I mean and you know it! You were close to him, closer than any of us. Why are you so hard-hearted? There's not much for you here, is there? A ramshackle playhouse in winter? At least we're warm at Greys."

"I grew tired in his service," I replied. "I was his for nine years – I was there through all the trouble, always to be relied upon. Like some old chair," I said disparagingly. "He agreed to my leaving him; he understood my reasons. I began a new life here. He has no right to break in upon it and disturb my peace."

"What am I to tell him, Giles? Oxfordshire is a long way to go with no answer."

"I know how far it is to Oxfordshire," I answered sourly. "Tell him what I have told you and speak it kindly. I wish him well; but I won't go to Greys where Frances is."

"You need not see her," Myton said. "My lord does not, scarcely at all. That is, they dine together; but they do not say much. The room is so quiet you can hear the noise of teeth!"

I smiled in spite of myself. "Myton, you do not tempt me! It may be cold at the Red Bull but our hearts are warm enough. Is it true?" I added. "They don't talk?"

"Sometimes they sneer and snarl. I would not call it talking."

"And –" I despised myself for asking it, "as for sleeping?"

"Sleeping?" teased Myton knowing what I would ask. "Aye, they sleep. At least, they go to bed."

"Alone?"

"Lady Frances has three lovely maids to share her slumbers."

"But he – does not?"

"He does not have three lovely maids, no. There is one of her pages I have seen him looking at."

"Devil take you, Myton – does he share her bed?"

"If I tell you that he does not, will you give me a favourable answer?"

"I cannot. I asked only out of curiosity. The ways of the household at Greys are none of my business."

In the month of April Myton was back. I was not at the playhouse and they sent him round to Lucifer's lodgings where I was copying a play. At his thunderous knocking I let him in, my lips and fingers smeared with ink – I had a foul habit of sucking my thumb when I wrote.

He sat down on the bed and spread himself. He looked weary, as well he might. His boots smelt of the mud of the field. I poured him some wine. I hoped he did not bring another letter; I hoped he did – the last was pressed within a book, along with the first celandine I picked, harbinger of spring.

"Well," he said downing the wine in one draught and noisily wiping his lips. "I suppose you think I have brought you a letter."

"And have you so?"

Wordlessly he removed it from his shirt. "I ought by rights to make you work for this."

I reached for it; he took it back. "What will you give me for it?" he said aggressively.

"Oh, have done," I snapped. "Take it back to Oxfordshire; I care not."

"Very well." He stood up. "Thank you for the wine."

"Come back, you fool," I said, betraying myself by my visible alarm.

"Fool?" he queried loftily.

"Forgive me – I spoke rashly."

"And the letter?"

"I would have it."

"You would have it, so rude and abrupt, young Giles?"

"I would have it, if you please; and thank you for the 'young'."

"You are his age, are you not?" He eyed me thoughtfully. "And I think you wear the better."

I hesitated, the letter in my hand. "Is he not well?"

"Put it thus – he is not one that loves Oxfordshire," Myton observed, "after having known Whitehall."

"The more fool he," I said and opened the letter.

"It occurs to me," I read, "that you have not the money for the journey. If that be the case, take from Myton the money that I send, and come to this place as soon as ever you may, which I trust will be within the week. It is very dull here, time passes slow."

"Would you believe it?" I marvelled. "He is so puffed up he thinks that nothing but poverty would keep me from him. Can you credit such self-conceit?"

"Ah, Giles, that's not the way it is," protested Myton. "It was his thoughtfulness to send you money – I have it here. He heard you were a player and he knows they are not rich."

"And then he only asks for me for his diversion; he would be entertained. Are there no travelling players in the land of my birth? There used to be. And books? And he can ride out, can he not? The fields of Oxfordshire are considered very fair."

"He can ride out," said Myton carefully, "but for three miles only in any direction from the house. He is forbidden by His Majesty to ride beyond that three-mile compass. Your fields are fair enough; but they are already somewhat known to him."

I felt ashamed for my jibing.

"It is not for want of money that I do not go to him," I said then. "I have a little. It is not a dismal life I lead. I live – as you see – comfortably enough."

"And not alone," Myton observed.

"This room belongs to one of the players."

"One bed," said Myton meaningfully. "Or one of you sleeps on the floor."

"One bed," I said.

"Ah, now we have it," Myton said. "This is the reason you remain deaf to his lordship's pleas."

"Commands," I corrected.

"If you will," he shrugged. "Why should he not command? After all, he was a great man in his time."

"You speak as if he were dead," I blurted out angrily.

"To the king and to the court he might as well be," Myton said.

"That's not true!" I cried. "I knew them when they were together, he and the king – they were very close. The king once said that once he loved a man he never could hate such a person, and believe me, he loved Robbie. I am sure he loves him still, in his heart."

"You are?" said Myton with a crooked smile. "Even now? With the Marquis of Buckingham the richest man in England after the king?"

I thought of Villiers strutting in his finery and Rob kicking his heels in a three-mile circle about the house of his wife's sister. I did not answer. "He is not yet pardoned then?"

"No, he is not, and it is his own fault for pleading not guilty."

"How else might an innocent man plead? Tell me that."

Myton shrugged. "A clever man would have gone for the pardon and to hell with principle."

"Rob was ever honest and direct. He never was at ease with deviousness and corruption."

"I think this time," said Myton smoothly, "there'll be a favourable answer to his letter, you being so warm in his defence."

"No – no," I stuttered. "I was speaking as I would of any man who had been wronged. No, keep the money; I would not take it. You have made the journey – it is yours."

"Is it because of this?" he pointed to the bed upon which he sat.

"No," I said. "I do assure you, no."

I did not think that he believed me. He stood up. "I shall not come again on this journey," he told me. "Let him find another fool to run his errands. I have done with it." He paused. "He would not agree with me, I know, but speaking for myself – well – it was merry in the Tower." He grinned. "Always something going on – visitors, good food, Lady Frances setting up little intrigues – and always the chance of some great one or other for your neighbour! But not now," he complained, the grin fading. He looked about, as if we could be overheard. I wondered fleetingly whether years of daily life within the Tower had caused this mannerism. He nudged me. "I'm quitting his service. I cannot stand the life at Greys. I cannot stand the country. You do well to refuse his offer, Giles. The lady Frances is half crazed and his lordship is as miserable as sin, gloomy as November." He fetched a deep sigh. "You would be out of your mind to tell him yes."

That was a month ago. Here I now was on a May evening, sitting with Lucifer at our table in The Three Pigeons, munching beef pie, drinking beer, and talking earnestly about the play. What is it that raises a play above the common? We both believed that we had seen a masterpiece. We had only seen it once, but we were muttering the lines that had already marked themselves upon our minds. Lucifer raved on about the lovely boy that took the lady's part and revelled in the villainy, repeating what he remembered, all in appropriate voices.

> – and make you one with me!
> With thee, foul villain?
> Yes, my fair murderess!
> Can you weep Fate from its determined purpose –
> So soon may you weep me!

I watched him with affection. I did not love him, but I loved our life together. Let him pursue Beatrice Joanna; I wished them well. He had been good for me and I was grateful. And he would say I had been good for him; it is no bad thing to find a dear companion to share one's time with – a warm shoulder in a bed, a drinking fellow, an unpossessive easy-going lover, one, moreover, with a roof over his head. In his friendship I had been very lucky and I knew it.

Joining him in sharing our remembrances of the play I spoke the lines that I had found impressive:

"Beneath the stars, upon yon meteor

Ever hung my fate."

Lucifer agreed. And then my mouth dropped open as I looked beyond him to the shadows by the wall and saw that Rob was standing there.

CHAPTER FORTY-FIVE

By rights I should not have recognised him for he was somewhat changed. He was muffled in some kind of dark shabby cloak with a hood, and at first gaze I thought his face more thick-set than I remembered it, the beard coarser, the hair darker. So stunned was I that I had not the wit to shuffle him from the inn parlour and hide him in a place of greater safety; and before I could speak he had sat down at our table, facing towards the room, obscured from the crowd by Lucifer's presence. Then the hood of his cloak slipped to his shoulder and the golden hair shone dazzling as a beacon. In great alarm I shoved my old felt cap upon his head, as one might snuff a candle.

"What in God's name are you doing here?" I whispered appalled.

"I wouldhae thought it plain: I am come for you."

"Haven't you seen the streets?" I gasped. "The dreadful images? Don't you know the playhouses and the corner ballads tell your story?"

"I told you," Rob repeated. "I am come here for you."

I turned to Lucifer. "Stay!" I hissed.

"Why?" both said.

"If you sit there he will not be seen," I said. "You shield him. For God's sake, Rob, crouch lower – they will kill you if they recognise you."

Doubtfully Rob squinted at the drinkers, who were paying him no attention whatsoever. He jerked his head at Lucifer. "Is this the man you live with?"

I told Rob his name. "And this is –" I began unhappily.

"He kens damn well who it is," growled Rob.

"I do," agreed Lucifer politely. "I am honoured, my lord." His face worked like a puppet's; in any other circumstances it would have been droll to see. I could see him totting up the points: *I was in the service of a lord. . . there was a time when others would have liked to take a cudgel to him. . . you have more than once spoke the name of Robbie as you slept.*

"Please speak low, Rob," I winced. "If they hear your voice. . ."

"Why do you not answer my letters?" Rob said in a passable London speech.

"I did answer, in a way. I always told Myton what to say. Oh, Rob, I wish you were not here! You should not be here. Three miles from the house, Myton said. And you are here in London," I said miserably.

"Aye," said Rob with grim satisfaction at my discomfort. "I risk God knows what on this fool's errand."

"I did not ask you to come."

"If I had waited till you asked me I would be an old man. I want you with me. I could understand you when you left me in the Tower, in that confined space. But now I am released and I can offer you a little more. It is a big house. I mean, not big as we have known in better days, but I have my own rooms. And when I get my pardon, which I will do, I know, I mean tae buy a house near London – I would like you in it, Giles."

"Accept," whispered Lucifer behind his hand.

"But *she* is there," I said slowly.

"Aye, she is there and she will be there and wherever I go she mun go wi' me and that is the way of it. I have accepted it and so will you."

"But why should I?" I seethed. "I don't need to. You know I hate her. I can never forgive her. Even to see her – even to think about her – my guts heave."

We whispered fiercely between our teeth. Lucifer, heartily embarrassed, sat on amongst it all, silent.

"So is she tae separate us?" Rob said. "I thought you said once that you loved me." He was looking down at the table. Now he raised his eyes. They were the most haggard eyes that I had ever seen, and shad-

348

owed, as they had been at the trial. It occurred to me that they might always be so. I remembered how they used to be when I first met him – mischievous and laughing.

"I did love you," I admitted.

"But now you do not? Is that the way of it?"

"I don't know," I said dumbly.

"Is it that you love him?" Rob indicated Lucifer.

"No!" said Lucifer and I together.

"No," added Lucifer gallantly and honestly. "His heart was always yours."

Rob nodded. I had the impression that this was what he had suspected.

"I don't sleep wi' her," he said. "I havenae' laid a hand on her in love since I was brought frae Westminster. She has her rooms and I hae mine. Naturally we do speak tae one another. Well, Anne is there, you see."

He turned to Lucifer. "I have a daughter, Anne. She's seven years old. Eight in December. An awfu' bonny sweet girl." He turned to me, a little aggressively. "Nothing like her mother!"

I thought suddenly of Tom's sisters laughing by the hearth, tossing apple peel and teasing us. I wondered about households where little girls were to be considered. The notion seemed an odd one.

"In order tae tempt you tae Greys," said Rob, "I am something at a disadvantage. It has in many ways little tae recommend it. As you point out, Frances is there and she is not an easy woman tae be with. You willnae' find her quiet over her sewing. When she is quiet it is the dreadful silence of despondency and melancholy. At other times she rants and raves. I want tae be honest wi' ye. I need not have told you that. You know Elizabeth – you have seen Lord Knollys. He is in his dotage – nearly eighty. It is my hope he willnae' dare tae tell the king I was frae hame, for fear he will have seemed a puir and doddering jailor tae me. It is true we hae an imposition on our movements frae the house. But we would be able tae go riding, within a three miles' compass, and there are woods where we could be alone. I have an annuity; but I have tae tell you that I am no' confident that Prince Charles will honour it when he becomes king, although he should do. Even so, I mun save all the moneys that I may for Anne for a dowry, and therefore I am nae sure even of such wealth as I have. I believe that one day I will hae my pardon frae His Majesty, but to be truthful, nor am I sure o' that. It is not a tempting picture that I gie ye, Giles; in short the only thing that I am sure of is my love for you, which has brought me here today, and the only thing that I may offer ye wi' any certainty is mysel'.

And also," he said quickly, as if that were perhaps not enough, "in coming intae Oxfordshire – although Greys is not near those parts you once knew – you would in a manner o' speaking be coming hame, and that mun count for something. And we would sleep together," he added as an afterthought. "Did I not say? But maybe seeing me you don't find that a pleasant prospect now? I am not as pretty as I once was."

Although there be who speak that kind of language in a search for compliments I had the disturbing sensation that Rob said it in genuine anxiety. He truly seemed to think I could no longer care for him because his beauty was not of that clear unspoilt comeliness that I first fell in love with – in short, that he was thirty-five and had known troubles. It occurred to me that when one has been singled out through beauty, has risen and achieved fame and fortune for those same good looks, one's being equalling in the eyes of the world that beauty which made one celebrated, then any marring of the same must be an erosion of one's self-worth, indeed, of one's very self. As I mulled over this extraordinary notion, Lucifer nudged me violently in the ribs.

"What is the matter with you, Giles? For God's sake, reassure him. If you don't have him, I will!"

Just as Rob began to look more comfortable, even to smile at Lucifer's remark, we became aware of a certain whispering about us, and I turned to find that we had all unaware become the centre of attention.

I had forgotten our surroundings as I listened to Rob, and now seeing the men in the inn grow restive I sensed we were like to be in some difficulties.

"That is the Earl of Somerset!" one loud bold voice announced.

The Lord be praised that even as he said it I could hear how ridiculous the accusation sounded. What would the Earl of Somerset be doing in The Three Pigeons, St John's Street? Someone even laughed derisively. I blessed him.

There were murmurs of assent, of disbelief. Rob stood up, ashen, backed against the wall. I could see he had a sword beneath his cloak. I prayed he would not draw it, not only because it would give truth to the outrageous claim but if he did not do murder he would be mown down by the cudgels of the mob, and either way the king would hear of it. I swore at myself for a fool, with my prevarications and my sensibilities, obliging him to put himself in danger for my sake. I had only to see him there, vulnerable and at bay, to have it brought home sharply to me what I must have always known – that I had never ceased to love him, loved him far more than I hated her, loved him now as much as ever; while into my thick skull penetrated the words which he had made me a gift of half unnoticed – that it was love for me that brought him here tonight.

"The Earl of Somerset?" one guffawed nearby.

"Aye – look at him – he is like his picture."

"He is not. He is nothing like. This is a country man – look at his clothes."

"It is the Earl of Somerset, I tell you. See how he fears us. Ask him where his wife is. Ask him," he sneered, "how he slew his friend."

As the crowd teetered on the verge of crediting the incredible, Lucifer jumped forward and held up his hand. In his lovely resonant voice that carried comfortably to those groundlings standing at the back, he said: "Friends, what madness is this? What have you drunk? This fellow is Giles's cousin out of Oxfordshire whom I have seen before. The Earl of Somerset!" he laughed. "In The Three Pigeons! In those old clothes and wearing Giles's old hat!"

Several now began to snigger at their folly. Lucifer declared: "The Earl of Somerset chatting with Giles? Giles, our dresser, who plays the cornet, and hammers down the boards! You'll tell me next that he and Giles are old acquaintances!"

He who had first shouted looked a little sullen, but the rest were plainly glad enough to find that it was all a mistake.

"Why did he jump up then?" grumbled the first.

"Would not you, to see you drunkards rush at him?" Lucifer retorted.

They settled back into their seats, a little sheepishly, laughing, telling the stories they had heard about the wicked earl and his more wicked wife; and Lucifer and Rob and I shuffled our way out of The Three Pigeons – some even shook our hands and asked our pardon.

In the street outside and further off Rob shook the hand of Lucifer. "I don't much relish the way you did it, but I'm grateful for your quick thinking." He added then with a flicker of a smile: "I do hae better clothes a' hame, y'know; and though I now am travel-stained I can look awfu' fine in satins."

"It is just lucky for us you were not called upon to speak to them," said Lucifer, modestly proud of his success.

I fidgeted. I did not think we were safe yet.

"Will you go with him?" Lucifer said to me. "I think I would if I were you."

"I will," I said. "Satins or homespun, he has always been the man I love."

"I think you should be telling this tae me," said Rob.

I said a fond farewell to Lucifer there in the street, and wished him luck with Beatrice Joanna. Then Rob and I went down St John's Street in the dusk and I picked up some belongings from my lodging and put them in a travelling bag. I would have found much cause to marvel, seeing Rob there, waiting for me, if I had had time enough to marvel; but I could not rest till we were clear of the city.

"Which way did you come into London?" I asked.

"Along the road frae Reading, and then Holborn."

"You rode along Holborn?" I blanched.

"I wore my hood."

"And do you purpose to return that way?"

"It's the way I know."

At the stable where Rob had left his horse I hired one for myself. There was no way of course that we could return the nag but Rob said he would send money and make all fair.

I was on tenterhooks as we rode along Holborn. The summer dusk obscured us, and Rob pulled the hood low across his face, but there were folk about, and here and there on doors and walls the smudges of pallor showed where the ghastly portraits flapped and the close-writ relation of the murder and the trials hung printed out for those in hibernation who had missed the fine details. Rob seemed calm enough, and often stopped to look about him, curious as to the changes that had occurred since he had last seen the London streets; but I was not composed of heroic stuff and was never so glad as when we struck the road to Reading and rode out into open country.

Somewhere in the wilds of nowhere, seeing lights and the innkeeper not abed, we put up at a wayside inn and were led by candlelight into an upper room. We dined there on cold meat and warm beer and bread hard enough to crack the teeth of lesser mortals; and would have gone at once to bed had it not been for the fleas. It made me laugh to see Rob's face as we unmade the bed, shaking the fusty sheet, turning it over, gingerly replacing it, and then the same with the blanket. I went round after Robbie, hanging up his clothes, and joined him in the bed.

We settled without speaking into a long embrace. There was so much to be said that we said almost nothing, only words of love and fond affection, as, tired and content, we set about to know each other's bodies once again. Rob who had ridden almost without pause from Henley was so saddle-sore and aching that he soon fell asleep; but I lay looking beyond him into the darkness with my arms about him and my heart full of love, listening to his breathing, stroking his hair. My giddy thoughts veered pendulum-wise betwixt the extremes of exhilaration and peace.

I awoke first and was first out of bed. The room was warm and musty. I opened the little window beneath the thatch with some difficulty, and a startled dove swore at me and flapped away. I stood and scratched – we had not fooled the fleas – and turned and watched Rob waking.

The sunlight fell upon his tousled golden hair, his eyelashes, the muscle of his naked shoulder as he moved. I suddenly recalled the moment when I first had seen the same, when we were young in Stamford and the king on his way south to claim his throne, and Jamie Hay lent Rob his bed and Rob had danced about in Jamie's gorgeous velvets.

I felt a surge of love so strong it caught me in the throat.

Beneath the stars, upon yon meteor
Ever hung my fate, mongst things corruptible.

Misgivings a-plenty I had about the life we were to share together, this is true. But as the sweet air of the meadows touched my cheek it seemed to me that it was no poor thing to go with my lover into Oxfordshire all on a May morning.

EPILOGUE

Two years have passed; it is the month of September, and in very different circumstances Rob and I were riding towards Royston. The difference was that we had royal permission to be clear of Greys. Commanded by the king! Requested even; for the letter Rob had with him was no legal document but the missive of a friend. Different also was Rob's appearance – the gentleman traveller – the tall crowned hat with the brim turned up on one side, the wired collar with deep lace edges, the tight-waisted peacock blue doublet and full gathered breeches, the knee-length soft leather boots. After some consideration we had decided he should have his hair curled and I spent many hours about this, for we would not want the king to think that Rob had gone to seed away from the royal presence. Even Frances had ceased her carping and treated the matter with proper respect, for upon this journey hung the future of us all.

A month ago a fair had come to the green, with its pavilions and stalls and entertainers. Wandering on foot amongst it all – the hobbyhorse seller, the gingerbread woman, the wrestlers, the protesting Puritans – we had found a fortune teller's tent and Rob had gone inside. He did not tell the gipsy woman who he was, but of course she knew. She told him that if he could see the king and speak to him all would go very well with him. His future would be bright. She saw changes. She saw a dwelling near a river.

Whitehall! thought Rob with an ache of longing.

He came away in great despondency of spirit. He did not need a fortune teller, he reckoned, to tell him that if he might be alone with James he might work something of the old charm on our monarch. But how to arrange it? He had written enough inadequately answered letters. A person could grow tired of useless begging. Particularly as Villiers would read the letters. How very gratifying it must be for him – once threadbare in Newmarket and now the richest man in the kingdom after James.

We had heard about his wild adventures in Spain, in search of a Spanish marriage for the heir to the throne. Villiers had won over the youthful Prince Charles, now twenty-two – something Rob had never bothered to do. Together they had slipped across to France and thence to Spain where they flit about in the mountains, and so to Madrid. The Infanta Maria was unenthusiastic. They came home with nothing achieved and much money spent, and Villiers was made Duke of Buckingham.

"Duke, no less!" gasped Robbie awed and sick. "Duke. . ." he marvelled continuously. "And all for nothing more than having good legs."

It was frustrating for us at Greys, so far from the hub of things. We heard news when it was already old. Gossip was very much second-hand. We heard that Charles had begun to assert himself and shaken off his fear of his father. We heard that someone had tried to introduce a new favourite on to the scene but James would have none of him. As to Villiers, we heard he was ambitious and ungrateful, that he made the king weep, that he was unstable and prone to nervous collapse and took to his bed at moments of stress; that he was ill; that he was well again; that the king had sent him melons, pears and strawberries when he was sick. We heard that Charles and Villiers had turned against James and his peaceful policies, and favoured war with Spain, and that Southampton and Essex had joined with Villiers, that Parliament had voted money for the war, that troops were sent to the Low Countries and the king was disregarded. We heard that Essex was yet unmarried.

Our life at Greys had not turned out to be as fraught with difficulties as I had feared. I was constantly with Rob, so I was well content; I had a little room adjoining Rob's, but at night we shared a bed – a manservant may do so if the lord requires it. We rode out each day and were together in the quiet woods. And as for Frances. . . to my astonishment she welcomed me with great delight. From the first moment of Rob's ebullient: "Look – I hae Giles wi' me!" she treated me with a benevolence bordering on tenderness. I believe that she associated me with her memories of the early days of her marriage, a sort of symbol of happier times. Incredibly she seemed to have a blind spot as to my kinship with Thomas, as if she had forgotten it or erased it from her memory. I remembered that she had always quite misunderstood my feelings regarding her, had considered me a friend when all the time I had been secretly hostile; the superficial politeness I had adopted to so many in my role as manservant to the Earl of Somerset must have been more effective than I had supposed. There were occasions now at Greys when she would seek me out and speak to me of Robbie, question me as to his feelings for her – was he truly as indifferent as he seemed? – and plead with me to speak of her with kindness to him, ask me to remind him of what she once had meant to him, and worse, thanked me for my patience and my sympathy; till I was fidgeting with embarrassment and unease. So taken up was she with her own self-absorption that the idea had plainly not crossed her mind that behind closed doors Rob and I might kiss as lovers; here I was grateful for her all-encompassing unhappiness which blinded her to everything outside its reach. I thought in time that I might come to pity her – the notion confused and astonished me.

Of course we spoke about the past; indeed, it was not so past that it was not the cause of all our troubles in the present. Often Rob would speak inconsequentially as he had done at the trial; as for instance after a silence, suddenly to thump a table and remark: "Why was not Paul de Lobell brought to trial? Is it a coincidence that he is brother-in-law tae the king's physician? Why was not Dr Mayerne made tae give evidence? Why did Mayerne not discover symptoms of poison? What kind of a physician is he? A bone setter, aye, as I have cause tae be thankful for, and there his talent ends." And then once when we were alone: "What if it wasnae' Frances at all? What if she only thought that she had weakened him wi' poison? What if some other suborned the apprentice? That poisoned glyster made up by Lobell, bypassing all the tarts and jellies – what if some powerful person ordered it, someone who hated Thomas more than she. . . ?"

"There is no future in this kind of speculation. . ."

"Och, I have had stranger thoughts than that," Rob said. "When I was there at Westminster, so tired and confused that I could scarcely see, let alone put my words together, and I was face tae face wi' Essex, I remember thinking we were not the foes I thought we were. Puir devil, I thought, you lost some of your hair and fingernails through what she gave you tae eat, and all the world made songs and jests about how you couldnae' raise your prick – I thought well, maybe you were dealt wi'

355

worse than me! But now, of course," he added soberly, "I dinnae' think so; for he is at court, and I am here."

But maybe not for much longer?

Within a week of that fortune teller's pronouncement Rob received a letter from the king, asking him to Royston. Not, you understand, into the house. This meeting must be secret. It would take place in the garden. Behind the house, if Rob remembered, there was an orchard, set within a wall. There James would meet with him. No flea-ridden inns either. Along the way there were noble houses where he would be welcome; James had forewarned them. All would be done in the style to which Rob once had been accustomed.

I long to see you, James had written.

So here we were, in the warm moisty September afternoon, drawing near to Royston. Not we alone either – servants from Greys were with us, making a dignified procession, worthy of the Earl of Somerset who visited the king.

"But do you think he'll have me back?" Rob said. Our dignified and nonchalant exterior masked the turmoil of our thoughts. "Will he want me back at Whitehall?"

"Would you want to go?" I said dubiously.

"Aye, I would," said Rob.

The last time we had seen the red brick hunting lodge had been when the news of the murder had broken, and Rob had dashed off to London in a panic to put right what he could, and James had wept into his neck and said: "When shall I see you again?"

Nine years ago. It seemed like another life, other people. I looked at Robbie. I had done my best with him; he looked handsome, noble and exquisite. He always carried himself well. He was strong; not weak and willowy like Villiers. Why, when he was sixteen he could throw a tree trunk with the best of those other Scots who passed the time in games. What would his life have been, I wondered, if he had never come to court, never caught the attention of the king? But no – there was nothing for him in the Border country. The rose was pulled, and young Tam Lin had to come from the forest, and through shape shifting reach beyond the world of balladry. And now all those flamboyant changes had led us here, to a garden in Hertfordshire, where the apples hung down low on the laden boughs.

Dismounted now, the horses tethered further off, I watched him walk through the long grass towards the figure that approached him from the house.

From where I stood I thought the king looked old and twisted. I was startled by the change in him. You would have thought each joint pained him as he walked. When he came face to face with Rob he reached for him and stumbled into his arms. Rob supported him and they clung together close, James noisy in his emotion – I could hear him weeping from where I stood. They remained close pressed together for an age.

Beneath the apple boughs, a line of bee skeps stood, big baskets of woven straw. From time to time a dozy bee, replete with summer sweetness, droned into its hole and disappeared.

A bee that's hatched in summer has but a few weeks of life and potency. A little longer if it be hatched in autumn. Every bee has his own place within the skep. The rigid positioning rules their lives. There is no place for one that's out of step. When the queen ages and is considered worthless, new young queens are found. Those for whom they have no use are destroyed. Those that remain live through the dark winter months and therefore they need to store large quantities of honey. They pass nectar on their tongues to other bees. Sometimes they dance.

Rob spoke with the king for a long while. I held the horses and I watched the bees. They know what they are about; they are wise, I thought, they are not as we, that bumble around aimlessly, believing ourselves so knowledgeable, thinking we rise, only to find we fall; thinking ourselves indispensable, finding ourselves lost in obscurity, easily replaced.

They talked in low voices, Rob with some animation; I heard something of what he said but only snatches. James responded with emotion, but quiet the while, preoccupied. Both seemed deeply moved, and more than once they kissed. At last Rob drew away from the king and came towards me, not looking back. The king gazed after him. I saw him drinking in the sight of Rob going away. Then he turned and walked back to the house.

Rob reached for his horse's bridle. I stopped him.

"What happened? What did he say?"

"God – he is all worn out," said Robbie, tear-streaked, much disturbed. "So thin and bony, so hag-ridden; he can barely stand."

"What did he want?" I interrupted brusquely. "What will he give you?"

"Och, I will get my pardon, that's for sure. It will be mine within the month."

"That's wonderful, Rob! At last!"

"And then we will be able tae quit Greys and live wherever we please; no bad thing."

"Did he speak about that?" I pressed. "Did he talk about where you would live?"

But Rob was following his own line of thought. He ignored my question. "He says that Villiers is worse than ever I was – which I think he thought was comfort tae me; and that Charles is no better. He says his peacemaking has come tae nothing and that he longs for his grave."

"But – what more? What more about you?"

"Nothing in the sense you mean."

"Why did he want to see you?" I persisted.

"He wanted tae hold me in his arms," said Rob, much moved.

"And is that all?" I blanched.

"That, from you, Giles?" Rob said with a wry smile. "I thought you found that a pleasing enough prospect."

"I am bewildered – I spoke without thinking," I apologised.

"He said he loves me. He said I was his dearest love. He said that I was looking very beautiful. I know he wants me back. As for the other matter. . ."

"The other – ?"

"That which parted us. I told him I was innocent. I told him again and again."

"What did he say?"

Rob answered: "I rather think he did not care one way or the other."

There was no sign of the king now. There was simply Rob and myself, and our two horses, and further off, beyond the wall, the servants we had brought with us, waiting on events.

"But I am sure that he will send for me again," said Robbie.

"Yes he will," I reassured him. "Of course he will."

"Now he has seen me, held me, it will only be a matter of time," said Robbie. "He will surely send for me."

"No doubt of it," I said, and lied.

Then Rob and I turned our backs on the garden and came away; leaving the bees about their business.

– THE END –

James died the following year and was succeeded by his son Charles I.

Pardoned, Robert Carr acquired a house in Chiswick where he lived with his wife, daughter and servants. He did not return to Whitehall. He died in 1645 aged 58.

Frances died in 1632 of cancer of the womb, aged 39.

Anne Carr, Robert and Frances's daughter, grew up to be sweet, gentle and likeable. She married the heir to the Earl of Bedford, a love match, settled at Woburn and became the fifth countess.

Robert Devereux, Earl of Essex, married again. The marriage proved unsuccessful and was followed by a separation. He commanded the parliamentary army in the Civil War but eventually resigned after blunders. He died in 1646.

George Villiers, Duke of Buckingham, after James's death the close companion of Charles I, became hugely unpopular and was assassinated in 1628.

Giles Rawlins, Thomas Overbury's cousin and Robert Carr's man, was a real person, who took a white powder into the Tower of London and was questioned about it, saw Thomas daily at his window in the Tower, and sent a petition asking that the death be investigated further. In anything other than that, his part in this story is fanciful.

In researching this story I relied heavily upon:
Cast of Ravens by Beatrice White;
The Murder of Sir Thomas Overbury by William McElwee;
The Notorious Lady Essex by Edward Le Comte.

It is from these books that I have taken the genuine letters of the period and the accounts of the trials of the Somersets.

The most recent work on this subject is *Unnatural Murder* by Anne Somerset.

Amongst many other books, especially useful were:
Jacobean Pageant by G. P. V. Akrigg;
James I and *The Jacobean Age* by David Mathew;
Essex the Rebel by Vernon F. Snow;
Simon Forman by A. L. Rowse;
Ben Jonson by David Riggs;
and *The Trials of Frances Howard* by David Lindley.

Send for our free catalogue to GMP Publishers Ltd,
BCM 6159, London WC1N 3XX, England

Gay Men's Press books can be ordered from any bookshop in the
UK, North America and Australia, and from
specialised bookshops elsewhere.

Our distributors whose addresses are given in the front pages of
this book can also supply individual customers by mail order.
Send retail price as given plus 10% for postage and packing.

*For payment by Mastercard/American Express/Visa, please give
number, expiry date and signature.*

_____

_____

Name and address in block letters please:

Name
_____

Address
_____

_____

_____